CONSENT

THE LOAN SHARK DUET (BOOK 2)

CHARMAINE PAULS

Published by Charmaine Pauls

Montpellier, 34090, France

www.charmainepauls.com

Published in France

Cover design by Kellie Dennis (www.bookcoverbydesign.co.uk)

ISBN: 978-2-9561031-1-0 (eBook)

ISBN: 978-1-5488248-0-8 (Print)

❧ Created with Vellum

Valentina

A baby.

I'm going to have Gabriel Louw's baby.

Gabriel Louw.

The most dangerous man in Johannesburg.

Oh, God.

I clutch a hand over my mouth to silence a sob and place the other over my stomach where our child is growing.

While the taxi takes me farther and farther away from my captor on my impulsive escape route, my mind reels with a thousand thoughts. How did this happen? Did I forget to take my pill? I'm sure I took it every day at the same time. I even have an alarm programmed on my phone. Did I slip up? How? When? I haven't taken any medicine that could've interfered with the contraceptive.

For the life of me, I can't think of an explanation. My rational mind, the part of me in denial, demands that I find proof that the pregnancy test is wrong, but my gut knows otherwise. The knowledge pounds in my ribs.

I'm pregnant.

And alone.

I have little money, no job, and I'm running from Gabriel Louw.

I'm in so much trouble. Now is not the time to figure out what went wrong. I need to think of how I'm going to stay alive.

"Where to, ma'am?" the driver asks.

When Gabriel finds out I'm missing, he'll go after my brother. I give the driver Kris' address and sink back in the seat, nauseous from fear.

He glances at me in the rearview mirror. "Everything all right?"

I lower my hand from my mouth and grip the door handle. I need to hold on to something. "I'm fine, thank you."

It feels like forever before we pull up at the clinic. I ask the driver to keep the meter running and skirt around to the back of the house where I won't be visible from any of the clinic windows. I try the kitchen door, but it's locked. I knock softly.

Please, Charlie, hurry.

For several painful heartbeats, nothing happens.

Biting my nail, I run from window to window until I spot Charlie. He's sitting on his bed, reading a comic book. I tap on the glass. The last thing I want is to scare him by pounding on the window. No reaction. I knock harder. I can't afford to attract Kris' attention. In the meantime, the taximeter is running a hole into the small amount of cash I have on me.

Tap, tap.

Finally, Charlie looks up. When he sees me, he calls out, "Va–Val."

I motion for him to be quiet with my finger on my lips and point at the window latch. Instead of opening it, Charlie hops from the bed and leaves the room.

Don't call Kris.

A moment later, the backdoor opens, and my brother steps out.

Beyond relief, I want to pull him into my arms and tell him we're going to be all right, but I have to act normal.

"Surprise, Charlie," I whisper. "I came to fetch you. We're going on a holiday, but you have to come quietly."

"Q–quiet," he whispers back, mimicking my earlier gesture with a finger on his lips.

There's no time to go through the house and gather some of his things. I lock up so Kris will be safe inside and throw the key through the bars of the open bathroom window. Hooking my arm through Charlie's, I lead him to the waiting taxi.

Inside, the driver and Charlie speak simultaneously.

"Where do you want to go?"

"Where are we go–going?"

Where are we going?

Where can I run to where Gabriel won't find me? A place like that doesn't exist. If I'm to keep my wits about me, I have to ignore that notion. I'm no longer responsible for only Charlie and myself, but also for a third life. I have no plan of action. I pinch the bridge of my nose.

Think, Valentina. Think.

"Ma'am, where to?" the driver repeats, more impatient now.

I can't afford a plane or bus ticket to anywhere for myself, let alone for two people. There's only one option left. Wherever we're going, I'll have to drive.

"Ma'am?" The man turns in his seat and gives me a piercing look. "Is everything all right back there?"

"Yes. We're going to Berea."

He regards me from under his bushy eyebrows and says with a hint of disbelief, "Berea. You sure?"

"Just drive. I'll give you directions."

He holds my eyes for another moment before turning back to the front and pulling away from the curb. I exhale in relief, and squeeze Charlie's hand to reassure him, happy that Kris hadn't seen us. Charlie has wound down his window and is staring at the buildings that whiz past, oblivious to the lump of concrete in my stomach and the maddening fear pumping through my veins.

I send a quick text message to Kris so she won't worry when she finds Charlie gone.

Charlie and I have to leave for a while. Sorry to sneak off like this, but the less you know the better. Thank you for always being a friend. Love you.

3

A block from my old flat, the driver stops. "This is as far as I go." He motions at the street ahead. "That's hijackers' paradise."

I pay the extortionate amount and usher Charlie out before the driver can pose the questions I see in his eyes. The minute we're on the pavement, he speeds off, happy to get out of here.

"Va–Val." Charlie kicks in his heels as I take his arm. "This is ho–home."

"Not anymore." I give him a bright smile. "This is only where our holiday starts."

I have precious little time. It's a matter of hours, minutes maybe, before Gabriel discovers me gone and puts a death warrant out for our lives. He'll track my phone and be on our tail faster than I can say disappear, but if I want Charlie to follow hassle-free, I have to make him happy.

We walk one block to a corner café where I buy Charlie a King Cone ice cream. While he sits down on the pavement to eat it, I call Jerry. The number rings and rings, and finally disconnects without going onto voicemail.

Darn it. Jerry is my only hope. I try the special number he gave me when he was still supposedly watching over Charlie. It's a number only me and some of his crime buddies have.

This time, he picks up with a hesitant, "Val?"

There's no time to beat around the bush. "I need a car."

"What?"

"A car, Jerry. Now."

"To buy?"

"Would I have called a car thief if I wanted to buy a car?"

He utters his refusal meekly. "I can't do it. What's going on? This isn't like you."

I've always condemned his shady business, but now isn't the time for my moral values to induce guilt. "After what you did to us, you owe me, damn you."

There's dejection in his voice. "Val…"

"Do you want to know what Gabriel Louw did to me because of your ignorant stupidity?"

"Oh fuck. Oh fucking fuck. You're running." His voice trembles. "You're running away from The Breaker."

"If he finds me, I'm dead. So is Charlie." And the baby I'm carrying. "Please, Jerry. You got us into this mess. Help me get out."

There's a long silence. I can almost feel the gears turn in his head. Just when I think he's going to hang up, he says, "Where are you?"

"Your place."

"Give me an hour."

"Thirty minutes."

"Goddamn, Val." He takes a breath, as if to calm himself. "Wait at the side of the building."

"Thank you. You better show up. When I hang up, we can't speak on this phone again."

He knows what I mean. I have to destroy the phone if I don't want Gabriel to track me.

"I'll be there." The line goes dead with a click.

Charlie has finished his ice cream. I make him clean his hands on a tissue and throw the wrapper in the trashcan so I can go around the corner and crush the phone under my heel. There are too many tiny parts to discern a tracker, not that I know what to look for, so I stamp on everything again, just to be sure, and dump the lot in the trashcan.

"Ready for our adventure?" I take Charlie's hand. "Let's go get our wheels."

We hide in an alcove from where I can watch the road. Thankfully, we haven't crossed any thugs, but they'll soon crawl out of their holes with the setting of the sun. I play a distracted game of noughts and crosses with Charlie, using a chalkstone I picked up in the road to draw lines on the brick wall.

Thirty-five minutes later, an orange station wagon pulls up. The bodywork is dented and the metal rusted where the paint has peeled. My jaw drops when the rickety vehicle comes to a stop next to us and Jerry exits.

"Jerry." I throw my arms in the air.

"What?" he says in an exasperated voice. "It's all I could do on short notice."

"How far will this thing get us?"

He pats the bonnet. "She's good. I checked her out. Engine is a make-over, the full Monty." He holds the key out to me. "Swapped the registration plate, too, but keep off the main roads, just in case."

"Thanks." I snatch the key from his hand. "Let's go, Charlie."

Jerry pats Charlie on the back as my brother rounds the car. "How's things, my man?"

Charlie gives him a high-five and a grin. When he's buckled up, I look at Jerry through the window one last time before pulling off, heading for the highway.

The engine makes a funny noise, and the body of the car rattles, but we make smooth progress and manage to get through Hillbrow without any hijacking attempts, courtesy of the state of the car.

Once we hit the N1, my frayed nerves finally unravel. My hands start shaking on the wheel. A hot flush travels over me, making me break out in a sweat. My stomach is so tight it aches. I fight the urge to throw up. The summer smog is brittle and dirty, but I open the window to fill my lungs with air. As always, survival mode kicks in and numbs me to the fears and dangers of our situation.

Charlie is looking through his window, humming a song. I manage to tweak the radio enough to find a Country and Western station he likes. Checking the petrol gauge, I groan inwardly. The tank is near empty. At the first petrol station after Midrand, I fill up and use my last cash to buy a few supplies from the Quick shop, which are mostly snacks for Charlie. I don't dare withdraw money at the ATM with my card. It will be too easy to track. I should have remembered to do that before I started out.

My gut twists and churns the farther we crawl away from Johannesburg, the city of gold that is ruled by a man as beautiful and ruined as the place itself, a man who'll kill us if he finds us.

When the skyline of Sandton disappears from my rearview mirror, a crippling notion of loss and loneliness hits me. The emotions throw me off kilter. Shock runs through me. I miss Gabriel. That makes me twisted and sick. It must be the hormones. Yes, I'm not myself. Uninvited tears sting my eyes. Swatting at them, I force my gaze on the road ahead.

Don't look back.

There is only Charlie, me, and my baby now.

We'll make it. We'll survive.

I have no idea where I'm heading until we hit the sign announcing the three-way split. If we carry on straight, we head north toward Polokwane. I don't know the area. The only remaining options are Bloemfontein or Durban. Durban isn't as far away as Bloemfontein, and the weather is less harsh. Without financial means, Durban is the better option. Plus, I can make it there on a tank of petrol, whereas I'll run out of fuel in the middle of nowhere, long before I hit Bloemfontein.

The sign for the N3 appears. I change lanes and enter the interchange that takes me over the highway and east. With a flick of the indicator, I decide our destiny and future.

Gabriel

THE GUY I took out this afternoon was scum, but today the violence leaves a bad taste in my mouth. All I want is to go home to Valentina, crawl into her body, and melt into her bed. Things between us have changed. No matter how much I lie to myself, she's no longer the toy I pickpocketed from her life. She's something--someone--I want enough to break every rule in the book to keep. She's no longer my captive. I'm hers.

My addiction has grown over the months to an all-consuming obsession. Despite the coldness inside of me, she awakens emotions I thought I didn't have. She makes me feel things I've never felt before--gratitude, regret, joy, and fear--and even if these feelings scare me shitless, I want more.

When I get home, I dismiss Rhett and Quincy and go upstairs for a shower. I don't want to face my girl covered in blood. Washing the stench of my sins away, I think about her and what I want to do to her body. The thoughts make me hard. If I wasn't so impatient to plant my cock in her body, I would've made myself come first so I can last longer, but my urgency is palpable. I towel myself dry quickly and dress in slacks and a shirt.

My heartbeat speeds up as I make my way to the kitchen. At this hour, Valentina will be ironing. It irks me to see her work so hard, to see her work at all, but it's not for much longer. The minute she falls pregnant, everything will change.

Silence greets me when I enter the kitchen. The counters are tidy and wiped down. Marie has already left for the day. An eerie emptiness presses down on the space. I don't like it. I quicken my step, putting my head around the scullery doorframe, but there's no one. A sickening sensation settles over my body. Every nerve ending tingles. Rushing to the maid quarters, I jerk open the door. Valentina's bed is made. Oscar is sleeping on her pillow. My leg hurts from the force I put on it as I limp to the bathroom.

Empty.

With a growing feeling of dread, I fling the cabinets open. Everything seems to be there. The cosmetics and bath salts I bought are neatly stacked. Back in her bedroom, I do the same with her closet. The clothes, shoes, jewelry, books, and other knick-knacks I got for Valentina are there. Still, something is wrong. I know it in my gut.

Standing there, absorbing the chill from the descending night, the molecules of my body go flat and cold. An overpowering sense of abandonment fills me. Then the fear hits, hot and liquid, rippling over me in a wave. If Magda did something to Valentina... If she hurt her... I swear to God I'll kill my mother.

Making my way down the hallway to my office, I dig my phone from my pocket and call Rhett.

He replies with a cheerful, "What's up, boss?"

"In my office. Now. Bring Quincy."

I hang up and rush through my office door, expecting an army or Magda, but what I see is a sheet of white paper on my desk.

All of my attention hones in on that scrap of paper. Instinct tells me everything that has just derailed in my life is summarized on there, and for three whole seconds I can't make myself move. I pinch my eyes shut, brace myself, and round my desk. It's in her handwriting. My hand shakes as I lift it to the light and read.

I can't honor my promise. I hope you'll forgive me.

Goddammit, no!

I crumple the paper in my fist and drag my hands through my hair. I feel like falling to my knees, but somehow I remain standing. Of all the things she could've done, this is the last I expected. Charlie means too much to her. My feelings are a mess of tangled, electric wires. I'm about to short-circuit, explode, and burn out. I want to find and hurt her, make her pay for her betrayal and for what she's putting me through. I'll take the skin off her backside and drag her right back. This time, I'll chain her to my bed until she understands the meaning of *property*.

Rhett and Quincy chase through the door, saving me from my dark thoughts. They both still at the state of me.

"What's up?" Quincy asks carefully.

I lower my hands to my hips. It's hard for me to speak. For a moment, I consider thrusting the paper at them, but I don't want them to witness Valentina's intimate rejection. I swallow, breathe in, and say, "Valentina's gone."

Quincy pales. "What do you mean, gone?"

It takes every ounce of strength I have to push out the words, and when I finally do, my mouth is bitter. "She ran."

Rhett's eyes go wide. "Fuck, no."

Quincy is the first to get to his senses. "Did she say something? Has someone seen her go?"

"She left a note." Since Quincy seems more in control than Rhett, I say, "Go to the guardhouse. Ask them when she left and how. With what? Did she go with a suitcase? Pull the tape. I want to know every fucking detail. Not a word to Magda or her guards." A dribble of cold sweat runs down my spine as I say it. This is the opportunity Magda has been waiting for.

Quincy is out of my office in a flash. I'm tripping over my thoughts in the orders I'm thinking up for Rhett. Track her phone. Pull her bank records for the last six hours. Put out word with our informants. Before I can voice anything, Rhett steps forward. Something in his demeanor makes me pause. His shoulders are hunched and his eyebrows drawn together.

"Gabriel..." he starts.

This is going to be bad.

He pauses and licks his lips. "There's something you should know."

Those words make me want to kill him. He knows something and withheld it from me. I stand quietly, waiting for him to continue.

"I think..." He lowers his head. "Maybe... I don't know for sure, but..."

My patience snaps. "Spit it out or I'll shoot a hole in your goddamn tongue."

He takes a deep breath and faces me. "Valentina asked me to buy her a pregnancy test this morning."

I reel in shock. "What?" I heard him fine, but I can't process what he told me. "Valentina thinks she's pregnant?" I say more to myself than him.

"If you think about it, she's been acting kind of emotional, lately."

I let the observation sink in. She's been through a lot with her accident and giving up her studies. Naturally, I attributed her sadness to those events. Now that Rhett mentions it, Valentina has been more tearful than usual. When I touched her last night, her breasts were bigger and tender, but I blamed her pending period for the changes.

Fuck me.

There are too many feelings assaulting me to make sense of anything––pride, joy, fear, hot fucking raving mad anger. If Valentina is pregnant and she ran, it can only be for one reason. I know how negative and depressed the women in my life felt about their planned pregnancies. How much worse must she feel about an unexpected one? She doesn't want the baby, and she's going to get rid of it.

Even if I expected the reaction, I'm filled with rage and heart-ripping anxiety. The rage is not for her, but for me. I could've prevented this disaster. I should've locked her up. I should've noticed when her disposition changed. I could've prevented her from killing our child, the child who is supposed to save her.

Pain rips through my insides when I think about losing an unborn baby, but I have no one but myself to blame. This is all my doing. I swapped her birth control pills for placebos. I deceived her in the most despicable way, and I'll take full responsibility for her actions. No matter if she's no longer pregnant, she's still mine, and I want her back.

"Gabriel?" Rhett has taken two steps back and is standing at a safe distance closer to the door.

"Search every trashcan on the property." There's a good chance Valentina took the pregnancy test with her, but I need to be sure. "Find that test and bring it to me."

I'm clear enough in my fucked-up state to realize I may be jumping the gun. There's a chance she's not pregnant, but I have to consider all options.

When he's gone, I call the guardhouse and bark out commands. I don't want the news to leak to Magda prematurely. Eventually, she'll find out. Until then, I need all the time I can get or Valentina is dead. I punch in the details to activate the tracker software installed on my phone. Her tracker is goddamn dead, which can only mean she destroyed the phone. To be sure, I dial her number, but it goes straight onto voicemail.

The day I kicked down Valentina's door in Berea, I gave her my phone to call her friend, the vet she's been working for. I saved the number on my phone when she was done. Scrolling to Kris' name, I dial the number with a shaking hand.

Her voice comes tired over the phone. "Kris, here. How can I help?"

"Gabriel Louw."

She goes quiet at the mention of my name.

"Is Valentina with you?"

"Why would she be?" Panic enters her tone. "What's wrong?"

I believe her. Her reaction is too genuine to be acting. "Is Charlie there?"

"You know he is."

"I think you better check."

"Even if he wasn't, I wouldn't tell you."

"Listen to me, and listen carefully. This is not the time for games. Valentina's life may be at stake."

"You useless son of a bitch. I'll bust your balls." She carries on with elaborate and colorful insults that are interrupted by a lot of barking. I assume she's walking through the clinic to the house. "I'll mince you up and eat you alive."

"Kris?" I keep my voice calm. "We both care about Valentina, each in our own way. Help me to help her."

She grows quiet at that, and for a moment, so do I. It's the first time I've admitted to anyone but myself that I care about Valentina. The words shock me, but they also free me. It's out in the open. No more hiding.

She inhales and exhales. The air that leaves her mouth is shaky. Her verdict is short and sweet. It has a sense of terrible finality. "He's gone."

Jesus.

I raise my face to the ceiling and search for calmness within myself.

"What the hell is going on?" she shouts.

"Is there a note?"

I can hear her footsteps clacking through the house. "No. Nothing." She's shuffling things around. Something hits the floor with a thud. "Fuck-all. All Charlie's stuff is here."

"Stay calm. I'll find her. Do me a favor. Call me on this number if you hear anything from her."

"Why will I give you shit?"

"Believe me, right now, I'm her only chance."

"The sad thing is I do."

I cut the call just as Rhett reenters my office, a zip lock bag in his hand. He holds it out to me. "We found it."

His solemn eyes tell me the news even before I reach for the proof. Two blue lines.

The air leaves my lungs. My weak leg twitches, and I have to grab the edge of the desk to maintain my balance.

I was right. Valentina could only have left for one reason––to get rid of a baby she doesn't want. It may just kill her if Magda has her way. It's the exact opposite of what I intended. My fucked-up, ingenious plan backfired.

Quincy comes rushing back. Words fall like verbal diarrhea from his lips. "She left on foot four hours ago. All she had with her was an overnight bag. I tried not to raise suspicion, but the guards know something's going on. I'm afraid…" He trails off as his eyes land on the bag in my hand. "Fuck. Is that what I think it is?"

"What now, Gabriel?" Rhett asks, his expression concerned. "What do we do?"

I don't hesitate in my answer. "We get her back."

"You better hurry," Quincy says. "The guards made noise. By now, Magda knows."

The stick with the evidence of Valentina's conception in hand, I march to Magda's office.

She sits behind her desk, scribbling on a notepad. "Valentina ran." Her expression is smug. "We're going after her with everything we've got. A team is already on the way to her brother."

"Stop them."

She throws down her pen. "Excuse me?"

I drop the evidence of my child in front of her. It takes her one second to connect the dots. In her eyes, I see her understanding. We both know I did it on purpose, and we both know why.

She pinches her lips together and leans back in her chair. "So, this is how you get what you want."

"Call off your men."

"You made a big mistake."

"That's your opinion, and you know I don't care about what you or anybody else thinks. Valentina is going to be the mother of my child. From now on, she's family. That wipes away her debt and keeps her and anyone remotely connected to her safe."

I don't say what I suspect, that the baby may already be gone. It doesn't matter whether I bring her back pregnant or not. Eventually, she *will* have my child, even if it takes years and thousands of rands of fertility treatments. I don't care. Somewhere in the back of my mind I know it's a lie. I do care. I do care if she wants to be a mother. More than that, I care if she wants *my* child. Unfortunately, when it comes to life and death, we don't always have the luxury of choice or answers to our questions. Maybe it's better that I don't know the answers. I already know I'm a monster, and she hates me. What I'm doing to her is selfish, wrong, and immoral, but I've never claimed to be a good man. I wanted her from the moment I saw her. I still do. More than ever. Letting her go is the one thing I'm not capable of.

Magda is still regarding me with contempt. I'll go as far as to say with hatred. Even as she speaks, she picks up her phone and dials a number. "You foolish boy. This goes to show men can never be trusted. It's too easy to lead them around by their dicks." A ringtone sounds on her phone, followed by a curt answer. "Scott, turn back. The hit on Charles is off." She listens to a reply. "We still want the girl, but bring her in unharmed." She cuts the call and glares at me. "You do realize you've given all your power away. Now, she holds the power over *you*. I hope this makes you happy."

It's been a long time since Valentina took power over me, and a man like me can never be happy. I'll settle for being content, and I'll be that when I get my precious property back.

My mother needs to understand one thing. "If a hair on her head is harmed, I'll take it as a personal attack on me and my family. All gloves will come off."

"This can never have a happy ending."

I don't want to hear my mother's prophecy, because it hits the instinctive knowledge inside me with a bullseye. "Just make sure your men understand. She's my responsibility. Anything they find, anything they hear, sniff, guess, or divine, I want to know."

"You will. I owe you a *fuck you* for getting tangled up between that whore's legs and screwing this up for the family."

I inch closer to the desk, towering over Magda. "Careful. You're talking about the mother of my child. This is your last warning. Insult her again and you won't like the consequences."

The smile that cracks her thick layer of foundation is artificial. "I'd love to see how you explain this one to Carly."

It's a low blow. Since considering the possibility that Valentina may be pregnant, it's something I've contemplated. I'll have to lie to my daughter, telling her some rosy shade of pink bullshit story about Valentina and I falling in love, when in reality nothing can be further from the truth. There's no way to ensure Valentina will keep her mouth shut about the circumstances of how we ended up in bed. I seduced her, but I did it against her will. There's little difference between my kind of seduction and force. For all I know, she'll take revenge in telling Carly how I stole, blackmailed, and tortured her for nothing but my pleasure, only so I can feed my sick addiction to giving her pain and orgasms. Her tears and pleas make me hard, but her climaxes make me explode. The combination of the two––her pain and pleasure––is the biggest aphrodisiac. Beyond that physical part, something else has started to develop, these *things* she makes me feel, like the agony that's slicing through my gut right now.

"I'll deal with it," I say bluntly. "No one says a word to Carly but me."

"Oh," she snickers, "I wasn't going to volunteer. I'll leave the unpleasant task to you."

"Good. I'm glad we understand each other." I walk to the door and turn. My smile is as cold as her eyes. "Congratulations. You're going to be a grandmother again."

I don't wait for her reaction. I go back to my study to start my own search.

It becomes apparent I have nothing to go on. Valentina destroyed her phone in no place other than that godforsaken area where she used to live, and she hasn't touched the money in her account. Even though she couldn't afford a plane ticket, I set up a search for travelers by plane and bus. Trains going farther than Pretoria are non-existent, so that leaves me with private taxis, but none in the Johannesburg area has crossed the city borders during the last few hours. My hackers plant bugs in electronic banking and medical servers to raise a flag if her and Charlie's names pop up anywhere on the system. I inform my network of colleagues and police informants to be on the lookout and offer a huge reward for any information on her whereabouts. Then I drive to Kris' house, who's shell shocked. She shows me Valentina's text when I finally convince her I'm only trying to keep Valentina safe, and demands to know why Valentina ran. I don't tell her about the baby. For now, it's best that only Magda, my bodyguards, and I know.

I take Rhett and drive to Berea. We knock on the door of every bar and business in a five-mile radius of her old place, but no one knows anything. By the time night falls, I'm sick. My concern is so great I can't even hate her for it. I only want her back. She's got no money, and the world is a very unsafe place. Valentina may be cold, hungry, or scared. She may even be in danger. Without money, her only option is a backstreet abortion, and those don't come without health risks. Feeling defeated, I get behind the wheel and drive to an unbearably empty home.

Valentina

The drive is strenuous. Because of the state of the car, it takes longer to cross the country at a slower speed than the legal limit. My back aches, and Charlie is getting restless, but after seven hours the lights of Durban finally come into view. Just as well. We're almost out of fuel. I have no idea where I'm going. I've only been here twice on holiday with my parents as a child.

A sign indicates the beachfront. The main beach will be much too dangerous with the criminals hanging around. I opt for one in a suburb and follow the road to a dark and empty parking lot. We can't stay here in full sight. It's asking for trouble. After circling the parking once, I find a spot where I can drive off the tarmac under some over-hanging trees. The hiding place isn't perfect, but it will have to do. I can't go another kilometer.

Charlie makes a lot of excited noise when he realizes we've reached our destination. I have to silence him like I did at home when we hid from the mob. Knowing he needs to stretch his legs after the long sit, I unlock the doors and help him crawl out from under the dense vegetation into the night. The tropical climate is warm and humid.

Hand in hand, we walk down the steep path to the beach. I use my penlight to illuminate our way, keeping vigilant and watching out for danger. You never know who lurks in the dark.

"Shh," I say. "We're not supposed to be on the beach at night. This is our secret, okay?"

Charlie nods enthusiastically. "Se–secret."

We stop at the bottom of the stone path to take in the scenery. The moon shines over the water, casting a light over the white foam of the waves. I take a second to register the salty air and the crush of the water as it curls and breaks.

"Do you remember the ocean, Charlie?"

"Swi–swim."

"It's night."

His tone becomes insistent. "Swi–swim."

"Tomorrow, okay? It's too risky at night."

"Swi–swim!"

I take his arm. "First you need to sleep to build up your strength."

I utter a sigh of relief when he allows me to lead him back up the path. Near the top, we climb over the sand, already wet from dew, to relieve ourselves in the dunes. Certain that the parking lot is still empty, I take him back to the car. For a second, he freezes.

"N–no."

"We're not going to drive anymore. I promise."

He shakes his curls. "No–no."

"Hey," I nudge him with an elbow, "this is our big adventure. We're camping."

"Ca–camping."

"Yes." I take his hand and guide him back to the car. "Isn't this exciting?"

I put the seats down and settle him in as best as I can, rolling my fleece into a pillow for his head and covering him with my jacket. When his soft snores fill the car, I allow my façade to drop. Pretending is exhausting. I don't know if we'll get through the night unscathed or where tomorrow's food will come from, but worrying ahead is useless, so I simply focus on getting through the night.

MORNING IS SURPRISINGLY COLD. I shiver in my T-shirt. My body aches from the uncomfortable position. Too wary of the possible dangers, I haven't slept a wink. Charlie shifts, yawns, and gives me a bleary-eyed look.

I cup his cheek. "How did you sleep?"

He doesn't answer, but he doesn't have to. The dark circles under his eyes say it all.

We crawl out from under the bushes. I bring my toilet bag from the car and find a garden tap at the top of the path to the beach where we can wash our faces and brush our teeth. I give Charlie the tooth-brush I bought at Quick and help him with his grooming. Dressing behind a tree, I pull my bikini on under my dress and try not to think about the fact that Gabriel bought it for me. Charlie will have to swim in his underpants until I can make another plan.

"Hu–hungry."

"Me, too."

Not having enough money left for food, I let Charlie finish the apple from his snacks and fill up his empty soda bottle with water.

"Ready for more adventures?" I shade my face with a palm, looking up at the road that snakes past the houses to the top of the hill.

Charlie groans, but he follows as I start walking. After an hour, we hit the first small commercial area. It's a strip mall consisting of a grocery store, a Wimpy restaurant, a bank, a pharmacy, and a liquor store. I stop at every store to ask for a job, but as expected there's nothing available. With an unemployment rate of over forty percent and me not having formal qualifications or referral letters, I have zero percent chance of landing anything, not to mention that the affirma-tive action law isn't in my favor.

By midday, we hit another residential area and a beach. I'm famished, and Charlie is tired. We stop at a beach kiosk selling ice cream and hot dogs. I count out my last few cents on the counter, but it's not even enough to buy Charlie an ice cream.

The man waiting behind us in the queue clicks his tongue. "Eish," he says in the local dialect, "you look hungry, little miss."

I turn to look at him. He has brown, wrinkled skin, like the coloreds who are a mix between black and white.

He shuffles past us to the front, goes through his pockets, and takes out a bill, which he hands to the vendor. "Give this lady and man each a *boerewors* roll."

I gape at him, blinking back tears. From the state of his clothes and the way the soles of his shoes flap when he walks, he's worse off than us.

"No, please." I hold up a hand. "It's very kind, but I can't accept."

He makes a tsk-tsk noise and rumbles off something in Zulu to the man grilling beef sausages on the gas grill behind the counter.

Before I can protest again, the vendor places two *boerewors* rolls with all the trimmings in our hands.

I avert my eyes, ashamed that we robbed this poor man of a meal, but too starved to refuse him a second time. "Thank you."

"You're very welcome."

Charlie has already dug in. We sit down on a bench facing the sea to eat. The bread is toasted and the beef sausage thick and juicy with fat. The *chakalaka* sauce is dripping with onion, peppers, and tomato. It has just the right amount of chili to give it a bite without burning. Charlie devours his in seconds and licks every drop of sauce from his fingers. I finish half of mine and give him the rest.

The man who bought us lunch walks past, a bottle of Coca Cola under one arm and a loaf of bread under the other. A worn jacket with patches on the elbows stretches over his crooked back. The stitches are visible where the fabric is pulling apart on the shoulders.

"Wait!" I jump up and run after him.

He turns and smiles. "Yes?"

"Do you have a number?" I wipe the windblown hair from my face. "I can call you when I get a job to repay you."

"Not necessary," he says with a shake of his salt-and-pepper head, "but you'll have a hard time finding anything here."

"You don't know of something?" I ask hopefully.

He laughs softly. "If I did, I would've told you."

"Thanks again for the food."

"Good luck." With a wave he's gone.

We're going to need more than luck.

To distract Charlie, I take him swimming. He hangs around in the shallow water until his lips are blue and his teeth are chattering before he lets me towel him dry. For a while, we lie in the sand, looking up at the clear, blue sky. It will be dark in a couple of hours. We need to head back to the car. While we walk I talk and sing to keep Charlie's mind off the effort, simultaneously watching out for unfavorable elements. At least here, in the residential area, we're safer.

At the strip mall, we sit down on the lawn of a small park facing the back of the shops to rest. This is what I tell Charlie, but I have an ulterior motive. When a waiter at the Wimpy brings out the trash bags, I tell Charlie to stay put and run across the road.

"Excuse me," I call as I near.

The man looks up. He has a skin as smooth and dark as oil and his apron is a pristine white.

"Are there any jobs here?"

He shakes his head. "*Aikona.*"

"Maybe some leftover food?"

He shakes his head again and dumps the bags in the trashcan.

"There must be *something* someone didn't finish. I'm not fussy."

"People take home what they don't eat in doggie bags." He pushes past me, heading for the door.

I grab his arm. "Please. Don't make me go through the trash."

He jerks free and slams the door in my face.

Swallowing my pride, I look around, and when I see no one, I lift the lid on the trashcan and tear open the bag on the top. The inside is a mashed-up version of breakfasts, lunches, and dinners with splatterings of coffee and milkshake. I push back my sleeve and plunge my arm in up to my elbow, but all I grab is mush. It will be easier to take out the bag, but it's heavier than I thought. I battle and grunt, and just as I'm about to free the bag from the bin, a hand closes around my throat. Uttering a shriek, I drop my loot.

"This is my beat," a voice growls.

I look up into a pair of bloodshot eyes. The man holding me stinks of brandy. His clothes are oily and his hair and beard dirty.

"Sorry," I mumble, battling to get the word out with the pressure he's putting on my windpipe.

From the corner of my eye, I watch Charlie. My heart sinks when he gets to his feet, his face scrunched up in fear.

"I didn't know." I lift my hands. "I won't come back here. Just let me go. My brother is on his way, and he's going to hurt you. I don't want trouble."

He glances over at Charlie. When he sees my brother's bulky frame moving toward us, he releases his grip on me. I scurry away as fast as I can, intercepting Charlie halfway.

"Va–Val?"

Charlie would never hurt a fly, but my threat worked.

"Let's go," I say, taking his arm and heading back to the road.

We have to wait an hour before the last visitor, a man who was jogging on the beach with his dog, leaves the parking lot where our car is hidden. Only then do we get into the car and settle for the night. Thankfully, Charlie falls asleep quickly, but I'm not so lucky. My mind works overtime. We need money. The only plausible solutions are to find a job, rob a bank, or beg. I don't want to beg or steal, but work is hard to come by.

The surprising part is I still miss Gabriel. I miss his arms around me and his mouth on my skin. My body needs him with more intensity than ever. If he was here, he would've kept me safe, like he protected me from Tiny, but what will he do to my baby? Will he blame me? Or hate me? Will he believe it was an accident, that I didn't plan this pregnancy to manipulate my way out of my debt? No. He won't believe me. A man like Gabriel never slips up, and he won't understand failure. There was a good reason why he gave me the birth control pills. He won't want this baby. He won't be forgiving or understanding. Yet, lying here, staring at the roof of our stolen car, I want to run both from and to him. He's the only man I simultaneously crave and fear.

A noise pulls me from my reverie. It sounds like an empty can being kicked on the tar. I look over to Charlie. *Please don't wake up and panic.* If he makes a sound, we'll be discovered. The metal clang becomes louder. Laughter follows. I turn on my stomach to peer through the back window. Four men are walking our way. They're kicking a beer can between them. The red end of a cigarette glows in the corner of one of the men's mouths.

I close my eyes. *Don't let them venture into the bushes.* My heart starts galloping as they come nearer and nearer, making a raucous racket. The walking and swimming must've exhausted Charlie, because he sleeps through the noise. My nails dig into my palms as I wait for them to leave, but they sit down on the side of the lot, and from the way they make themselves comfortable, they may stay for a while. They talk and talk until the conversation turns into an argument, but I don't understand what they're saying. They're speaking in Zulu. One of the men puts a six-pack of beer in the center of their circle, and they each crack open a can. Another chooses a song on his phone and plays it at top volume. Charlie stirs, but he doesn't open his eyes.

They're getting wilder, laughing and smoking pot. The smell is unmistakable. When they take out flip knives and start throwing them at stray cats, I break out into a cold sweat. On top of that, my bladder is full, and I don't know for how much longer I can hold. As long as the men are here, we're trapped. The feeling is nauseating. Right now, I'll do anything to be back in Gabriel's strong arms, except sacrifice my baby.

After a long time, one gets up and walks into the bushes, heading straight for us.

My throat closes up. I stop breathing. A short distance from our car, he stops and opens his fly. Aiming straight at us, he relieves himself in the bushes.

Don't let him see us.

A tilt of his head, one missing leaf or the shine of the moon on the body of the car, and we'll be discovered.

He shakes himself dry, zips up, and, to my utter relief, turns back to his buddies.

My body is a shaking mass of nerves. I'm shivering all over, feeling cold to my core. I stay awake, hardly breathing, watching their every move. After what feels like an eternity, they get up and walk away. The air leaves my lungs in a gush of relief. To be on the safe side, I wait ten minutes before I dare it out of the car and near the lot. There's no sign of the men. I make quick work of emptying my bladder behind a bush and flick on my penlight. On the tarmac lies a burned spoon caked with blood, an empty plastic bank bag, and several dented beer cans. We can't stay here. It's only a matter of time before we're caught, raped, and murdered.

THE NEWSPAPER HEADLINE at the stand we pass the next morning doesn't help to ease my nerves. A family was tortured to death in their home last night for their television and laptop. Charlie walks next to me, grumpy and sulky. This is no joyride for him, either. I wish I could talk to him and ask his advice. I'll give anything for a shoulder to lean on, for someone to share a small part of my burden. Determined not to sleep in the car, we walk farther today in my quest of finding a job. At the grocery store, I manage to beg a few expired loafs of bread, and this keeps us going for two days.

When Charlie swims, I rinse his clothes and let them dry in the sun. At night, we sleep hidden between the tall grass in the dunes. It's more comfortable, but colder and wet. Charlie develops a cold, but I refuse to give up hope. More than once I'm tempted to withdraw money from the bank--I still have the monthly allowance Gabriel paid me--but the minute I do, Gabriel will know where we are. I may as well sign our death warrants.

After a week, there's no more pretending that this is a holiday. Charlie doesn't believe me, any longer.

"I want to go ba–back," he begs.

I pat his leg. "Soon." What else can I say?

Another week of going hungry and washing under cold beach showers, and I finally hit the jackpot. We're outside a dry-cleaning store when a Chinese man drags a woman out by her collar, screaming in Mandarin. I don't understand a word, but from the shirt with the burned hole he holds up as he shouts, it's not difficult to gather what the rift is about. He goes back inside and returns with a handbag that he throws at the poor woman. She cries and begs in English, saying she's sorry, but the man is a statue with his finger pointing north. When she realizes her begging has no effect, the woman leaves with hunched shoulders, clutching her bag to her chest.

I jump at the opportunity. An hour later, I'm hired. The only reason the man, Ru, is taking me on is because he can pay me cash under the table. This is his way of avoiding social charges, and it suits me. There's no money trail that leads to me. The pay is low, but he lets Charlie stay with me while I work, and for half of the money he pays me per month, he gives us a room with a toilet and basin in the back. It has a door exiting onto the street so we can come and go freely when the shop is closed.

The room is dirty, but with Charlie's help we clean it with the products from the shop, scrubbing away fungus in the basin and grime in the toilet, the origins of which I don't want to consider. The mattress is stained with coffee and semen, but I cut plastic trash bags open and tape them around the bed.

The following day, we go back to get my clothes from the car, but the long walk isn't worth the effort. Someone broke into the car and stole our belongings, down to our soap and toothbrushes. When I tell Ru about our misfortune, he allows us to take clothes from the box filled with unclaimed dry-cleaning.

The money I earn is barely enough to feed two people. Our new lifestyle isn't so much different from our old one in Berea, except back then I still had my dream of making a better future for us. My dream may be dead, but my hope's still alive. We'll get through this. I work long hours, sweating over the ironing board while Charlie plays solitaire at the plastic table in the corner we use for lunch breaks. The rhythm is harsh, and my pregnancy doesn't help. I've never been more tired in my life.

I soon discover another reason why Ru's happy not to have me employed on a formal contract. He can treat me however he likes. He makes me work twelve hours per day instead of the legal eight, but I don't dare complain. It's hard to put one foot in front of the other after ironing from six in the morning to seven at night with an hour lunch break. Most evenings, I fall asleep the minute I hit the mattress next to Charlie.

After a few more weeks, three months to be exact, my jeans are stretching over my stomach, and I can't fasten the button any longer. There's nothing else in the box of unclaimed clothes to fit me, so I keep the two ends of the waistband together with an elastic band I wind through the buttonhole and around the button. Some women are lucky and don't show much for the first four or five months of their first pregnancies, but I'm not one of them. I have a definite bump. If my boss noticed, he doesn't say anything.

Nausea hits me on and off at all times of the day and night. Sometimes I vomit, and sometimes it's only a sickening sensation in the pit of my stomach that lasts all day. I'm losing instead of gaining weight, which must be because of the vomiting. Our future may not look bright, right now, but I can work on it. We're alive. All I have to do is get through this pregnancy and have a healthy baby.

It's in April, during the first week of my second trimester, when I hand a well-groomed lady her dry-cleaning that I faint.

I come to my senses lying on my back on the floor. Someone is slapping my cheek. Shit, it stings. Ru is bent over me, speaking in loud, angry words.

"Stop shouting at her," the lady says. "She needs a doctor."

I push onto my elbows. "I'm fine."

"You're not." The woman looks down to where my sweater has moved up, exposing the pants I keep closed with an elastic band. "You're pregnant."

This evokes a new marathon of words from my boss. He spurts

them at me with animated hand signs, which mostly points at my stomach.

The woman pushes him away. "Stop it right this second or I'll call social services."

This shuts him up.

"You need to see a doctor," the woman says.

"I'm fine, really." I let her help me into a sitting position.

She purses her lips while studying me. "I'm taking you."

"No, I just need a minute."

"Don't worry, I'm paying."

I want to die of shame, but concern for my baby overrides my pride. "I have to tell my brother where I'm going, or he'll worry."

"I'll wait."

I tell Charlie to stay in our room and lock the door. When I get back to the front shop, Ru starts protesting again.

"I'm reporting you," the woman says, waving a finger in his face.

Unhappy but pushed into a corner, he lets me go, leaving him in the lurch in the middle of a workday.

"I'm Cynthia," she says as we get into her luxurious car.

I don't reply, praying she won't think I'm returning her kindness with rudeness. The less anyone knows, the better.

She drives me to a fancy clinic and introduces me to a lady friend who's a gynecologist. When the receptionist asks for my identity document, I start to argue, but she tells me it's standard procedure, and I can't see a doctor if she hasn't registered my details. I don't have a choice but to hand mine over. Cynthia gives the receptionist my address, and when I say I don't have a phone, she gives her the number of Ru's shop.

As if understanding my fear, Cynthia pats my hands. "Don't worry. This clinic is very discreet. No one will know you were here."

After an ultrasound and blood tests, the doctor tells me I'm fine and my baby is healthy, but I'm undernourished. She prescribes vitamins and a protein shake, which my Samaritan pays for at the pharmacy.

"Thank you," I say when Cynthia drops me off at the shop. "I don't know how to repay you."

"You've been pressing my husband's shirts for over three months. Besides, I was going for an expensive lunch date with a friend. I'm happy to have used the money better."

Not having more words, I exit the car and make my way back inside where I'm met with a very angry Ru.

He points at my stomach. "No baby. No want no baby. Go." He waves his hands at me. "Out. Go."

My hope shatters, and my world ends. "I'm okay, I promise. It won't interfere with my work."

"Out. Tomorrow. No baby." He pushes me toward the backroom. "No baby. Tomorrow. Gone."

I unlock the door and stumble inside in tears, finding Charlie on the bed playing solitaire. I look around the shabby but clean room with the cheap sheets I bought from the flea market and the boxes covered with colorful cloth that serves as our table. I don't even know if the car is still in the bushes by the beach. Everything we had is gone, including my job.

"We'll be fine," I say, brushing my hand over Charlie's head as I walk past him to the two-plate stove. "How about scrambled eggs for dinner?"

Charlie loves scrambled eggs. I turn my back on him so he doesn't see my hopeless tears. Gripping the counter, I let them flow. It's my fault we're in this mess. If I hadn't slipped up with my birth control, Charlie would've been safe, warm, and in bed with a full belly. I have to find a new way of putting a roof over our heads and food on the table, but I'm so, so tired. I don't have the strength left to fight this never-ending battle of survival. How long before I let my brother and baby down? Tomorrow, we're back in the street. Oh, God, what am I going to do?

Silent sobs shake my shoulders as I lift my eyes to heaven and pray for a miracle.

Something.

Anything.

Gabriel

IT'S BEEN three months and a week since Valentina ran. I thought I knew agony when Sylvia left, but nothing compares to this torture. Not knowing is the worst. Is Valentina alive? Is she well? When I'm not looking for her, I get through the days by focusing on business and through the weekends by spending time with Carly.

The first breakthrough comes from Magda. I'm pouring over our financial statements when she walks into my study and throws a photo of a vehicle number plate on my desk.

"This is how she left."

I drop everything to look at the picture. For the first time in months, my frozen heart starts to thaw. My fingers tighten on the glossy paper. "How did you find this?"

"I found Jerry."

This reminds me how powerful my mother's network is. I've been trying for months to locate that orange-haired mongrel with no success.

"Where did you find him? How?"

"Does it matter?" She perches on the edge of my desk. "Connections."

Valentina hasn't touched her money, which leaves only one explanation. "He gave Valentina a stolen car. False number plate?"

"Exactly."

"And?" I hold my breath.

"Nothing so far, but I've put out word that we're looking for a car of this description. I have a few friends in the traffic department."

Since our initial argument, Magda's become a lot more cooperative. As she came to acknowledge that Valentina could potentially bear me a child, she's been putting her full weight behind the effort of tracking Valentina. For the first time ever, I have the sense that our family--at least my mother and I--are standing together. It doesn't make us like each other, but our tolerance levels are higher.

Despite my concern and anger, I admire Valentina for staying hidden for so long. The odds have never been in her favor. It was only a matter of time, and that time is now.

A DAY LATER, we have information from the Kwazulu Natal Traffic Department. The good news is they found the vehicle. The bad news is it's a burnt-out wreck. Today's flights to all airports in Natal are fully booked, and I can't wait until tomorrow.

An hour later, Rhett, Quincy, and I are on our way to Durban. I take the Jaguar while they follow with the Merc so we can split up if needed. I instruct my bodyguards to talk to the people residing in the area where the car has been found, and I visit the site. What I see raises the hair on my arms. The car has been hidden behind some bushes under trees, something clever that Valentina would do, but the state of it makes my skin crawl. There's dissolution in the vandalised carcass. The tires are missing, the seats have been ripped out, the dash torn to pieces, and the windows shattered. In the midst of the chaos, in a circle of black, burnt grass stands the broken framework of the car. There's no telling how long ago the destruction took place, but the pungent odor of soot still coats the soil. Is her body somewhere in the bushes, vandalized, too? Even if Magda's contact at the police department ensured me the area has been thoroughly searched, I can't get the ghost of that thought out of my head.

Quincy and Rhett join me an hour later. An old man living in a beachfront house saw a young woman and man matching Valentina and Charlie's descriptions hanging around the beach, but it's been days since he last saw them. I'm about to search the dunes when a text message comes in from my hacker.

Bingo.

Valentina Haynes visited a private clinic. *Today*. I stare at her address and phone number that appear on my screen, waiting for the next line to say it's a hoax, but no other information follows.

"What is it?" Quincy asks.

"Rhett, Quincy, bring the car. Follow me."

Rhett's voice is both hopeful and frightened. "You found her?"

I'm not going to jinx my luck by saying yes. I make my way with long strides to my car. Rhett catches up with me as I open the door.

He places a hand on my arm. "Gabriel?"

There are a thousand questions in the way he speaks my name, and I understand each of them. I know what he's asking. "I'm not going to hurt her. If they're both there, take Charlie for a drink until I give you further instructions."

He drops his hand, letting me get into the car.

I send the address to Anton, my PI, with instructions to get information on the dwelling. I want to know what kind of building it is, who owns it, and if tenants are registered.

The few kilometers I drive to the address on my GPS are the longest of my life. Every single traffic light is red and seems to take forever to change. It's early evening when we pull up in front of a dry-cleaning store. The store is already closed. My spirits sink. I pull up the information Anton sent to my phone. The business is owned by a Chinese immigrant. If he gave Valentina a job, she's not registered as an employee in his records. I get out and motion for Quincy and Rhett to follow, weapons pulled in case. The area isn't as bad as the city center, but you never know. If need be, I'll wait out here all night until the shop opens in the morning. It won't hurt to look around in the meantime.

We move around the building. A light shines from the single window in the backroom, but a curtain obscures the view. My pulse racing, I test the doorknob. Locked. A nod at Rhett communicates my command. He knows what to do. Stepping back, he takes aim.

3

Valentina

Wiping my eyes with the back of my hand, I take a few deep breaths and get a hold on myself. One thing at a time. Dinner first and then packing. I'm breaking the eggs in a bowl when a shadow moves across the curtained window. My heartbeat picks up and warning prickles pop over my skin. Maybe it was someone passing by in the street. Holding my breath, I prick up my ears and sharpen my gaze. No sound comes from outside. There's no further movement. Several seconds pass with nothing happening. I'm almost letting the air out of my lungs in relief when the doorknob turns.

The action is quiet and ominous. Someone is trying to break in.

I can't move. Escape. We need to escape, but the door to the shop is locked, and Ru is the only one with a key. Five more seconds and then the adrenalin takes effect. I drop the whisk, looking for a weapon. At the same time, I gauge Charlie's position. He's still on the bed, which puts him closer to the door. Grabbing the vegetable knife, I put myself with quiet steps between Charlie and the door. Thank God for Rhett's self-defense training. My experience is limited, and my physical state is weak. My only chance is to catch our attacker off-guard. As soon as the door opens, I'll stab. My hand holding the insufficient weapon shakes. Charlie looks up and notices the knife. Before I can silence him, he yells. His scream breaks my concentration. A loud thud falls on the door. The doorframe rattles. Whoever is outside now knows we know he's there. The element of surprise is lost. There's no more breaking in quietly. He's kicking down our door.

When the door flies into the room a horrible spell of déjà vu washes over me. For the second time tonight I'm frozen, but this time I'm frozen in a moment in the past. Like in my memory, Gabriel steps over the broken wood into the room. Rhett and Quincy are on his heels, but I can only focus on the man I ran from and the gun in his hand.

He found us.

He's going to kill us.

Charlie stares at the three men, confusion marring his features. Since our first violent encounter with Gabriel, after all the visits to Kris' place, Charlie considers Gabriel a friend. Quincy and Rhett block the only exit while Gabriel crosses the floor with his characteristic limp. He wears a black suit and white shirt without a tie. His body is as broad and big as I remember, and there's menace in every line of each rigid muscle. The dull light of the room isn't enough to wash out the scars on his cheek. He missed a haircut or two. Wisps of curls reach his ears.

He stops in front of me and looks down at me with the darkest expression I've ever seen. From the way his chest heaves, whatever is going on inside his head is intense. Retribution is intense. So is killing. There's only one thing I can do to try and save our lives.

I fall down on my knees and fold my arms around his legs. Looking up at him with all the begging I'm capable of, I whisper, "Please, Gabriel."

The gun in his hand shakes.

I can't control my shivering. Even my voice trembles. "It's not Charlie's fault. Please don't hurt him."

"Come on, buddy," Rhett says, taking Charlie's arm, "let's go grab a milkshake."

"Milk–milkshake." Charlie doesn't hesitate. He trusts Gabriel and therefore his friends.

They're going to shoot my brother in the back alley. I start to cry, hugging Gabriel's legs harder. "Please don't hurt him. I'll do anything, anything you want."

His stance is passive as he regards me. The only movement is a tick in his temple. "They're just taking him for a drink."

So that Gabriel can shoot me without Charlie bearing witness?

Rhett and Quincy exit the room with my brother, leaving me alone with Gabriel. My tears fall faster. My pride won't let me grovel for myself, but I'll do anything for my baby. Degrading myself like I've never done, I kneel down farther and kiss his feet, my tears spoiling his expensive shoes.

"Please, Gabriel, I beg you. Please, don't kill us. I'm sorry. I'm so, so sorry. I'm sorry for running, but I didn't have a choice."

My breath catches in fear when he grips my hair and guides my head up to meet his eyes again. Caressing my scalp with the barrel of the gun, he takes a plastic bag from his pocket and dangles it in front of my face. "Is this why you ran?"

As my eyes focus on the object, an involuntary gasp escapes my throat. He knows. I lift my gaze slowly back to his. The ice in his blue eyes pierces my heart.

I shake my head, forcing out through dry lips, "I didn't fall pregnant on purpose. I swear to God. Gabriel, you have to believe me. I don't know how it happened, but I promise you it was an accident."

He hooks his hands under my arms and pulls me to my feet. His voice is quiet. Dejected, almost. "I believe you."

I sag in his arms. How can he be so blasé? The life I carry means nothing to him. He's still going to kill me. The only question remaining is how. Gathering inhumane strength, I push away and stand up straight. "Are you going to shoot me?"

He regards me with a strange light in his eyes. "No, Valentina, I'm not going to shoot you."

I lift my chin a fraction, ignoring the warm tears that trickle down my cheeks and drip on my sweater. "How are you going to do it?"

"Do what?"

"Kill me. Strangling? A knife? Poison? Or will you break my neck?"

The ice in his eyes splinters. The fragments turn dark. "I didn't say I was going to kill you."

My thin bravery slips. "What then?" I throw the words at him. "Torture me?"

"I prefer to call it punishment." He grabs my face and digs his fingers into my cheeks. "For running. For putting your life in danger. For not talking to me before stupidly fleeing."

More tears spill from my eyes, running over his fingers. "I thought you wouldn't believe me. I knew you'd be angry about the baby."

His hold slackens. "I *am* angry about the baby." His shoulders drop as he lets me go. "You should've talked to me."

He'll force me to do what I feared all along.

"What now?" I whisper.

"Now I take you back to where you belong. We'll work through the rest when we're home."

Meaning he'll make me get an abortion. Cupping my hands over my stomach, I take two steps back.

"I beg you, Gabriel." My lips tremble violently. "Please, don't hurt my baby."

When the last word leaves my mouth, the moment freezes. Gabriel's eyes widen, and his face pales, the color making the embossed scars on his cheek stand out with an angry red. Time stretches as he stares at me in shock. The horror I never wanted to see is etched on his face, giving me insight into his soul. No, he wasn't taking me home for an abortion. He hoped I would've taken care of it, by now. He's disappointed the problem is still here, growing in my belly.

The spell keeping him immobile breaks, and he limps back to me. We're two broken people in a twisted situation with an innocent life trapped between us, a life I already love more than my own.

"Please," I beg when he towers over me, "I'll take your torture or punishment, and I promise to never run from you again, no matter what, if you let my baby live."

"*Our* baby," he says harshly.

He's right. It's his baby, too, but we aren't two people in a relationship who make consensual decisions. Gabriel decides.

"Yes, our baby," I agree. "Don't make me do something I can't live with. Please."

"You want this baby," he says with a tinge of disbelief, "knowing how it'll complicate your life?"

"It's not his fault he was conceived. It can't be undone, and I'll deal with it, whatever it takes."

His left eye jumps, and his nostrils flare. I have no idea what he's thinking, only that it's upsetting. I understand why he's unsettled. I know how this must look. Many young girls in my neighborhood got themselves knocked up to catch a man or to escape a debt. It must be hard for him to give me the benefit of the doubt and to battle the idea of becoming an unwilling father.

"I won't ask anything from you," I continue hastily, biting back my tears. "I won't make this problem yours. You have nothing to worry about. I don't expect your money or time. I will take care of everything. You won't even know the child is there."

All I see is incomprehension as he digests my words. For some reason, he seems confused––it's a lot to take in––but as he doesn't object immediately, I allow myself to feel hope.

"Please?" I ask softly.

"Why?" is all he asks in return, as if he can't get his head around my request.

"Because I already love him."

"Him?"

"I have a feeling it's a boy."

He says nothing. We stand, facing each other, while unnamable emotions play off between us. I hold my breath as I wait for his answer. My life, Charlie's life, and my baby's life are in Gabriel's hands. The next word that falls from his mouth will be the verdict that decides my child's future, the difference between life and death, and I can't do a goddamn thing about it, because I'm still Gabriel's property for the next nine years.

The sound I'm waiting for doesn't come, but he gives me better. He wraps his arms around me and pulls me to his body. The minute his strength envelops me I collapse, my knees caving in while my hands fist in the shirt under his jacket. It doesn't matter that I can't stand, because he is there to catch me. I breathe in his spicy and clean scent, enormous relief making me dizzy and, now that I'm no longer alone, also leaving me weak.

"I was so afraid," I whisper, letting out a tremulous breath and clutching his clothes as if they're my lifeline. "I was so afraid every day."

"Shh. I'm here now."

His hands are broad and strong on my back, and I sink deeper into the strength he provides. The way he holds me is hesitant. I sense he wants to say more, but after another heartbeat, he scoops me up in his arms, snatches my bag from the makeshift table, and carries me to his car.

I know men like him, and I know the gift he just offered is greater than any I could've hoped for. More than believing me when I said I didn't fall pregnant on purpose, he forgave me for running, and he's allowing me to have a baby he doesn't want. He didn't have to. He could've dropped me off at a clinic with instructions and fetched me back as his toy. Men like Gabriel don't do well with pregnant toys. A big belly won't serve his needs. Or maybe I'm done being his toy. Whatever the case, I'm filled with relief. I lean my head on his chest in gratitude.

He opens the door, lowers me in the passenger seat, and fits my seatbelt. He removes his jacket and dumps the gun in the cubbyhole. The jacket goes on the console between our seats and my bag at my feet. When he takes the wheel, I dare to ask again, "Charlie?"

He squeezes my knee. "Don't fret, beautiful. He'll be fine."

After fastening his seatbelt, he steers us into the traffic and dials Rhett on the hands-free kit with a single instruction. "Take Charlie home."

I lean my head back, for the first time in three months not worrying about dying. With the earlier adrenalin wearing off, I feel like a washed-out ragdoll. I don't care about what waits for me at home. All that matters is that we're safe.

Gabriel cups my neck and pushes my head down in his lap, my body cushioned on his jacket. I keep my eyes open and absorb his power. His thigh muscles bunch under my cheek as he steps on the clutch and changes gears. I watch his enormous hands as he grips the wheel and takes charge of my destination. The feeling I once had of placing myself in his hands, trusting him to be a good driver who'll bring me safely to my destination, is now real. I rely on him to drive us six hours straight through the night and deliver us home. There's not a doubt in my mind he'll navigate any pitfall without falling asleep or crashing the car. Gabriel is too decided, rational, and faultless for that. His chest rises and falls with steady, deep breaths, the reassurance I need that he's securely on his course and knows what he's doing. I can let my guard down. For once, I can rely on someone else to take control.

I nestle deeper into his lap, letting his warmth enfold me. Masculinity radiates from the flex of his muscles as he manipulates the powerful engine of the car. He doesn't break the speed limit, and this further reassures me. He turns up the heater and puts the radio on a classical music station that helps soothe me.

Once on the open road where he doesn't have to change gears, he brushes a palm over my head, tangling his fingers in my hair. For a while he rubs the tresses between a thumb and forefinger, and then he strokes my shoulder and arm. He runs his hand over my back and comes to a stop on my waist, his fingers playing gently over the side of the bump that used to be my flat stomach. I turn slightly to find a more comfortable position, and Gabriel doesn't change his hold on me. He keeps his fingertips on the curve of my belly, lightly, yet protectively.

The moon is visible from the passenger side window where it breaks through the clouds. It moves with us, bringing along the milky-way stars. There's something soothing about the sound of the tires rolling on the tar and the music playing softly in the warm background while I'm cocooned in a strong man's lap as the cold, dark night speeds past outside. Finally, the comfortable, luxurious safety of it all lulls me to sleep. I fall down a rabbit hole of deep, exhausted, crazy dreams where property like me is cherished.

Gabriel

ALL THE WAY from Durban to Johannesburg my insides shake. How easily I could've lost her. She's a survivor, one of the strongest I know, but even survivors eventually run out of luck. This is my fault. This is my backhanded, conniving doing. Valentina ran to protect our baby. She believed I wouldn't want it. I can't blame her. From her perspective, I'm the monster, and it's true. Only a monster would kidnap her, train her to fuck him, and then make her pregnant without her consent. Only a monster would believe the worst of her, expecting her to run to get rid of our child. A good man would've seen things for what they are. Valentina isn't capable of hurting an unborn child, even if that child is a monster's.

The guilt mauls my mind to pieces all the way home. I hate myself for who I am and for what I'm going to do, because I won't tell her. I won't tell Valentina why she fell pregnant. I'm too needy. I want a small part of her affection and approval too much. Why make her hate me more than she already does? Why make it harder on her? It'll be best for both of us to keep the untruth alive. She never needs to know. This is what I tell myself when I park the car in the driveway.

While she was sleeping, I called Magda to let her know the status of the situation. I also checked with Rhett on how Charlie was doing. They were behind me by one hour. I instructed them to let Charlie sleep at the guardhouse when they arrive. It was a long twelve-hour drive to Durban and back, but I barely feel the strain. Superhuman strength drives me where my woman and child are concerned. A glance at the dash clock tells me it's three in the morning. The house is quiet, everyone asleep. Just as well. I want time alone with Valentina before facing Magda and the rest of the staff.

My precious bundle stirs when I lift her from the car and carry her inside, but I press her face to my chest, urging her not to break her sleep. I take her upstairs and lie her down on my bed, trying not to disturb her too much when I remove her clothes. After undressing, I get under the covers beside her and pull her to my chest. My body molds around hers, every part just like I remember, except for the soft curve of her stomach that presses deeper into my groin. The rest of her has lost weight. Her bony shoulders and thin arms cut straight into my conscience, and still I'm perverse enough to grow hard. I want to both possess her and revere her by not touching her. With all the willpower I possess, I force my dick down. For now, her mind is in a subconscious world, and like the bastard I am, I hold her naked body close while she can't deny me.

Valentina

WAKEFULNESS PULLS AT ME, but I'm not ready to open my eyes. I'm still in my cocoon, warm and safe, only, now it's softer and more comfortable. Slowly, reality returns. I'm in a bed, in a pair of strong arms. Naked. I lift my eyelids to find Gabriel watching me. Immediately, I tense. When is he going to order me to the gym for my punishment? As stiffness invades my muscles, his eyes grow hard, and his deformed face twists into a cold mask, but he doesn't loosen his hold.

His voice is clipped. "How do you feel?"

I sweep my hair behind my ear, self-conscious about our nakedness. It's been three months and my body has changed. "Fine, thank you."

"Stay." He throws the duvet off his body, but makes sure I'm covered.

His chiseled ass bunches, and the muscles in his broad back flex as he walks to the bathroom. A second later, the water in the shower comes on.

Not sure what to do, I look around the familiar room. The same medical equipment from before is still here. I'm not going to lie in bed awaiting my punishment naked. I get up and walk to the closet to borrow one of his T-shirts so I can make it to my room with my modesty intact, but when I open the top drawer my T-shirts are neatly folded on the shelf. So are my underwear, shorts, and nightdresses. Drawer after drawer holds my clothes as well as new garments I've never seen. I lift a blouse to read the label. Everything is in my size, or at least my pre-pregnancy size. Baffled, I go through the closet. My jeans, dresses, jackets, and pants are organized by colors.

"Those won't fit, now," his deep voice says behind me.

I jump and twirl around. Gabriel stands in the door, a towel wrapped around his waist and his chest wet with drops of water. Instinctively, I cover my breasts and below my stomach, a warm flush working its way over my body. Without looking at my naked parts, he takes a T-shirt from the top shelf and hands it to me. It's one of his.

"We'll have to do some shopping," he says.

I pull the T-shirt over my head hastily. Thankfully, the hem reaches my knees. I motion at the cupboards. "I don't understand."

"I had your things moved over."

"Why?"

He takes down a shirt and drops the towel. I have to look away as he starts to dress. "We'll rectify the clothes situation as soon as possible. I apologize about that."

More confused than ever, I say, "You couldn't know. That I'm still pregnant, I mean."

The look he gives me is a strange one. A shadow invades his eyes. He pulls on a pair of slacks, not bothering with underwear.

"How *did* you find out?" I ask carefully.

"Rhett was worried about you."

"Ah." It's a nice way of telling me Rhett ratted on me without blaming Rhett.

Feeling increasingly uncomfortable, I find a pair of panties and borrow one of Gabriel's sweatpants with an elastic waistband that accommodates my rounder waistline. I have to roll the pants up several times.

"Back to bed," he says with a dark expression.

I can't stand the tension, any longer. "Gabriel…"

He turns to me. "Valentina?"

"Just take me to the gym and get it over with."

For one second, two seconds, three seconds he stares at me, then he crosses the floor and puts his hands on my shoulders. "I'll never hurt you while you're pregnant."

The air leaves my lungs in a gush. I'm relieved, but not reassured. "Only after?"

He doesn't answer. He only points at the bed and makes me get back in.

"Don't move."

"Charlie?"

"Later."

He kisses my forehead and leaves the room. What am I supposed to do? Sleep? Not ready to test Gabriel's patience, I stay put. The door opens not five minutes later, and Marie enters with a tray. She gives me a scowl and dumps it on the nightstand. There are eggs, bacon, toast, baked beans, and coffee. The smell of the food makes me feel sick, but I fight it down. Before I can say thank you, she's gone.

Gabriel doesn't leave me alone for long. When he returns, it's with Dr. Engelbrecht. A frown runs over his features when he looks at the untouched food, but he doesn't say anything. The doctor runs tests similar to the ones I took in Durban and notes everything on his computer.

"I know it's hard when you're feeling sick," the doctor says, "but if you don't want intravenous feeding, you'll have to eat something."

"She'll try," Gabriel says.

Once the doctor is gone, Gabriel gives me a piercing look. "Put on your coat and shoes."

"Where are we going?"

He takes his jacket off the clotheshorse, but doesn't answer.

I don't have a choice but to obey and follow him to his car. Before starting the engine, he kisses the knuckle of my amputated thumb and places my hand on his thigh. We drive in silence. It's only when we park outside a redbrick building that I dare to question him again.

"Gabriel, what's going on?"

He turns off the engine and faces me squarely, his body a block of hard muscle that takes up all the space on his side of the car. Tightening his fingers on mine, as if he's expecting me to pull away, he says in an unwavering voice, "We're getting married."

4

Valentina

"What?" I cry.

I try to pull away, but he holds fast, a silent warning creeping into his eyes.

"We're getting married," he repeats.

"Now?"

"Here, now, today."

If he punched me in the stomach, he couldn't take my wind out harder. "Why?"

He gives me an even look. "You're pregnant with my baby."

I'm feeling more hysterical by the moment. "That doesn't mean you have to marry me."

He lets go, opens his door, and comes around the car to open mine.

When I don't move, he puts his head in. "Get out of the car, Valentina. Now."

Kicking and screaming won't do me good. He'll carry me into the building if he has to. My only chance at getting out of this is to reason with him.

I step out on shaky legs, holding onto the door for stability. "You don't have to marry me just because I'm pregnant."

He narrows his eyes. "Do you think I won't man up to my responsibility?"

"I told you, I don't expect anything from you."

He puts his nose a hairbreadth from mine. "Has the thought that I'm doing this to protect you crossed your mind?"

The sucker punch he dealt me earlier is nothing compared to this knockout.

"Do you know how many enemies I have?" he continues, grabbing my arms. "Do you know what they'll do to you to get to me? The only thing that makes anyone in the business untouchable is being family."

Everything he says is true. I know how the business works. My child hasn't been born, yet, and there's already a sword hanging over his head. The fact that he's Gabriel's child is enough to put both our lives in danger. I understand what he says, but marriage isn't what I want. It's not what Gabriel wants. Not like this. Marriage is for love.

"There must be another way."

"This is the only way. You can do it the easy way or fighting. The judge has been bought. He doesn't care if you say yes or no. We *will* be married."

His fingers dig into my arm as he pulls me up the stairs and through the door. Some of his men have followed by car and are guarding the entrance. He doesn't give me time to protest or speak until we stop in front of a door with a metal plaque that reads Judge EL Viljoen.

I hang back when he moves forward. He turns with an irritated look.

"Gabriel."

"What?"

I run my sweaty hands over the fitted trench coat that won't fasten over my bump, any longer, to dry my palms. "I think I'm going to be sick." Bile pushes up in my throat.

He cups my face. For the first time since I've met Gabriel his eyes fill with something keen to dearness. "Take a deep breath." He gives me a hard, possessive kiss and ushers me inside.

Barely five minutes later, we're married.

Husband and wife.

The nausea I've managed to hold down boils over. We're scarcely outside before I empty my stomach in a flowerbed. Gabriel is next to me, his arm around my shoulders. He holds my hair out of my face and rubs my back as dry heaves wrack my body. Tears mix with my anguish, shaking my shoulders.

"It's all right, beautiful. Breathe in and out."

I take a steadying breath and scrape some dignity from the bottom of the barrel of my control, enough to straighten my back and suppress more tears.

Gabriel takes me back to the car and fastens my seatbelt. Shell-shocked, I stare at the platinum band with the floating diamond on my ring finger that matches the one on his, except that his has a black diamond. Mine fits perfectly. There's no way he got the rings this morning. He already had them before we left the house. The hasty marriage isn't something he cooked up last night.

He gets in and traces his thumb over my jaw. "Feeling better?"

I hold up my left hand, fingers splayed. "How long have you been planning this?"

His expression becomes guarded. He starts the engine and puts the car into gear. "Since I found the pregnancy test."

"Why are you doing this? Why give up your bachelorhood to protect *me*?" Seriously, why does he care? "My debt can't be worth *that* much to you."

Instead of answering, he pulls off, his guards following. We drive in silence until we hit the road heading toward Lanseria.

"Where are we going?"

He cups my knee. "We need someplace tranquil to talk."

"Charlie--"

"Will be fine. Rhett and Quincy are taking care of him. Today is about *us*."

My worry is not completely eased, but I don't have a choice. I have to trust Gabriel. Now that we're back, I have to let Kris know. I hate that I made her worry.

"Do you mind if I call Kris?"

He takes his phone from the console holder and hands it to me.

"Thank you."

Gabriel has her number saved in his contacts. Why doesn't that surprise me? She picks up with a rushed greeting.

"Kris, it's Valentina."

"Val! Where are you?"

"Johannesburg."

"Are you all right?"

"I'm fine. We're fine."

"What happened? Did Gabriel find you?"

I glance at him, knowing he can hear her, but his face is a stoic mask.

"Yes," I say.

"Tell me what's going on. I'm going out of my mind."

"I promise to explain everything, but not on the phone."

"When can I see you?"

I look at Gabriel.

"Tomorrow," he says.

"Tomorrow," I repeat.

"Today. You owe me a fucking explanation."

"You're right." I rub my eyes. "But I can't do it now. It'll have to wait."

"Val--"

"Kris, please."

She must hear the desperation in my voice, because after a sigh, she says, "Okay. Tomorrow and not a day later. I'll be waiting."

"I'm sorry for making you worry."

"I'm just glad you're safe. We'll talk tomorrow."

I don't know how I'm going to explain. I both fear Kris' judgment and crave her support.

I hand Gabriel back his phone and look through the window. We're heading toward Magaliesburg, passing the airport.

"How do you feel?" he asks.

"Nauseous."

I swear there's a hint of a smirk on his face.

"What's so funny?" I snap.

There's a definite twitch to his lips this time. "It's cute."

"It's cute that I feel like puking?"

"It's cute that you're having pregnancy symptoms."

He places his palm on my stomach, but pulls it away immediately, as if he's worried his touch is unwelcome. The sad and sick thing is I go cold when his touch is gone. Only pride prevents me from asking him to hold me.

After thirty minutes, the road starts twisting up the mountain. I don't usually get carsick, but the winding road doesn't help. I have to focus on my breathing not to empty my stomach again.

He pats my knee. "Almost there."

I close my eyes and lean my head against the headrest. When I open them again, we pull through the gates of Mount Grace. I sit up straighter. I've always wanted to come here. I heard it's beautiful.

It's that and much more. The mountain resort is hidden in the lush hills, surrounded by a forest. The main building has stone walls and a thatch roof. Everything shouts luxury and extortionate rates. When we enter the lobby where several well-dressed guests are conversing, I feel self-conscious about my clothes, but Gabriel's arm is around my body, sheltering me against his side. A concierge rushes forward and greets Gabriel by name.

"Your room is ready, sir. Would you like me to escort you?"

"We'll have breakfast, first. My wife is pregnant, and she needs to eat."

"Of course. What may I get you?"

"Everything," Gabriel says, "and my men will order from the menu."

"Yes, sir."

Gabriel's guards follow, but they keep enough of a distance to give us privacy. We're escorted to an indoor garden where a table is set with silverware and paper-thin bone china. Evergreen creepers ornate the glass walls that give a view of the mountains and the valley.

"Not too cold?" Gabriel asks as he takes my coat.

There's a bite in the autumn air, and the day is overcast. "It's warm enough inside here, thank you."

He seats me before taking the opposite chair. A waiter arrives with coffee and an assortment of herbal teas. I opt for a mint infusion, as coffee doesn't agree with my stomach, of late. More waiters deposit silver-covered platters on the tables lining the sidewall. They lift the lids to reveal every kind of breakfast food imaginable. There are sausages, bacon, fried potatoes, eggs, porridge, pancakes, cereal, fruit, nuts, croissants, sweet pastries, cheese, and a variety of cold meat cuts. Gabriel's men are not seated with us, but there's enough food to feed ten times the small army.

"This is too much," I protest.

"I didn't know what you could stomach. Besides, I didn't want to waste time pouring over a menu. It was easier to simply order everything."

"The guards can eat with us. At least not all the food will be wasted."

"The guards are fine." He turns to the headwaiter. "Pack up whatever we don't eat and deliver it to the homeless shelter."

"Certainly, sir."

Gabriel turns to me. "There. Happy?"

"Shall we serve, sir?"

"We'll manage, thank you."

The staff exits discreetly, leaving us alone.

"We need to get some food into your body," he says. "What do you fancy?"

"Just some fruit." I look at the spread. "I'm sorry, but the smell of everything else makes me queasy."

"Don't ever apologize for how you feel." He gets up and places a selection of fruit on a plate, which he carries to the table. "Orange?" He spears a piece on a fork and brings it to my mouth. Piece by piece, he feeds me until half of the plate is gone and I assure him I can't eat another morsel.

"You didn't eat enough in Durban." His expression turns somber. "Your stomach probably shrunk. We'll have to fix that."

"It's just the pregnancy. Aren't you hungry?"

The way his gaze trails over me detonates sparks on my skin. He still wants me, and my body hasn't stopped wanting him. Not for one second. Not even after he bullied me into marriage. The conditioning of old kicks in. My panties turn damp as he takes my hand and rubs a thumb over my wrist.

As quickly as he took my hand, he lets it go. An uncomfortable silence follows as he serves himself a full English breakfast and eats while I sip my tea.

He only speaks again when he pushes his empty plate aside. "We need to talk. I know you don't want this, Valentina, but there's no turning back. You asked me why I gave up my bachelorhood to protect you. You're going to be the mother of my child. You and our child are my responsibility, and I've never been scared of my responsibilities. You're family, now. Your debt has been wiped clean. You never have to fear for your or Charlie's life again. We're going to be a family, and I know it won't be easy. All I ask is that you try. I won't deny you anything within my means to give. Ask and you'll have whatever your heart desires."

I swallow at the end of his speech. "Charlie and I, we owe you nothing?"

"You have no more debt."

What he offers is noble, but I have to understand if we're equals. "Are you saying I'm free?"

A stony expression replaces his earlier tenderness. "No."

"Then nothing has changed in terms of what I owe you."

He leans back in his chair, putting distance between us. "Oh, but it has. Everything has changed." He holds my eyes. "Before, it was nine years. Now, it's forever."

The statement startles me. I bite my lip to stop it from trembling. How clever. He changed the game, the rules, and the implications.

What did I think a ring on my finger meant? I'm still a toy. The only difference is this time it's for life.

Leaning over the table, he grips my chin, but there's nothing tender in the gesture. It's dominant and brusque. "It'll be easier for both of us if you don't let your disappointment show so easily."

With a jerk of my head, I free myself. "Why must it be forever?"

"You're mine, Valentina. I'll never let you go."

"Why?" I whisper again, needing to understand so badly it eats a hole in my soul.

"I don't need a reason. When I first saw you back at Napoli's, I wanted you, so I took you. Now, I've decided to keep you."

The teacup is shaking so much in my hand I have to put it down. "What about what I want?"

"I said I'd do everything in my power to make you happy. Our time together doesn't have to be miserable. It can be good. Just accept the way it is, and things will be easier for you."

The part of me that needs to be loved rebels. "I'm still your property."

"As my wife, you'll be respected and protected."

"As long as I stay."

His expression darkens. "You ran from me once, but I won't let you run twice. The next time it happens, the person who'll suffer is Kris. I'll ruin her, break everything she's built in her life, and kill her. Do you understand?"

The food pushes back up in my throat. It feels like a knife is twisting in my stomach.

"I asked you a question, Valentina."

Tears blur my vision. I don't want to cry in front of him. I don't want him to know he has an effect on me. Blinking away the moistness, I give him the answer he wants in a voice hoarse from suppressed tears. "Yes."

"Good." Pushing back his chair, he comes around to my side of the table and wraps his arms around me. "In time, you'll get used to it."

I don't say anything. A deep-sated knowledge presses down on me. Gabriel is a man of his word. He did what he said he would. He found a new kitten, and this time, he's not letting it go. All I can do is pull up a protective barrier around my heart. If I'm to survive this new arrangement, I need to be strong, but the first cracks are already showing. He'll break me, after all.

AFTER OUR WEDDING BREAKFAST, Gabriel takes me for a walk in the garden. True to his word, he tries to make this good for me. He has his arm around my shoulders, ensuring I don't slip on the stepping stones that are wet from dew, and points out bird species.

At the edge of a pond, we stop to admire the view.

"I was thinking," he says, "that maybe you'd like to do charity work."

I look at him quickly.

"Now that you're not studying or working," he continues, "you'll have time on your hands. I know you had your heart set on being a vet," he rubs a finger over the knuckle of my missing thumb, "but how about starting a dog rescue program? I'll sponsor all the money you need."

It's too much, too fast. I haven't made peace with my new future, yet. I need time for everything to sink in and to adjust to my new circumstances.

"Thank you. I'll think about it."

He touches my cheek. "You're pale. Still nauseous?"

"A little."

"Come on. Let's get you to the room."

I don't ask for how long we're staying or why, assuming this is our pretense of a honeymoon.

The room is spacious and comfy with decorations in neutral colors. We have no luggage, but the bathroom is stocked with everything I need, including a toothbrush, comb, fluffy robe, and slippers. The tub stands against a ceiling to floor glass window that reveals more stunning views of the valley.

"Do you mind if I have a bath?" I ask. "I've been washing in a basin for three months."

A shadow crosses over his face when I mention the basin, but he doesn't comment on it. "Sit over there." He points at the wicker chair in the corner. "I'll run you a bath."

Emotionally, I feel depleted. I flop down in the chair, watching Gabriel prepare a bath with oil that smells of lavender. My life is no longer my own, but I'm too tired to fight it. Sometimes, swimming upstream becomes too exhausting. Will it be terrible if I, just for a while, go with the flow? Maybe, when I get my strength back I'll fight again, but now isn't that moment.

"Come here," Gabriel says when the bath is filled with steaming water, holding out his hand.

Disobedience comes with a price. Pushing to my feet, I cross the floor and stop in front of him. A moment of silence follows as he looks at me, his thoughts impossible to read. When he finally acts, it's with determined, strong movements. There's nothing insecure or hesitant in the way he grips the hem of the T-shirt and drags it over my head. Burying his fingers under the elastic of my underwear, he pushes both the panties and sweatpants to the floor. As his fingertips skim over my legs up to my hips, my body heats, coming alive under the light caress. The power of his touch is familiar. I'm both devastated and ecstatic to discover his magic still works on me. I crave his body, but feel guilty about wanting the man who tied me to him with the invisible chains of marriage, and worse, Kris' fate. As always, he leaves me no choice. I'm powerless to prevent his touch or my arousal. I'm powerless to do anything but feel.

A flutter of nervous anticipation races through my belly, burning my core as his hands fasten on my waist. Instead of lifting me into the bath, he walks me backward to the window until my back presses against the glass. The crisp chill of the autumn air penetrates my skin, but heat runs down my spine. He arranges me like a butterfly pinned for framing and takes a step back. For several seconds, he only looks at me, his gaze trailing from the top of my head to the tip of my toes. There's fire in his eyes, but it's his hands I want. I crave them on me with a desperation that makes my breath shallow and my breasts heavy. When he finally comes closer again, his clothes brush against my skin. It takes all of my self-control not to rub up against him in search of the contact I need.

Holding my eyes, he reaches between my legs. My body trembles when he lightly outlines my folds.

"I'll understand if you don't want this," he says. "I know how it is with a pregnant woman."

The fact that he's giving me a choice comes as a big surprise. It's the last thing I expected from him. But I do. I want him there and deeper. Cupping his hand, I guide his middle finger inside.

He lets out a groan and rests his forehead against mine. "You're wet. I trained your body too well."

There's no arguing that fact. Every long and frightening night of my freedom I yearned for him, for the way he now gathers my moisture and spreads it to my clit. I gasp when he presses the pad of his finger on the nub and holds the pressure without giving me the stimulation I need. Forcing my hips to be still, I wait for permission to have my release. His breath chases over my face as he keeps the stance, his hard-on a thick rod against my hip.

His jaw flexes as he grinds his teeth. I don't know why, but he fights wanting me. Me? I've given up a long time ago. I'm a realistic girl. I know I'm an object, something to satisfy his sexual cravings for dominance and manipulating my pleasure, but I've come to accept his control over my body as I'm coming to terms with my new captivity. I'll never be free or loved, and I'm not going to deny myself the only thing I have––unequalled physical passion. If this is what my life has been reduced to, I'll take what I can get. I'm not masochistic enough to refuse the breadcrumbs when I'm starving. There will be other things that can fill the hole in my heart and the hankering for love in my soul. A career, a child, finding joy and gratitude in each moment. In this moment, I can have a piece of Gabriel by giving him what he wants most. My pleasure. My submission.

Cupping his beautiful, masculine, scarred face, I guide his lips to my breast, showing him what I'm prepared to take and give.

"Valentina." My name is a broken sound on his lips. He brushes his mouth over my nipple. "Are you sure about this?"

I drag my hand through his hair, tugging on the strands. "Isn't this what husbands and wives do on honeymoon?"

He looks up at me with the kind of intention that's fierce enough to scare. "No." The word is loaded. It slips out on a huff of strained control. "This is *not* how husbands and wives behave."

I know what he means. Husbands and wives make love. They don't devour each other with a hunger that borders on obsession, on something so perversely pleasurable it feels wrong.

The air leaves his lips on a gush, a moment of sublime surrender. The fight to keep his distance melts into the kiss he plants on my breast. He groans when his tongue touches the tip. With a catch of his breath, he draws me deeper.

My knees buckle at the scorching hotness of his mouth as he licks and bites. Gone is the cotton wool in which he wrapped me earlier, and back is the man I'm addicted to. He lets go of my sex to squeeze my other breast between his fingers. His mouth moves to that peak, sucking with a force that pulls blood to the engorged tip. When I moan, he lets go with a pop.

He rubs a palm over the curve. "Jesus, I gave you a hickey on your tit."

I don't care. My body has worn his marks before, marks harsher than the red spot on my breast. His name falls needy and breathlessly from my lips.

Contained desire replaces the predator look of a moment ago. Once again, Gabriel is in control. He kneels in front of me and hooks my leg over his shoulder. Folding his hands around my waist, he helps me keep my balance while his mouth goes to the juncture of my thighs. He watches me as he teases my folds with his tongue, running the tip over my heated flesh. When he bites lightly into my labia, I jerk and try to move away, but his big hands keep me in place. It's the grueling way in which he sucks on my clit and runs his teeth over the aching nub that has my toes curl with unbearable pleasure. He pulls back, all the while holding my eyes, and parts my pussy lips. His gaze leaves mine to study the flesh in the V of his fingers.

"You are so fucking beautiful," he whispers. "You have the prettiest cunt I've ever seen."

I flush at his vulgar compliment, but he doesn't give me time to process how I feel about the crass words, because he sinks the thumb of his free hand into my channel. My thighs tremble when he pulls out and pushes back in a few times.

"That's it, beautiful. I want to make your whole body shake with pleasure."

That's exactly what happens when he uses two fingers pressed together to spank my clit.

"Gabriel!"

My nails dig into his shoulders for support as my body prepares for release.

"I know you like this."

Yes, he does. He knows this from the first time he spanked my pussy with his belt.

"Come for me," he growls, looking up at me with dark possession.

Two more taps, and I do as he demands, coming with a violent spasm that locks my muscles and arches my back. He covers my clit with his lips and sucks me through the orgasm until I'm trembling with aftershocks. My head is tilted back, and my eyes are closed, but I feel him straighten and work open his fly.

He kisses the shell of my ear. "I'm going to fuck you right here against this window."

No one can see us––our bathroom is practically overhanging an abyss––but the thought of being seen in such a compromising position makes me tense. The slick head of his cock touches my stomach. I open my eyes to look at him. His face is close to mine, not turned away to shelter me from the scars as before.

He brushes our lips together. "What a gorgeous sight you must be with your ass cheeks pushed up against this window."

He grabs my ass and spreads the cheeks, opening me up to the view of the outside world. "What a turn-on to see those wet pussy lips." He nips at my neck, freeing his cock. "Any man on the other side of this window will come in his pants."

As he speaks, he aligns his cock with my entrance and presses an inch inside. I moan at the thick intrusion, needing him to drive deeper, but Gabriel isn't to be rushed. Male grunts and female whimpers fill the space as he enters me painstakingly slow. It takes him a while to work himself fully inside. I'd almost forgotten how big and thick he is. By the time he's buried up to his balls, he's perspiring, and his face is contorted with strain. He flattens me against the glass with his body, bends his knees, and gives a few shallow pumps.

"Mine. Mine. Mine." He accentuates each word with a shove that drags his cock over the sweet spot that makes my womb tighten with a new building need. It's too little and too much.

"Pleeaasse," I beg.

He pulls out almost completely to give me more friction, and penetrates me carefully. He cups my hips between his large palms as if I'm as fragile as our breakfast china. His heat envelopes me from the front while the cold window cools my back. At this rhythm, the contraction that announces my orgasm is a slow-detonating pool of pleasure that ripples out over my entire body.

"Ga––" I swallow the rest of his name as I come.

"Yesss," he grunts, "come on my cock."

My inner muscles clench around him as he speaks the wicked words. My skin is still tingling from the orgasm when he pulls free, turns me toward the bath, and places my hands on the edge of the tub.

"Hold on for me."

With much gentleness he enters me from behind. His thumb presses on the pucker of my ass, adding extra sensations as he pumps in and out of my body, swaying us both with an easy rhythm.

"Look at that," he says, grabbing my hair and turning my head toward the mirror on the wall.

The muscles of his legs and ass bunch as he pulls out, drives in, and grinds our groins together, over and over. The motion makes my breasts sway. Holding onto one hip, he palms a breast and rolls my nipple, making me contract around him.

He groans and pinches. "Yes, squeeze my cock just like that. Make me come."

When I clench my inner muscles, he falls forward with a curse, catching his weight with his palms on the edge of the tub. His chest is pressed against my back. Even if I can't take him any deeper he thrusts his hips up, claiming every piece of me he can.

I feel the exact moment he snaps, the moment every part of his body goes rigid and his cock grows thicker inside me. When he reaches for the bath oil, I'm reminded that Gabriel is still the hard lover from before. I squirm when the cap lifts with a click, but he holds me down with a hand between my shoulder blades and squirts the liquid down the crack of my ass.

I know what this means even before he penetrates my dark entrance with a finger. For a while he takes me with shallow pumps, and then his finger slips in all the way. When I'm used to the sensation, a second finger joins the first, and then a third.

"Will you be a good girl if I let up, Valentina?"

No matter how well he prepares me, anal will never be my favorite, but Gabriel loves it. I want to give him this. I look back at him from over my shoulder and give a small nod.

"Good kitten."

He lifts his palm from my back and grabs the root of his cock, positioning it at my tight entrance. His free hand moves between my legs. It burns when he opens me with the broad head of his cock, but his deft fingers are manipulating my clit in just the right way, rolling the over-stimulated nub with the perfect amount of pressure. The way into my backside is a slow process that takes a long time during which he stops frequently to let me adjust. When the burn gets too much, he pinches my clit, setting my nerve endings off with a good kind of pain. By the time his whole length is buried inside, I'm shaking, but the pleasure is always bigger than the pain.

"I want to make this good for you," he says in a strained voice.

I cry out when he starts moving, feeling a dark and demented pleasure work its way through the pain up my spine. I gnash my teeth together as he increases his pace, trying to accommodate the carnal feelings so different from my usual orgasms. I crave with ferocity, but I don't know what. It's only when he plunges two fingers into my pussy and scissors them that I understand what my body wants. I need to come so badly it feels like torture. I'm on the edge, but the anal penetration isn't enough.

"Touch yourself," he commands, understanding my body better than I do.

I find my clit and rub while he fucks me with his fingers and cock. I'm not cognizant of time or place, only of him and our bodies as he pushes me to the darkest of pleasures, to a point where no person should go. He fucks me into floating bliss, always pushing the boundaries to physical highs I'm frightened I won't survive but somehow always do, and he's right there with me as he curses and cries out his climax. Coming inside me while driving me past my limits and beyond, he makes me lose myself in the best and worst way possible.

Before I can guard my tongue, the words tumble from my mouth, drowning out even the powerful orgasm burning through me.

"I love you, Gabriel."

5

Gabriel

A man like me can only hope for the words she utters, but they catch me off-balance. I stumble back, ripping my cock too quickly from her ass and making her whimper. She freezes. Her back is no longer rising and falling with the heavy breaths of earlier. She's as shocked as I am. The statement tumbled from her mouth without premeditation. Unlike my usual type of woman, she didn't express the ultimate sentiment of affection to manipulate me, because there's nothing to manipulate. Her fate is sealed. The ring on her finger is the proof. She's mine—forever—but the spontaneity of the words doesn't make them truer than when Sylvia or Helga spoke them. This is what I trained her to think. To believe. Sex and emotions go hand in hand for women. My weapon with Valentina has always been sex, and her words confirmed I won the war. Yet, instead of feeling victorious, I feel like a jerk. Bleak, cold self-loath fills my gut.

Covering her body with mine, I fold my arms around her and give her the only thing that can make me feel better--the truth.

"You only think you love me because I trained you so." I kiss her neck to soften the ugly deliverance.

Finally, her chest expands as she inhales. When she pushes up, I don't prevent her.

She turns in my arms to face me. Pride clashes with embarrassment in her pretty, big eyes. "You're right," she lifts her chin, "because I hate you more."

There it is, the naked truth, stripped from pretenses and a dollied-up version of our unconventional relationship when sex is taken out of the equation.

I cup her face. "I know, beautiful."

The sad part is, I do. I always did. The minute I saw her and decided what I was going to do with her body, I knew she would hate me. I just wasn't prepared for how much it would hurt, and that comes as a surprise. Sure, I care about her like I've never cared about another woman, not even my ex-wife, but the plan was always to maintain my superior position of power over her. Feelings were not supposed to weaken me. How could I foresee this petite woman would make me feel so many different things in the short span of half a year?

I'm crowding her space, not backing away so she can move, but she's not trying to escape. She faces me bravely with her pale cheeks and blurry eyes. I recognize the emotion in that expression. Defeat. It's the point at which she realizes how utterly I've ruined her. She needs me, and she hates it, but she doesn't shy away from the reality. She embraces the pain and makes it her own with that same sense of survival that allowed her to accept my ownership, give up on her dream, and carry my unwanted baby.

In return for her life and body, her dreams, and one-sided, warped love, I wrap my arms around her and give her comfort. She doesn't deny herself the little I offer. She buries her face in my chest and leans against me, allowing me to support her weight. I scoop her up in my arms and lower her into the water before getting undressed and into the tub myself. I pull her back to my chest so that her head rests on my shoulder. The water covers everything except the contracted tips of her breasts that float like enticing cherries on the milky water. I lather soap into the sponge and drag it over her smooth shoulders and the crests of her breasts. I wash gently between her legs where it will be tender and rub my palms over the toned muscles of her thighs. It's on her stomach where I linger the longest, folding my hands around the miracle unfolding in her womb.

I'm amazed that she allows me to touch her at all and pathetically grateful. I couldn't come near Sylvia from the minute she fell pregnant to the day Carly was born. Reluctant to break the moment, I don't have a choice when the water starts to cool. I pull the plug, help her from the tub, and hand her a towel. We dress silently, both lost in our thoughts. When I look back at her, my heart fills with an overwhelming, intense fucking sadness. Against the expanse of the window, she looks lost and unbelievably neglected, a bride in my oversized clothes. Fragile, damaged, and irreparably broken.

"Come to bed." It's midday, but I want to hold her.

She blinks as if returning from someplace far. I don't like it. Even the moments she retracts within her head are too far away for my liking. With the backdrop of the mountains and wild nature, she's terrifyingly destructible. Small and vulnerable. The swell of her waist reminds me that her delicate condition makes her ten-fold more frail. An overpowering sense of protectiveness consumes me. The fear that something should happen to her or that I could lose her pushes a burning sensation up in my throat. The thought of anyone's hands on her other than mine will drive me to my knees.

Suddenly, I need to know. I told myself if I could have her back it would be enough, that I wouldn't ask questions, but I'm not strong enough to stand by my intention.

"In Durban, did you touch another man?"

She gives me a startled look. "No."

"Nobody?"

"The only man who's ever touched me is you." She looks uncomfortable. "Except for that one time."

I cross the floor and kiss her lips to shut her up. I don't want her to think about the rape. Due to all of my energy having been focused on finding my runaway girl, I haven't made progress with tracking her assailants. Enough of those thoughts. I took her body hard, and she needs to rest. Maybe I need to hold her more than she needs to be held, but it doesn't matter. I take her hand and pull her down next to me on the bed. Fully clothed, I put my arms around her and cradle her against my body. She relaxes, her limbs molding around mine like puzzle pieces that fit just right.

"What would you like to do later?" I ask, stroking her hair.

"This is enough, Gabriel."

I kiss the top of her head. It can never be enough. I can never get my fill of her, and that scares the fuck out of me.

We nap for a couple of hours, have a late lunch, and take one of the short hikes to the waterfall after I checked with the hotel guide that the walk isn't too strenuous for my pregnant bride. The air and exercise do us both good. I needed to clear my head from Valentina's gut-eating revelation of love and hate, and she has a glow on her too-pale cheeks when we get back at sunset. Not willing to share her with others, I selfishly order dinner to be served in front of the fireplace in our room. When the staff have cleared the dishes and stoked the fire, we play a game of Scrabble. Our behavior strikes me as odd. This isn't something I'd ever have done with Sylvia, and certainly not on a honeymoon, but we aren't a normal couple celebrating our newly taken vows.

Even if my need for Valentina is already fierce again, I take her to bed without fucking her. In her fragile state, I'm worried of wearing her out, and after this morning's marathon tonight seems too soon. Despite not satisfying my sexual urge, I'm wholly and strangely content to simply sleep next to her, a definite first for me.

When the sun wakes me with a pale glow that sifts through the large windows of our room, I can't pretend that our mountaintop castle of glass is forever, any longer. The fairy tale of last night is over. It's time to go back to reality and all the problems our new situation will bring, including breaking the news to Magda and Carly. I start with Magda, sending her a text message to inform her we're married. Let her make of it what she will.

Valentina is quiet on the way home. The first thing she does upon our arrival is to check on Charlie. Her worry was for nothing. He's in his element, playing a game of cards with the off-duty guards in the staff quarters. The walk to the house seems like a good time to bring up our living arrangements.

"Charlie will live with us from now on."

She stops dead and gapes at me.

"Aren't you happy?"

"Of course, I am. I just assumed he'd go back to Kris."

"You're my wife. That makes him family. He can take one of the rooms upstairs. I'll send someone for his things, today. You can take charge of redecorating or whatever it is you women do."

"Thank you." She squeezes my fingers.

I bring her hand to my mouth and kiss her knuckles. "I don't want you to do anything strenuous while you're pregnant. No physical labor."

"I'm pregnant, not sick."

"I won't take risks with your health."

At my stern tone, she remains quiet.

The clothing consultant is waiting for us at the house with a selection of pregnancy outfits for Valentina to choose from. I thought it easier for her to shop at home than do the tiring clothes hunting. It wasn't my intention to stay while she tries on some of the dresses, but I find tremendous joy in sitting on the couch while she parades for me. Being conservative in her spending, I have to talk her into taking more than a couple of pants with adjustable waistbands and A-line dresses. My favorites are the fitted ones. It'll show off her belly beautifully. Sitting there and watching her, my chest expands with pride. She's going to make me a father, a precious gift I thought I'd never have again.

With the consultant gone, I hand Valentina the ideas I jotted down for her to start an animal rescue program, as well as a new phone. She's a bright and ambitious woman. The last thing I want is for her to be bored. We rehired our old cleaning company plus a server for our evening meals, and Marie is back in the kitchen. My wife will not dirty her hands like she was forced to when my mother made her our maid.

Think of the devil, Magda walks into the lounge as Valentina tells me she's going upstairs to change out of my clothes.

"Val." Magda approaches stiffly. She doesn't hug Valentina or kiss her cheek like she did with Sylvia when I brought her home after our wedding, but she makes an effort to be polite. "Welcome back." She motions at Valentina's stomach. "How are you?"

My petite wife's hands fold over her belly in a protective manner. "I'm fine, thank you, Mrs. Louw."

"Call me Magda. We're family now."

"All right, Magda."

Magda brushes her hands over her dress. "I'm going to be brutally honest, because there's no other way of saying this. I'm not happy with the turn of events, but whatever our past, whatever your debt, that's behind us. You're a Louw, now, and family comes first. You'll have all the benefits that come with our name, and in return I expect you to be loyal. Understood?"

"Yes."

Magda is worried that Valentina will rat to the wrong people in government, people who abide by the law, or worse, our enemies.

I put an arm around Valentina's waist. "She understands."

"Good." Magda looks between us. "I'm also not happy about the way you snuck off to tie the knot. And like this." She motions at Valentina's attire and pulls up her nose. "Really, Gabriel, shame on you to make a lady marry you in such a state. It should've been done properly, in a church, with guests, and with the public exposure my son deserves. The best we can do now is a newspaper announcement."

I don't argue, because she's right. Shame on me. Like every other woman, Valentina deserved a pretty white dress, flowers, a three-layered cake, and the whole nine yards, but I was too frantic to secure her safety. Plus, I wanted those invisible handcuffs on her the second she was back in my bed, where she belongs.

"Well, then," Magda gives a tight nod, "shout if you need anything."

When my mother's stifling presence is gone, I put my hands on Valentina's shoulders and turn her to me. Her muscles slacken as the tension leaves her body. Magda makes her nervous.

I brush a thumb over the smooth skin of her cheek. "I have business to take care of this afternoon, and I won't be home for dinner. I'm going over to Sylvia's to break the news to Carly."

Apprehension fills her eyes. "How will she take it?"

"She'll be fine." I give her a reassuring squeeze, even if I have my doubts. "If you're going over to Kris', or anywhere for that matter, the guards will go with you."

She doesn't contest the new invasion of her privacy. Valentina already knows when a battle is not worth fighting.

I kiss her lightly. "Call me if you need me or if you're not feeling well."

"I'll be fine," she says in a chastising tone.

I chuckle and kiss her again. She will be. She's too strong to be anything else.

Valentina

THE AIR in the house is suffocating. No matter where I turn, Magda is there.

"What on earth are you wearing?" she exclaims when I come downstairs in a calf-length wool dress with boots. "This shows every roll and bulge on your body. You want to hide your stomach, not draw attention to it. Try a short dress that you can wear like a blouse over a pair of slacks, and go for flats. These heels," she waves at my boots, "look like a prostitute costume for Halloween. A scarf is always good to round off your appearance. I'll take you to Hermes in Sandton tomorrow. They have a new range in neutral colors for winter."

In short, she wants me to dress like her. Ignoring her comments, I escape to the kitchen for a cup of tea. Marie enters with a bunch of coriander as I switch on the kettle.

"How are you doing, Marie?"

Her mouth droops on one side. "Shlut."

It takes me a while to figure out what she said. Suddenly, my thirst for a warm drink is gone.

"Where's Oscar?"

She doesn't answer.

I find him sleeping on the dryer. "Hey, baby. I missed you." I scratch behind his ear and am rewarded with a purr.

Curiosity drives me to my old quarters. The room is bare. The bed has been stripped, and the curtains are gone. It feels unreal to see the space so empty. A part of me belongs here. Strangely, I'm sentimental about my first intimate moments with Gabriel that took place in this room. I recall with uncanny clarity the first night he came to me. If he were a less skilled lover, would my reaction to him have been different? Somehow, I doubt it. The truth is I'm as attracted to Gabriel as I'm frightened of him. His darkness has long since invaded my heart, making me a soul mate to the unspeakable needs that drive him.

From far-off, Magda calls for me. I escape outside to see Bruno. At least he's happy to have me back. After playing with him for a while, I follow the path to the staff quarters. Quincy is with Charlie.

He gets to his feet when I enter. "Mrs. Louw."

"Please, I'm still Valentina."

He gives a small nod. "How are you?"

"I'm good."

"Are you?"

"Yes, of course." My smile is forced as I move to Charlie. "Still playing cards?"

"He plays a mean game of poker." Quincy laughs. "He cleaned out the coin jar."

"Thank you," I say gratefully. "I'll take him off your hands as soon as I get back from Kris'."

"No sweat. We're having fun. Gabriel mentioned that you'd go. The guards are ready when you are. Shall I call Kris and let her know you're on your way?"

"That will be kind, thank you."

It took time getting used to Rhett or Quincy driving me around when Gabriel wasn't available, but now I have an entourage of two cars and seven men.

"Isn't this over the top?" I ask my driver.

He doesn't answer, and for the rest of the way we're silent.

Kris comes outside the minute we park. The men take up positions around the property.

"Val!" Kris takes me into a hug and holds me at arm's length. "Are you all right?"

"Perfect."

She glances at the men. "Are they really necessary?"

"Gabriel seems to think so. Let's go inside."

She takes my arm and leads me to the practice. "I cleared my schedule when Quincy called. I just have to finish the midday medications."

"Oh, Kris, you shouldn't have." She needs the consultation money.

"I want to talk to you without interruptions."

"I could've come tonight."

"I couldn't wait. Come on, take the tray."

I take the tray with the pills, syrups, and syringes, and follow Kris to the hospital kennel. Boxes are stacked in the corner and on every free surface. Reading the labels, I shoot her a questioning look. "A computer? And printer?"

She administers an injection to a Pug. "More like computers and printers, as in plural."

"Did your ship come in?" Nobody deserves it more than Kris. "Did you inherit money from a long-lost uncle?" I tease. "What happened?"

She finishes with the injection and closes the cage before turning to me. "Gabriel, that's what happened."

"What?"

She waves her arm at the boxes. "All of this is from him. It came last week. There are also an ECG and X-ray machine in the backroom."

"Where are you going to put all this stuff?" The practice is bursting out of its seams as it is.

"An architect came to see me about plans for extending. The plans include a reeducation pool, Val."

I gape at her. "Gabriel?"

"Yes."

"Did you accept?"

"No."

"What did he say?"

"He told me to drive everything to the garbage dump if I don't want it." She carries on with her administrations.

"That sounds just like him."

"Why did he do it?" she asks, wiping her hands on her overcoat and giving me a piercing look.

"He didn't say?"

"Nothing."

"Shall we have some tea?"

"All righty."

We finish the round of medicine and go to the house. In the kitchen, she takes two beers from the fridge.

"No thanks. I'll stick with tea."

I switch on the kettle while she cracks open the can and watches me from under her lashes.

"What the fuck, Val?"

I sigh and lean against the counter. "I'm really, really sorry about running off with Charlie like that. I couldn't tell you. I didn't want to put your life in danger."

"Gabriel stormed in here looking like a madman. The guy is normally a freaky, frightening shit, but the way he looked that day scared the bejesus out of me. Why did you run?"

"I thought... I was worried he'd make me do something I didn't want to."

"Like what?"

I grapple for words, trying to find the most tactful ones.

"Like what, Val?"

"I'm pregnant."

"Jesus." She turns her head to the ceiling and drags a hand over her face. When she locks eyes with me again, there's sympathy in hers. Her gaze slips to my stomach. "How many months?"

"Four."

"Too late for an abortion."

"I didn't want one."

"Why not? Did you fucking plan it?"

I give her an incredulous look. "Of course not. I took my pill every day." I fiddle with the teabag. "I don't get where I went wrong."

Her sigh is labored. "It happens. The pill isn't one hundred percent effective. There's always the one percent exception, but why did you let the pregnancy come this far? No one would've blamed you if you'd ended it. Your circumstances aren't exactly normal."

"It's not the child's fault."

"Neither is it yours." Her voice turns bitter. "It's Gabriel Louw's fault."

"It takes two to tango."

"I'm not naïve, Val."

"He didn't rape me."

"No?"

"No!"

"Can you honestly tell me you gave him your consent?"

"Yes. Actually, I begged him." I take down the tin with sugar so Kris won't see the shame in my eyes.

"I told you he was fucking with your mind. Please don't tell me you love him."

I can't face her. "I told him those exact words yesterday."

"You did not."

"I also said I hated him more."

"What is this? A love-hate thing?" She walks to my side and lowers her head, searching for my eyes. "What do you think you have with him, Val? You still owe him money, and nine years of slave labor."

I pour the water over the teabag. "He wrote all of that off."

"Because of the baby?"

Cupping the mug, I turn to her. "We got married yesterday."

Her jaw drops. Her gaze goes to the ring on my left hand. For several seconds, she only stares at it, as if she can't make sense of what it is. Finally, she clasps a hand over her forehead and starts pacing the room. Neither of us speaks while she processes the news.

When she finally stops, it's to stare at me with incomprehension. "Explain it to me, because I don't get it."

I shrug. "I'm going to have his baby. Making me family was the only way he could protect me."

"Are you listening to yourself? You're a member of the Louw family. You're mafia, Val."

"They're not mafia. They're loan sharks."

"What the hell ever. Same difference. You married into the mob."

"Well, it's done. I can't take it back."

"Damn right, you can't." Her gaze shifts back to my stomach. "How does he feel about the baby?"

I swallow. "I'm sure he's not ecstatic, but he was man enough to face his responsibility." I don't say marriage had a lot to do with Gabriel's obsessive possessiveness of me.

She holds up a finger. "Let me get this straight. You found out you're pregnant, but couldn't get it over your heart to terminate it, and frightened that Gabriel would make you have an abortion, you ran, taking Charlie with you, because you knew Gabriel would come after him when he found you gone. And then?"

"Then I got Jerry––You remember my old neighbor?––to give me a car, and we drove to Durban. That's where Gabriel eventually caught up with me."

"And instead of killing you for running, he married you."

"Yes."

"Do you know how fucked-up this sounds?"

"I know the situation isn't ideal, but Charlie is safe, and so am I."

"My God, Val, you're going to be a mother. Is this what you want?"

"Maybe it's not what I would've chosen, at least not for another few years, but it happened, and I'm dealing with it as best as I can."

"What about your life?"

"What about it?"

"Is it going to be centered around the mistake you and Gabriel made?"

"My child is not a mistake."

"That's not what I meant. A life without love can get terribly lonely."

"I'll have my baby, won't I?"

"I'm not sure you will."

A feeling of dread creeps over me. "What do you mean?"

"You grew up with the business. You're not stupid. This child will be Gabriel's first and yours second. If his family is against you, they may not give you much of a say in how you raise him. In fact, if they want to, they can take him away from you."

"He's mine." I put a hand on my stomach. "Nobody takes him away from me."

"That's not how the family works," she says gently.

She's right. Gabriel holds all the power, but I can't face it. Not now.

"Listen, Val, just do me a favor. Get a job. Find something to occupy your mind, something that'll make you happy."

I sound immaturely bitter. "For in case I end up not having a child to take care of, you mean?"

"I care about you, kiddo. That's all."

"I know." I look away. "Gabriel wants me to run a charity project for strays."

"Do you?"

"I don't know. I've kind of lost my passion."

"Maybe it'll come back."

"Maybe."

"I'll always be here for you, no matter what. You know that, right? I just don't want you to look at the situation with blinkers and get a shock when reality hits."

"I know."

"Hey," she nudges me, "have you had lunch?"

"No."

"How about I cook us something and we talk about disposable versus eco-friendly diapers?"

"I have a better idea. I'll take you out to lunch and baby shopping."

"Don't grab the arm when I offer the little finger. There's a big difference between talking and actually walking through aisles filled with bottles and pacifiers."

"We'll also talk about your new practice. Are you going to keep the equipment Gabriel sent?"

"I haven't decided, yet."

I leave the tepid tea on the counter and take her hand. "You'll have to hire more people if you do."

"And set up a baby playpen for when his mom comes to visit."

I swipe at the tears building in my eyes. "Damn hormones."

"Here." She fishes a tissue from her pocket. "The best remedy to get over pregnancy hormones is tiramisu at Roma's."

"Yuk." I make a face. "The thought alone of coffee liquor and cream makes me sick."

"It's for me, not you. Looks like I'll need a double portion, today."

A laugh bubbles from my throat. "You're horrible."

"Love you too, kiddo."

Gabriel

ON THE WAY TO BEREA, I call Dorothy Botha. The psychiatrist greets me by name when she answers.

I dive straight in. "I need advice. When's a good time to call?"

"You can speak. I'm not with a patient."

"I need to break important news to Carly, and I was wondering how to go about it."

"What kind of news?"

"I got married, and my wife is pregnant."

A silence follows. "Does Carly know about your relationship?"

"We kept it secret. She was our maid."

"I see." The silence stretches even longer. "Does Carly like her?"

"Let's just say she doesn't hate her. After what you said about

73

Carly's insecurity of losing me or her mother to a new spouse, I want to make sure I handle this correctly."

"I'm afraid it's too late. You handled it wrong the minute you decided to get married in secret. Carly hasn't been a part of the unfolding relationship or the events that led to your decision."

"Things were complicated. What do you suggest?"

"In a situation like this, I'd say go for honesty."

"Impossible. This is not a rose-colored fairy tale, Ms. Botha."

"If you can't tell all the facts, be as honest as you can. Tell Carly why you excluded her and be frank about your feelings. It may help her to express how she feels about your rash decision. Expect a negative reaction, and whatever you do, don't get upset. What she'll need is love and understanding. Give her time to deal with the news and to adjust, but make it clear that your decision won't change, if that's the case. It's important to show her stability and to reassure her that your love for her is unaffected."

"So, I just blurt it out?"

"No, you use tact. Give her a prompt to prepare her, something like, 'Carly, you remember Ms. So-And-So?'"

"Got it."

"Good luck. I'll chat to Carly about it during our next session."

"Thank you."

"My pleasure. Oh and congratulations."

I rub my aching neck muscles when she hangs up. As I've said to myself so many times during the last few days, I only have myself to blame.

The first thing on my agenda is to have a word with Jerry. I've been looking for him ever since the burglary at Valentina's old flat, the scruffy bachelor apartment I now own. The cockroach has been hiding from the day I took Valentina, but now that Magda has found him, he crawled out of the drainpipes, thinking he's safe from me. There are things that don't add up, and I want answers.

As per my instruction, Rhett and Quincy follow in the Merc. I needed privacy for the call I made to Ms. Botha. They park behind me in front of Jerry's building. The beggars on the sidewalk recognize my face. They scatter when I exit. From windows higher up, mothers shout in Xhosa and Sotho for their children to run inside.

Scott, my mother's bodyguard, gets out of the Merc with my two guys. This wasn't the plan.

He greets me with a curt nod. "Mr. Louw."

"Scott," I say, acknowledging him, and turn to Rhett. "What's the meaning of this?"

"Mrs. Louw sent him with us."

My mother has never sent a babysitter before, and she didn't send Scott out of motherly concern for my wellbeing. I've been in situations a lot more dangerous than this one. In any event, we're here, and I don't want to waste time.

"Quincy, stay with the cars," I instruct. We may be feared, but some dumb idiot or teenager on a drug high may get it into his head to steal the vehicles or the tires.

"Yes, boss." He takes out his gun, making sure it's visible.

"You guys come with me."

We climb the rusted steps to Jerry's floor. I pull my gun while Rhett bangs on the door.

"Who is it?" a voice calls from inside.

I don't feel like breaking down a door, today, so I cock my head at Scott who replies.

"It's Mrs. Louw's guy, Scott."

The key turns in the lock, and the door swings open. The minute the cockroach sees me, he reverses the action, trying to shut the door, but my foot is already wedged between the wall and the wood.

Knowing he's trapped, he swallows and backs up into the room. "What do you want?"

We enter the interior that looks and smells surprisingly clean.

"I'd like to ask you a few questions." I close the door and lock it.

His eyes follow the action. "About what?"

"Where were you hiding these last few months?"

"I wasn't hiding."

"No?" I move around the room, taking in the shelf above the television stacked with decks of cards and an early edition of Monopoly. I love this edition. Eloff Street, one of the main arteries of Hillbrow, is still a prized property in this board game.

"I was visiting family," he says, his eyes darting between Rhett, Scott, and me.

"Right." I lift the Monopoly lid. All the pieces, including the car, hat, shoe, iron, and cat, are there. "Or maybe you ran because you thought after taking Valentina I'd come for you."

He utters a nervous laugh. "Hey, I didn't do anything wrong."

"You took Charlie gambling, didn't you?"

His face pales a shade, but he keeps up the bravado. "Where's the sin in that?"

"Let's see." I take out the silver cat and study it in the light. "Maybe the fact that he's got brain damage and doesn't know the meaning of debt?"

The way he licks his lips reminds me of a lizard catching flies. "I don't understand."

"What don't you get?"

"Why are you here, asking about this?"

"Who broke into Valentina's flat?"

"I only heard about it from the neighbors. I told you, I wasn't here."

I advance on him, swinging the gun by the trigger guard. "Why did you give Valentina a stolen car?"

"Because I felt bad, okay?"

"Bad about getting her and her brother killed?"

He backtracks until his legs hit the couch. "You killed them?"

"I was going to, but you knew that."

"I didn't know for sure." He lifts his palms. They're sweaty and shaking. "Look, I didn't know a goddamn thing. I only did what your mother told me to do."

I freeze. I heard him perfectly well, but reflex makes me ask, "What?"

At the same time the word leaves my mouth, a shot rings out.

6

Gabriel

The body remains standing for two beats before it falls backward onto the couch. Jerry's corpse is staring wide-eyed at the ceiling, his mouth forever shut.

Slowly, I turn. Scott has his gun raised. The barrel is still smoking.

Anger makes my jaw lock tight. It takes three calming breaths before I can speak. "What the hell just happened?"

Scott lowers his weapon. "He was disrespectful."

If Scott was my man, I'd put a bullet in *his* brain, but he answers to Magda. In two strides I'm in front of him. I can't shoot him, but it doesn't mean I can't do *this*. I pull back and plant a fist under his jaw, sending him crashing into the coffee table.

Rhett aims his gun at Scott. His first priority is protecting me. Scott may be working for my mother, but, right now, in Rhett's eyes, he's an enemy. One wrong move and the curly head is dead. Scott knows it. From where he lies on the floor, he drops his weapon and raises his hands.

"No hard feelings," he mumbles, moving his jaw from side to side.

I walk closer and stop over him, gritting out my words. "I wasn't done."

"He wasn't going to tell you anything," Scott says.

Bullshit. He was going to tell me a whole lot more, and I want my answers. Going down on my haunches, I grab Scott's right hand and push back his middle finger. "Guess what, Goldie Locks? You're going to stand in for the man you killed."

He grunts when I apply pressure. "You can't touch me. I'm on Magda's payroll."

This does it. Black dots pop in my vision. "The thing, you see, is I don't give a fuck."

Uncertainty creeps into his eyes. The way his pupils are bouncing around as he takes stock of the room tells me he's considering his options. Fight or flight. He tries to pry his finger free, but I push back more. Before he snatches the gun on the floor, I use my free hand to slide it in Rhett's direction. When his fist comes up, I grab and squeeze until he gnashes his teeth.

"Why did you shoot him, Scott?"

He spits next to my feet. "Fuck you."

"If that's how we're playing, very well." A bit more pressure and his finger snaps above the knuckle.

A chilling cry fills the room. For such a big man he has a high-pitched voice. He'll make a good soprano.

I let go of his fist and move to his thumb. "You have nine fingers and ten toes left. This can take a while."

He grunts and wheezes as I bend the digit back. His muscles tighten. He thinks I won't see the blow coming, but I've been on the block far longer than him. I duck when his fist whizzes past my face and retaliate with a few punches in his ribs. Another one in his stomach takes out his wind.

"Fuck. Ouch." He coughs and gurgles. "Fucking shit."

Snap. That was his thumb.

His cry is ugly this time. From the doors slamming and the feet running on the landing, I gather people are fleeing the building. A gunshot is nothing new. Most people wait it out, hiding behind locked doors. Screams, they're a totally different ballgame. Nobody wants to be tortured, and if the neighbor isn't talking, chances are whoever is making him scream will come for you.

Scott is rolling around on the floor, curling into a fetal position. "You shit. You broke my thumb."

"If I do both trigger fingers you're out of business. Won't be much of a guard without a trigger finger, will you?"

"I know fuck-all." He grunts through his pain.

"I'll ask you one last time. Why did you shoot Jerry?"

"I was following orders."

I jerk him into a sitting position. "Whose orders?"

"Mrs. Louw's. All I know, is she told me to take care of him." His look is cutting. "It's not my job to ask questions."

I believe him. Rhett gives a small nod. He agrees.

"Take him back to the car," I say.

As Rhett is helping a bent-over Scott downstairs, I go through the flat, but find nothing of interest. Popping the Monopoly cat in my pocket, I close the door and join the men.

"Drive Scott home," I tell Quincy. "Rhett, keep a gun on him, just in case."

Scott is fuming when they bundle him into the back, but he's quiet. He's too clever to insult me again.

Pulling off ahead of them, I race north on Jan Smuts Avenue with the speed of the devil. I need more answers, and Magda will give them. She's working at the loan office in Yeoville today.

I barge straight into her office without knocking. "Why did you order Scott to shoot Jerry?"

"Gabriel." Her manner is non-startled as she gets up and rounds her desk. "He was a nuisance."

Mad anger coils through my insides, pulling my gut tight. "A nuisance? That's enough reason for a killing?"

"That's not it, and you know it. He was starting to cause problems."

"You know what I think?" I close the distance. "I think you wanted to shut him up."

A laugh bubbles from her throat. "Shut him up?"

"He was about to tell me what you ordered him to do."

"Me? Give him an order? Are you out of your mind? The only contact I had with Jerry was to get more information on Charlie Haynes' whereabouts."

"I find that hard to believe."

"You'd believe that low-life car thief over me? Jerry was scared. Of course he'd spew all kinds of bullshit." She crosses her arms. "Believe what you will, I did your job for you. Jerry gave your wife a car––a stolen car, may I add––to run away from you. If you were man enough he would've been dead the minute I gave you the information."

"My first priority was finding Valentina. After that I had other priorities."

"Like fucking her?"

To prevent myself from strangling Magda, I plaster my fists at my sides. "You won't speak about my wife like that."

"Calm down." She drops her arms. "Since when can't I call a spade a spade?"

"You're vulgar."

"I'm honest."

"Are you?"

"I don't have time for your games. Scott killed Jerry because we had to show the world no one messes with one of us, and Valentina is one of us. Giving her a car was as good as messing with you or me. The next time she runs, her friends will think twice about aiding her in her silly quests."

"It won't happen again."

"It better not. It won't look good for you if your own wife runs away." She walks back to her chair and sits down. "Anything else?"

My words are measured. "Not today."

"Good. Now get out of my hair. I have work to do."

At the door, I say over my shoulder, "Oh, by the way, Scott has a couple of broken fingers."

The charcoal lines around her eyes crinkle. "That was a childish thing to do."

"He may also have a few broken ribs." The words give me enormous satisfaction. "If he ever gatecrashes one of my parties again, on your invitation or not, he won't leave alive." I wink. "Keep that in mind if you value him as a member of your staff."

Her eyes are spitting venom as I shut the door.

In my study at home, I add Jerry's Monopoly cat to my jar of charms. One for each life I've taken. I may not have pulled the trigger, today, but the intention was there. In my book, intention is as good as action.

The jar is disturbingly full. It sits on the corner of my desk to remind me of who I am. I can put a face to every memento in that jar. I tell myself every one of them was justified, a necessary kill in this constant war of survival, but I'm losing my appetite for the killing. My path has been set, and I've been following it as my heritage demands. With this new path I'm walking with Valentina, it feels as if I'm veering farther and farther away from where I came. I don't know where the hell I'm going, but I know I can't go back. I want to walk this road with her too much, her and my baby.

⁂

THE AFTERNOON DRAGS on with affairs that keep me occupied until late, and when I finally pull into Sylvia's driveway it's close to seven. Dinner is served at eight. I'm hoping to get the big talk with Carly out of the way before we sit down for the meal.

Sylvia waits at the door, a hand on her hip. "Hey, Gab. Gabriel," she corrects, catching herself. Her smile is sweet and filled with the womanly self-assurance of someone who knows she's physically desirable. "You had me wondering about this hasty dinner all day."

"I didn't mean to give you extra work."

She laughs softly and holds out a hand for my jacket. "Don't fret. My cook did all the work." She deposits the jacket on the coat stand. "Are you going to tell me the reason we're having dinner with Carly, or are you going to make me sweat it out another hour?"

"Where's Carly?" I look around the foyer and up the staircase. I don't want my daughter to overhear anything prematurely.

"In her room. I'll call her down in a second. Shall we have a drink?"

She's already on her way to the lounge. I follow, looking around the foreign space. I've been in Sylvia's house a few times, but it still feels unfamiliar. Overly stuffy. Too perfectly decorated. No pets, books, or shoes lying around. Nothing to hint at life. Carly's toys were never splayed on our stairs or even the playroom carpet. Will Valentina allow life into our home? My chest fills with something warm and light as I picture trains, fire engines, and stuffed toys littering our floors.

"Here you go." She hands me a glass of Scotch on the rocks and takes one for herself, which she clinks to mine. "Now, tell me the purpose of this secretive family meeting."

It's probably better that I prepare her before I speak to Carly. I mull over the words, but there's no easy way of saying it. Finally, I settle for short and sweet. "Valentina and I got married yesterday."

Her hand stills with the glass halfway to her mouth, her red nail varnish standing out against the white of her skin where she grips the tumbler. Her eyes grow large, and her lips thin.

"She's going to have my baby."

Pulling back her arm, she slaps me across the cheek. I saw the blow coming. I could've stopped it, but I allowed her the violence as an outlet for her shock.

"You son of a bitch. How dare you humiliate our family like this?" Her voice rises. "You married the *maid*?"

"You know making her our maid was Magda's idea of getting the payback she believed we deserved."

"She caught you, didn't she?"

"Actually," I give her a cold smile, "I caught *her*."

"Why?" She bangs the glass down on the mantelpiece, drops of alcohol sloshing over the sides. "You could've had Helga or any other woman of your social standing."

"I don't want any other woman." My words are measured. "I want *her*."

"How old is she?"

"Twenty-three."

"Is this some kind of midlife crisis? Is this why you have to go for a girl fifteen years younger than you? You have to prove to yourself you still have it?"

"Is that why you're getting engaged to a younger man?"

"Fuck you, Gabriel. It's not the same."

"No, it's not, because your decisions when it comes to relationships and marriage are not based on love or affection, but on which move will serve your financial and political position best."

"Love and affection?" She utters a laugh. "Are you telling me you *love* her?"

"I don't know about love, not anymore, but whatever I feel is the closest thing I've ever felt to being happy."

"You're a fool."

"I was a fool for loving you once."

"You still do."

"Maybe--you'll always be the mother of my child--but I want her more than any woman I've ever wanted."

The color drains from her cheeks. Rage fills her violet-blue eyes, but she maintains a calm voice. "I will *not* acknowledge that woman or her child."

"It's my child. Your disagreeable nature will make things more difficult for all of us, but that's your choice."

She pushes out her chin. "I'll call Carly and give the two of you a moment. Come through to the dining room when you're ready."

As her heels click over the marble, I take a long sip from my drink. A moment later, my daughter comes bouncing down the stairs.

"Dad!" She gives me one of those rare hugs. "Dinner in the week? At mom's house? What's going on?"

I leave my drink on the table and pull her down next to me on the couch. Through the open door, I spot Sylvia making her way to the kitchen. When our eyes meet, she gives me an accusing look.

I pull my attention back to Carly. "How's school, princess?"

"Good. You've seen my grades."

"How about living with your mom? Is it working out well?"

"Yes. Is this about asking me to move back to your place?"

"Of course not." I'm stalling for time, but by God it's difficult to broach the subject. "I have news." I put a bright smile on my face. "Very exciting news."

"Dad," she sweeps her hair behind her ear, "what is it?"

"I got together with someone."

"As in dating? That's great!"

"Actually, it's a lot more serious than dating. We already took it to the next level."

"You're engaged?" She shrieks. "Oh, my God! Who is she?"

"Not engaged, Carly," I say gently. "I jumped the gun and married her."

Her smile drops. She stares at me with the disappointment I expected but hoped not to see. "You're married?"

"Yes."

"W–when?"

"Yesterday."

"I–I don't understand. Why didn't you say something? Why do it in secret?"

"It was an impulsive decision. It's not that I didn't want you there for an important event. It just happened on the spur of the moment." This is the closest to honesty I can get.

Her mouth pulls down. "Oh, my God, I have a stepmother."

"I don't want you to think of her as a stepmom. Sylvia is your mother. She's my wife, and it'll mean a lot to me if you can be kind to her."

Her bottom lip starts to tremble. "Who is she? I mean, do I even know her?"

"Yes, you do."

A frown pulls her eyebrows together. "Who?"

"It's Valentina."

Before the name is out she's on her feet. "Dad, no! How could you? She's our maid!"

I get up and place my hands on her shoulders. "Carly, calm down, please, and listen to me. There's nothing wrong with being a maid."

"She irons my clothes and cleans my room, for God's sake!"

"She *was* our maid. Not any longer. We have a cleaning service for that, now."

"A maid! Could you not have made a less humiliating choice?"

"There's nothing humiliating about being a maid. Valentina was studying to become a vet before she started working for us, and she only came to work for us because she owed a lot of money and didn't have a choice."

She jerks free from my hold and turns her back on me.

I groan inwardly. "I thought you liked her."

"Is it the money? Did she marry you for your money?"

"No."

She twirls to face me again. "What then?" Her laugh is wry. In this moment, she looks so much like her mother. "Don't tell me you're in love."

"She's going to have a baby," I say softly.

Like Sylvia, her eyes grow big. Shock washes over her features, leaving her pale and silent.

I take her hand. "This doesn't change how I feel about you. I'll always love you. I'm sorry you had to find out like this, but I hope you'll accept Valentina as a part of this family."

She pulls away, clasping her hands behind her back. "I'll be seventeen in a month. You don't think it's a bit late to start a new family?"

"It's not a new family, princess. We're all family."

"She's *not* my family, and she'll never be!"

With a sob, she runs from the room. I'm torn between going after her and giving her space. I decide on the latter. I guess that went as well as it could. In time, she'll come around.

Sylvia leans her hip against the doorframe and swirls the liquor in her glass. "Congratulations, Gabriel. I hope you're happy."

She watches me with contempt as I cross the floor, a look not unfamiliar to me. It's the same one she gave me in bed, right before I touched her.

Craning her neck up at me, she continues, "I suppose dinner is off. I don't know about Carly, but if she feels like I do, she's lost her appetite."

"I understand."

She flattens her body in the frame for me to pass. As I go for my jacket, I'm acutely aware of my limp and the way her eyes burn on my back.

"Goodnight, Sylvia. I'll call Carly tomorrow."

The ice clinks in her glass. "You do that."

I see myself out and drive the short distance home. I like to tell myself Sylvia bought a house close to ours for Carly's sake, but it's always been the prestige of the neighborhood. Like Magda, Sylvia comes from a long line of descendants where money is everything and cast is determined by birth. The house staff doesn't mix with the proprietors. In her eyes Valentina will always be the servant. Up until today, I never realized how many of Sylvia's values are embedded in Carly.

When I get home, I find Valentina on her knees in our bathroom with her head over the toilet.

Rushing to her side, I wipe the hair from her face. "Damn, Valentina. Are you all right?"

A feeble wave of her hand is supposed to send me away. "Just morning sickness." Her body convulses, but her stomach must be empty, because nothing comes out.

Concern burns in my gut. "I thought this was only supposed to happen in the morning."

She takes two steadying breaths. "All times of the day." Her laugh is weak, but not without humor. "This baby doesn't like pasta."

I wipe my hand over her clammy forehead. "What did you eat?"

"Fettuccini with cèpe mushrooms. I had lunch with Kris at Roma's." She turns around and slumps against the toilet. Her face is pasty white and dark rings mar her perfect eyes. "About that..." A stern look invades those bleary eyes. "What are you doing sending Kris all that stuff?"

I bent down and lift her into my arms. Even at four months pregnant she weighs nothing. The worry weighs heavier on my shoulders. She looks exhausted. From the way her body is reacting, I poisoned her with my seed. I let her down on the rug and start to pull the dress over her head. Obediently, she lifts her arms.

"I asked you a question, Gabriel."

I unhook the clasp of her bra and push the straps down her arms. "She's your friend."

"Is that your motivation for spending a fortune on her practice?"

The panties follow next, but her boots prevent me from removing the stockings. "The way things were going, her practice wasn't going to survive much longer."

"If I stay, Kris gets a revamped practice, and if I leave, she's dead."

"Yes."

My answer is harsh, but she needs to understand the lengths I will go to. The knowledge that she's here against her will is a bitter pill to swallow, but I will gobble down flames, fire, and toxic waste if that's what I have to do.

I crouch down to unzip her boots. "Why bring it up? Are you planning on leaving?"

"No."

Right answer. "Then let Kris enjoy the gift and stop worrying about it. Except for the nauseating pasta, how was your lunch date?"

Her expression brightens. "Good. I missed Kris. She's a good person, you know."

"I don't doubt it."

I remove her boots and then the stockings, allowing my fingers to linger longer than necessary.

"You're back early." Her look is thoughtful. "How did Carly take the news?"

"Not well, but she'll come round."

"Oh, no, Gabriel. I'm so sorry."

"It's not your fault."

"It is. If I hadn't gotten pregnant––"

My gut twists with guilt. "I don't want to hear you talk like this."

If I were going to come clean, now would be the time, but my decision is made. She opens her mouth, but I still her with a finger on her lips. No more talk of our inside-out, right-in-every-wrong-kind-of-way relationship. No more talk, at least not for the rest of tonight, not while her naked body is right in front of me. Going down on my knees, I cup her hips and pull her toward me. She gives two tiny steps, but the momentum makes her stumble into me. I press my lips against her abdomen and hold them there until her gasp startles me.

"Oh, wow." She utters a delighted giggle. "I felt him."

My throat tightens with an unknown emotion. "The baby?"

"He moved." She stares at her stomach in wonder. "It felt like butterfly wings."

We laugh together as I splay my hands over the tight skin of her belly while she cups her hands over mine. I'm unable to process the wonder unfolding beneath my palms. She's a miracle, and she makes my life happier for this incredible gift.

"Do it again," she says, lifting her hands to give me access.

I plant kisses all over her belly, starting with her navel and ending on her pubic bone.

She says my name like it's a happy word. A ten-megawatt smile burns on my face.

"Did it work?"

"Yes." She laughs again, her eyes filling with reverence. "Oh, my God, Gabriel." She takes my hand and moves it back over her stomach. "Can you feel it?"

"It's too early, beautiful. Tell me what it's like."

"It tickles inside."

A happy glow transforms the pale face with the dark rings. It's a beautiful moment I don't deserve, but I take it greedily. I'd stay on my knees forever to be part of these magical milestones Sylvia wouldn't share with me. For another moment longer, I hold her to me, pressing my face against her warm skin, inhaling the raspberry fragrance I associate with her. I'm reluctant to let go, but she's probably tired and weak from the bout of sickness. Tearing myself away, I run a shower.

There's enough space for us both to stand comfortably, but I sit on the bench and drape her over my body, unwilling to break our contact. She lets me take care of her, washing her body and hair.

When we're both dry, I carry her to our bed. My only intention is to hold her while she rests, but when her hand wraps around my shaft, my willpower dissolves. I roll over her, keeping my weight on my arms, and kiss her lips. She gasps as my cock sinks into the heat of her pussy, and then there are only moans as I make love to her, slowly and reverently.

COME MORNING, I force myself to leave our bed. Valentina is sleeping, and if I stay another second, I'm going to wake her with my cock in her pussy. Again. We made love until late, and she needs her sleep. I can't act like a goddamn horny teenager around her all of the time. The problem is I want her more than ever. With enticing curves and pretty features, she's always been my perfect little toy, my pet, but now she's a goddess. When I fell for her, it was for her strength and loyalty. This time round, I'm smitten by her unconditional love for the life she carries and her uncomplaining nature in dealing with the pregnancy curveballs.

Some women get sick, some feel tired, some have backache, and some develop cravings, but Valentina has everything. This pregnancy came at her with the full-blown force of a hurricane. I'm in the shower when she storms into the bathroom and vomits her guts out.

I'm out in a flash, wrapping a towel around my waist. I let her finish before helping her up.

She wipes the back of her hand over her mouth. "I'm sorry you had to see that."

Tangling my fingers in her hair, I push her cheek against my chest. "You've got nothing to be sorry about. We're in this together, baby."

She puts an inch of distance between us and gives me a grateful, guilty kind of smile that shatters my heart, because I don't deserve one drop of her thankfulness and especially not her guilt.

She touches her wild morning hair. "I must look a mess."

"You've never looked more beautiful."

This time her smile blinds me with its radiance. She cups my cheek on the scarred side of my face. "You're sweet."

"Sweet?" I advance on her, trapping her against the vanity. "Is that how you'd describe me?"

"Like sugar."

"Sugar, eh?" She shrieks when I catch her around the waist and lift her onto the counter. "You're doing serious damage to my reputation."

"Just a big, old, fluffy, sweet bear," she taunts.

"Old? Fluffy? Now you're asking for it." I tickle her sides, inviting more shrieks and a wild bout of screaming.

"Stop," she says through tears of laughter, trying to catch my wrists.

I catch hers instead and pin them to the mirror above her head. I want to look at her. She's insanely gorgeous when she wakes up and even more so when she's happy. Laughing tears cling to her eyelashes, making them appear darker. Traces of the same wetness run over her flushed cheeks. Silky hair tumbles in curls over her shoulders. Her breasts are firm, their new weight pulling them slightly down. Under my unabashed scrutiny, her nipples harden, pulling her areolas tight. I'm standing between her legs, her knees brushing up against my hips. My cock stirs. My breathing quickens. The mound of her shaved pussy presses against my dick where it rises under the towel. I rip the towel from my body and cover the taps to protect her back before bending her knees and placing her heels on the edge of the countertop. She's spread wide, and it's all for me.

I place the pad of a finger on her clit. "Mine."

"Yours," she echoes, her breathing shallow.

"I want to make you burn."

"Then touch me."

The laughter and playfulness are gone. That's exactly what I'm going to do. Touch her. I shouldn't, but I'm not strong enough to resist. My conscience says she needs to rest, but my lust says she's awake, anyway. Fuck my good intentions. I need her. I need her pleasure. I need her *intense* pleasure. It's too soon to take her like at Mount Grace. Fucking her ass like that, I kind of lost it after not having had her for so long, and I don't want to lose it again. I don't want to hurt her, at least not in a non-erotic way.

I squeeze her wrists. "Keep your hands up."

Fear mixes with excitement in her eyes. She wants this, because this is what I taught her. This is how I made her. It's all she knows.

Reaching over her for the wall cabinet, I take out the orgasm oil I saved for an occasion like this. I unscrew the cap and deposit the bottle on the counter. She watches me with wide eyes, licking her lips nervously.

All of my attention hones in on her pussy. Carefully, using the fore and middle finger of one hand, I part her lips, exposing the treasure buried between them. Her clit is engorged. Wetness glistens around her slit. She's turned on. Hell, so am I. My cock is about to combust, and I'm only looking at her. Holding her open, I turn the bottle upside-down and wait for a drop to form at the dripper nozzle.

I catch her gaze, silently commanding her eyes to hold mine. "This is going to feel warm, but it's perfectly safe."

She communicates her trust with a small nod.

"Good girl."

I drip the stimulant oil on her clit and massage it into the nub. Her flesh swells and turns a shade darker. Heat penetrates the calloused skin of my fingertip. I can only imagine how hot her delicate clit must be burning. The sight of that delectable flesh turning to a torturous blaze under my ministrations is enough to make me ejaculate without touching my dick, but I tear my gaze away to read the expression in her eyes. Her head is resting against the mirror, her face turned to the side. Two more seconds, and the hotness will turn into a quick-lasting, intense inferno. Right on cue, her eyes fly open. Red blotches color her cheeks.

She utters a low moan. "It burns."

"I know, baby."

I stop the massaging, giving her time to absorb the sensation. As the intensity climbs, her clit swells. Her feet slip from the counter. She tries to relieve the sensation by closing her legs, but I need to watch. Pushing open her thighs, I trap her body with the weight of mine and press my oil-coated finger on her asshole.

"Want to burn here, too?" I ask, kissing her shoulder.

"No." She squirms under me. "Please."

"Then keep your legs open."

She rotates her hips, trying to press her burning parts on the cold marble, but I catch her legs to keep her still. She gnaws on her bottom lip and tries to be quiet as she rides the wave that burns through her genitals, but her whimpers are becoming louder.

"Please, Gabriel. I need to come."

The stimulant makes her clit pulse with need, and the bite of heat will only make it hotter when she comes. Her pussy is wet with her arousal, the lips dark pink and swollen, inviting me to sink my cock into the soft, warm depth beyond. On the brink of exploding, my cock spills pre-cum. I part her folds with one hand and flick her over-stimulated clit with my nail. Every time my nail connects with her skin she dilates a little more and screams a little louder. I count every flick, measuring the pressure carefully. Too hard or soft and she won't find release like this. She comes on the eleventh count with a wail that lifts the roof. Her pussy contracts around nothing but air, but it won't be empty for long. I press the head of my cock on her clit, rubbing in circles to prolong the orgasm. She clamps her legs around my hips. The heat that drove her to this high penetrates the tip of my penis and burns down my shaft in a slow, agonizing mixture of painful pleasure. The urge to spear into her is fierce, but I count to five, take a few deep breaths, and enter her carefully.

Her pussy is tight, hot, and wet with a distant echo of a burn. I stop when I'm buried to the hilt. This is what I always want, to take her so deep she doesn't know where she begins and I end. There's an endless need to my rhythm as I start pumping. She drops her arms to grip the basin for support as I shove into her, making her back collide with the mirror. I need her to come again, with me this time. Having made it my business to understand her body, I know how to make that happen. Gripping both nipples between my fingers, I use the hard tips as leverage to bounce her curves. The clench of her pussy on my cock is the reaction I'm after. I thrust harder and pick up my pace. Her body tenses, and her legs hug me tighter.

"Come, beautiful." I release her nipples and grab her breasts in my palms, kneading the flesh as my own climax starts to build at the base of my spine. "Goddamn. Fuck."

My load explodes like hot jets of lava. I bite back another curse and fall over her, trapping her body between my arms.

"Goddammit, Valentina." I rest our foreheads together while I catch my breath.

By the time I feel more or less steady, she's still lying back against the mirror, her muscles like mush.

"Don't move."

I turn on the shower and rinse us both, taking care to wash her gently. When she's dry, I coat her genitals with a vaginal balm to alleviate any lingering burn and just to be sure her asshole, too.

Wiping my fingers on her inner thigh, I search her eyes. "How are you doing?"

Her smile is soft and sleepy. "Mm."

I wish I could take her back to bed, but our first appointment will be here in thirty minutes. We don't have time for more than a chaste kiss. "Get dressed and come down for breakfast. You need to eat. After breakfast, there's someone I'd like you to meet."

"Who?"

"Just do as I say."

"I'll go check on Charlie, first. It was his first night in his new room."

"Let him sleep. He was up late with Rhett, watching movies."

"This is new to him."

"He'll be fine."

"I just--"

My palm lands on her naked backside. *Smack.* "Are you deliberately provoking me to spank your ass?"

For a crazy moment a new bout of lust flares in her eyes. It looks as if she may consider that forbidden spanking, but then she turns to brush her hair.

My phone buzzes on the nightstand with a message from Magda. Our appointment arrived early. Thank God Valentina doesn't ask more questions. I have no idea how she'll react to the man waiting for us downstairs.

7

Gabriel

By the time I get downstairs, Christopher van Wyk and Magda are conversing in the lounge. Magda introduces us. He's a close friend, and this was her idea.

"I'm early," he says, shaking my hand, "but I didn't know how traffic would be from Pretoria."

"Why don't you join us in the dining room?" I offer. "We can talk over breakfast."

Magda is in the middle of pouring coffee when Valentina comes down the stairs. Like a fool, I stop what I'm saying to stare at her through the open door. She's crazily, inhumanely, angelically beautiful. Her hair has more volume, and her face has a pregnancy glow. Maybe some of it is the post-orgasm endorphins coursing through her blood, but the pearly quality of her smooth skin is something I've only seen with expecting mothers. The blue dress is fitted, showing off the roundness of her full breasts and stomach. There's a spark in her eyes as she looks straight at me, a telltale sign of secrets, of moments in bathrooms only we share.

"You were saying?" Christopher urges.

"I–uh…"

Valentina saves me by stopping in the door.

I get to my feet. "Let me introduce you to my wife. This is Valentina. Valentina, meet Christopher van Wyk. He's a hypnosis psychologist."

Christopher comes around the table to shake her hand. "Pleased to meet you, Mrs. Louw."

Magda tenses when Christopher attributes Valentina with our surname, but she plasters a smile on her face. "Christopher is a friend. I wanted you to meet him, Valentina."

"Me?" Valentina takes the chair I hold for her.

"Since Charlie is now part of the family," Magda says, "I want to look into all possible treatments."

Valentina looks at me quickly, a question in her eyes.

"I didn't have time to tell you." The truth is I didn't want to give her the opportunity to refuse.

"We've already tried everything," she says politely.

"Not hypnoses, I'm sure," Magda says.

"No, not hypnoses, but I've met with all the specialists in Johannesburg. Nothing can reverse the brain damage."

"We're not talking about repairing damage," Christopher says, taking his seat again. "We're talking about making sure he's comfortable and happy."

"I assure you, Charlie is as balanced and happy as he can be."

"Hypnoses can help him be more autonomous." Magda brings her cup to her lips. "He needs more stimulation and friends. There are wonderful institutions in Johannesburg that can provide that."

Alarm flashes across her pretty features. "Gabriel, you said he could live here."

"He can." I cup her hand. "I only want you to consider all possibilities now that money is not an issue."

"He needs me." She glances at the people around the table like a trapped rabbit. "I'm his only family."

"Shh." I pull her chair closer to mine and put an arm around her shoulders. "I don't want you to get upset. The decision remains in your hands."

"You'll let me decide?"

"Of course."

Her tense shoulders relax a fraction. "What does the treatment entail?"

"A few sessions of hypnoses," Christopher says, "during which Charlie will go into a state of deep relaxation. He'll come out of the sessions feeling centered and at peace. I've used my technique in similar cases to help with insomnia, loss of appetite, speech problems, ticks, repetitive actions, involuntary cussing, anti-social behavior, and incoherent thoughts."

"Charlie has a short attention span, and he repeats syllables, but he eats and sleeps well."

"We'll do an extensive evaluation beforehand," the doctor says.

"If it's in Charlie's best interest..." She looks at me.

"It is," I say. "There are also legal issues you neglected, such as declaring Charlie financially incompetent and formalizing your guardianship. We'll look at that after breakfast."

Her gaze flickers between Magda and me. She doesn't trust us, and I don't blame her. She always took care of her brother without help, and we were going to kill him, after all.

"You're not alone any longer," I whisper in her ear. "I'll take care of everything."

Valentina

AFTER BREAKFAST, Gabriel gives me documents to sign to declare Charlie financially incompetent and to secure my guardianship. I'm eager to see how my brother is doing this morning, but Charlie wakes late. I'll have to have a word with Rhett about the movie nights. Charlie is happy with his new bedroom, especially the flat screen television mounted on the wall.

I make Charlie a breakfast of tea and toast, and introduce him to Bruno, but the two don't hit it off. Bruno must sense Charlie's apprehension. Usually, Charlie doesn't venture outside unless lured by someone dangling a reward in front of his nose, but I give him strict instructions about asking before going to the garden. I don't think Bruno will attack him, but I prefer to be over-cautious. To get Charlie out of the house, I decide to take him shopping with me after lunch.

When I tell Gabriel about my plan, he's pleased that I'm getting out and spending money. He walks us out and hands me a set of keys.

My fingers fold around the key ring. "Keys to the house?"

"Yes." He chuckles. "And your wheels. Sorry it wasn't ready when you arrived, but there was no stock on the floor. I had to order it."

There are five cars parked on the curb of the circular driveway. To who do they all belong? Maybe the guards or Magda and the cleaning service staff.

"Go on," he says, indicating the remote in my hand.

When I press the button, the indicator lights of a Porsche Cayenne Turbo lights up.

"That's very kind, but--"

"Don't say you won't take it," Gabriel says darkly, "because it's my job to provide for you."

"All right, I won't say I won't take it, but it's a big car. I just need something small."

"It's a safe car with enough space for a pushchair, carrycot, feeding chair, nanny, and whatever else women need when they go out with a baby."

The wayward look of panic in his eyes as he rumbles off the items makes me laugh. I punch him playfully on the arm. "I won't need more than a pushchair and definitely not a nanny."

"No?" He seems surprised.

"My mom and I were close."

He still looks at me with his brow raised in question.

"I want to raise my child myself. I want to experience everything, both the hard and joyful parts." Kris' words suddenly haunt me. I wrap my arms around his waist and look into his eyes. "You'll let me take care of our baby, won't you?"

The tenderness in his touch as he brushes the hair from my face reassures me. "Anything you want. As long as it doesn't tire you too much."

Going on tiptoes, I kiss him. "Thank you for the car." I learned my lesson. There's no point in arguing.

"My pleasure. Drive safely."

He nods at the guards standing next to a black Mercedes as Charlie and I get into my new car. I know they'll follow, but I also know it's for our safety.

"Mi–milkshake. Can we have mi–milkshake?"

"We're going to buy Gabriel a gift, but we can stop for dessert. In fact, we can do better than milkshake. How about a banana split?"

Charlie's mouth drops open. I swear there's a drop of drool on the side. I pat his leg. "I know. You haven't had many of those. Not nearly enough."

We drive to a nearby mall in Rosebank. After Orange Grove, Rosebank is the suburb with the largest Jewish settlement. It thus comes as no surprise that I run into someone from the Jewish business from way back.

"My goodness," Agatha Murray cries, "aren't you the Haynes girl?" She looks Charlie up and down. "You must be Charles."

"That's right. How are you?"

"You probably don't remember me."

It's hard not to remember her. Agatha has the same look from when she removed her false teeth and slurped her tea from the saucer in our kitchen. From head to toe, she's dressed in black, always a lacy dress with a cloak and hat. She's been dressed that way since her husband died, a long time before Dad passed away. She must own a thousand hats. I've never seen her with the same one. Today, she wears a box style creation with a crow feather bouquet and a big, faux diamond that keeps the lot together.

"Oh, no, I do remember," I say.

"Sad about your parents. So wrong."

Charlie starts to shuffle his feet. He's getting impatient.

"And Charles," she says when her eyes are drawn by his movements. "What a tragedy."

Tragedies are not on my topic list for the day. This morning's meeting with Christopher already made me feel guilty enough. "Nice running into you."

"I suppose Charles would've taken over the business if not for the accident. He was always a big chunk of a boy, all muscles and the tallest of his class. Do you think he would've become the big boss, maybe run the mafia?"

I glance around to see if we're being overheard and keep my voice low. "I'm glad he's not part of that criminal lifestyle."

"Criminal or not, at least you wouldn't have ended up as poor as church mice. Are you still in Berea?"

"We moved."

"Where to?"

"I really have to go."

Bony fingers close around my left hand. Before I can pull back, she lifts my ring finger to the light.

"Will you look at that?" She gives a hen-like cackle. "From the size of this rock it's not Lambert Roos' ring." She studies the ring, turning my hand left and right.

Self-consciously, I pull away.

"Lambert didn't have a choice, you know. He wanted to marry you. He wasn't all bad, back then." She sniffs. "A bit lazy, but not all bad. Everything was set up for your engagement the day you'd turn eighteen, and the next thing you know, the Portuguese break down their door and threaten to kill everyone if they take you in. Said it would be a war between the Jewish and Portuguese. Just like that, they cut you loose. I think the payoff also had a lot to do with it."

"What?" I forget about Charlie's fretting and my irritation. "Why?"

"Don't know. Probably money. Money's always the motivation in the business, isn't it?"

I stare at her open-mouthed. My father was part of the Jewish mob, but they had an agreement with the Portuguese in the south.

"Anyways," she waves a hand, "all water under the bridge. That life is gone. Not many of the old gang is left." Her eyes take on a far-off look.

"I–I'm sorry. I have to go." Grabbing Charlie's arm, I drag him along the walkway.

"Wait! You haven't told me who you married."

Not wanting to listen to more, I rush head-on into a flow of pedestrians. Scratching open the old wounds of how my father died was too painful. I do my best to shake her words as I sip a fruit juice while Charlie gobbles down a banana split with all the trimmings. While we are in the café, Kris calls, asking how I am, and somewhat manages to distract me from my guilt trip.

"I need help at the practice," she says. "Can you come back?"

I owe her. "I'll be happy to. Can I bring Charlie?"

"I was hoping you'd offer. He did a great job walking the dogs."

We agree that I'd start next week on my old salary. I don't need the money––Gabriel transferred a ridiculously big amount to my account––but spending his money doesn't feel right. I should earn my own.

"Come over for lunch tomorrow," she says. "We'll talk about the logistics."

After our dessert, we hit the shops. I want to get Gabriel something for his birthday. We haven't spoken about it, but the big party, the one where I was supposed to work, took place while I was in Durban. It's pathetic, but I care. I can help it as little as I can help how he makes me feel with his touch. Even as I crave my freedom, to be allowed to make choices like any other human being, I meant it when I said I love him. I lied when I said I hate him more. My love for him has quietly blossomed inside of me, growing from the tiny kernel he planted. By the time I noticed the tree it was too late. It hurt when he told me I didn't mean it. Maybe that was why I retaliated by saying I hate him, and the fact that those hurtful words didn't have any effect on him wounded me even worse. Yet, always true to his word, he's making this good for me, and this is the happiest I've been in a very long time, since that tragic day on the thirteenth of February. Giving him something for his birthday is my way of showing appreciation. The only problem is that I have no idea what to get him. Gabriel has everything.

We walk around the mall until Charlie gets tired, and I have to make a decision. Coming to a stop in front of a bookstore, an idea hits me. It doesn't take long to find the book I'm looking for. I pay and have it wrapped. Forty minutes later, we're home.

With Carly living at her mom's, Magda has dinner served later. It allows her and Gabriel to work late. Charlie won't last that long, so I cook him spaghetti bolognaise and serve it with a salad in the kitchen. We unpack his clothes Gabriel's men brought over from Kris' and explore his new gadgets, which include a PlayStation and a stack of games, courtesy of Gabriel. He's settled for the night when Gabriel comes home after nine. Dinner is not until ten. He'll work another hour in his office. The gift clutched behind my back, I knock on his door.

His deep voice is laced with impatience. "Come in."

Uncertainly, I pause in the doorframe. He looks stressed and busy. I'm disturbing him.

Leaning back in his chair, he works his tie loose with one hand and holds the other out to me. "Come here."

I walk around his desk and stop next to him.

He stretches his neck to look around me. "What do you have behind your back?"

"A gift."

"A gift?"

"For you," I say shyly. He's going to think it's a silly idea.

"For me," he parrots. Warmth fills his eyes and then appreciation as he trails his gaze slowly over me. He pats his knee. "Then you better come over here and give it to me."

One more step puts me between his legs as he opens them to accommodate me. With his hands on my hips, he lifts me onto his lap, making me straddle him. The dress rides up over my thighs, exposing my underwear. I still have my hands clutched behind my back, so he can't let go of my waist without risking my balance, but he stares at the triangle between my legs as if he wishes to touch it with every fiber of his being.

"That's a real pretty gift," he muses. "I can't wait to open it."

The knowledge of how much he wants me fills my core with heat and my heart with a deeper kind of warmth. I bring the present from behind my back. "This is what you need to open."

A smile tugs at his lips as he lets go of me with one hand to take the gift. "What's the occasion?"

I cup his face, feeling the roughness of his beard between my palms, and kiss his lips. "Happy birthday. I'm..." It's hard for me to say this, but I have to get it off my chest. "I'm sorry I wasn't here. I'm sorry I ran. I'm sorry I put our lives in danger. I should've spoken to you, trusted you, but--"

"Shh." He stills me with a kiss. "There's nothing to forgive." His expression becomes pained. "No more of this talk, understand?"

I nod.

He holds up the gift. "You want me to open this now?"

"Whenever you like."

"Grab the armrest. I don't want you to fall."

When I do as he's instructed, he tears the paper away and holds the book up to read the title. "Baby names."

"I didn't know what to get you. You have pretty much everything, so I thought you could choose his name."

In our kind of families mothers name their babies. It's an unwritten and unbreakable rule. Their reasoning is that as long as they suffer the pain of childbirth, the choice is their privilege and right. The pain of childbirth has always been a foolproof bargaining chip, and the details thereof is an argument men aren't prepared to take on.

Gabriel swallows hard. He stares at me with a piercing gaze. "You'll let me?"

"It's not a real gift, but--"

The book falls onto his desk, and his arms come around me. "You'll really let me?"

"If you're fine with it."

"Valentina…" He presses our foreheads together. "You have no idea how much this means to me."

"I was hoping."

"Thank you." He gives me the gentlest of kisses, his trimmed beard scraping my skin. "It's a beautiful and unselfish gift."

"Do you have any ideas, yet?"

His lips tilt in one corner. "You're not supposed to say until the baby is born."

"I'll never be able to wait that long!"

He nips my bottom lip. "Looks like you dug yourself a very deep hole, but don't worry, you have five months to conquer your curiosity."

"You're evil."

The smile vanishes, and his expression turns serious. "Yes, I am, but no matter what I am, you're mine."

Before he can say more gloomy things, I kiss him again, running my fingertips over the rough ridges of his scars. He's my darkness and my love, and he has no idea how truly I am his.

Gabriel

MY MEN INFORM me of my wife's run-in with Agatha Murray. It's accidental, or I would've picked up a call to or from Agatha's number on Valentina's phone. Yes, I'm a creep. I check my wife's calls, but it's as much for her protection as my peace of mind. Our business is dangerous. Even if most men play by the rules and only a crazy idiot will lay a finger on my wife, there are always the nutcases who would cross the line. Besides, she's still a forced wife, one I keep on a tight leash of pleasure and threats, and I prefer to be prudent when a mob family member like Agatha suddenly walks onto the stage.

Not wanting to raise the issue in front of Magda, I search out Valentina after breakfast. She exits Charlie's room with a laundry basket. What the hell? The thing is so big it blocks her view. She almost bumps into me. The collision is only prevented because I catch her waist.

Worry makes my voice sound angry. "What are you doing?"

She blinks. Her big, innocent eyes are wide. " Laundry."

I take the basket from her hands. "You're not supposed to carry heavy things." Scrap that. "You're not supposed to do the laundry."

A sweet smile flirts with her lips. They're full and pink, and so fucking kissable. "There's nothing wrong with my hands."

"I don't care. We have a service for this."

"Don't be difficult."

"You haven't seen difficult, yet." I put the basket aside, tangle my hand in her hair, and drag her to me. "I can show you, but it'll cost your tears and pleasure."

Those soft lips part. She moans. A soft ripple runs over the delicate skin of her throat as she swallows. When I pull her head back farther to look into the dark pools of her eyes, she sags against me, her body warm and supple. Her pupils dilate a fraction, and her gaze becomes lustful.

My words turned her on. Me, there's no word for what I am. Combusting, maybe. Exploding. Trapped between our bodies, my dick pulses against her stomach, showing her how she affects me. What I want is to rip off her clothes and fuck her right here against the wall. I may go crazy if I don't.

Dragging my lips over her throat, I kiss a path up to her jaw. "Would you like that, beautiful? Do you want a bite of pain with your pleasure?"

Her breath catches. "Yes."

I graze her earlobe with my teeth. "Why?"

"It feels good."

The sadist in me roars. I want to spank her, whip her, belt her, but not while she's pregnant. The confirmation that she wants this is enough. Letting go of her hair, I catch her face between my palms and crush our mouths together. My tongue spears through her lips without waiting for her to open. She whimpers, and I swallow every sound. My hand moves up under her dress, finding the elastic of her underwear. My fingers are a hairbreadth away from penetrating her pussy when someone clears a throat behind me.

Fuck. Not now. I let Valentina's lips go with a sound close to a growl, blocking her body with mine until I've lowered her dress to protect her modesty.

Magda walks past us with a scowl. "You have a room, for God's sake."

That was a bucket of cold water on our moment. Valentina's cheeks burn like light bulbs. She averts her eyes and tugs a strand of hair behind her ear.

"We have a meeting in ten," Magda calls from the end of the hall.

Taking my wife's hand, I intertwine our fingers. "No more laundry or any housework for that matter."

"Laundry isn't hard work."

My tone doesn't leave room for arguing. "No laundry."

She consents with a huff.

"My men told me you ran into Agatha Murray, yesterday."

"Oh." Her brow furrows, as if the memory is unpleasant. "Yes."

"You look upset. What did she say to you?"

"It was nothing."

"Valentina, don't lie to me."

"Nothing important, anyway."

"It is to me."

Her shoulders sag. "You're impossible."

I take her other hand and pull her body against mine. "I have a video conference in five minutes. Start talking."

A sigh moves her breasts against my chest. "She said the Portuguese threatened Lambert's family with a war if they took me in. Apparently, he was bribed not to marry me."

Every muscle in my body tenses. What the hell do I make of the information? It's as I suspected. Lambert didn't turn his back on his promised bride because he didn't want her. He was forced to. The question is why.

The kiss I place on her lips is gentle. It's my way of rewarding her honesty. "Be a good girl today. I'll see you for lunch." I squeeze her hands and set her free.

"Gabriel?"

I grin like a teenager. God, I love it when she says my name, especially with that sliver of shyness, as if she's about to ask me for something and she thinks I'll refuse her. If she only knows, I'll bust my balls for her.

"Valentina?" I let her name roll over my tongue.

"I won't be here for lunch today."

"Where are you going?"

"To see Kris. With all the extensions in the practice..." She wrings her hands together.

"What is it?"

"She wants me to work with her again."

Kris did what I'd ask of her. This will be good for my girl. She's not the stay-at-home type. "Do you want to?"

"I'd like that."

"Good."

Her face lights up. Everything sparkles from her eyes to the happy blush on her cheeks. "Really?"

"Really. Be safe."

Her look turns serious. "You, too."

My cock rages in protest as I walk away from her. I'm done. Finished. Beaten. There's no more walking away from her. Ever. I can't exist without this scrap of a woman.

Valentina

I MORE OR less abate my nausea with two crackers and ginger ale before getting ready to meet Kris. Charlie and I are halfway to my car when Rhett comes jogging up the driveway. From the way sweat drips from his body, he's been out for a long run. Things between us have been awkward since Gabriel brought me back, mainly because I've been avoiding him. It's not his fault, but I'm still upset that he betrayed me. In the end, before I ran, I felt like we were becoming friends.

"Hi," I say to be polite without breaking my stride.

He grabs my wrist as I pass. "Valentina."

I look back over my shoulder. "Yes?"

"Can I talk to you?"

"I have a lunch appointment."

"It'll only take five minutes."

From the steel in his gaze, it's clear he's not going to budge.

"All right."

He relaxes marginally and releases my grip. "I had to tell Gabriel."

"I understand."

"You don't. Magda's men were going to kill you. The only way to keep you safe was to play that pregnancy card. Magda will never hurt the mother of her grandchild."

"Oh." Understanding blooms in my senses. "I thought Gabriel... I thought he..."

"Was going to force you to get rid of the baby?"

"Yes."

"Well, now you know."

"I owe you a thank you, then."

"I'll settle for you not being angry with me."

"I wasn't angry. You work for Gabriel, and your loyalty lies with him. I just felt betrayed."

A look of hurt washes over his face. "I didn't want to compromise your trust, but as I said, if I'd kept my mouth shut you would've been dead."

I look at Charlie quickly, but he doesn't react to the statement.

Rhett holds out his hand. "Friends?"

"Friends."

We shake on it.

"How are you doing?" His gaze trails to my rounder belly.

"I'm good when I'm not nauseous, vomiting, or crying for nothing."

He grins. "I hope you're giving Gabriel a go for his money." His face sobers. "Is he treating you all right?"

"Yes." I don't want to discuss my relationship with Gabriel. "Very well."

"Good." He pats Charlie on the back. "I have to get ready for door duty. See you around."

The atmosphere between us is lighter. There's some of the old banter in his manner as he calls back, "At least the baby saved me from training you."

"Not by a long shot."

He turns and skips backward. "How come?"

"The minute he's born we're back to basics."

He groans, but there's a grin on his face as he jogs away.

———

WE FIND Kris in the kitchen, frying veal schnitzels. The smell puts me off, but I swallow down my nausea.

"Sit down," she says. "Food's almost ready."

"Yum–yum." Charlie takes his usual seat at the table and sticks a napkin into his collar.

I pour the water while Kris dishes up rice, schnitzels, creamed spinach, and cinnamon pumpkin mash.

"So," she says between two forkfuls of food, "I've decided to go for it."

"The plans for extending?"

"The pool, the new operating room, the bigger kennel, everything."

"Good for you."

"I reckoned it's rude to stare a gift horse in the mouth."

My suspicion grows. Kris is too much of a principled person to change her mind overnight. "Is Gabriel behind this?"

She makes big eyes. "You know he's paying."

"I mean, did he tell you to do this for me?"

Caught out. Her cheeks flame. "He might've mentioned it'll be good for you to get back into a business you enjoy."

"You'll shove your pride and do it for me?"

She reaches over the table and cups my hand. "He's right, you know. Giving up your studies was damn hard. Nobody knows how much that meant to you better than me. You lost a thumb, and you can never be a veterinary surgeon, but so what? What's wrong with being a clinical vet?"

"That's not what I had my heart set on."

"Then get your heart set on something else." She points her finger at me. "You still have the passion. I can see it in your eyes."

"I'm not going back to uni."

"Are you sure?"

"I don't have the heart for it any longer."

"What about something different in the field?"

I stab at a piece of meat. "What's your idea?"

"Practice management."

"You want me to run your practice?"

"If you're not going to be a vet, so be it. I can do with another vet on the staff, but I need someone to run the business more. It will free up my time to be a vet and not a manager."

My interest is piqued. It sounds challenging and exciting.

She scoops up the rice with a piece of bread and pops it in her mouth. "More, Charlie?"

"Mo—more. It's goo—good."

She places another helping on his plate and holds the spoon to me, but I shake my head.

"We'll need a receptionist," she says, "and a vet nurse, maybe even a bookkeeper, and a makeover. A nicer reception area. I'd like to run a rescue center in conjunction with the practice. We have enough space in the back where the vegetable garden used to be. God knows, I don't have time to plant a blade of grass, anyway."

I can't help but laugh at her contagious enthusiasm. "Slow down. We'll first need a financial plan."

"We?" She puts down her knife and fork. "Does that mean you're in?"

"All right, I'm in."

She grabs my hand on the one side and Charlie's on the other. "The three musketeers."

"The three of us," I echo.

"Way to go, kiddo."

Charlie, who picks up on the vibe, chants with Kris. "Way to go-go." Laughter transforms his face. For a moment, he looks exactly like he did at the age of fifteen, before the accident.

I cup his cheek. "You like being a dog walker, don't you?"

He agrees by banging the end of his knife on the table until I have to put my hand on his arm to still him.

"Finish up," I tell him. "Kris has to go back to work."

She looks at my untouched food. "Still feeling queasy?"

"Yep. There's no telling when it will pass. I wish I was one of those lucky women who only felt sick during the first trimester or not at all." A thought strikes me. "I hope I won't let you down when it gets time to deliver this baby. Nobody in their right mind will employ a pregnant woman, let alone for such an important job."

"We'll work around it. Don't worry."

"Thank you." I mean it. Kris has always been my lifebuoy, and she's just thrown me a big one, thanks to Gabriel.

She pushes her plate aside. "How are things going at home?"

"Good." I can't help the smile or heat that creeps onto my face when I think about Gabriel's reaction this morning. "Wonderful, actually."

Her brow lifts. "Really?"

"Why do you ask as if it's impossible?"

"Wonderful in what sense?"

"Gabriel is good to me. He's kind, attentive, generous, loving…"

"Loving?"

"Yes."

"You forgot to mention controlling, possessive, and jealous."

"Yes, he's controlling, but in a protective way." He'd also threatened my best friend's life, but she doesn't need to know. As long as I stick to my end of the bargain, Gabriel will keep his word. "Let's not forget this new practice management wouldn't be possible without his generosity."

"True, he does a hell of a good job of taking care of you, but that's material."

"As I said, there's more to him than his money."

"You fell for him."

There's no more denying it. "You know I have."

"De–dessert," Charlie says, licking his plate clean.

"Don't do that," I chastise. "It's not polite."

"There's flan in the fridge," Kris says without turning her attention away from me. "Help yourself, Charlie." She takes my hand again. "Val, what are you doing? Playing house?"

"What's wrong with that?"

"It's nothing but role play if he doesn't love you. Does he?"

I avert my eyes. "Probably not."

There's understanding and sympathy in her tone. "There's your answer."

"The thing is we're living together, we're legally married, and we're going to have a baby. Most of the time, we're happy. I'm not going to fight it any longer." Anyway, I don't have a choice. "We can't always have everything we want, but we can be happy with what we have."

"Okay." She squeezes my fingers and lets go of my hand. "I'm behind you. One hundred percent. No more questions asked."

"Thank you," I whisper.

"I may not agree with what Gabriel does for a living, but I'm grateful to him for pulling you out of Berea. That area is only getting worse. With Jerry being murdered and everything that––"

"What?" I grab her arm, my fingers digging into her flesh. "What did you say?"

"Shit. You didn't know."

"Jerry?"

"Yes."

"When?"

"Yesterday. I'm sorry, Val. I thought Gabriel told you." She adds apologetically, "Maybe he doesn't know."

Gabriel must know. Berea is his territory. He knows about every-thing that happens there. A sickening knowledge grows in my gut.

"How?" I ask.

"Shot between the eyes. A neighbor found him in his flat."

"Do they have a suspect?"

"The newspaper article didn't say. I don't think the police are going to make a big effort for a car thief murdered in Berea."

They won't. A killing happens every twenty-five minutes. Jerry is one thief less to deal with, and nobody cares if his killer is caught.

Suffocation hangs like a cloak over me. The air in Kris' kitchen is suddenly too thick to breathe.

Checking my watch, I keep my face even. "We'll let you get back to work. Thanks for lunch." I'm already on my feet, clearing the table.

"Leave that for me," Kris says. "I'll do it tonight."

"I'm not letting you come home to a dirty kitchen."

With Charlie's help the dishes are done and dried by the time Kris is ready to reopen the practice. I walk to the car on shaky legs, barely conscious of what's happening around me. Gabriel's guards parked across the road acknowledge me and get into their cars when we do. I make sure Charlie is buckled up and drag a few deep breaths into my lungs. Alone with Charlie who won't notice, I let the truth crash over me. My hands shake on the wheel as what Kris keeps on reminding me––the same thing I ignored and tried to forget––hits me hard.

My husband is a murderer, and he killed the man who helped me escape.

8

Valentina

The drive home passes in a haze. I can't remember if I stopped at any traffic lights. All I can think about is that Jerry is dead because of me, and my husband killed him. Yes, Jerry was a scumbag who got me into this dire situation, but it doesn't mean he deserved to die.

I put Charlie's favorite cartoon on in his bedroom and storm to Gabriel's office, not caring that my face is streaked with tears or that my mascara is running. Gabriel looks up when I open his door. The smile freezes on his face as he takes me in. He pushes to his feet, the ever-present flinch giving away the strain the action puts on his leg.

"How could you?" I cry.

"Valentina." His voice is harsh, authoritative. "Calm down."

"Don't tell me to calm down. You killed Jerry!"

A mixture of sympathy and regret soften his features. "Who told you?"

"It's in the news." The last thing I want is to implicate Kris.

Rounding his desk, he takes my shoulders. "I should've told you, but I didn't want to upset you."

"Why? Was it because he gave me a car?"

"It's not what you think."

I slam my palms on his chest. "You son of a bitch."

He catches my wrists. "Calm down, please, or I'll be forced to tie you up."

At that, I still. Gabriel never makes idle threats.

"Will you be quiet if I let go?" He sounds genuinely concerned. "All this screaming and crying can't be good for the baby."

I want to hate him, but I can't. Not even when I think he shot Jerry. My shoulders slump.

"Will you listen?" he asks.

"Yes."

"Calmly," he insists.

I don't have a choice but to agree. "Calmly."

He lets go of me slowly, testing me. When I don't move, he brushes his thumbs over my cheeks, wiping away the tears. "It was Scott who shot Jerry."

"Magda's bodyguard?"

"Yes."

"Why?"

He takes a deep breath and holds it for a moment.

"Tell me," I urge. "The truth."

"He helped you run, and he shouldn't have. She had to make an example of him."

There is doubt in the way he speaks the words. I get the feeling he doesn't believe himself. "You were there?"

"Yes," he says gravely.

Pushing his hands away, I cover my face. "Oh, my God, Gabriel. It's my fault. He died because of me. Why didn't you stop Scott?"

"He didn't give me a chance. Valentina, look at me." He grabs my arms and pulls my hands away from my face. "Jerry was no saint. He got Charlie into this mess."

My look is cutting. "You mean he got me enslaved to you."

His glacier eyes turn hard, and his hold tightens to the point of pain. "You don't understand the meaning of the word slave. I made

115

you a princess, but if you want to be treated like a slave, that can be arranged."

Of all the cold, hard truths, this one cuts the deepest, because it's another affirmation of what Kris keeps on telling me. Gabriel doesn't love me. I'm an object. He can turn me from princess to slave as his mood changes.

The pain in my heart makes me lash out at him in anger. "What I want doesn't matter, anyway. You'll do with me as you please."

"What you are to me is entirely in your hands. You can live in comfort and be cherished or be chained in my basement and sleep in a cage."

"But I can never leave."

"No, you can never leave."

"Then I'm nothing but your prisoner."

"That's one way to see it. The other way of looking at it is that you're my wife."

Sobs push up from my chest and find their way to my lips. I was doing so well on make-believe until a couple of hours ago. How can it hurt so much? Why didn't I listen to Kris? Why did I make myself vulnerable? Now it's too late. I fell for him, and it fucking hurts that he's not falling right back for me.

"I don't understand." I wrap my arms around myself and take a step back. "Why me? Why are you doing this to *me?*"

He eliminates the space between us with one, easy step. "I already told you, I don't need a reason."

"I hate you!" I accentuate the statement with a fist on his chest.

His words are tender, compassionate. "We've already established that."

I don't have the strength to fight alone any longer. I can't fight him and myself. He made me fall in love with him knowing he'll never love me back. How can any man be so cruel?

"Please, Gabriel, if you feel anything for me, anything at all, set me free." It's my only hope at salvaging what's left of my heart.

His wraps his arms around me and pulls me close, carefully, as if I have wings of rice paper. The embrace is what he offers. This is his answer. He won't set me free. What I get in return for love is a consolation hug.

"I hate you," I say, sobbing in his arms, hating myself more because I can't even mean the damned words.

He kisses the top of my head. "I've got you, baby."

The man who inflicts the pain is the man who offers the balm, holding me against the warmth of his body and whispering soothing words in my ear. Gabriel is a constant that never changes. He takes care of me now like he does after lashing me with his belt or palm. His behavior when he emotionally hurts me is the same as when he physically tortures me. I don't have the strength not to take this olive branch he offers. I don't have the strength not to fall into him. As always, he's there to catch and carry me through his cruelty. As he lifts me into his arms and moves toward the stairs, I already mourn my surrender.

Gabriel

EVERY LIVING BEING fights for one thing. Freedom. I claimed a woman and took that away from her. Instead of putting her in a cage, I clipped her wings to prevent her from flying away. In time, some caged creatures are tamed. Some remain wild forever. Valentina falls in the latter category. Her spirit is too strong, but my will is stronger. My need is fiercer. I'll break her, over and over, make her submit to me time and time again, until we both blow out our last breaths.

She's my black kitten.

She's my forever.

Her tears move me, but not with the perverse lust I feel at her erotic pain. This pain cuts me. I carry her to our bedroom and nudge the door open. This is one of those occasions I want to love her gently, giving her comfort to make up for what I won't give––the freedom she is fighting for. The love she deserves.

Making quick work of undressing us both, I lower her to the bed and cover her body with mine. I feel between her thighs to test if she's ready and find her slick. Always wet for me. I don't wait. I put my cock at her entrance, part her folds, and pierce her pussy.

When she moans and writhes I give her more, and when she starts panting I give everything, taking her body to a place where pleasure is freedom. She clings to me with her arms and legs while her orgasm crushes through her. Our coupling is uncomplex, pure, and complete. Trapped in each other, our bodies connected, for a few blissful moments we both forget.

Valentina

COME MORNING, I go back to pretending. It's the only way to survive. It's not like anything other than my heart is suffering. Lots of people are worse off. Look at poor Jerry. I have it good. I'm lucky. It could've been me with a bullet in my brain. Who needs freedom and love? I'm done wallowing in self-centered pity. There are other people to consider.

Today is the first day of Charlie's new treatment. I gave my consent, because I couldn't come up with any arguments why we shouldn't try. We have nothing to lose. I wait anxiously outside the television room where Christopher is working with Charlie. I asked to stay with my brother, but Christopher said it would hamper his efforts and inhibit Charlie. Gabriel sits next to me in the hallway on Magda's infamous Louis Vuitton love seat, the one Oscar almost ruined, holding my hand. He acts like a good husband, and we don't speak about yesterday.

I jerk from my thoughts when the door opens. Christopher exists first.

"How did it go?" I ask, jumping to my feet.

"Very good. We made progress."

"Really?"

Charlie follows. He looks happy, calm, and very awake, awake as in present in the moment.

"Hey." I touch his arm. "How do you feel?"

"Gre–great."

"Are you hungry?"

"Sta–starving."

"How about a burger?" Gabriel asks. "I can start the barbeque."

"Bu–burger."

"Wood or gas?" he asks.

"Woo–wood."

Charlie loves a wood fire. He can stare at the flames for hours.

"Let's go take care of lunch, then. Afterward, we're up for a game of football with the guards."

Gabriel takes Charlie and leaves me alone with Christopher. As much as I resent my husband, I love him for this.

"Do you think the sessions will make a difference?" I ask.

"I do." The doctor shifts a briefcase from one hand to the other. "We'll start with general relaxation exercises and then work on speech."

"How much of his old memories does he have left?"

"It's hard to say. I can only know if I take him back into the past. Why do you ask?"

"I just wanted to know if he remembers us the way we were before the accident."

"Ah." He puts down the briefcase and removes his glasses. "Mrs. Louw––"

"Valentina, please."

"Valentina," a note of caution slips into his voice, "it'll never be like before."

"I know. I was just hoping…"

"It's normal to miss the old personality, the person before the brain damage, but it's not conducive to dwell in the past. It's better to accept the present and to optimize on what we've got."

"I understand." I miss my brother so much. I long for the Charlie I destroyed.

He looks at me with scrunched-up eyes. "Maybe you could use some hypnotherapy yourself. You lived through a traumatic experience with the accident, and the trauma is often ongoing for the ones left to take care of the injured."

"Oh, I'm fine."

"It won't do harm trying. Isn't that what we said for Charlie?"

"Really, I'm all right."

"Let me know if you change your mind."

I hold out my hand. "Thank you. May I walk you out?"

His handshake is firm. "I want to say goodbye to Magda before I go, but don't worry, I know my way."

Gabriel

WE'RE at the dinner table. Magda is at the head and Valentina opposite me next to Charlie. Our server enters with the wine.

"No wine for Charlie or me, thank you," Valentina says, as every night.

"Water, ma'am?"

"Sparkling, please."

Magda raises a finger. "Still. Sparkling will give you indigestion."

Valentina doesn't argue, but I pour my wife a glass of sparkling water. Magda's look is condescending, as if I'm a child who obstinately defies her for the sole purpose of creating conflict.

When the roast is served and Valentina adds salt, Magda says, "Not so much salt. It's not good for the baby."

I pin Magda with a look. "Her blood pressure is fine."

Magda takes a sip of wine. Her gaze moves over Valentina. "You couldn't fit a tighter dress?"

The black dress was my choice, and Valentina looks stunning in it. It shows off her growing belly just the way I like. I want the world to see she's carrying my seed in her womb.

Valentina shifts on her chair, but I wink at her. "I like it."

Magda makes a sarcastic sound. "You would."

"May we please eat in peace, now?" I ask pointedly.

Pinching her lips together, Magda gives me the stink eye.

For a while we eat in silence, except for the noise of Charlie's cutlery. He has a habit of hacking everything on his plate to tiny pieces.

Halfway through the meal, Magda is on her third glass of wine. From time to time she shoots an irritated glance in Charlie's direction, her eyes focused on the knife he drags through the meat.

As if she can't stand looking at him butchering his meat any longer Magda turns sideways in her chair, cutting Charlie from her peripheral view. "Any news from Carly?"

The food goes stale in my mouth. Magda knows it's a sensitive subject and one I don't care to discuss at the dinner table. I swallow and take a drink. "Nothing new."

"I miss her." Magda sighs. "When is she coming home? Isn't her weekend visit long overdue?"

Charlie drops his knife. It makes a loud clang as it hits the plate. Magda jerks. She pinches her eyes shut for five seconds, probably counting to get control over her patience.

"I said––" she starts.

"I heard what you said. Sylvia and I don't work like that, and you know it. Carly is old enough to decide when she wants to visit. She knows her room is always ready."

"Maybe you should force it, Gabriel." Her gaze keeps on flittering to Charlie who's pinching each miniscule piece of food on his plate with a loud clank of his fork. "You're too easy on her."

Charlie takes a bite and chews exactly ten times before he swallows. He repeats this with every morsel.

Magda turns to Valentina. "You should take the room on the left of yours for the baby. Have you thought about decorating?"

Valentina glances at me. "Gabriel and I haven't discussed it, yet."

The sweet, incredible woman she is, she'll allow me to be a part of creating a room for Connor. That's what I decided to call him, after my great-grandfather whom I greatly admired.

121

I give her a smile, telling her how much she pleased me. "What would *you* like?"

"I was thinking bright colors like green and blue with a jungle theme. Something happy."

If she wants monkeys and elephant tusks on the walls she can have that. She can have anything she wants.

As usual, Magda has to throw a spike in the wheel. "Green and blue?" She chortles. "It won't fit with the rest of the house decor. I saw a beautiful crib in whitewashed wood with a beige, hand-embroidered duvet. It will look perfect with off-white walls and sand-colored curtains. We should replace the carpet with tiles. A carpet will get too dirty with a baby."

Valentina sits up straighter. "Thank you for your input, but it's not my style."

It's the first time Valentina defies Magda so openly, and Magda doesn't like it. I, on the other hand, am ecstatic that my tiny wife has enough backbone to stand up for what she wants.

"Well," Magda looks between us, "this is still *my* house."

It's a winning statement to an argument. There's not much Valentina can say to that, and the smug look on Magda's face says she knows it.

I've been toying with the idea of getting our own place, and now my decision is made. The atmosphere in this house is way too tense.

Gabriel

IT TAKES another three weeks of cajoling before Carly agrees to come over. She doesn't agree to a weekend visit, but I settle for the Saturday lunch she proposes. To make it as relaxed as possible, I plan a barbeque by the pool. It's late autumn, and the water is too cold to swim, but the day is sunny and pleasantly warm. An outdoor lunch will do us all good.

Carly doesn't say a word in the car on the drive to our house.

In the driveway, I switch off the engine and turn to her. "Is there anything you'd like to talk about before we go inside?"

She stares straight ahead with her arms crossed over her chest. "Like what?"

"Like the fact that Valentina and I are married and we're going to have a baby."

"You said it all, didn't you?"

"Don't be a wisecrack. Do you want to talk about how it makes you feel?"

She shoots me a dirty look. "Embarrassed?"

"I'm sorry if my choice embarrasses you, but she's a good, strong woman, and I'm proud of her."

"Like you're proud of Mom?"

"This has nothing to do with me and your mother. Your mother chose a different path, and I accepted it. So should you."

Turning her face away from me, she picks at the hem of her blouse. "You treat her differently."

"How?"

"You love her more."

"Please don't compare her and your mother. It's not fair to either."

"Did you love Mom?"

"Very much."

"Why did it change?"

"People change. Sometimes, we grow apart or want different things."

"Did Mom want different things, or was it you?"

"Pointing fingers and laying blame won't help. It is what it is. We need to accept it and move on."

She snorts. "You certainly have."

"Would you rather see me alone for the rest of my life?"

"Not alone. Just with someone different. She's a gold-digger."

"Listen to me, Carly. Valentina didn't ask to be put in this situation. If it's anyone's fault, it's mine. This is hard for her, too. Will you at least try to make an effort?"

"That's why I'm here, isn't it?"

"Good. I appreciate that. Before we go inside, there's more you should know."

She turns her head to me quickly. "More? How much worse can this get?"

"Carly," I say sternly. I'm trying to be patient, but her attitude doesn't help.

"Okay, okay." She rolls her eyes. "I'm listening."

"Valentina's brother is staying with us."

She gasps. "Are you moving her whole family in?"

"Just her brother."

"Why must he live here?"

"He has brain damage and needs a lot of care."

"Oh, dear God." She makes a face. "A disabled person in our house?"

"I'm proud of the way Valentina takes care of him."

"Give her a gold star on her forehead or something. Doesn't she have other family who can take him in?"

"No and that's not the point. I offered."

"How crazy is he?"

"He's not crazy. He lost some of his cognitive functions. Mostly, he repeats parts of words."

"This is going to be the Mad Hatter's crazy tea party."

"I won't tolerate this kind of talk, understood?"

She blows out a puff of air. "Can we go inside, now? It's hot in the car."

"Remember what I said. This is not Valentina's fault."

She gets out and slams the door. I take a few deep breaths. Admittedly, I haven't expected her to be ecstatic. I don't blame for her being upset, but I can't stand by and let her be mean to Valentina for something that's my fault.

I grab Carly's bag from the back and follow her inside.

"We're outside," Magda calls when the slamming of the door announces our arrival.

Instead of heading to the deck, Carly snatches her bag from me and veers toward the stairs. "I'll meet you at the pool. I'm going to change."

Some of the tenseness leaves my body when I step outside and see Valentina. She's dressed in a tight dress with her hair pulled back. God, she's beautiful. The size of her belly doesn't faze her, but Valentina has never been conscious of her physical beauty. The fact that she doesn't know how desirable she is only makes her more desirable to me. A tendril that escaped the elastic feathers over her temple and a flush marks her cheeks--telltale signs that she's been busy. She's bustling around the veranda table, which is laid with green crockery and bright yellow napkins. A bunch of sunflowers is the center decoration. Magda is lying on a deckchair, reading a book, and it looks like Charlie is doing origami the way he meticulously folds the paper napkins.

I cross the deck and pull Valentina to me with a hand on her hip. "Hey, beautiful."

She smiles at me. "I made potato and beetroot salad with garlic bread. There's mud pie for dessert. Do you think it'll do?"

"Perfect."

I make sure she gets how much I appreciate her efforts with a soft kiss. The red of her cheeks darkens.

She first glances at Magda and then at the sliding doors. "Where is she?"

"Changing. She'll be down in a minute."

Carly takes her time to join us. By the time she walks through the door wearing a swimsuit and sunglasses pushed back on her hair, I'm on my second iced tea.

She kisses Magda's cheek, but ignores Valentina and Charlie.

My blood starts to simmer, but I remind myself I'm solely to blame. Forcing patience, I count to ten and say, "Carly, don't you have something to say to Valentina?"

She turns to Valentina as if she only notices her now. "Oh, yes." She flops down in a chair and flips her sunglasses over her eyes. "Get me a lemonade. Plenty of ice. While you're at it, bring me a towel."

9

Gabriel

My vision unravels at the edges. Who is this mean girl? Carly has always been difficult, but this disrespect crosses a new line. The tea sloshes over the edges as I slam the glass down on the table. In two strides I'm next to Carly, pulling her up by her arm. She looks at me with a start, her cocky attitude slipping. Magda drops her book and jackknifes into a sitting position.

"Dad!"

Carly protests as I drag her through the sliding doors back into the house. It's time the two of us had a talk. Not like the talk we had in the car. A serious talk.

The first available room is the reading room. I push her inside and am about to slam the door when Valentina rushes up.

"Not now," I growl. This is between Carly and I.

Her soft hand on my arm pauses me, and it's the look in her eyes that makes me falter. I can't resist this begging, wide-eyed appeal.

"Just five minutes," she says.

Educating Carly in manners is my responsibility, but it's also

Valentina's right to stand up for herself. With much difficulty, I remove myself from the room, but I can't move farther than around the door where I stop to eavesdrop shamelessly.

"You're upset," Valentina says.

"Damn right, I am."

"I understand. The news about the baby must be hard to deal with. It came as a shock to me, too."

"You only got pregnant to trap my dad."

"It was an accident neither of us planned."

There are tears in Carly's voice. "How long have you been sleeping with him?"

"That's private," Valentina replies gently, "and not your business."

"Did you seduce him?"

"No."

"Then what?"

"I don't understand your question."

"He said you didn't ask for this." There's a long silence before Carly speaks again. "Did he ... force you?"

My heart stops beating. Valentina hates me. She has no reason to protect my daughter from the ugly, raw truth. Yes, I forced her. I made her beg first, but I gave her no choice. Not really.

The tremble in Valentina's voice is so minute, if I didn't know her as well as I did, I would've missed it. "Why would you ask that?"

"It happened to friends of my mom. The maid is pregnant with the husband's baby, and she said she didn't have a choice because he forced her."

Valentina's voice is firm and reassuring. "It didn't happen to us."

"He didn't ... rape you?"

"Absolutely not. Please don't think about your father that way."

"So, you're not a victim."

"No, I'm not."

"If you're not a victim, I can't feel sorry for you."

"I'm not asking you to feel sorry for me. I'm asking you to try for us to get on."

"Why? Why should I? I don't even like you. You're lower class and poor."

"Fair enough. Then try for your dad's sake."

"I'm not doing anything for his sake. He didn't talk to me before marrying you to see how I would feel, so why should I consider his feelings?"

"He loves you, Carly. Don't push him away. If we put a bit of effort into it, we can all get along."

"Give me one, good reason why I should get along with *you?*"

"You're going to have a baby brother or sister. Doesn't that count for anything?"

Carly goes quiet. For several seconds, neither of them speaks. Finally, Carly says in a broken voice, "I've always wanted a brother or sister, just not from you."

"We can't change that it's me, but I'm sure this baby is going to love having a big sister."

Carly sniffs. "You think?"

"I do. I was hoping you'd help me with some baby shopping."

"Those tiny shoes and cute bunny-ear pajamas?"

Valentina laughs. "And a teddy bear. Every baby needs a teddy."

"Oh, my God, I know exactly where to go. Tammy's big sister had a baby last month. You should see the cute baby dresses and matching headbands we got for her. Can I help with the room?"

"Yes, you may."

"Not the painting, though. Oh, and I'm not changing diapers."

"No paint. No diapers. Got it."

Carly excitedly babbles on about baby powder, mobiles, and blankets.

For the first time in months, I hear Carly laugh. I lean my head back against the wall and swallow hard. I don't deserve Valentina's cover-up, but I take it anyway.

Valentina

WE PARK in front of a two-story house with a circular entrance hall like an abstract castle tower. The pillars framing the entrance are a modern, off-kilter version of the Arc de Triomphe. The house is painted gray, black, and burgundy. I've never seen anything like it.

"Where are we?"

Gabriel turns off the engine, but doesn't answer. He exits and comes around to help me from the car. It was a long drive to the northern suburb of Broadacres, and we got stuck in traffic. I stretch to relieve the ache in my back. His hand moves to my lower back, his fingers gently massaging the sore muscles.

At the glass doors, he hands me a key with a red ribbon looped through the hole.

"Gabriel, what is this?"

"Our new house."

Incapable of forming words, my gaze shifts from the keys to the doors. Behind the glass, there is a large, open-plan, furnished space.

"Aren't you going to open it?" he asks with a quirk of his lips.

I fumble to fit the key in the keyhole and eventually manage to let us inside.

Our footsteps echo on the slate tiles. A spiral staircase leads from the tower to the first level. To the left is a lounge and at the back a kitchen. The finishes are in industrial steel.

"Come." He takes my hand and walks me through the house.

The ground floor includes a wine room with walk-in fridge, an office for Gabriel, a soundproof cinema, an indoor barbeque facing a heated pool, a Jacuzzi, bar, bathroom, sauna room, and gym. The kitchen leads to a pantry and scullery, and the scullery to maid quarters and a double garage.

He gauges my reaction as he leads me upstairs. "Do you like it?"

The decoration is minimalistic and modern. I can see why Gabriel would like it. "It's very impressive."

Satisfied with my answer, he shows me four spacious bedrooms, each with an en-suite bathroom.

From the main bedroom, we step onto the balcony that has a view on the pool.

"Charlie can have the bigger bedroom on the right, and we can break a door from ours to the one on the left for the baby."

I lean on the balustrade and look up at him. "Why?" Magda has a big house, and up to now Gabriel has been content to live there.

"I want you to be happy. I want you to buy what you please, decorate as you like, and paint the walls green if that's your thing."

I have to laugh. I can't imagine the gray walls of this house being a crazy green.

He cups my hips and presses our lower bodies together. "Just promise me the nursery will have a jungle theme. I kind of have my heart set on it."

More laughter bubbles over my lips. Baby and decoration talk is so unlike Gabriel.

"I want this to be good for you, Valentina." He brushes the hair from my face. "Having a baby won't be easy. I want you to be as comfortable as you can be."

"Thank you," I whisper, not for the house, but for his efforts.

He kisses me and smiles against my lips. "Does that mean you like the house?"

"I do."

"Then we move next week."

I weave my fingers through his thick hair, keeping him in place. "I don't care where we live, as long as you never stop touching me."

The smile is gone. His expression sobers. "I trained you so damn well."

"Does that mean you like it?" I ask, throwing his words back at him.

"Like it?" Heat invades the icy blue of his eyes. "I love it. I fucking live for it."

As his fingers go to the zipper of my dress, I melt for him, wanting what he can give me long before he offers. Whether he drags me to Berea, Broadacres, or hell, it doesn't make a difference. As long as he feeds on my pleasure, his arms will keep me warm, and I can go on pretending he gives a damn about more than my body.

THE MOVE TAKES place the following Monday. By Tuesday, we're settled. Since the house came fully furnished, all we had to transport were our clothes and Gabriel's office equipment. On one of the nights Gabriel works late, I invite Kris over for dinner to show her our new home. I would not have felt comfortable inviting her to Magda's house. At least here, I can do as I please. The freedom feels amazing. The irony of that sentiment doesn't escape me. I'm anything but free, but as the days go by and my stomach grows bigger, a new numbness dulls my senses until I don't think about my captivity, any longer.

The intercom buzzes as I'm caramelizing the sugar with a kitchen blowtorch over the crème brûlée. Oscar, who now lives with us—as does Bruno—jumps from the priceless silver bowl on the coffee table.

"I'll get it," Rhett calls from the gym.

Rhett and Quincy reside with us in the staff quarters meant for the maids. Each has an independent studio with a kitchenette and bathroom. Gabriel insists that one of them stays with me when he isn't home. The guards stationed at our gate aren't live-in. They work on a shift basis. The living arrangements with Quincy and Rhett worked out well, since I don't want a live-in maid and prefer to take care of the cooking myself, maybe because of the memories that role evokes. Due to the size of the house, we were forced to hire a cleaning service that comes in twice a week. The rest I can handle between working at Kris' clinic and completing a mini MBA to help me master business management. The household, work, Charlie, and studies keep me busy, but I've never been an idle person, and I like to feel useful.

"Here's your guest," Rhett says, holding the door for Kris.

"Thanks, Rhett. Dinner is almost ready. Would you like to join us?"

"Yeah." His smile is enthusiastic. Rhett loves home cooking. "Let me grab a quick shower."

Going over to Kris, I give her a hug. "How was the traffic?"

"Not too bad." She looks up at the double volume entrance, turns in a circle, and whistles through her teeth. "Wow."

"Do you like it?"

"Too modern for my taste, but it's ... wow."

"Charlie, come say hi," I call into the cinema room. "Kris is here."

Charlie bounces through the door and takes her in a bear hug as if he hasn't said goodbye to her at the practice only three hours ago.

Kris sniffs the air. "Smells like Beef Stroganoff."

"Good olfactory skills. Wine or beer?"

"Beer."

"In the fridge. Help yourself."

Kris grabs a can and looks around while I set the food on the table.

"There are an awful lot of glass doors and windows."

"I love the light."

"What about security? I don't see burglar bars."

"Each door and window is fitted with a bulletproof metal shutter. No metal cutter can get through the steel. In case of an emergency, we can bring them down in seconds with the push of a button. We have a control panel in the kitchen and upstairs in our room."

"You don't fool around."

"You know Gabriel."

"Yeah, this sounds like him. That man is crazily protective over you. I don't want to see how he's going to be when the baby is born."

Rhett enters the kitchen, his hair wet. "Is that Stroganoff I'm smelling?"

"Spot on," Kris says.

He rubs his hands together. "Shall we eat before it gets cold?"

Kris chuckles. "Hungry?"

I dish up, and Charlie serves the water. Rhett doesn't drink when he's on duty.

"Val tells me she can shoot a bullseye. Is it true?" Kris asks Rhett.

He gives me a chastising look. "You're not supposed to advertise it."

"I only told my best friend." I grin. "I was proud."

I'll have to pick up the self-defense training after the birth, but I convinced Rhett to take me to the shooting range when Gabriel stays out late for business.

"My lips are sealed," Kris says, "and I think it's a good thing that Val knows how to defend herself."

Rhett gives Kris a half-smile. His ass will be on the line if Gabriel finds out.

"How's Charlie's sessions going?" Kris asks, thankfully changing the subject.

"Good." I pat Charlie's hand. "Christopher says he's making progress. Aren't you?"

"Pro—progress."

Kris raises her beer. "To Charlie's progress and the best practice manager in the world, who can now also shoot like a pro."

Our laughter is interrupted by Rhett's phone.

"Excuse me." He looks at the screen. "It's Quincy. I have to take the call."

He leaves the table and walks to the far corner of the lounge, but the acoustics of the open space carry his words to us.

"What?" He pauses to listen. "Okay. Sure. No worries. I'll tell her."

My armpits zing with pinpricks of foreboding. "Is Gabriel all right?"

He walks back to the table, his expression troubled. "It's Carly. She's been arrested for possession of drugs. Gabriel is at the police station. He'll be home later than planned."

Kris covers her mouth with a hand. Only Charlie eats without a care in the world. My appetite for food is gone. All I want is to be with Gabriel.

"There's nothing we can do," Rhett says. "We may as well enjoy our meal."

By the time Kris leaves, there's still no new news from Quincy or Gabriel. Rhett goes to bed, and I watch a movie with Charlie to distract myself, but I can't concentrate on anything. Finally, there's nothing left to do but ship Charlie off to bed and wait. I shower and change into a nightdress before making myself comfortable on the sofa in the lounge with a book. My gaze keeps on flickering to the door, watching for Gabriel's headlights at the gate.

It's well after three in the morning when he returns.

When I open the door, he grabs me to him and buries his head in my neck. "What are you doing up?" He kisses the soft spot on the curve of my shoulder. "It's late."

"Is she all right?" I pull away to look at him. "Did the police lay charges?"

He closes the door and turns all three deadbolts before taking my hand and pulling me to the bar. He pours me a tomato juice, for which I developed a sudden craving, and a Scotch for himself.

"No charges."

"Did your lawyer get her off?"

"Not my lawyer. Magda."

He doesn't have to say more. Magda has questionable connections with the police.

He sits down on one of the barstools and pulls me onto his lap. "The police raided a nightclub." His icy eyes turn stormy. "They found a gram of coke on her."

"Oh, Gabriel." I place a hand on his cheek.

"She's sixteen, for God's sake." He cups my hand and rubs his jaw over my palm. "Sylvia said she didn't know. She said Carly sneaked out."

"The drugs?"

"Carly said a friend gave it to her. She swore she tried it only once. Tonight was supposed to be her second time. I think the arrest was a good lesson. It scared the hell out of her, especially since she's under the legal age for access to that club." He absent-mindedly strokes my hair. "She promised me she'd never do it again, but how can I trust her, now?"

Wrapping my arms around him, I lean my head on his chest, offering him the little comfort I can.

"Valentina." He grips my chin and tilts my face up to him. "I don't know what I'd do without you."

Like he's always there for me, I'm there for him. He knows he can count on me, no matter what. It's an invisible bond that becomes stronger with each passing day. I don't know if it's the baby or the time we spend together that brings us closer, but it doesn't matter. I've never felt more connected to anyone than I feel to Gabriel, and that scares me.

"Don't leave me," I plead.

It's an irrational fear I contribute to my pregnancy hormones and a strange request coming from someone who begged to be set free less than a month ago. I want to stay, but out of my own free will, and until Gabriel lets me go, he'll never trust or believe me when I say I love him and I won't run.

Instead of pointing out the shift in my demands, Gabriel brings our lips together and kisses me tenderly. "Never. I can never let you go."

Embracing that knowledge, I lean into him, immensely grateful for my imperfect world.

Gabriel

THE MONTH that follows is the happiest of my life. I have setbacks with Carly, but our relationship has never been better. She visits every weekend. Valentina suggested she chooses a room and decorates it herself, which Carly appreciated. We celebrated her seventeenth birthday with a quiet lunch at home, and afterward she did baby shopping with Valentina. Although she'll never see Valentina through my eyes, they're getting along, mostly due to Valentina's efforts, for which I'm forever indebted.

Business is calm for a change. Magda has finally accepted my decision to move and for once we're not knocking heads. The distance is what we needed. We get on better not living under the same roof. Quincy and Rhett dote on my wife, and only her devoted attention to me and me alone makes me swallow my jealousy. We had a door fitted between our room and the nursery, and Valentina bought the paint. Bright green. I'm sure it's just to piss Magda off, but I'm game.

As far as the world's concerned, we're newlyweds. Hell, as far as I'm concerned, this is as normal as it gets. I can't keep my hands off her, and she needs my invasive advances. I can love her hard or hold her in my arms watching a movie. It doesn't matter whether we're swimming with Charlie or clearing the table after our meals, I love every minute with her. I love the way her belly swells with the life we created. Every time I look at her, I have this godawful fear that it's not real, that it's too good to last. Like an infatuated person I drift on the cloud I fabricated, blind to anything but my wife's pleasure and my own euphoria.

On one of those warm and sunny winter mornings the Highveld is famous for, we're lounging by the indoor pool. I have Valentina's legs in my lap, massaging her feet. She moans as I work on her pressure points. I steal glances at her bikini-clad body. With her six-month belly she looks both like a pinnacle of strength and vulnerability. Charlie discovered a love for water. He's a strong swimmer. Nevertheless, I keep an eye on him as he's doing laps from the shallow to the deep end. Later, I'll fetch Carly for the weekend. We have a barbeque planned. There are only us, Rhett and Quincy, and a couple of Carly's girlfriends. Afterward, the plan is to relax with a couple of movies. I'm looking forward to the afternoon. The low-key, family time is exactly what I need. Oscar jumps from my towel as my phone vibrates.

I check the screen. Sylvia. Carly must be running late, as usual. I flip the button to answer and am met by a noise so foreign and bizarre that my mind refuses to place it. I sit up, every muscle going tense.

"Sylvia?"

A series of incoherent words mixed with hysterical sobs follow. I move Valentina's feet aside and stand, my only awareness the acute pain that shoots into my hip and the numbness that settles over my heart.

"Sylvia, take a deep breath and tell me what's wrong."

Her sobs become more distant. There's a scratching noise before another voice comes on the line.

"Mr. Louw?"

"Who are you? What's going on?"

"I'm a paramedic, sir. Mrs. Louw is not in a state to speak, right now. We have to ask you to come to the Garden Clinic."

"What happened? Who's hurt?"

"It's your daughter, sir." There's a short, horrifying pause, and then the words I can't face. "I'm terribly sorry."

10

Gabriel

My chest shrinks. My ribs constrict my heart. Static noise buzzes in my head.

My little girl. *My little girl.*

"Gabriel?"

Valentina's voice reaches me through the ringing in my ears. The sound is far-off and distorted.

Only thirty-seven years of experience allows me to put one cognitive thought in front of another. Tell Quincy to stay with Valentina. Get the car. Drive to the clinic. Call Magda on the way.

"Gabriel?"

I turn to my pregnant wife, seeing nothing but her belly and our unborn baby. "It's Carly," I say on autopilot. "She's in hospital."

"What happened?" she asks in a small voice.

"I don't know." But I do. Please, no. No. Dear God. I can't survive it. There's still hope.

She pulls a wrap around her body. "I'll come with you."

"No."

The word is harsh and angry. It wasn't my intention, but I can't control my intonation. I need space. I need to break down in the car so I can be strong before I get to the clinic. Sylvia won't want Valentina there, and I don't have enough presence of mind to deal with what awaits *and* protect Valentina. Most of all, I don't want to expose Valentina to a hospital with germs and a stressful situation in her fragile state.

Hurt invades her eyes, but she quickly clears it. "All right. Let me know, please. Let me know if you need me. Anything."

Drops of water splash over the side of the pool where Charlie is swimming. The white smell of chlorine fills my nostrils. The lazy buzz of a bee turns at my ear. Oscar licks his paw and washes his face. A breeze stirs the lavender in the hothouse at the edge of the pool and carries the scent through to the deck. The clean flower fragrance is infused with the fresh odor of a mowed lawn. The smells mix with the chlorine from the water to create a summer perfume right in the middle of winter. Our little artificial paradise. Every detail is magnified. Every impression is clear and clutter-free. It's the adrenalin from the shock. I take everything in and imprint it in my mind, instinctively knowing things will never be the same. Life will never be as carefree and happy as it was this morning.

I give Valentina a peck on the lips. "Lock the door behind me."

In the lounge, I grab my shirt and pants from the back of the sofa. Stripping from the wet swimming trunks, I leave them in a mangled puddle on the floor and pull the pants on without jocks. While I button up my shirt, I call Quincy on the phone. I'm not wasting time walking to his room.

"I'm going out." I grab my wallet and jacket from the kitchen. "Keep an eye on Valentina and Charlie. They're by the pool."

Once I clear the gates, I floor the gas, breaking every speed limit and pissing off more than one minivan taxi. It's only a matter of minutes before I turn myself into a road rage victim.

I use the voice control to call Magda.

"I'm on my way," she says. "Sylvia's boyfriend called me."

The parking lot at the clinic is thankfully empty. I curse my leg as I run too slowly to the entrance and barge through the doors.

"Carly Louw," I announce at the front desk.

The receptionist avoids my eyes. "Lounge number six, sir."

"It's Louw," I repeat. "My daughter has been admitted." She'll be in the emergency wing, in an operating room, or in intensive care. Not the lounge. Please God. Not the lounge.

"The others are waiting for you, sir. Lounge six."

Not the lounge. Not the lounge.

"Sir?"

"Yes." I turn toward the private rooms, every step slower than the last.

Not the lounge.

My palm flattens on the door, right under the six. Once I push the door open, I can never go back. Once I cross the threshold, my life will never be the same. But the world turns under my feet and around me, and there's no choice but to move forward with time. I apply the necessary pressure, propelling myself into the room.

The door clicks softly behind me with a bizarre finality, enclosing me into the reality sealed in the lounge. My gaze goes around the space, my eyes connecting with each person who shares my fate. Sylvia is hunched over. Francois, her boyfriend, strains under the effort of holding her up. Magda stands next to them, her Gucci handbag swinging uselessly back and forth in her hand. Facing them is a chaplain. He stops talking at my entrance. Magda's eyes find mine. This is what my eyes must look like––barren and empty. She gives me a small shake of her head, preparing me.

"Mr. Louw." The chaplain bows his head and grasps my shoulder. "I'm sorry."

They still have to say it. Someone has to tell me.

Sylvia lifts her head. Anger and blame twist her features, but not acceptance. I feel so much sympathy for her, right now. That's the worst suffering––the road to acceptance.

"Tell me." Don't tell me. Until it's spoken, it isn't real.

The chaplain squeezes my shoulder. "Your daughter ... eh..." he glances at a piece of paper on top of the Bible he clutches in his hand, "...Carly, is gone."

140

"Gone?" I say.

The clergyman falters under my hard look.

"Gone where?"

"Mr. Louw."

He says my name like it's an appeal. An appeal for what? An appeal not to make him say it?

"What?" I challenge.

It's Sylvia who steps forward. "She's dead. She's dead, Gabriel. She's dead!" Flinging herself at me, she hits my arms and slaps my face. "It's you! It's you! It's all your fault!"

I take her blame and punches, wishing to God she'd hit me harder so I won't feel the torch burning a hole through my heart.

The chaplain and Francois reach for her simultaneously, trying to pull her off, but she renews her attack, shouting and sobbing with snot flying from her nose. I hold out an arm, holding both men off.

"Why?" she cries, looking at me for an answer. "Why, Gabriel? Why?"

Why? Yes, please, someone, tell me why. I don't know. I can only look at her.

At my silence, she collapses against my chest, grabbing fistfuls of my jacket. "I'll never forgive you. It's you. It's you and your games. You and your wife and new baby."

At the mention of my wife and child, I loosen myself from her grip, holding onto her elbows to keep her stable.

Francois takes her shoulders, and Sylvia allows herself to be led to the corner where he rocks her in his arms.

Magda regards me with a stoic, pale face. "She overdosed on sleeping pills."

I can only manage a nod in both acknowledgment and thanks. I needed to know.

"They pumped her stomach," she continues, but doesn't say more. She doesn't have to.

"Would you like me to pray for her?" the chaplain asks.

Praying won't change that she's *gone*. Dead. Praying won't bring her back.

"We should discuss the funeral arrangements." I need to do this. I need to keep busy.

Francois shoots me a 'you can't be serious' look.

"About counseling––" the chaplain starts.

I don't hear more. I'm already out of the door. Counseling will help as little as praying. No one in that room can console me. I can't console them. I just want out.

SO YOUNG.

Her face looks angelic. Peaceful.

The doctor draws back the sheet to cover her. "We made arrangements for her to be transported to the morgue." He hands me a hospital bag with her belongings. "I'm sorry for your loss."

I nod without cutting my eyes away from the shape under the sheet.

"Whenever you're ready," he says.

The door shuts with an agreeable click. At last, I'm alone with my girl. I move the sheet aside to take her hand. Her skin is cold when I press my lips to it.

"I'm sorry I failed you, Carly."

My voice breaks. Scorching tears burn my face and trickle down my neck into the collar of my shirt. Inside, I'm pulp. A mushed bruise. It's only my conditioning that allows me to construct a stoic wall on the outside. I've taken plenty of lives, but I've never lost one. My dad, yes, but that was different. We weren't close. I've never been cut open, exposed, and left vulnerable. I'm a hollow shell of weakness, easy prey for any enemy, and I dare them all to take me on, take me out, and end this misery for which I'm solely to blame.

I failed.

Where did I go wrong? Was I too hard on her? Too soft? Why did I not see it coming? Did I spend too little time with her? Was I too self-absorbed? Was it my lifestyle? Did she find out what I do for a living? I should've refused when she said she was moving back to her mom. I should never have driven her home the day she confronted Valentina before we even started the barbecue. I should've insisted she stay. I should've forced her to talk. I should've been more patient. I should've taken her home with me after the drug scare. I shouldn't have ignored my gut. I shouldn't have lived in my ignorant bubble of selfish happiness.

Regrets, regrets.

Someone, God, anyone, please fucking tell me where I went wrong. I want to tear the sky in two and scream at life for explanations, but all I do is go down on my knees and press my forehead to my daughter's dead hand. I pray to know. I *need* to know, but there will be never be an answer. No understanding. No absolution. No forgiveness. Only guesses and guilt. Only should haves and what ifs.

When they come to take her, I find Magda waiting in the hallway. The exterior she works so hard on maintaining breaks, and her unspoken accusations show through the cracks.

"Francois took Sylvia home," she says. "The doctor gave her a tranquilizer."

"I'll take care of the funeral arrangements."

"You better. I doubt Sylvia will manage."

"Can I give you a lift?"

"Scott will drive me." She hesitates. "Will you be all right?" Her voice breaks on the last word.

For a brief moment, she pulls me to her, enveloping me in her embrace. It's the first time my mother put her arms around me. It feels foreign, and after a heartbeat she pulls away. The cracks in her veneer break all the way open. Tears stream down her cheeks, running black mascara rivulets through her foundation.

"I'll never forgive her for what she did to this family."

It takes me a second to understand who she's talking about. It's easier to shift the blame, but not even Magda can be so blind.

"It's not Valentina's doing."

"It's the baby," she whispers, "and everything else."

Dumping *everything else* in my lap, she leaves me with that heavy burden and walks away. She's right, of course. I've always fucked up everything in my life. My relationships. My daughter. Valentina. *I should be under that white sheet. It's me who doesn't deserve to live.* Albeit, ironically, here I am.

Parking in the garage at home, I sit quietly for a long while. The life has been sucked out of me. I'm numb. I can't cry, rant, or rave. I can't sleep or eat. I can't work or think. Most of all, I can't face myself. I sit in my car, because I simply don't have the willpower to do anything else.

The door connecting to the house opens and the light comes on. Valentina stands in a pool of tungsten brightness that shines through the thin fabric of her nightdress. It throws a spotlight on the roundness of her body, the lies and mistakes I planted in her belly.

"Gabriel."

My name is a sob. She must've heard. Scott or someone from Magda's staff would've called Quincy. She doesn't come closer or speak. She waits for me to make the first move, to see what I need.

Steeling myself, I force my body to comply and exit my car. Her arms reaching for me are too much. I don't deserve her sympathy or soothing. I did this to her. I did this to Carly. I'm destruction. I'm a monster. A look of pain filters into her eyes when I sidestep her embrace.

"It's late," I say, facing away from her. "Get some sleep."

As I stalk away, her soft whisper reaches my back.

"I'm sorry, Gabriel."

I keep on walking. It's what she wants. It's best for her.

I take a blanket and pillow to my study. There's not a chance I'll sleep, but I need the pretense of routine like I need the Scotch I pour. I down the hard liquor and pour another, then another. Alone, I fall on my knees and wail into the pillow, grieving for the life I created and destroyed.

At some stage, I must've passed out, because I wake with a headache from hell and my throat on fire. It's five in the morning. Quietly, I walk through the big house, going from room to room of nothingness and empty meaning until I've done the full round and am back in my study. The bag from the hospital sits on my desk like a shrine, a reminder that will never let me go.

My hands shake as I reach inside. It's like plunging your arm into a box full of snakes. I don't know what I'll pull out or how it will poison me with further self-blame and sorrow, but I can't stop myself. I remove a white tank top and blue shorts. Underwear sealed in a plastic bag. Her favorite pair of sandals. A raw sound leaves my throat. The clothes are familiar, yet strange. Not on her body, they look like someone else's, and the estranged sentiment scares me. I want to hold onto every memory, not lose a single fiber of intangible emotion or the lifetime of movie reels imprinted in my head. Her first tooth, her first smile, her first step. God, it hurts. It cuts and cuts until I'm nothing but meat shredded to the bone.

I fall into my chair, fighting my shirt collar and tearing at the button strangling me. I'm sorry. I'm so fucking sorry. Forgive me, Carly. I'll never forgive myself. My hands curl into fists. I bang them on the desk so hard my knuckles bleed. I want her back. I want to turn back time. Smoldering anger burns through my body, shaking my muscles. Every ounce of that thick, black fury is directed at myself. How could I not know? How did I not see?

It takes several deep breaths before I somewhat calm myself. I have to behave rationally. For everyone else's but my own sake. I have to wear the mask and carry on.

My attention goes back to the paper bag. Turning it upside down, I give a shake, longing for more. Something. Anything. A sealed envelope drops out with a clank. Inside is something bulky. I run my fingers over the paper ridges. It feels like a chain. I break the seal and let the object slide out. It's Carly's platinum butterfly pendant, the one I gave her for her seventeenth birthday. Picking up the chain, I hold it up to the light. It dangles from my fingers, the butterfly soaring like a pendulum from left to right, right to left.

"Fly free, princess." I press the silver wings to my lips. "Goodbye."

Goodbye. This is where I make my peace, find my acceptance. It'll be a long road to healing, and I honestly don't know if I can do it. Holding the pendant over the jar of keepsakes, I let the chain run through my fingers, allowing it to slip from my grasp, link by link. It drops with a clink on top of the mementos. This is where it belongs, with all the other lives I took. I wring my hands together, intertwining my fingers until it hurts.

This was the last time.

The last one.

I'm done killing.

Valentina

THE NIGHT IS one of the longest of my life. I toss and turn and tiptoe downstairs several times to check on Gabriel. The door of his study remains closed. Not a sound comes from inside. Only a shard of light seeping from under the door confirms his presence. What do I do? How do you make something like this better? Sick with helpless grief and self-blaming worry, I pace between the kitchen and lounge until the first light pierces the awful night.

The sun is weak today with mist clouds gathering in the sky. The day feels broken. Everything feels broken. My heart shatters for Gabriel. I burst into tears every time I recall Quincy's horrible words, the way he looked at me with concern and pity as he stuttered the news, because I play a guilty part in this tragedy. The pregnancy was hard for Carly to take. Even harder was the implied meaning that her father and I were intimate in secret, right under her nose. If I hadn't fallen pregnant, none of this would've happened. Carly would've been blissfully unaware and maybe still alive. Yes, definitely alive. The more I think about it, the more I cringe in shame and burning sin. This is my fault. If I didn't beg Gabriel to selfishly let me keep the baby he never wanted, this wouldn't have happened. Will Gabriel ever forgive me? Can I forgive myself? I can't deal with the answers, so I focus on the most pressing matter––taking care of Gabriel.

My gaze alternates between the rising sun obscured behind the clouds and the study door. When the door is still closed by eight, I take a hasty shower and check on Charlie before starting the tasks of the day on autopilot. I feed Oscar and Bruno and cook breakfast for Quincy, Rhett, and Charlie.

Quincy watches me from under his lashes as I prepare a tray for Gabriel. "How is he?"

I avert my eyes. "I don't know."

"He hasn't come out of his study," Rhett says in understanding.

I add sugar to the tray. "He needs time."

"Of course." Rhett gets to his feet and reaches for the tray. "Let me take that for you."

"I've got it," I say hastily. "Finish your breakfast."

What I mean to say is that I need to see Gabriel. I ache to see him, to soothe him, to tell him how sorry I am, if he'll even listen to me.

At the door, I balance the tray on the table in the hallway and knock.

His voice sounds simultaneously strong and tired. "Who is it?"

"Valentina." I clear my throat. "I brought you breakfast."

The sound of his chair scraping over the floor reaches me through the door, followed by his uneven footsteps. The door opens on a crack.

"Gabriel--"

"I'll take it."

Picking up the tray, I hand it over and lick my dry lips in preparation for what I want to say, but the shadow of the door falls over me as he shuts it in my face with a curt, "Thank you."

"You were right," Rhett says behind me, making me jump. "He needs time."

I flush with shame that Rhett witnessed the rejection of my condolences. It's a clear reflection of Gabriel's judgment. I feel like guilt is carved on my chest. First my father and Charlie, then Tiny and Jerry, and now Carly.

"Yes." I take several steps away from the door. "He needs space."

"Val." Rhett reaches for me. "Are you all right?"

"It's not me who's suffering." Tears burn in my eyes. "I wish I could take it away for him."

"I know." He gives my shoulders a reassuring squeeze. "I know how you think, Val. It's not your fault."

Unable to look him in the eyes, I turn my face to the side.

"It's not your fault." He accentuates his words with a gentle shake.

"Sure. Yes." I twist free. "I'm going to start lunch. We'll probably have visitors popping in throughout the day."

So MANY PEOPLE stop by to pay their condolences I lose count. Business associates, mafia, government officials, employees. They all arrive in dark suits with respectful faces and expensive flowers, muttering words of sympathy and solace. Gabriel sits in the lounge, receiving the drips and drabs of guests who never dwindle enough to grant him a moment of solitude. The only way I can make myself useful is to bake savory and sweet pastries and prepare salads and casseroles, which I serve as the hour of the day demands. Savory snacks in the morning, lunch from twelve to two, and sweets in the afternoon with tea. Quincy and Rhett help to load the dishwasher and unpack the crockery in a continuous cycle. Charlie is happy to take charge of brewing fresh tea and coffee.

Magda arrives shortly before teatime. Despite her brave composure her face is ashen. We face each other in a strained atmosphere by the door. Since our move, she hasn't been over to visit, not even to see the house. No matter our history, my heart aches for her loss.

I place a hand on her arm. "Magda, I'm sorry."

She shakes off the touch. "If it wasn't for you..."

My stomach dips, and my insides twist, guilt eating at my gut. I step aside to let her in. "He's in the lounge." I motion at the group crowding the sofas.

Sylvia arrives a few minutes later on the arm of her boyfriend. Her hair is neatly plaited in a French braid, and she's wearing makeup, but she looks haggard. Her eyes slice through me, and then her gaze drops to my big stomach. The way she looks at me makes me feel dirty, like I cheated or did something wrong. Was I wrong in surrendering to

Gabriel's advances? Shouldn't I have been stronger? A better person would have resisted. Indefinitely. I feel like I'm standing in a spotlight about to receive judgment.

"This is her," she says to Francois. "This is the reason my Carly committed suicide."

11

Valentina

The subdued conversations around us drone out Sylvia's words. Nobody but her friend and I heard. For that, I'm profoundly grateful. I'm not sure I can handle the whole room's eyes on me in the midst of Gabriel's grief.

A switch in her flips, and I no longer exist. She looks right through me. Like Magda, she walks to Gabriel's side to receive the sympathy and support she deserves. I didn't expect anything different, but it makes my standing clear. Gabriel and I may be married, but only in name. To everyone else I'm still the maid, the slave, the toy, the imposter. I can't even deny it. All of those things, I am. The only people who pay me kind attention are Michael and Elizabeth Roux.

Elizabeth hugs me by the door. "How is he doing?"

I can only shake my head.

"Come here." Michael takes me in bear hug, holding me for two seconds to his big body.

Up to now, I haven't realized how much I needed a hug. There's nothing sinister in the gesture. The only vibe he gives off is of platonic affection. I immediately like him more.

Elizabeth hovers a palm above my stomach. "May I?"

I try to give her the bright smile of an expecting mother, but my effort flies half-mast. "Sure."

She places her hand on my belly and looks at Michael with sparkling eyes. "Oh, my God. I swear I feel the baby kick."

"He's been kicking up a storm since this morning."

"You're beautiful, Valentina. Truly stunning. Isn't she, Michael?"

"Breathtaking," he says with a kind light in his eyes.

"I think I'm making the baby active." Elizabeth removes her hand. "He obviously likes me." She looks toward the lounge, taking in the guests. "Poor Sylvia." Her attention returns to me. "Poor Valentina. She hates you, doesn't she?"

"Is it that obvious?"

Elizabeth makes a sad face. "The way she looks at you..."

"I deserve it."

Michael grabs my hand. "No, you don't, and if you ever say something so self-degrading again, I'll get Gabriel's permission to spank you myself."

A baritone voice resonating from behind us makes me jump.

"What was that, Michael?"

The three of us turn in unison. Gabriel is standing two steps away, his white shirt and black tie pristine, as if he hasn't been wearing it since early this morning. He appears together, like he has a handle on everything. Only the haunted look in his frozen-over eyes gives him away.

"I was just telling Valentina not to put herself down," Michael says.

Gabriel's eyes find mine. They penetrate my soul, making me cold inside. "Is that so?"

"Our deepest condolences, my man." Michael places a hand on Gabriel's shoulder. "There are no words."

"No, there aren't," Gabriel says.

"Gabriel." Elizabeth embraces him. "If there is anything, anything at all..."

"Thank you."

"Congratulations on the wedding," Michael continues. "We're happy for you."

"Yes," Gabriel says without looking at me.

Inwardly, I cringe. If I had any doubts about Gabriel's feelings toward me, I don't any longer. He thinks like Magda and Sylvia. It's only his sense of responsibility and honor that prevents him from tossing his true thoughts in my face.

Elizabeth saves the moment by asking Gabriel questions about the funeral planning. All the while, he ignores me without ignoring me. He pretends I'm not standing next to him, but we're so aware of each other our bodies hum.

The atmosphere is uncomfortable. The stress is too much. Every muscle in my body is clenched. A band tightens around my abdomen, squeezing and holding for three seconds before releasing. After two beats the pattern repeats, but it doesn't hurt. My first Braxton Hicks contractions.

Needing to escape the tense situation, I offer to get Elizabeth and Michael a drink, but Gabriel stops me before I can walk away.

His fingers curl around my upper arm. "No."

I stare at him in surprise. "Excuse me?"

"Go upstairs and rest."

Is he trying to ship me off? Is he ashamed of me? Of everyone seeing the evidence of what happens between us in the size of my belly? Hurtful feelings scorch through me, but this isn't the time or place. This isn't about me. Or us. This is about him and Sylvia. This is about Carly.

"All right." I smile brightly for his guests. "Let me know if you need me."

I purse my lips as another contraction hits. Gabriel holds my gaze for two more seconds, his eyes too knowing, too piercing. When the invisible vice on my belly snaps, I offer Elizabeth and Michael a polite greeting and free my arm from Gabriel's hold, turning for the stairs, but he doesn't let me go. His palm presses on the small of my back.

"I'll walk you."

I can't be alone with him, right now. I'm afraid of the intensity of what I felt a moment ago, and most of all of his honesty. "I'll be fine. Stay with your guests."

And he does. He turns around and walks away.

In our room, I sit down on the bed. My hands smooth out the comforter that knows our secrets, our shame. Grief and blame tear me apart. My heart breaks a thousand times over for the man downstairs. I'm powerless to console him. How can I? I'm an ugly, dirty link in a chain of events that led to Gabriel's daughter's death.

Gabriel

MAGDA IS GETTING impatient with me. She taps her nails on the desk upstairs in Napoli's. "It's been a month. You have to move on."

A month since Carly is *gone*, and I can't get my shit together. With moving on, Magda means killing, of course. Some jackass in Braamfontein crossed the line when he burgled our office. A month ago, I wouldn't have hesitated. I would've taken the idiot out without blinking an eye, but I made a promise to myself, for Carly, and I won't betray my daughter's memory.

I turn my back to her, facing the window that overlooks the gambling floor below. "Told you, I'm done. I'm out."

There's anger in her voice. "Without you, we'll go under."

"You have Scott and a thousand others you can recruit."

"*You* are my son. Albeit a useless one, and thanks to--" She cuts herself short, gulps in some air. A shaky breath slips into the silence. "Now we don't have an heir."

Damn right, we don't. My son won't end up like me, just like it was never my intention to marry Carly off to a criminal worthy of running our shady business. What Magda won't see is that we never had an heir, and we never will.

"It's your business." I turn back to face her. "Do with it what you will, but I'm leaving."

Scorn deforms her mouth. "What will you do? How will you live?"

She's got me by the balls and from the way that scornful smile grows into a spiteful grin she knows it. I have no idea. I have a wife and soon I'll have a child to take care of. People hate me. Enemies have grudges. I need to keep my family safe, and the only way to do it is to have money. State of the art alarm systems, ammunition, and guards cost bucks. Big bucks.

I cast out my feelers carefully. "I could still run the office, take charge of our business affairs."

She throws me a snide look. "In our business the only bosses respected are the ones who get their hands dirty."

"We could clean up the business."

She slams her fist on the desk. "This isn't how this city works, and you know it." She points a finger at me. "Try and run a clean loan shark business and see how far you get. The competition will ruin you in a day, and if they don't, the police and government will. They'll take kickbacks from someone willing to pay it, and we'll be finished. Over."

The sad part is she's right. If you can't do bribes and play dirty, you're going down.

"I will not see my hard work to build this company up to where it is go down the drain." She accentuates her statement with a nail she pushes on the polished wood of the desk.

I won't break my vow. That leaves only one option. "I'm sorry, Magda. I guess that means you're on your own."

Her body goes rigid. Pushing back her chair, she rises stately. It looks as if her back is about to snap. The fine hair on her upper lip and chin trembles. Her nostrils expand and shiver like a buck smelling lion.

She presses her palms flat on the desk, regarding me from over the rim of her glasses. "You're making a mistake."

"This is the only right thing I've done in my life."

Her arms are shaking so badly she has to lock her elbows. I've never seen her this mad.

"It's *her*, isn't it?" she hisses. "It's *her* idea. *Her* doing. *She* planted this in your dim-minded head."

My defenses rise. "Leave Valentina out of this."

Her eyes narrow to slits. "I should've known. Should've guessed this is her game. She's always been too holy for us."

I take a step toward the desk. *"Leave her alone."*

"This is what it's come to, then?" She straightens, balling her fists at her sides. "You'll choose her over your family, over your own mother?"

"She *is* my family, and yes, she comes first."

Magda reels at my words. I may as well have slapped her. The color of her skin takes on an ashen tone. For a few seconds, emotions suspend between us––shock, betrayal, disappointment, anger. They pollute the air and poison the blood that's supposed to be thicker than water.

When there's no other expression but disillusionment left on her face, she says flatly, "Get out."

I throw her words around in my mind. *This is what it's come to.* To be honest, we've always been heading this way. I was always the son who disappointed. She took my choice and gave me a gun, but I'm not that boy any longer. I'm the man Magda bitterly hoped I would never be.

Rapping my knuckles on the desktop, I give her my resignation with a tight nod and turn my back on her and the future I've been building all my life. A part of me feels sorry for her. Not only did she lose her only granddaughter, but also the ambitions she had for her son. I won't be her successor. I won't salvage and nurture the business she busted her balls for. It will go with her to her grave, and what I've done for this business will take me to hell.

Outside, I stop on the landing for a breath. I lean my palms on the balustrade and inhale deeply. This is where it all started. This is where I laid eyes on Valentina for the first time. She looked so young and damn innocent in her white uniform and so strong. She was standing right there, at that table, and when the croupier grabbed her arm, I wanted to chop off his hand for laying a finger on her. The minute I looked into her scared but defiant eyes, I wanted her. She was a challenge and a mystery. She was brave and naïve. So damn hot and so damn untouchable. Unobtainable, and yet, just there, within my reach. Every contradiction in the book. The woman I wanted, and the woman I had to kill.

It seems like three lifetimes ago, but it's only been a year. If I were a better man, I'd right the decision I took here that night by setting her free. I'd cut her lose like I cut the cords with The Breaker, but I'm not a good man. I can never let her go. This is my unrepented evil. She's my biggest sin.

Looks like we came full circle. It ends where it began. With her. Somewhere in between, I lost Carly. My marriage, the baby, the changes in our living arrangements, it was too much. My ruthless lust for a woman I stole drove my daughter away from me, pushed her right over the edge. My burden doesn't feel lighter when I descend the stairs and walk the hell away from who I used to be. It only grows heavier the nearer I come to the house. I can't lay that godforsaken burden down, because it will mean I have to set Valentina free, but I can't look at her, either, because it means I'll have to face my guilt.

Valentina

AS THE DAYS MOVE ON, Gabriel grows further and further away from me. He's closed up in himself, and no amount of probing or baiting can lure him out. To suffer the loss he did is shattering, and the grief is devastating. He eats well and exercises every day. His body is the same rock-hard, strong one I remember, but the man inside has changed. Is he even in there, in the darkness that's become his mind? No matter how much I talk or touch, I can't get through to him.

From the dark circles marring his eyes, I know he's not sleeping, even if he no longer sleeps next to me. After the funeral, he moved into the spare bedroom. He doesn't go to work or see friends. He stays at home all day, but well away from me. When he's not closed in his study or working out in the gym, he's doing DIY work around the house. I watch him with his shirtless body up on the ladder, and my body doesn't care that he's still in grief or that he blames me. It only wants what it's being denied––my husband's touch.

Abstractly, he's never been my husband, of course. Our house of cards, my make-belief reality, has come crushing down, and the man who taught me to be hungry for his caresses is now withholding them from me. This makes me sad. Since he hasn't been inside me for weeks, I feel obsolete, like a purposeless burden. When he didn't give me a choice, I didn't want to be his toy or his wife, and now that I'm neither, I desperately want to be one or the other, preferably both. I'll settle for anything he gives. There has to be hope, because he still gets hard for me. It's difficult to hide when he's working out in his sweatpants or swimming in his trunks.

Tonight, I cook his favorite dishes––lamb roast, green beans with bacon, and fried potatoes––and set a table with candles outside. Rhett, Quincy, and Charlie are dining inside, as usual. The falter in Gabriel's step when he comes downstairs and sees the romantic setting in the garden almost has my courage failing.

Meeting him at the bottom of the staircase, I take his arm and lead him outside, not giving him the choice of heading for the dining room.

Without a word, he seats me and takes the opposite chair.

His gaze moves over the meal. "What's the occasion?"

"Just dinner."

For the first time in a month he meets my eyes directly. "Just dinner?"

"And spending time alone. We're always with the others, not that I'm complaining. I like them, but..." Damn. My courage fails me.

The look on his face stops me before I can work up the nerve to finish my sentence. A veil falls over his eyes, and a shutter clicks in place. The silence stretches as he regards me with an emotion that slowly breaks through his unreadable expression. Under the thick surface of his mask, I recognize pity.

He pities me. He must think I'm pathetic. Irrational anger spreads through my veins. This is his doing, what he made me. If I'm needy, it's his fault. If I want him, he's to blame. How dare he sit there and judge me, feel sorry for me for wanting him? Tears prick at the back of my eyes. No matter how fast I bat my eyelashes, I can't blink them away. One slips free, two... Goddamn. Do I have to show weakness after weakness?

The mask slips another fraction as he reaches across the table and takes my hand. "Don't."

Don't cry? Don't want? Don't feel? I want to shout and hurt him like I'm hurting, but I sniff my tears away and force my irrational hormones down.

"I'm trying so hard..." My voice cracks on the last word. I can't carry on speaking for the fear of sobbing all over the roast.

He rubs a thumb over my knuckles. "You don't have to try, beautiful."

I don't have to try what? Staring at him through my tears, I will him to explain, but he doesn't.

He brings my hand to his mouth and kisses the back. "You need your strength. Shall I dish up for you?"

My heart shatters into tiny shards. It takes everything I have to take my rejection gracefully and not jump and fight him like a bitch in heat. I nod. When he's busy dishing food onto my plate I quickly wipe my eyes with the back of my hand. It'll be easier for him to just let me go.

"Gabriel?" I wait until he faces me. "Set me free."

His eye turn hard. "I already told you it's not going to happen." He puts down the spoon. "Eat. Your food's getting cold."

I vowed to take whatever I could get. Looks like I'm settling for being an unwanted responsibility.

KRIS PICKS up on my change at work. She drags me outside to the garden table for lunch and sets down a box of chow mein takeout in front of me. I feel bad that Charlie is eating alone inside, but when I mention it, she shakes her head and points a chopstick at me.

"Stay put. We're going to talk."

I groan.

"You can give me that look all you like," she shakes out a napkin in her lap, "but you're going to spill the beans. What's eating you?"

"Hormones." Lately, I've been using that a lot as an excuse.

Her chin sets in the way that says she won't give up. "How are things at home, with Gabriel, I mean?"

I don't want to saddle Kris with my problems, but I do need a friend to confide in. "Not well. He's a walking corpse."

She stuffs her mouth with noodles and mumbles, "Sounds kind of normal with what he's going through."

Immediately, I feel selfish and bad for thinking of my needs when I should be placing his first.

"Mourning takes time," she says.

"He hasn't been back to work, and he hardly leaves the house."

"He doesn't need to work if he doesn't want to. He's got enough money."

"I'm worried about him sitting in his study all day."

"I'm sure he's doing stuff."

"I wish I knew what to do to help."

"Give him space." She takes another big bite. "And be patient."

When I don't say anything for several seconds, she stops eating and looks at me again. "You want things to work out with him, don't you?"

This is the crux of the problem. "Yes," I whisper.

"You feel you shouldn't because of how the two of you started."

"I don't know what I feel. I only know I want this to be real. I don't want to pretend, anymore. I want a real husband who loves me for me, not an owner who married me so his enemies won't decapitate me."

"Whoa." She laughs. "It sounds harsh when you put it like that."

"But true."

"Yeah. Harsh, but true. What are you going to do?"

"I was hoping you'd tell me. What should I do, Kris?"

"I guess it depends on what you want."

"I want him."

"Then fight."

"Fight?"

"Yes. Give him another few months to mourn and then start walking around naked. That should catch his attention."

I swat at her with my napkin. "We have other people living in the house."

"I know. Maybe that's part of the problem. You need time alone. Send the guys away and bring Charlie over to me."

"You're a good friend."

"I'm practical."

"You're still a good friend."

She checks her watch. "Eat your food. We're back on in five. See? I'm practical."

That gets a laugh out of me.

PULLING weeds from the vegetable garden, I sit flat on my ass on the ground as I can't bend down anymore. Dr. Engelbrecht, who does a house call every second week, tells me I'm gaining too much weight. Some of it is water retention, but for the most part it's unhappiness. I gobble down ice cream with peanut butter sauce when I'm sad, at least since I'm pregnant. The extra weight restrains my movements, and I still have two months to go.

The July midday sun beats down on my head. Even in winter, it's hot. I seem to have an internal heater inside, making things worse. Unless I want to faint from overheating, I better seek out the cool interior of the house. As I'm battling to lift my heavy body, a pair of hands clasps my elbows and helps me to my feet.

I look up into Quincy's face. "My knight in shining armor. Thank you."

"Where's Gabriel?" He looks pissed off. "Wait, don't tell me. In his study."

"This is hard on him, Quincy." I don't know if I mean me, the baby, or Carly's passing. Probably all three.

"Yeah." He motions at my stomach. "This is not hard for you."

"It's not the same."

He looks like he wants to argue, so I say quickly, "Charlie has a session with Christopher. I'm going to make a fresh pitcher of iced tea."

"Need help?"

"I'm good, thanks."

He watches me broodily as I make my way back to the house. Christopher is already there, chatting to Rhett. I show the doctor and Charlie into the cinema room with an uneasy feeling. The last few sessions left a mark on Charlie. He was agitated afterward, but Christopher wrote the mood swings off to a normal mid-phase of the therapy. Today, I wait by the door, immediately noticing the tense set of Charlie's shoulders as he exits.

I grab his arm before he can escape. "How did it go?"

"Po–pool." He jerks free and skirts around me, heading for the sliding doors.

"I made iced tea," I call after him. "It's apple and cinnamon." Charlie's favorite.

He gives me a backward glance, but walks away with quick steps. He's irritated and won't be swayed.

Christopher follows next. "Well, I'll be on my way, then."

"Can we please talk for a moment?"

He glances at his wristwatch. "I have another appointment."

"Five minutes?"

He can't refuse me without being rude, but the corners of his mouth turn down. "All right." He puts his briefcase down and takes the tea I offer.

"Charlie's been irritable of late. To be exact, since your last four sessions."

"I told you it's normal. We hit a barrier in his development, and breaking through it is hard work, but once we're through he'll be fine. Better than fine."

"What are you working on?"

"I'm not at liberty to discuss that. It may compromise our goal if you interfere." I open my mouth to object, but he stills me with a hand in the air. "Trust me, all caring relatives interfere. It's human nature. We can't stand seeing our loved ones suffer. Just remember that all great results come with hard work."

I'm not reassured, but he downs his drink and leaves the glass on the table. "Great iced tea. It reminds me of my grandmother."

"Thank you," I mumble as he sees himself out.

I'll give it two more sessions, and if Charlie is still worked up, I'll stop the treatment. Sometimes Charlie gets impatient, especially when he can't express his feelings, but mostly, he's just a big, huggable bear. I don't want him to be unhappy, ever.

Gabriel

DAYS WEAVE into nights and nights into days. Time is one, slow, never-ending, torturous cycle. Most days, I pour over photo albums with pictures of Carly from when she was born up to her death. I study each picture, hunting for details and information I may have missed before, like on how many photos she wore her blue T-shirt with the red heart. I never realized how much she liked it. Had I known, I would've packed it in a box and kept it with her first baby shoes, her favorite rattle, and the doll she slept with until she was five, the one whose hair she cut off, believing it would grow back. My life is a box of memories. Full, yet empty.

I'm making an effort to carry on with my life. The money in my bank account won't last forever. I accepted a management job at one of Michael's firms, which is nothing but charity from his side. He's turned out to be a good friend, and no matter how hard it is to pull my head out of the sand, I refuse to disappoint him.

Magda and I are still not on speaking terms. She sent me an email stating whatever happened between us, her grandchild will always be welcome in her house, and she hopes I'll change my mind.

Tough luck. I'm on my way to a new future that doesn't involve loan sharks or breaking bones. I need to do this for me, but also for the people who depend on me to take care of them.

I'm about to leave for my first day on the new job when Quincy steps into my study.

Adjusting my tie, I say, "I'm running late."

The wide stance he takes makes me look, really look, at him. His fists are balled at his sides and his jaw is flexed. He is mad. Furious.

"We're going to talk, Gabriel. Now. This has gone on for long enough."

"Talk about what?"

"You want me to spell it out for you?"

What the fuck is eating him? "Why don't you?"

"Your neglect of Valentina."

It takes a moment for his words to register. "My neglect of--" And then they sink in. "What?" I glare at him. "It's none of your business."

His stance becomes wider. "Is she your wife or isn't she?"

My temper starts to slip. "Of course she's my wife."

"Then act like a husband, and if you can't, let someone else."

I see fucking red. Burnt black with orange, melted edges. "Keep out of my business," I growl, "and out of my wife."

"She deserves better. You got her pregnant. Now treat her right."

Grabbing his lapels, I lift him off his feet. "If you're wise, you'll shut your mouth."

He doesn't look scared in the slightest. "Can't face the truth? Not man enough to hear it?"

Before I can stop myself, I slam my fist into his jaw. He goes flying, hitting the floor with a thump. At that very moment, the object of our discussion walks through the door. Valentina freezes, looking from me to Quincy who is sprawled out on the tiles. It's him she rushes to.

"Quincy! Are you all right?" She gives me a startled look. "Gabriel, what's wrong with you?"

The jealousy I had tapered down to an art during the last few months bubbles back to the surface, ugly and acidic in my throat. She's *mine*, and she's carrying *my* child. Nobody gets her, no matter how much better a man he is.

Before I say or do something I'll regret, I leave Quincy in her concerned hands and set off for work. I'm not going to tell her about it until the time is right, until I know it's working out. She doesn't need to worry about where the money is going to come from.

***

THROWING my full weight behind my resolution, all I eat, drink, and live for is work. I'm adjusting well in the company and get on with Michael. I respect him as a friend and boss. Elizabeth is his second-in-command. She often asks about Valentina, but gives up when she gets nothing out of me. It feels strange to work my way up in someone else's business, but I'm grateful for the challenge. It keeps my mind off darker thoughts. The kinder they are to me, the harder I work to earn it. I want to prove my worth to them, but mostly to myself. This isn't my father's business or my mother's money. I'm earning my own way, and it's harder than I thought. I spend long hours at the office, coming home after eleven when the rest of the house is asleep, and leaving before they wake. Little by little, day after day, I stitch back a resemblance of a life.

***

Valentina

IT'S seven in the evening when Magda's car pulls up to our gates, and Scott announces her through the gate intercom. What is she doing here? Did Gabriel invite her for dinner? Since the funeral, she hasn't been back to the house. Even if Gabriel doesn't say as much, they must have had some kind of fallout.

I brush down my dress, a nervous habit that stuck with knowing how much she disapproves of my choice of clothes, and meet her at the door.

Her manner is urgent. "Is Gabriel still at work?"

"You'll know better than me."

"Me?"

"He works with you, doesn't he?"

"He hasn't told you?" She makes big eyes. Behind her faked expression, she seems pleased. "He works for Michael and Elizabeth Roux, now."

Wow. That's like pushing a needle under my nail and twisting it. The fact that he didn't tell me something this important hurts in ways I don't care to examine.

"Come in." I step aside, wondering how much I should ask. I don't want to give her ammunition to shoot down the already crumbling walls of whatever warped relationship Gabriel and I have left. I'm holding onto the ruins with both my hands, digging my nails into the broken bricks as I dangle over the wall, but I'm not sure cracks of that size can ever be filled.

She looks around the space. "Where's everyone?"

"Charlie is upstairs, and Rhett is in his room."

"Quincy?"

"With Gabriel."

"Ah. Good. I was hoping we could talk alone. Can we go somewhere private? I don't want to be interrupted."

An itch crawls down my spine. I should say no, but my gut is stirring, and red flags are waving in my mind.

"In here." I lead her to Gabriel's study, the nearest room with a door.

"I'm surprised he didn't tell you he left our company," she says once we're inside. "Then again, he doesn't tell you much, does he?"

Why did he hide it from me? And Rhett and Quincy? Are they in on this, too? I can't help how defensive I sound. "What's that supposed to mean?"

"I bet he never told you why you fell pregnant."

That itch from earlier spreads over my skin, making every nerve-ending tingle in alarm. "What?"

"He replaced your birth control with placebo pills." She pushes a USB key into my hand. "Here's the proof, and the reason why he chose *you*."

1 2

Valentina

Gabriel did what? I don't believe it. He wouldn't. Never. Why is Magda doing this? My gut warns me this is only the beginning. Magda planted a path of destruction in my palm, and my feet are firmly on it. My fingers clamp around the key in my hand that will, if true, destroy me. The heartache I felt at Gabriel's rejection is nothing compared to the pain slashing through my insides. I prefer a hundred lashes of his belt to this. Anything, but not this. If Magda is right, he purposefully deceived me. He lied to me. Worse, he let me believe it was my fault. My nails cut into the skin of my palm around the piece of plastic. I ache in every corner of my soul.

"I'll leave you to it." Magda walks to the door. "I assume you prefer to watch this in private. If I were you, I wouldn't waste time in packing my bags." A victorious smile marks her grand exit.

For some time, I stand rooted to the spot. My body trembles, and chills run over my skin. This is game over. It hurts, really hurts. Why me? The answer I want is in the palm of my hand. Releasing my fingers one by one, I stare at the black object with Magda's company logo. My hand shakes as I carry it to Gabriel's desk and open his laptop. When the screen comes to life, I hesitate. Once the key hits the slot, there's no turning back. I won't have a choice but to face the facts. My hand hovers next to the slot.

How could you Gabriel?

I insert the key and bite my nail.

As the file is loading, Charlie appears in the open door.

"I'm hu–hungry."

"I'll be right there. How about folding the laundry while you wait?" Charlie loves pairing socks.

"Lau–laundry." He disappears in the direction of the scullery.

I turn my focus back to the computer. A folder named *Valentina* sits menacingly on the screen. Shiver after shiver creeps over my arms. It's eerie to see my own name and wrong to open something that doesn't belong to me, something that Gabriel is clearly hiding. I make a last brave effort to abort my mission, which is driven on the ugly fuel of curiosity, pain, and humiliation, but my finger is already hovering over the mouse. Will Gabriel give me honest answers if I question him? Probably not. The final thought that sways the balance and brings my finger down is the knowledge that Magda knows more than me.

Click-click.

The folder opens. My heart stops pumping for a beat. I hold my breath and bite my lip. The folder contains two files. The one is titled *Birth Control* and the other *Evidence*. I open *Birth Control* first. It contains a sound file. Confused, I click on it. It's a recording of a telephone conversation. The voices belong to Gabriel and Dr. Engelbrecht. They're discussing my health. Guilt and fearful anticipation heat my cheeks as I listen in on a conversation not meant for my ears.

"I want a placebo birth control pill," Gabriel says.

"You want her to fall pregnant?" Dr. Engelbrecht asks.

Gabriel doesn't hesitate. "Exactly." He doesn't even sound ashamed. No remorse, no explanations.

"Tomorrow?" the doctor says.

There is a smile in his voice. "Perfect. We need to repeat the examination to make sure she's healthy and susceptible. I want her to have a fertility shot to help things along."

It takes a full minute to register the words. I rewind and play the conversation over. Over and over. With each repetition more anger boils through my veins until my body feels like a coal stove ablaze with a fire. Shaking uncontrollably, I go back to the beginning and listen to the conversation again. I can't help myself. I keep on lashing my soul with the hurtful truth, punishing myself for my naïve ignorance. My heart doesn't want to accept what I've heard, even if my mind already believes it. I cover my mouth with a hand and place the other on my stomach, over Gabriel's planned intention, the baby I love more than myself. I feel sick. When I've played the conversation back at least ten times, I stop. I've listened to every nuance and intonation of Gabriel's voice, searching for feelings and motivations that aren't there. Why did he do it? Why did he lie to me? Why me? Magda's words spin in my head. *And the reason why he chose you.*

It takes every ounce of courage I have left to open the second file. This one is a video clip. Fear snakes down my arm, making it feel heavy as my finger pauses above the keyboard, but my hand has a life of its own as it moves down and hits enter.

The image is grainy and blurry, but slowly comes into focus. It's not a feed from a security camera as I expected, but a home movie. The lens is pointing at the floor. Whoever is carrying the camera is walking. A pair of polished, black shoes fall on the wood. There are voices in the background. They are excited, loud. There is something else, another voice my mind refuses to decipher. A feeling of foreboding heats my body, making my palms clammy. I want to turn the recording off, but I can't. The unfolding pictures hold my eyes as if they're glued to the screen. The shouting becomes louder, clearer. There's cheering. The camera lifts, and the room comes into focus.

"You got that, Barney?" a voice says.

"Yeah, hurry up. I'm rolling."

The walls are covered in wood paneling with framed pictures of dressed-up dogs playing cards. In the center is a big table covered with green felt. A pool table. My mouth goes dry. My body temperature drops ten degrees, and ice lodges in every pore of my skin. Frozen in horror, I watch as four men drag a struggling girl onto the table. Two of them grab her arms, and two her legs, while a fifth starts tearing her clothes. Her screams are futile. The more she pleads, the harder they laugh. Sobs wrack her thin body. She tries to kick and gets a fist in the stomach. Her eyes are pinched shut as the man who destroyed her clothes works his pants over his hips. He's fat and gray. She keeps her eyes closed as he does the unthinkable, but I don't. I watch every violating move of his body, every painful slap of his palm as it falls on her cheeks. Through the lens, I watch each face that looks on, that laughs as it's his turn to smile for the camera. The coldness spreads through my limbs when the man in the center, the one with his pants around his ankles, falls over the girl's body. Something hot and wet runs over my face and explodes in drops on the keyboard. The camera moves around the table, capturing every angle of the unmoving body that lies on top. When it comes to the side where her dark hair trails over the edge, the rapist stands up right in front of me. His head is bent, obscuring his features as he pulls up his pants and fastens his belt. Then he lifts his face and looks straight at me. My throat constricts. I try to swallow, but I can't. I can't breathe. The cold spell of my body ripples over my skin, freezing me inch by inch, until I can't move a finger or toe. When the extreme coldness reaches my scalp, it's replaced with scorching heat. I've seen the face of my rapist many times before. Right here, in my husband's study. It's standing on his desk, looking back at me now. Paying witness to my shock, he regards me with a mocking smile.

Owen Louw.

Gabriel's father.

169

13

Valentina

Everything happens at once. A painful contraction folds me double. A dull ache drives into my brain until my vision turns blotchy with spots. And my water breaks.

It's too early.

These are nothing like the Braxton Hicks contractions I got used to. The pain drives me to my knees. Gnashing my teeth together, I wait it out, and when the band of agony lets go, I grab the desk and pull myself up. I use the desk phone to dial the emergency number, inhaling and exhaling while I wait. Just as someone takes the call, the second series of contractions hits.

I clench my teeth and groan.

"Hello?" the operator says. "Can you hear me?"

Please don't hang up.

Click.

Damn. No! Putting one hand on the furniture, I use the desk, chair, and wall for support to make my way to the lounge. Dizziness slows my progress. My head hurts as much as my abdomen. Just then, Charlie exits the scullery with a basket full of socks.

"Go get Rhett," I say as calmly as possible, even as every bone in my body is shaking. There's a good chance I'm going to lose the baby.

Charlie takes one look at me and drops the basket. "Va–Val!"

"It's okay. Where's Rhett?" I continue to the kitchen, but another contraction stills me before I can get to my phone that's lying on the counter.

It hurts like nothing I've felt. My head is going to explode. I count through it. One, two, three, four, five. Another few steps. My cry isn't loud, but it's a wretched sound. "Rhett?"

He flies from his room, his hair wet and a towel wrapped around his waist. "Val, did you call me?" His eyes fall on the wetness on my legs and feet, and then they grow large.

"The baby," I whisper, tears dripping from my eyes. "Call an ambulance."

The thought that runs on repeat through my mind shows in the way he shakes his head in silent denial.

Too early.

We don't stand a chance with a premature home delivery. If I don't make it to a hospital on time, my baby is dead. I cry harder as Rhett gets our private ambulance service on the line and gives them our address, but the crying only makes the pain in my head worse. All the while he rubs my shoulder. I'm grateful for that point of human contact. I'm scared to go through this alone.

"They're on their way," he says in a clipped voice when he hangs up.

"Call Kris. She needs to stay with Charlie." I grunt as another contraction pulls my abdomen into a sharp point of pain.

Breathe. In, out. In, out.

While Rhett makes the call to Kris, I speak to Charlie. "I'm going to hospital, like we talked about. You're going to be all right. Kris is coming to see you. Ask her to cook whatever you like. There's lots of food in the fridge."

"She'll be here as soon as she can," Rhett says on a huff.

"Can you be brave for me?" I ask Charlie.

"Bra–brave."

"Good. I love you so, so much." I want to say more, but I can't speak through the next contraction. I have to lean on Rhett for support. Impatient for it to lift, I blow out a breath and drag in air. I have little time before the next one comes. "You've always been a good, big brother to me, Charlie. Never forget how much I love you."

"God, Val." Rhett's voice is choked. "Don't talk like that."

"I'm good." I give him a reassuring pat on the arm. "I just want him to know."

"He knows." Rhett shoots a worried look at Charlie. "How about watching a movie until Kris comes?"

"O–okay."

As Charlie heads for the cinema room, Rhett carries me to the sofa. He pushes a pillow under my head and strokes my hair. "You're strong. You're going to be fine."

My smile is weak, because my heart is not in it.

Please don't let my baby die. Please don't let him pay the price.

Rhett has his phone pressed to his ear when sirens sound in the distance. "Damn you, Gabriel, pick up," he mutters under his breath.

I don't know how I feel about Gabriel being here, right now, but this is still his baby, too.

"Quincy?" I offer, grinding my teeth through the pain.

He's already scrolling through his contact list when the intercom buzzes, but gives up on the call to open the gate from the control panel in the kitchen. Rhett rushes for the door and lets the paramedics in. Despite the fact that he's still only wearing a towel, he runs next to the stretcher as they wheel me to the ambulance.

He grips my hand. "I'm not leaving your side."

"No. Stay with Charlie." He could drown in the pool or explode the gas in the kitchen. There are too many potential accidents waiting to happen in this house. When it looks as if he's going to argue, I beg. "Please, Rhett."

Reluctantly, he gives in, but his expression lets me know he's not pleased.

"I'll call Quincy," he calls as the paramedics load me into the back of the ambulance and one of them takes up a position next to me.

We're speeding off when the medic starts bombarding me with medical questions about my health history and the pregnancy while he listens to my heartbeat and takes my blood pressure. His eyes flare when he reads the gauge.

"Except for the contractions, do you have any other pain?"

"My head hurts."

"Blurred vision, seeing spots, or sensitivity to light?"

"Spots."

His frown deepens. "Nausea or vomiting?"

"Nausea, but I've been nauseous since the beginning of the pregnancy."

"Dizziness?"

"Yes."

He connects me to a tocometer to measure my contractions and tells me he's sending the information to the hospital ahead of my arrival. He doesn't say there's nothing to worry about, and I'm glad he doesn't give me meaningless reassurance.

Thanks to Gabriel's private medical insurance, I've been pre-admitted for the delivery at the brand-new Broadacres Clinic a short distance away from home. We clear the gates less than twenty minutes later. A male nurse is waiting at the emergency entrance to escort me to an examination room in the delivery wing where an obstetrician takes immediate charge. With him are two nurses. He's studying a tablet as one nurse helps me undress and pull on the hospital robe while the other prepares a drip. The nurse helps me into a bathroom for a urine sample before leading me to a gynecology chair where the doctor takes a blood sample and does a physical examination. The look in his eyes when he finally lifts his head reflects my fears.

"Mrs. Louw," he says in a soothing voice, "you're nine centimeters dilated, and your contractions are two minutes apart. You're in the active phase of labor. It's too late for an epidural. We're going for natural unless there are complications, all right?"

"Can't you stop the contractions? It's too early for the baby."

The way he looks at me is so calm that his next words floor me

173

completely. "You have severe preeclampsia. Are you familiar with the term?"

I frown at him. "Vaguely."

"Your blood pressure is too high. If you don't deliver the baby now, you risk developing eclampsia or seizures, which can be life threatening." He softens the blow with a pat on my leg.

"What?" Shock resonates through me. "My baby! What about my baby?" I bite my lip as pain sharper than before contracts my body.

"We're going to do our best. The rest is in God's hands." There's a sense of urgency but also confidence in his movements as he starts to prepare, pulling on scrubs and a hair cap. "Can we call someone to be with you?" He glances at the screen of the tablet. "You have only your husband listed."

The only people I want are Kris and Charlie. They're the ones who stood by me regardless, who never lied to or deceived me, but this isn't a situation I can expose Charlie to, and it's better that Kris takes care of him.

"No," I say, "there's no one else."

"Get the anesthesiologist on standby," the doctor says to one of the nurses.

The nurse pushes a needle into my arm and connects it to a drip while the doctor takes a seat in front of my bent legs.

"Push when I tell you," he says. "On the count of three. One. Two. Three!"

The contractions are coming faster and harder. I need all my energy to breathe through them. I don't have enough strength left to think, let alone to talk, so I put everything out of my mind except the one task required of me––delivering this baby.

14

Gabriel

The meeting runs overtime. While our investor drones on about the real estate market, I check my watch. It's almost eight. My phone vibrates on the tabletop. I glance at the screen. It's a message from Quincy.

Call Rhett.

Something's up. Being in a meeting, I'd ignored Rhett's earlier call, but both my bodyguards won't be trying to reach me if it's not important. Excusing myself, I leave Michael to chair the meeting and make the call in the hallway.

Rhett's voice is strained. "Valentina's on her way to the Broadacres Clinic."

Every sinew in my body is a string about to snap. "What happened?"

"Her water broke."

I go cold. I clench the phone so hard my fingers hurt. "Hold on." I shake like a puppy in a storm. My leg is dead weight dragging behind my body as I hurry back into the meeting room and whisper my emergency in Michael's ear.

"Go," he says, grabbing my shoulder, "and let us know." His eyes are laced with concern as they follow me out of the room.

In the hallway, I text Quincy, telling him to bring the car around, and revert back to Rhett's call.

Speaking as I walk, I ask, "Where are you?"

"At the house. I'm waiting for Kris to arrive to stay with Charlie. As soon as she gets here, I'll go to the hospital."

"How did this happen? Did she lift something heavy?" Dear God, did she...? "Did she fall?" I should've been there, dammit. Maybe she tried to clean under the bed again or carry the laundry basket downstairs.

"I don't know." Rhett sounds lost. Frightened. "Magda arrived, I went for a shower, and the next thing I knew, Valentina's in labor."

"Wait." Magda arrived? My hackles grow ten inches long. "What did Magda want?"

"I don't know. I assumed it was a social visit."

It doesn't add up. I'm in the lobby, scanning the street for Quincy. "Did you see her?"

"No. I only opened the gate. Valentina met her at the door. I went for a shower to give them privacy."

"Is she still there?"

"She left before Valentina's water broke."

Spotting the Jaguar pulling up to the curb, I race for the passenger side. "Good." I don't want Magda there when I'm not home. I get inside and cover the phone with a hand. "Broadacres Clinic," I say to Quincy. "Hurry. Valentina's having the baby."

Quincy pales. He puts the car in gear and takes off with screeching tires.

"I'm on my way," I say. "We'll be there in twenty."

Luckily, at this hour, there's little traffic. We take the quieter roads and make it to the clinic in just under my predicted time.

Quincy drops me off at the front entrance. "Go. I'll park the car."

As a short month ago, I rushed to the reception desk, but this time I ask for my wife. As a month ago, the receptionist tells me to stay put. A doctor is on his way to meet me. I turn to stone. My organs transform into lead. I haven't been directed to a lounge, but it's the same.

A young man in a white coat approaches me. He doesn't waste time with a greeting.

"Mr. Louw, your wife is in labor."

I'm like a lion ready to pounce. I want to be with my woman. "I know. Take me to her."

"Shortly." His tone is assertive. "First, I need to bring you up to speed." He turns and starts walking, not looking to see if I'm following.

When we enter a small visitor's room, everything inside of me turns heavy. My stomach is a ball of granite. My chest cavity is filled with rocks.

He closes the door and turns to me. "Your wife has severe preeclampsia as a result of hypertension. The only way to prevent further risks is for the baby to be delivered immediately, but we're battling to stabilize her blood pressure. We're administering magnesium sulfate intravenously. If her body doesn't react to the magnesium, she may develop eclampsia. In other words, she may have seizures. We've already explained the condition and possible consequences to her. Before you go into the delivery room, we need to do the same." He takes a breath and plows forward. "There's a chance she may not survive the birth."

My legs turn to stone pillars. My fault. My doing. "How big a chance?"

"Right now, I'd say fifty-fifty, but it depends on how she reacts to the medication."

My first irrational reaction is anger. "Our private doctor examined her every two weeks. Why didn't he pick this up?"

"Preeclampsia often only starts at the onset of labor."

"She wasn't due for another two months. What went wrong?"

I'm screaming at nature, at God, and at the day I replaced her birth control pills with placebo ones. If I can find what triggered the untimely contractions, maybe I can go back in time and change it. Maybe I can find the mistake and flog myself to reverse this process, to take her back to before her water broke. Or maybe I simply need to punish myself for not carrying that laundry basket for her. If I flog my back to bloody strips for letting her bend down and clean under the bed, maybe God will forgive me and spare her life.

"It's hard to say," the doctor says. "A physical shock could've triggered the birth, emotional trauma, illness… there are many factors. What matters now is that you support her." He grabs my shoulder. "You have to be strong for her, Mr. Louw. It's what she needs most."

I haven't realized that big, fat, slobbering tears are streaming over my face until he hands me a tissue from a box strategically placed on the table. If she dies… No, no, no. I can't face it.

"Ready?" The doctor gives my shoulder a squeeze. "We should go."

Another minute later, I'm showering and scrubbing in a change room, donning the scrubs a nurse put out for me. My chest is so tight it's difficult to breathe. The beat of my heart is like the slap of a hammer on a block of marble, chipping away at the corners and edges, carving deep grooves into the memories of my moments with Valentina.

Please, God, save her.

I'll give my life, instead. Don't make her pay for my mistakes. Don't let her pay the ultimate price for my selfish lust and hardheaded will to keep her. Save her and I swear I'll make this right. I'll take a vow on my knees to undo every wrongdoing, every self-serving sin I committed against her. Even if it kills me, I'll set her free.

I'll let her go.

Fuck, that thought cuts crisscrossed lashes into my heart. Retribution is a bitch, and I deserve every bit of it.

"Let's go, Mr. Louw."

The nurse leads me down a long hallway with too bright lights. It's like walking down a tunnel toward the end. There's mercy in life and peace in death. I don't want her to have peace yet, not before she's lived the full and happy life she deserves. I want her to grow old and see her grandchildren married. I want her to have whatever she wants. I want her to have the mercy.

The woman in the white uniform holds a door and motions for me to enter. My world crashes to pieces before those pieces are reconstructed to form the picture facing me. My wife lies on a bed, straining with all her might. Her face is as white as pottery clay, and her slender legs are shaking in an unnatural way, as if she's having a fit. She's trying to give life to the baby I put in her womb, and suddenly her frail limbs look too vulnerable for the task. Her hair is plastered to her brow, and her skin shiny with perspiration, but the set of her mouth is determined. Strong.

Jerking from my immobile state of shock, I rush to her side and take her hand. The stump that used to be her thumb is another reminder of who I am, one more piece I took away from her.

"You can do it, beautiful."

What lies in front of me is a broken creature, an angel with torn wings and pieces of her soul and body missing. Despite the injuries, she still fights to fly. I lift her hand to my mouth and kiss her fingers. Her skin is cold.

"Please, Valentina." I beg for forgiveness. I beg for her to fight harder and not to leave me. "Fight," I whisper.

For all her brave efforts, things are going wrong. The nurses are tense, and the doctor's instructions are strained.

"The baby's not descending," the obstetrician says.

Valentina wails when he pushes a forearm on top of her abdomen and works it down. I want to tear the motherfucker's limbs apart. I want to rip the cause of her pain away and crush his skull against the wall. It's only sheer willpower that prevents me from stabbing him with the scalpel. My anger is directed at the wrong person. The root of all this agony is standing next to the bed, clutching her hand.

"Emergency caesarean," the doctor declares with a new note of urgency.

One of the nurses lays a hand on my arm. "Please move aside, sir."

I jerk free. "I'm not leaving her."

"Mr. Louw," the doctor's voice is stern, "for the sake of your wife and child's lives, leave. We don't have time."

Grabbing her face, I kiss her like I may never kiss her again. There's too much to say, but no time, because orders are being called, and Valentina is pulled from my arms onto a gurney. I strain to hold back when they take her. Walking next to her, I keep one hand on her stomach and grip her fingers in the other.

I press her palm against my mouth, stifling the emotions that won't let me speak, because I have to say this.

"I love you." Each word is broken. Each word is meant. Each word is beautiful in its own, ugly, wrong way.

We approach the operating wing doors.

"You can wait in the visitor's area, Mr. Louw."

"Wait." Valentina grips my wrist. "What's his name?"

"Connor," I say, fighting to keep my voice from breaking. "His name is Connor."

And then she's gone.

The doors to the operating wing swing shut, and I stand alone in the long hallway with the bright lights.

TEARING out of the hospital clothes, I pace and pray, repeating my vow. I feel like dying. Is this punishment for my sins?

Rhett and Quincy arrive. They're here more for Valentina than me, and I can't blame them. She has that effect on people.

"How's Charlie holding up?" I ask Rhett.

"He's fine. Kris is cooking dinner. You don't have to worry about him."

"Val?" Quincy looks as if he fears my answer, but couldn't stop himself from asking.

"I don't know," I say honestly. I give them a brief explanation of the situation.

"Fuck." Quincy clenches his hands together and flops down in the nearest chair.

"Coffee?" Rhett asks.

Sensing he needs to keep busy, I agree.

Armed with dark, bitter coffee, we nurture our fears, thoughts, and blame as we wait. When I can't stand it, any longer, I limp up and down the hallway. It's taking too long.

I've lost count of time when the door at the end of the hall opens and a doctor exits. Quincy and Rhett get to their feet. They stare at the doctor as if he's grown horns. With sure steps, he walks over, stopping short of me. His look is direct and factual, void of emotion. Standing--praying, hoping, despairing--I await the news. The stones are grinding on each other in my chest. Every breath I take hurts.

He looks at the three of us. "Mr. Louw?"

"That's me."

"It's a boy."

15

Gabriel

"It's a boy," I murmur.

I'm a dad.

Rhett, Quincy, and I stare at the doctor. None of us speak. We wait in the worst silence of my life.

The obstetrician gives me a tired smile. "Your wife pulled through."

The earth tips under my feet. I have to grab the chair back to stay upright.

She lives.

A boy.

Thank you, thank you.

I'm conflicted and raw, knowing the sacrifice I'll pay for her life, but my joy far outweighs the torment of giving up my child and the woman I love.

"He was born at thirty-six past three," the doctor continues. "One point one kilo. Thirty-nine centimeters."

My voice is gravelly. "How are they?"

"They're both doing well. You can see your wife in an hour, when she comes to. Your baby has been placed in an incubator. A nurse will take you to see him."

"He's only twenty-nine weeks. What complications can be expected?"

"Anything, but, statistically, survival rates for his age are above ninety percent and disability less than ten."

I swallow past the lump in my throat. "Thank you."

He pats my back. "Wait here. And congratulations."

Rhett is at my side the minute the doctor is gone, grabbing my arms as if he senses my physical weakness. "Congratulations, Gabriel."

A smile transforms Quincy's face into a goofy mask. "You have a son." He pulls me into a hug and slaps my back. "Well done."

"She's alive," I say, still needing to convince myself. "She's going to be all right."

There's a note of pride in Rhett's voice. "She gave it a good fight."

"She's a strong one," Quincy agrees.

They wait with me until the nurse returns to take me to my son. I stop in front of the incubator that separates us. For now, this is as close as I can get to him. He has patches on his tiny chest, a pipe in his nose, and an IV in his leg. Damn, he's small, drowning in the white diaper. So fragile. So perfect.

I place my palm on the glass. "Connor." I ache to touch him, to hold him against my chest and feel his heart beat in his brave little chest. "You made it. You're going to grow up big and strong. A good man." With a mother like his, he won't have a choice.

Big, shameless tears run through my beard into my smile. They're happy tears. Tormented tears, tears to welcome, and tears to say goodbye.

He looks just like me, at least the me before my scars, but he has Valentina's full lips. I don't know for how long I stay like that, drinking in his features while he sleeps like only the innocent can, but my hip is aching from the long stand when a nurse touches my arm.

"Would you like to see your wife?" she asks in a bright voice. "She's awake."

Would I like to see my wife? What kind of question is that? I don't bother to reply. I don't even have flowers or a stuffed toy. No balloons or diamonds. Only lies, deceit, and freedom.

The nurse stops in front of a door in the maternity wing. "Here you go. She suffered blood loss and is still weak, but you can stay as long as you want. No visiting hours apply. Don't tire her, though."

That's part of the advantage of a private clinic and room. I brace myself and push the door open. Valentina is surrounded by white sheets. Her eyes are closed, and her lips slightly parted. Her breathing is even, but her skin reflects the color of the sheets. My gut turns inside out. It's hard to see her like this.

I make my way over quietly, trying not to disturb her, but her eyelashes lift when I reach the edge of the bed. For three hammering heartbeats, she stares at me, her soft eyes awash with emotions. Fuck, that look unsettles me. The twisted, tormented expression coils around my chest and squeezes the air out of my lungs. The single tear that slips from her eye and spills down her cheek is a stake in my heart that leaves a hole that can never heal.

I grab her fingers and squeeze. I want to climb on top of the bed and hug her to me, but I don't want to disturb her wound and hurt her. Instead, I will myself to be content with perching on the edge.

I stroke the hair from her brow and trace my thumbs over the fragile skin under her eyes. "How do you feel?"

"Did you see him?" she croaks.

"He's perfect, Valentina. So perfect."

She lets out a gush of air that makes her shoulders sink back into the mattress.

"Rest." I kiss her cracked lips. "I'll be right here."

Her eyelids flutter close, and her breathing changes. In a second, I lose her to sleep. It's the anesthetic still in her system. Unable to tear away, I lie down next to her body and carefully pull her to me. I watch her until a new shift of staff comes on duty and a nurse pops her head around the door.

"The doctor is going to examine her, now, if you'd like to go home and have a shower," she offers in a curt manner. "Maybe you'd like to eat something, too. You'll need your strength to support your pretty young wife and that handsome son of yours."

Dragging a hand over my beard, I look down at my crumpled shirt and suit. I must look a mess. My mouth tastes foul, and my throat hurts. Hunger hasn't crossed my mind, but I feel unstable as I get to my feet. I'm reluctant to leave her, but get out of the staff's hair so they can care for the precious creature on the white bed.

On my way out, I check on Connor. After washing and warming my hands, I lay them on his back. He's so small my palm envelops his whole upper body. Dearness, pride, protective instinct, and love hurt my chest.

I pass my first diaper changing test, and when I place Connor like the nurse shows me, he holds onto my thumb with his fist, his grip surprisingly strong. It physically aches when I have to pry his minis-cule fingers loose.

I put my fingertip on his heart. "I love you, son."

No cell phones are allowed in the maternity wing. Outside, when I switch my phone on for the first time again, there are ten missed calls from Kris. Damn. In my panic, I completely forgot to let her know the status of events.

Quincy sits in a chair against the wall when I enter the reception area. He jumps to his feet when he sees me. "How are they doing?"

The smile that cracks my face is a string tied to a helium balloon. I'm going to float right up to the clouds. "Good. She's tired. He's perfect." I take in his disheveled hair and five o'clock shadow. "What are you still doing here?"

"Wasn't going to leave without you. Rhett went home to check on Charlie. Kris was going ape shit. She freaked out when she couldn't get hold of you, so Rhett told her the news. I hope you don't mind."

"Thank you." I mean it like never before. I don't know what I would've done without these two men. And Kris.

"You're welcome. You look like shit. I'll drive you home."

It's nearly six in the morning. A new day has dawned. The rays of the sun wash over the windowsills like the hands of a clock, marking my time that's running out. It feels as if I spent ten thousand nights in here, and every step I take toward the sunlight is heavier than the one before. Each mile I put between us is a mile closer to never. I swallow the knowledge of what I have to do, putting it away to deal with later, alone. For now, we need to celebrate life.

At home, an excited Charlie and Kris meet me at the door.

Kris embraces me, tears spilling down her cheeks. "Congratulations. I was going out of my mind. Tell me everything. I made breakfast."

She leads us to the table by the kitchen and makes me relay everything that happened over eggs, bacon, and toast. I only focus on the medical aspects and go into a long and detailed description of Connor, leaving out the part of how this is going to play out. When they've oohed and aahed, I kick-start myself into action. Kris can't afford to close the practice for the day and knowing how little sleep she got last night, I offer to organize a temp through Dial-a-Temp for the day, but she stubbornly refuses. We still have to talk about Valentina's maternity leave and how it will impact Kris' practice, but I put it on the backburner for now. The priority is for Valentina and Connor to rest and grow strong.

Feeling better after a shower and changing into a clean suit, I dial Michael and inform him of the news. I have five days of paternity leave, but will swing past the office later this afternoon to tie up a few loose ends.

Five days to say goodbye. That's what I give myself. I'm not going to brood over it. Not yet. There are shitloads of things to do in five days. The nursery isn't ready. Except for a few outfits and a box of diapers, we haven't gotten around to the baby shopping. Valentina needs a crib, pushchair, carrycot, car seat, breast pump, and various other devices that babies require. After doing some shopping, I want to go past the clinic again. Eager to get on with the chores so I can get back to the two people I care most about in the world, I get some of the cash I stashed for the baby shopping in the safe from my study. I'm about to walk out of the room when my open laptop catches my attention. I always keep it closed when I'm not using it. It's a security thing, knowing how easy a hacker can access the webcam and study what's going on in our house. Every hair on my body bristles. Someone snooped around. There's information on that computer that can implicate me in crimes and murders. Deliberately, I haven't erased the evidence of financial embezzlement and bribes we made for Magda's business. You never know when you may need it, like to blackmail yourself out of a dire situation when your life is threatened.

Treading carefully around the desk, I study the top for signs of disturbances, but all the papers and files are in place, painstakingly neat and square, just as I left them. I hit a random button to repower the screen. A folder I don't know appears. The name sets my heart racing. I nearly go into cardiac arrest when I open it and read the file names.

Fuck. Shit. No.

My eyes fall on the black stick with the Louw Unlimited logo inserted in the USB flash drive.

Magda.

Magda told Valentina. She told her what I did. According to the files staring back at me, she did more than that. She gave Valentina the fucking evidence. Throwing the pile of bills on the desk, I clench and unclench my hands. I do this several times to prevent myself from hitting something. Valentina knew. She had our baby knowing what I did to her. Magda had no right. Why? I never meant for Valentina to suffer the awful truth. Goddammit! I take my anger out on the chair, kicking it until a sharp pain rides up my leg and lances into my hip.

What did Magda show Valentina? A recording of my conversation with the doctor? I open the file with a shaking hand. Just as I thought, an audio file of my call to Engelbrecht opens. I listen to the whole, dire speech, hearing what Valentina heard, trying to imagine what she felt, what she thought. I kind of guessed what the content of that file was even before I clicked on it, but I have no clue what the so-called *Evidence* folder contains. What other proof is there of my deceit?

A nasty foreboding sits in the pit of my stomach. This feels heavy. Dirty. Suddenly, I'm impatient. In my haste to open the file, I miss-click and have to do it again. What opens is a video clip. A blurry picture fills the screen. It looks like a low-quality home movie. As the images unfold, ice-cold dread fills my veins. The dread turns to boiling hot, melting fucking lava. Anger explodes in every blood vessel of my body. Rage makes me shake. My organs tremble as I witness a younger version of Valentina in her worst nightmare. I recall the uncontrollable shiver of her body as she knelt before me and told me her secret. I feel her pain and see her humiliation as six grown men caused those feelings for their pleasure. I want to kill them like I never wanted to kill. I want to make them suffer a thousand times more. I want to chop off their limbs and throw them at Valentina's feet. I will drag them through stones and thorns until they don't have an inch of skin left on their bodies. I simmer in my fury, forcing myself to watch every cruel second, wishing that every second is the last of her torture. It's gruesome to behold and sheer agony to witness, but I push on, because the video contains something I've been after for the better part of a year--the identities of Valentina's assailants.

Somewhere in the back of my mind a warning pops up. Something is familiar, but I can't place it. When one of the fuckers speaks again, the fog lifts from my mind. I know that voice. Barney. He was—oh fuck. No. One of my father's cronies. One by one, their ugly faces drift onto the screen. The whole damn team. If my father covered up their crime, if he shoveled dirt over the despicable act he's no better than them. Then the camera turns, and I look into the eyes of the man who raped Valentina—the man who gave me life.

Sweet mother of Jesus. Shocked and sick, I fall into the chair, staring at the black screen. Several facts pierce my mind like burning arrows. One, my father raped Valentina while his friends held her down. My own fucking father. Two, Magda knew. She knew about the rape, and she never told me. Three, this has something to do with why Magda wanted Valentina dead. The debt was only a smokescreen. And four, what Valentina saw in this folder triggered a shock big enough to set her into labor and risk both her and my baby's life.

Charcoal flecks of burnt-out ashes drift in front of my vision. Slowly, determinedly, I rise to my feet. I lock the USB stick in the safe and take my keys. Magda works in Brixton today. The drive there takes too long. It's mid-morning when I park in front of the loan office. Only the Merc is outside, meaning Scott is my only obstacle before I get to Magda.

I slam my hands on the glass doors and push them open. Scott, who sits behind the front desk, jumps to his feet, reaching for his gun. Before he can grip the shaft sticking from the hip holster, I plant a kick in his stomach and a fist on his jaw. He falls backward, his body connecting with the wall. I use the momentum to grip his hair and throw him face-down on the floor. With a knee in his back, I restrain his wrists and wrestle the pistol from his holster. I flick off the safety, cock the gun, and push it against his temple.

He stops struggling, knowing he's as good as dead. "What the fuck, man?"

"Where's Magda?"

He grunts as I push up his arm. "Back office."

"Who's with her?"

"She's alone."

She usually is. The office is soundproof. She won't hear me rough up Scott unless she walks through the door.

"Why did she go to my house, yesterday?"

"I don't know." He curses and whimpers in pain. "You're breaking my arm."

"That's the idea," I snarl. "Where did Magda get the tape?"

"What tape?" He turns his head to the side and gulps air through his mouth. "Ah, fuck, that hurts."

"The one she left at my place. Yesterday."

"I don't know what you're talking about."

I push harder, inviting more swearing, this time mixed with snot and tears.

"An old tape. Home movie."

"Fuuuuck. Stop."

He squirms like a worm. I let go an inch, giving him room to breathe and speak.

He pants and hisses. "I dug up a video tape in the graveyard."

"Which one?"

"Rosettenville."

"Which grave?"

"Haynes, Charles."

I shove again, inviting a howl. "He's not dead. If you lie to me, you son of a bitch--"

"It's his plot," he screams, "for when he dies."

"When?" I accentuate my urgency with putting strain on his elbow. "When did you dig it up?"

"Ah, fuck! For the love of God." Air wheezes through his teeth when I let go. "Yesterday."

"How did you know it was there?"

"Charlie."

"He told you?"

"He told the shrink."

"Who, Christopher?"

"Yessss."

That bastard. That's why Magda insisted on the hypnotherapy. She needed to find a tape she was looking for. Some pieces fall into place, but there's still a big, dark hole in the middle of the picture.

"Why did she give the tape to my wife?"

"I don't know! I don't even know what's on the tape."

I reached my limit with Scott. He doesn't know more. Gripping the gun by the barrel, I bring the shaft down hard on his head, knocking him out cold. Just in case, I retrieve the cable ties Magda keeps with various other torturing tools in the bottom drawer and tie his hands and feet. I put out a closed sign and lock the front door before heading to the back office to get my answers.

Magda hops from her chair and rounds her desk, calling for Scott before the door shuts behind me.

I advance on her. "He can't help you."

Her eyes slip to the gun in my hand. "Be reasonable, Gabriel."

"Like you were when you gave Valentina the tape?"

She pales to the color of whitewashed wood, the surface of her skin uneven and rough. "She showed it to you?"

The diabolic side of me wants to play with her. A rabbit and a fox. "Were you hoping she wouldn't?"

She holds up her palms. "All I wanted was for her to leave. I only wanted my son back."

My voice grows louder with each syllable. "You thought she'd run knowing my goddamn father raped her."

"Yes, I thought it would drive her away. You haven't been yourself since she came into your life. She's destroying you, just like she destroyed your father."

"*She* destroyed *him?*" Every one of my limbs is shaking. "He's the one who took her innocence, her youth––God, Magda, they beat her to an inch of her life––and *she* destroyed *him?*"

Her eyes are magnified behind her glasses. "She seduced him!"

"She was thirteen fucking years old," I grit out.

"I saw the way he looked at her, even when she was that young. Do you know how that feels? It's the way she walks, with her ass swaying and her tits pushed out. It's what she wears, those short skirts and tight tops." She points a finger at my chest. "She did it to him, and she's doing it to you."

I can't believe what I'm hearing. "How long have you known?"

She looks away.

"You will tell me," I say. "Today's the day we come clean."

"You weren't supposed to find out, not like this."

No. Neither was Valentina. God, not like this. "I did, so start talking."

She faces me slowly. "What are you going to do with the tape?"

She needs to understand how serious I am. I'll frighten her into talking, and if that doesn't work, I swear to God I'll torture my own mother. "It will go to the authorities, the ones you don't own."

She trembles from the hem of her dress to her neatly trimmed hairline. "It'll destroy us."

"We're already destroyed. It's over, Magda. We're over. The business is over."

Her Adam's apple bobs as she swallows. "Don't do this, Gabriel."

"Why not? My father is a rapist. My mother is a criminal, and I'm a killer."

"We do what we must to survive."

"Don't fucking justify our sins."

"You say that because you're under her spell, just like your father."

"No, Magda. I'm in love with her. I love her like I've never loved a woman. I'll go to hell for her, and I won't blink an eye to send you to jail for what you knew and covered up, so start talking."

For five full seconds she stares at me. Just when I think she's not going to answer, she says, "Your father thought he killed her. He said no one needed to know, so he told Barney to destroy the tape. Only, Barney never did. He held onto it, as a bargaining chip, maybe to blackmail your father with later, who knows? Valentina survived. We learned about it when she was already well on her way to recovery, because Marvin and Julietta kept it quiet. Your father--"

"Stop calling him my father." I can't stand to be related to him.

"Owen was sure Val knew their names. He arranged a hit to take out the whole family."

Ugly words sit on the tip of my tongue, but I will them away so she can finish this nightmare of a story.

"Before the hit could take place," she continues, "Barney ended up dead. Shot down in his own front yard. Then Marvin paid Owen a visit and said he had the tape. Got it from Barney. He gave us a printout that clearly showed your--" She catches herself. "That showed Owen's face as proof. He said the tape was hidden, and if we touched his family, it would go to the police. At the time, when Owen was running the company, we didn't have many connections in the force. The police were waiting for a reason to arrest Owen. Even a speeding fine would've done. We didn't have a choice but to call off the hit."

Now I understand why Magda worked so diligently to buy her way through the police force. There was method in her madness of having as many of them in her pocket.

"What was the payback?" Marvin would've wanted revenge and compensation for what had been done to his daughter.

She gives me a long, sad look. "You."

I stumble a step, the full weight of my body pressing on my half-lame leg. "What?"

"The deal was that you'd marry the ruined Valentina, and Owen would give half of the business to Marvin."

I battle to take in the information, but it makes sense. Marvin would not only get an upgrade in terms of a suitor for his daughter, but also a hell of a payback, not that any money could make up for what they did.

I force the question from my dry lips. "What happened?"

"Owen wasn't going to let himself be blackmailed. Charles was fifteen and a dangerous factor to be reckoned with. He was protective of his sister. I told Owen Charles would never let this go. He would bide his time and take revenge. Not having a choice, Owen agreed to Marvin's demands, but the minute Marvin was gone, Owen called in his guys and told them to find the tape and kill the Haynes'. Instead of a hit, it was supposed to look like an accident."

"The car that went off the bridge…"

"Our men cut the brake cables."

"Julietta?"

"The bank robbery was staged. She was the real target."

"Why did Owen let the children live?"

"Owen spoke to Val at Marvin's funeral. It was clear she didn't recognize him. She didn't put two and two together. You've seen from the tape…" She looks away again, unable to meet my eyes. "You've seen from the tape she never opened her eyes, and Charles wasn't himself any longer."

"Why take the risk?"

"Owen wanted that tape, and Lambert Roos told us Marvin had given it to Charlie to hide. Charlie was the only one who knew where it was. We tried talking to him after the accident, but Charlie couldn't remember. He didn't know what we were talking about. He was totally incoherent. A complete vegetable."

"The mafia cast the Haynes kids out, and Lambert rejected

Valentina. Owen ordered them to do it, didn't he? Was it because Valentina was betrothed to me?"

"I had no intention of ever bringing that woman under our roof. Do you think I wanted a constant reminder by looking into her face, every day?"

"Then why tell Lambert to break off the engagement?"

"Owen didn't want them to have the Portuguese mafia's protection. If the truth came out, it would be a war between us and them." Her eyes turn flat and shiny like silver coins. "No one was allowed to take her in, but no one was allowed to touch her or her brother, either. He said it was just until he'd found the tape, but I knew it was for a different reason."

"What reason?"

"He became obsessed with her."

"Why would you say that?"

She opens the top drawer of her desk. Taking out a scrapbook, she throws it in my direction. I stride to the edge with more doom than curiosity in my heart, but we've come too far not to break the lid wide open and let all the maggots out. Flipping open the pages, I reel in shock as I stare at photo after photo of Valentina, all taken from afar. I only get to the third page before my gut turns on itself and bile pushes up in my throat. That explains how Valentina survived—relatively––unharmed in Berea.

Magda splays her fingers and rests her fingertips on the desktop. "We kept on looking, searching everywhere. We turned their house upside down and swept every nook and cranny of Marvin's workshop, but the tape never turned up. Yet, Owen kept on delaying their killing, using that damn tape as an excuse."

"When Owen died you ordered Charlie and Valentina dead to prevent them from ever talking and to take revenge on Valentina for your unjustified jealousy. The debt was just an excuse so no fingers from the mob family could be pointed at you."

"Yes. I paid Jerry to take Charlie to Napoli's."

"That's why you had Scott shoot Jerry. No witnesses."

"Yes."

"The break-in in Valentina's flat?"

"We'd searched the flat before, but when I heard she was selling it, I had to be absolutely sure the tape wasn't there."

Then I fell for Valentina, not only unknowingly honoring Owen's promise to marry his only son off to the girl he raped, but also making Magda's biggest nightmare come true, dragging the memories of my father's hideous crime over her doorstep. What a big fucking ironic turn of events.

Her voice shakes. "I told you not to fall in love with her. I begged you."

I'm dead inside for the people who conceived and raised me. My family no longer exists.

"Your brilliant plan to have Charlie hypnotized worked."

"It did. He told Christopher where the tape was hidden."

"And then you thought you could kill Valentina by showing her in brutal detail what the father of her husband did to her?"

"I'd never kill the mother of my grandchild. I only hoped she'd leave you."

"Well, you almost killed her."

"Almost?" she asks in a small voice, very unfitting for Magda.

"Valentina went into labor yesterday from shock. Not only did she almost lose my baby, she also almost died."

Joy flares in her eyes. It's brief, lasting only a split-second, but I don't miss it. She would've been glad if Valentina was dead, maybe even relieved if my child was dead, too. This, I can't forgive. I don't care that she shot me and turned me into a killer. I enjoyed being feared. I won't lie. What I won't accept is a threat to my child and the woman I love, the woman this family has wronged in every way. We took her virginity, her parents, her brother, her home, her money, her fiancé, and her protection. We brutalized her, disfigured her body, destroyed her studies, her dreams, and her life. I forced my child into her body, and now she knows. She knows the ugly truth.

Magda breaks my train of thought. "What are you going to do, Gabriel?"

"Make this right."

"I see." Her tall, straight body hunches. She looks fifty years older. "This is what it comes to, then."

"It should never have started." Owen should never have laid a finger on Valentina.

Her gaze is desolate as it searches mine. "What now?"

"It's in Valentina's hands. It's her call if she wants to lay charges or send the tape to the Jews."

She purses her lips, as if in deep thought. After a while, she asks quietly, "Boy or girl?"

"It's a boy. His name is Connor."

"Connor. You kept it in the family. That's nice. Gabriel…" She hesitates. "There is something you need to know about Carly's death. I don't think the baby was the reason for her suicide."

"What are you talking about?"

"Sylvia and Carly came over for lunch the day before she passed away. They had an argument about Carly going out to a party with her friends. Sylvia wouldn't let her go. She said after what happened with the drugs she couldn't trust Carly. Carly was being dramatic, accusing Sylvia of ruining her life. She said she'd rather be dead, and if she were, Sylvia would be sorry. I don't think she meant to overdose on Sylvia's sleeping pills. I believe it was another one of her attention seeking stunts that had gone terribly wrong."

I don't have to ask why she didn't tell me before. She wanted me to feel guilty about keeping Valentina. It was a matter of, 'See, I told you so.' Nevertheless, some of the weight lifts off my shoulders.

"Thank you for telling me."

She nods.

I look at her one last time, because when I walk out of here, I never want to lay eyes on her again.

"Goodbye, Magda."

She doesn't answer. She's still nodding, her head bobbing up and down, when I leave her office without bothering to close the door. I don't get as far as the front desk when the shot goes off.

16

Gabriel

The all too familiar sound of a bullet leaving the barrel of a gun tears through me. I stop dead. The metal explosion vibrates in my skull before the walls absorb the last echoes. My first reaction is to listen. For sounds of life? That she missed? I don't know.

Silence.

My body is heavy. I'm slow in turning and heading back to the office. My fingers hesitate on the knob of the open door. I can't breathe. It feels like I'm ten years old, under water in the swimming hole, counting to sixty. The weight of the door moves in my hand. I don't want to push it open wider, but I don't have a choice. Just like when I was twelve, Magda took my choice away when she pulled that trigger. The door swings open all the way, a crack of light falling over my shoes. I know what awaits, but the sight shakes me. Magda is slumped face-down on her desk, blood everywhere. In her hand, she clutches the gun with the ivory shaft, the same gun she used to shoot motivation into me.

Her unmoving body looks unreal. She's too strong to be splayed out like this. Too proud. Too much of a fighter. This must've been the end of the fight for her. It sure as hell is for me. My chest deflates and rises. Air fills my lungs, one painful drag after another, while her words tumble around in my skull.

This is what it comes to.

Pulling my phone from my pocket, I dial a friend, Captain Barnard at the Brixton police station, and explain what happened, minus the back history surrounding my father. Minutes later, detectives swamp the office.

Barnard gives Scott, who is coming to, a sidelong glance. "What happened to him?"

"I restrained him for questioning."

He writes something on a notepad and regards me from under his brows. "You and Magda had a fight?"

"A disagreement."

"What about, if I may ask?"

"A family matter that concerns my wife."

"I see." He continues to scribble. "Did you kill her?"

"No."

"It's suicide then?"

"Yes."

"Ah ha."

"May I go? My wife just had a baby."

"I'll let you know if you need to come in for further questioning."

Barnard's tone borders on boredom. He wasn't a friend of Magda, which is why I called him. He resented the criminality her loan shark business brought to an already crime-ridden Brixton.

Fighting claustrophobia, I rush outside and stop in the sunlight. What do I feel? Guilt? Relief? Sorrow? Pity? Magda and I were never close, but she was my mother. Good or bad, family is family, and I alone am left to carry the sins of ours. My life is falling apart, so I do what I've always done. I carry on.

The world weighs on my shoulders when I call Rhett to give him and Quincy the news before they see it in the media. Rhett offers to fetch me, but I decline.

"I do have another favor to ask," I say.

Rhett is a reliable rock, as always. "Shoot."

With the funeral to take care of, I won't get around to everything. "Can you and Quincy help with some baby shopping?"

He hesitates for a heartbeat. If it weren't for the circumstances, the fear in his voice would've made me smile. "What kind of shopping?"

"The stuff babies need. You know, a pushchair, car seat, crib, those kinds of things."

He swallows with an audible gulp. "Uh ... I guess."

"Good man. Take my cheque book." Rhett has signing power. "It's in my office."

"Wait," he says when I'm about to hang up. "What colors? What models?" His tone rises with a hint of panic. "Where do you buy stuff like that?"

"You'll figure it out. It'll make Valentina's life easier when she comes home."

Mentioning Valentina seals the deal. There's no lengths my guards won't go to for my woman.

With my bodyguards taking care of the shopping, I have time to go home and pack clothes for Valentina and Connor before stopping at a florist and jewelry store. Armed with a pair of diamond earrings, a chocolate bouquet, a humongous flower arrangement, and a giant stuffed crocodile, I drive to the clinic. Diamonds in my pocket, flowers under one arm, crocodile under the other, chocolates gripped in my hand, and an overnight bag swinging from the other, I walk through Valentina's door.

She's propped up on the pillows in bed. I stop to take her in. Her long lashes fall over her cheek as she stares at her hands. Chocolate-and-wine-colored curls tumble over her shoulders, partially obscuring the soft curve of her breast under the hospital robe. The bronze glow is back on her cheeks, this morning's paleness gone. The sight of her makes me weak. I must be turning into a big fucking crybaby, because I'm fighting back tears for the third time since yesterday. Just as I think she's not going to look at me, her lashes lift, and her brown eyes meet mine. Rivers of sadness flow through their depths, leaving muddy traces I swear I can see all the way to her soul.

Reluctant to start the unavoidable subject we need to discuss, I stall for time by placing the crocodile at the foot end of the bed. "For Connor."

A smile plucks at the corner of her lips. "You don't think it's too small?"

I shrug, shifting the weight of the flowers. "I thought it would go with the jungle theme."

Her gaze moves to the white and blue lilies.

"For you." I put the flowers on the bureau against the wall. "They smell good."

"Thank you."

I leave the chocolates next to the flowers and unzip the bag. "I packed you and Connor some clothes." I transfer the items to the closet. "If I forgot anything, just say, and I'll bring whatever you need." I finish by unpacking her toilet bag in the en-suite bathroom.

When I return, I catch her big, questioning eyes on me. Unarmed, with nothing weighing down my arms, I'm exposed and vulnerable. I have no choice but to give her what she really deserves––the truth.

My bad leg aches when I cross the floor and stop next to the bed. I can't help myself from reaching out and cupping my woman's cheek. For a heart-stopping moment, she presses into my palm, and then the heat of her skin is gone.

I let go, my fingers trailing over her jawline and down her neck. "How do you feel?"

Her lashes lower, half-moons obscuring her expression. "I'm good."

A wall breaks within me and emotions flood my composure. My voice trembles. "I'm sorry." Flopping down on the chair next to the bed, I grab her hand and press her fingers to my lips. "I'm so fucking sorry." For deceiving her, for the pain she suffered, for almost losing her to death. After Carly, I wouldn't be able to cope with losing her or Connor, too.

"Why?" Her breath catches on a sob. "Why did you do it?"

The question is loaded. There are so many answers to that one, single question I don't know where to start.

"I know everything, Gabriel."

Not everything. And it will kill me to tell her. I nod and swallow, trying to find my voice. "I know you know, beautiful."

Tears make her eyes shine like gold nuggets in the clear water of a river. "Why didn't you tell me?" Her hand trembles in my hold. "Did you get a kick out of making me relay the whole, ugly affair? Why me, Gabriel? Did you need to finish what your father had started?"

A wave of sickness rolls over me. "God, no. No, Valentina. I didn't know it was him until I found the USB in my computer this morning. I've been chasing the men who did this to you since the moment you told me. You have to believe me. I swear to God, if they weren't already dead, I would've killed them with my bare hands for what they did to you." My tone drops to a whisper. "If I could, I would've made my father pay."

"How...?" Her voice breaks. It takes a moment before she can speak again. "How did Magda find the tape?"

I stare at her for three full seconds. Longer. This is the part where she'll hate me even more, if that's possible. "Charlie."

"Charlie?"

"Your father killed Barney for the tape. He gave it to Charlie to hide."

"Barney. He was with your father." The color leaves her cheeks. "My father killed Barney? And Charlie remembered?" Her eyes grow large as understanding bleeds into them. "The hypnoses?"

"Yes," I say somberly. "That's how Magda found out Charlie buried the tape in the graveyard, in the plot your father had bought for him."

Resolution marks the square set of her shoulders as she steels herself for what's to come. "You better start from the beginning."

I tell her everything Magda said, leaving nothing out. I tell her my father was a sick bastard obsessed with an under-aged girl, and his obsession led to the destruction of not only her, but also my family. I tell her how the mafia paid and threatened Lambert Roos to call off the betrothal, and that I was supposed to take his place, ironically *have* taken his place. I tell her about Jerry, the trap Magda set for Charlie, and maybe the hardest part, that I was supposed to kill her, but that she already knew. She knew the nasty fact and still tried to build something with me. This is how big her heart is, but no heart can be big enough to process and forgive the depth of what I'm laying at her feet now.

She hears me out to the very end, and when my words dry up, she asks, "Why did you trick me?"

I rub her fingertips over my lips, back and forth, back and forth, pleading with my eyes for understanding as I gather my words.

"It was the only way to save you."

"From Magda."

"Yes."

"Why did she do it? Why show me the tape?"

"Giving you the tape was her way of trying to drive you away. I don't believe it was her intention to force you into early labor."

She stares at me for the longest time while silent tears streak her cheeks. Finally, she whispers, "What now, Gabriel?"

There's so much loss in her tone. The words sound broken coming from her lips. What now? How does one move on after something like this? How does she pick up the pieces of her life and build a new one? My heart aches for her, but my girl is strong. She's loyal, determined, loving, and brave. She'll make it.

"Magda is dead. She put a gun to her head when I confronted her this morning."

Her complexion pales further. "No."

No longer able to keep my distance, I climb next to her onto the bed and pull her into my arms. The minute my body molds around hers, she snaps. Big, insufferable sobs shake her shoulders. I soothe her the only way I know, holding her close. I push Valentina's head against my chest, willing her to purge her soul with bitter tears.

Valentina's cries must've alarmed a nurse who comes into the room and asks if we're all right. Taking in Valentina's state, she addresses me. "Post-natal blues. If it doesn't go away within a couple of days, call her doctor." She straightens the bed sheets and leaves without posing further questions.

I take the box from my pocket and place it on Valentina's lap. "I wanted to get you something memorable so you never forget how brave you were." I kiss her lips. "Always remember that you fought and survived."

The words are charged. We both know what I really mean. She survived my family. If she can survive Gabriel Louw, she can survive anything.

"Open it, please," I say when she doesn't reach for the box.

After a second, she pulls the ribbon free. Painstakingly slow, she removes the wrapping paper and regards the golden logo on the velvet for what seems like ages before she lifts the lid.

She bites her lip. "I can't."

"Don't say no. This is for me, not you."

"Will it make you feel better?"

Nothing can make me feel better. "Yes."

She lifts the diamonds from the box and fixes them in her ears. They suit her perfectly. She looks like she was made for flawless, brilliant stones. I take my time eternalizing the picture in my mind.

"Thank you," I say, feeling those two words to the bottom of my soul.

I'm not ready to go, but there's much to take care of. A lifetime's planning needs to happen in five days. I take her telephone from my pocket and leave it on the nightstand. Cupping her face, I kiss her forehead. The past is a thick, dark cloud stifling the air between us. Nothing can be said or done to take it away. All I can hope is that my decision will make it better.

Valentina

INSIDE, I'm hacked to pieces. My soul is broken. There's nothing left of the woman I once was or the one I could've been. I'm still a burnt-out volcano––ashes and black––but where that burn was fueled by fear and anger when Gabriel first broke down my door, now it's the result of inconsolable sadness. The crater that used to be my heart is bubbling with emotions of loss, shame, deceit, and worthlessness. I've lost so much of myself I don't know if there's enough left to build myself up from the cold embers of destruction. Gabriel's father took something from me I was supposed to save for the man I'd one day love. He took more than my innocence. He took my ability to have a normal relationship with a normal young man. Maybe that's why I fell for Gabriel. Maybe I can only have unhealthy, unequal, anything-but-normal relationships with older, twisted men. Owen Louw took my joy for life and gave me nightmares and shame instead. Because of a moment in time when he took something he shouldn't have wanted, I lost my parents and my future. I lost my beautiful Charles to a boy in the shell of a man. Because of Owen's crime, we became outcasts who lived in poverty with the cruelty of people like Tiny. When the time came, we would've paid the ultimate price––our lives.

Then there was Gabriel. Because of him, Charlie and I didn't die the day he came for us. I'd like to believe there was more than lust. A small part of me likes to think it was the kernel of something greater, something deeper. I have to believe he feels more than a physical attraction or even a sick obsession, because the seed of pleasure and pain he planted in me germinated to undeniable attachment and care. The fragile stalk of affection that shot up in my heart from the rotten secrets of our past grew as thick and sturdy as a tree. That tree may have sprouted in the fermenting layers of deceit, but that very compost made the branches rise high and strong. The addictions Gabriel gave me are woven like ivy around that trunk. They are grafted with the plant and the roots. They are part of who I am. In the center of it all is one, encompassing emotion. Love.

Despite everything, I love Gabriel. It'll take time to forgive and deal with my past, and great effort to work toward trusting Gabriel again, but there's positive in the negative. If not for that fatal day of thirteen February, I'd be married to Lambert Roos, living a loveless life in a run-down house in the south of Johannesburg with five or six kids, putting red lipstick on just to get through the day. If Magda hadn't orchestrated Charlie's debt at Napoli's, I wouldn't have walked in the night I laid eyes on Gabriel. If Gabriel weren't supposed to have killed me, he wouldn't have saved me. I'll always mourn my parents and what happened to Charlie. My scars will never fade completely, but my past doesn't have to dictate who I become. I choose not to be a victim. Owen may have broken my body and ruined my youth, but I won't give him my spirit.

Gabriel broke me, and he made me whole again. He taught me the meaning of love and gave me a beautiful baby who takes that love to a whole different level. When he took me from Berea, he didn't give me a choice, and I've floated in the blameless absolution he offered for far too long. Gabriel's prisoner or not, it's time to take a stand. Back then, I took an unwilling vow to pay off the debt for nine years. Now I'll make my promises willingly. I'd never want a killer as a father for Connor, but Gabriel works for Michael, now. There's nothing left standing between us. I *choose* this love. It's mine to have and to hold, and I'll give it my damnedest best shot until death do us part.

Gabriel

THE NEXT FEW days pass in a blur. Between painting the nursery and arranging Magda's funeral, I stay with Valentina and Connor as often and long as possible. Quincy, Rhett, and I have the baby equipment covered, or at least I think so. I have no clue if the milliard things we bought remotely covers everything, because I hadn't been involved in preparations for Carly. That was taken care of by a nurse and interior decorator. Readying a room for Connor gives me immense pleasure. I install a baby monitor with webcam so Valentina can watch him from anywhere in the house. I put up barriers at the top and bottom of the stairs, protective covers on all the corners of the tables and counters, and baby locks on the cupboards with cleaning and hazardous products. I fix a lockable cover on the Jacuzzi, put bars in front of all the upstairs windows, and install an alarm and fence around the swimming pool. Certain that the house is baby safe, I pull out all the poisonous plants in the garden, as well as cover up the fishpond. I read on the internet a toddler can drown in as little as two centimeters of water. I take Charlie to visit Valentina and Connor and prep him on being a good uncle. Rhett and Quincy are at the hospital more than home, eager to try out all the contraptions they bought and disappointed when they're told they'd have to wait until Connor can maintain his body temperature and has gained sufficient weight.

Magda's funeral is the day before Valentina comes home. I arranged it like this on purpose, not wanting her to be a part of the event. Magda doesn't deserve her parting wishes, and I doubt Valentina would want to pay her any. The service is private, for family only, which means just me. It's not that I don't want her friends and business associates to pay their respects. I just can't face the sharks who'll circle the waters, waiting eagerly for bits of bait as to how I'm going to handle the business promotions, new appointments, pay-offs, and bribes. It seems fitting that it's me alone to witness Magda's weakest moment, when her coffin is lowered into the earth. Even in death, she takes her rightful place next to my father, the way she'd bought the plots years ago. The old graveyard in Emmarentia is full now with no more space for a soul. My body won't rest here, and that, too, seems fitting. I said my goodbyes before she died. I cut my ties the day in Napoli's.

In the late afternoon, Magda's attorney reads her will. It doesn't come as a surprise that she'd added a clause. I'm still her sole heir, but the wealth can only be bequeathed or redistributed in the event of my death. Always thorough, Magda made sure I can't give Valentina or my only surviving child a cent. Magda's hate for the girl we ruined stretches beyond life, all the way to her grave. Valentina can't lay a finger on the Louw family fortune, not even as my lawfully, wedded wife, since we got married outside of community of property. Not until I'm dead. Which poses a problem if I'm to give her the freedom I pledged on her life. There's no way I'm sending her and my child penniless into the world.

I guess I'll just have to die.

17

Valentina

Every day Gabriel visits us at the hospital. Kris, Charlie, Rhett, and Quincy are frequent visitors, too, but no one is as caring and considerate as Gabriel. I only have to mention thirsty, and I have a bar fridge in my room stocked with every imaginable brand of mineral water and fruit juice. Even when I don't say anything, he spoils me with gourmet meals from my favorite Italian delicatessen and raspberry scented bath products. He massages my back and rubs my feet. When he's not with me, he's kangarooing Connor and changing his diaper. I see the good father who loved--still loves--Carly, and get a glimpse of how life can be.

On the day of my discharge, Gabriel waits for me with a bunch of blue and white balloons. Such thoughtful and kind actions, but I want him to stop these exaggerated efforts to make up for the past and simply be himself. I just want us to be. In time, things will fall into place, and we'll find our measure of normality. I have to hold onto this belief.

To Gabriel's protest, I decline the wheelchair. I started walking a bit every day, eager to gain back my strength. Rhett and Quincy help cart everything from the room to a pickup Rhett organized for this purpose. With the gifts I accumulated, it's not a light task. Even if I'm happy to go home, it's hard for me to leave without my baby. Clutching Gabriel's hand, I pull back when we reach the main doors of the clinic. Being as in tune with my emotions as he is, he understands the reason for my panic.

Strong arms fold me into a safe and warm cocoon. "He'll be fine." He kisses my lips. "He's a fighter, like his mother."

That evokes a smile, which seems to please Gabriel, but his own is weak in return. I wish I knew what's going through his head. Magda's suicide and the knowledge of what his father did must be excruciatingly tough on him. It's going to be hard to work our way to happiness, but I have a truckload full of determination and endless love in my heart.

I intertwine our fingers. "Shall we go home?" I want him to know I'm ready, that I'm taking this next step willingly.

He swallows and nods, but doesn't move toward the door.

"Gabriel?" I loosen his arms so I can step back and look up at him.

His expression shifts. His scars scrunch up with the narrowing of his eyes, as if he's studying a portrait to commit it to memory. His beautiful, disfigured face softens, and the set of his jaw slackens as his translucent blue gaze drifts over me. This is huge. I don't know what this sudden look of sad affection means, but I know it's the kind that can rip your feet from under you. Just as I'm about to speak, a smile wipes the dooming sorrow from his face.

His voice is unfaltering and strong, washing away my fear. "After you, beautiful."

During the drive he tells me about the changes he made at home.

"I know you want to breastfeed, but I got an electric steam sterilizer, just in case Connor has to drink from a bottle for a while longer." He glances at me. "And a food processor for later when you want to make puree. If you want to, of course. There's nothing wrong with buying ready-made baby food. I just thought––"

I cup his knee. "Thank you, Gabriel. Everything will be perfect."

At home, he takes me on a tour to show me what he mentioned in the car, insisting on carrying me up and down the stairs. It's as if he's lecturing me before going on a long trip. Despite my earlier burst of energy, I'm tired by the time we finish and happy to take a short nap.

The men prepare a welcoming dinner of burnt lamb chops and lumpy mashed potatoes. I feel cherished and something I haven't felt in a long time--welcome. This is home. This is *our* home.

After dinner, Gabriel carries me to the shower and washes my hair and body. He takes extra care with drying me, careful not to press on my stitches. Kneeling at my feet, he stares at me with a molten look in his eyes.

He plants a trail of kisses up my legs to my thighs, his palms following the path. "God, you're beautiful."

"I have a lot of flab to get rid of."

"There's nothing to get rid of." His hands glide over my hips. "You're perfect."

I brush my fingers through his thick hair. "You're a liar."

"Not about this. Not about you." He places a gentle kiss under my incision. "This amazing body gave me a beautiful son." His eyes fill with regret. "I'm sorry, Valentina, but I'd do it all over again to keep you safe."

"It's okay." I cup his cheek when he presses his face to my stomach. "What you did was wrong, but I don't resent having Connor."

There's more to discuss, but we have time, and for now I forget everything as his fingers move to my center.

"We're not supposed to…" I moan when he parts me gently.

"I won't penetrate you. Just a taste."

His tongue licks over my folds, finding my aching clit. The hot wetness of his mouth feels amazing, but the pleasure makes my womb contract, and that hurts. I groan in frustrated disappointment when he stops.

"Sorry." He gives me a sheepish look. "I couldn't resist."

He picks me up and carries me to the bed as if I'm made of paper-thin glass. Shifting in behind me, he holds me to his body, skin against skin, until I drift off to the promise he made in the clinic when he whispered he loved me. When I said those same words to him, he didn't believe me, but it doesn't matter. I have all the time in the world to convince him. One day, if I'm lucky, I may hear those precious words coming from his lips again.

I WAKE UP ALONE. The sheets on Gabriel's side of the bed are cold. He can be in the shower or working out in the gym. Only, I know he isn't. There's an instinctive knowledge in my soul. A dark feeling folds foreboding wings around me. My heart flaps in the cage of my ribs.

"Gabriel?"

I get out of bed and pull on a robe. Making my way downstairs as fast as my stitches allow, I call his name again, but all I get is my echo in the empty space.

"Valentina?" Quincy steps into the kitchen, concern etched on his face. "Is everything all right?"

"Gabriel." I walk to the kitchen as if I'm walking on pins. "Gabriel's gone."

"Hey." He rushes to meet me and takes my arm. "He left early to take care of business. He'll be back after breakfast."

I sit down in the chair he pulls out for me. "Where did he go?"

"The Brixton office."

"With Rhett?"

"Yes."

Even knowing Rhett is with him doesn't make me breathe easier. "Why?"

"With Magda gone, there's a lot to iron out."

We haven't talked about the business or what his plans are, yet. Maybe he feels it doesn't concern me. "He works for Michael. Does that mean he's going back to the loan business?"

Quincy looks uncomfortable. "I don't know about that. You'll have to ask him."

There's still such a huge gap between Gabriel and I and where I stand in our relationship.

"Can I make you a cup of coffee?" Quincy asks with a scrunched-up brow. "Maybe tea?"

I clutch my stomach and push to my feet. "I need to speak to him. Now." I can't shake this horrible feeling crawling over my skin.

"Whoa." He pushes me back into the chair. "Stay put. Gabriel will skin me alive if you tear your stitches. I'll get your phone. Where is it?"

"Thank you," I whisper. "On the night stand in the bedroom."

"I'll be right back." He bolts up the stairs, taking them two by two.

I don't care that the bed is unmade or that my clothes are scattered over the floor where Gabriel dropped each item last night after meticulously studying every inch of my body, not as if he was saying goodbye. Worse. As if he'd never set eyes on me again. My throat tightens. I grip the chair, battling to breathe.

Quincy comes bouncing down the stairs with my phone and holds it out to me. "Here you go." He does a double take. "Jesus, Val. You're as white as a sheet. Are you okay? Shall I call a doctor? Gabriel said I must call Dr. Engelbrecht if you don't feel well."

I take the phone with a shaking hand. "I just need to hear his voice."

I scroll through my call list and push the dial. Pressing the phone to my ear, I wait impatiently for the call to connect. If only I can speak to him, this irrational fear will let me go. My world will be all right, my life aligned.

Hope plummets with an uneasy turn of my stomach when his phone goes straight onto voicemail.

"Gabriel," I wet my dry lips, "please call me. I need to hear your voice. I need to tell you things, too many things I can't say over the phone." I start to cry. "I want to tell you how much I love you, and that I'm staying because I want to. I want to give this relationship my best shot. I want to make the vows I took real. Please, please, Gabriel, don't take this chance away from me. Don't leave without giving me a chance to say this. You owe me, do you hear me? You owe me this chance." My tears run in rivulets down my face. "Please, call me back."

I hang up, utterly devastated. Lowering my head to my hands, I weep like never before.

"Val." Quincy's breathless voice reaches me through my sobs. "Good God. What's happening? What can I do?"

Through my tears I see him crouch down in front of me.

"He's at work, sweetheart. He'll get your message and call you back when––"

The ringtone of his phone cuts him short. The sound is loud and obtrusive, like bad news.

His face freezes when he glances at the screen. His voice is ominous. "It's Rhett." He forces a smile on his face, but his heart isn't in his words. "See? He'll tell you everything's fine." He straightens and walks to the corner, keeping his back turned to me. "What's up, Rhett?"

For a while he doesn't speak. He only listens. The set of his shoulders grows tighter and tighter. They pull inward, and his head lowers between them until it hangs from his neck like a wilted leaf. He turns an inch, as if he wants to look at me, but he doesn't. He cuts the call and drops his hand without saying a word. He doesn't have to. It's written in his body language. When he finally faces me, the sorrow I see on his face weakens my knees.

"Val." He swallows and looks away, then returns his eyes to mine. "You have to be strong."

18

Valentina

My head moves from side to side automatically, already denying the words Quincy hasn't spoken yet. "No."

He walks back to me, drops the phone on the table, and takes my hands. "There was an explosion."

Heat boils through my veins and freezes over. I stare at Quincy in a silent stupor.

"I..." His Adam's apple bobs, and his eyes blur behind a veil of moisture. "I'm sorry." His voice lowers to a whisper. "Gabriel was in the building."

I can't think. I can't process what he said. Only my body is reacting to the vicious words, starting to shake uncontrollably.

"Rhett is on his way with a police officer." He blinks several times, but his tears overflow. "You've got to be strong, now, stronger than you've ever been."

I don't feel strong. I'm not strong enough for this. This can't be happening. From afar, someone calls my name.

"Val." Quincy gives my shoulders a gentle shake. "I'm going to help you upstairs. You're going to get dressed."

I move on autopilot. It's all I can do to keep myself together, but like a mended vase full of glued cracks, my foundation is already weak. Nothing is coherent, and nothing is powerful enough to protect me from this onslaught. It's Quincy's steady hand that gives me guidance, leaving me in the dressing room to finish a mundane routine so I can face the world.

Randomly, I take clothes from hangers, not giving thought to color or style. I don't remember dressing or brushing my teeth, but my breath tastes like mint, and my hair is untangled when there's a soft knock on the bedroom door. I open it to find Rhett standing on the doorstep, looking forlorn and haggard. His shoulders shake as he takes me into a brief hug, taking care not to press on my wound.

"There's a sergeant downstairs," he says when he manages to regain his composure.

"I know."

Taking my arm, he helps me to the lounge where a woman in a blue uniform waits. Looking at her young face, I feel sorry for her. What a terrible task.

"Mrs. Louw," her voice is steady, respectful, and filled with sympathy, "I'm terribly sorry to inform you that your husband perished in an explosion this morning."

Perished. What a strange choice of words. Like food or a lifeless commodity. "Won't you please sit?" I take a chair because my legs won't carry me.

She perches on the edge of the sofa and glances at Quincy and Rhett who hover at my side. "Do you prefer we speak in private?"

I follow her gaze. Like a watch losing time, I'm a second late in making intellectual connections. "Oh," I say as I catch her drift. "They're employees and friends. You can speak in front of them."

"Very well." She shifts her attention back to me. "An investigation will have to be conducted, but we suspect foul play."

Something inside my chest pinches. "You mean it wasn't an accident?"

"We found evidence that says otherwise."

"What kind of evidence?"

"Plastic explosives."

I clamp a hand over my mouth. "Oh, my God."

"Your husband had many enemies." She says it like a statement. "Did he have any threats, of late?"

I can think of a hundred people off the top of my head who would've threatened Gabriel, especially with Magda gone, but that's not where my thoughts are dwelling. "The body." I sink my nails into the fabric of the seat when I think of him blown to pieces. "Did you find a body?"

"Not yet, but the debris hasn't been combed through."

I look at Rhett. "He could've gotten out."

Rhett's look is haunted. "I saw him go inside, Val. There's no other way out. No backdoor or windows."

Anger surges in me. "What the hell was he doing there? Why did he go back?"

Rhett places a hand on my shoulder and says gently, "He had to deal with the business after Magda's death."

The sergeant clears her throat. "What time did your husband leave the house this morning?"

I turn back to her. "I don't know. When I woke up he was gone."

"We left at six," Rhett said, "as I already told you."

She ignores him, keeping her attention fixed on me. "I'll let you know what we find." She reaches inside her pocket and pulls out a business card. "In the meantime, if you have any questions or information you think may be helpful, don't hesitate to call."

I take the card with numb fingers, staring at the name without seeing it.

"Good day, Mrs. Louw." She gets to her feet. "Again, I'm truly sorry for your loss."

Rhett sees her to the door while Quincy stays at my side.

"Who did it?" I ask Rhett when he returns.

"If I knew, Val, he'd already be dead."

I hug myself to contain my shaking. "Someone knew he'd be going there."

"Everyone knew," Quincy said with a note of despair, "and the sergeant is right. He had many enemies." His tone darkens. "As do you."

"He's not dead. I don't believe it."

"Val." Rhett goes down on one knee, putting us on eye level. "He's gone. He walked in there, and two minutes later an explosion rocked the place." He shakes his head. "I'm so fucking sorry. No one and nothing could've survived the blast."

The connection between us is still there. Could it be like a ghost limb? Would I feel the itch long after my soul mate has been amputated, like with my thumb?

Before I can analyze my thoughts, Charlie comes downstairs wearing his batman T-shirt and pajama bottoms. I go to him with outstretched arms, needing his comfort even if he doesn't understand. I lean my head against his chest and whisper, "Gabriel's gone."

"Gabriel's go–gone."

At the affirmation, my whole being shatters. My legs cave in. Like a lump of dead weight, I plummet to the floor. All I want is to curl up and stay there, but at witnessing my distress, Charlie starts pulling at his hair. He needs me. Connor needs me. In a flash, Quincy and Rhett are there, helping me to my feet.

"We've got you," Quincy says. "You're going to be all right, do you hear me? It'll take time, but eventually you'll be all right."

The words don't soothe me, because I don't believe them. Without Gabriel, nothing will be all right, so I put my strength in hope, in this strange connection that still seems to simmer between us.

"We'll find him," I say to Quincy, "and *then* I'll be fine."

A look passes between him and Rhett.

"There's been too many damn funerals in this family," Rhett grits out, "and I'll be damned if we add another one to it." He marches me over to the kitchen and calls for Charlie to follow. "First things first. You have to eat. I'm cooking."

THE POLICE GIVE clearance for the Brixton office two months after the explosion. It didn't take two months to sift through the debris for evidence. They just didn't have the staff to attend to it before. What they give me is a report and a plastic bag with Gabriel's distorted wedding band, the only item they salvaged. This token--his ring-- announces that he's gone for real. Had I not believed so strongly he's alive, I would've collapsed on the spot. The police report states human remains were recovered, but are unidentifiable. The only link to the body destroyed in the blast, confirming the deceased's identity, is the platinum ring. Officially, Gabriel has been declared dead. Officially, I'm a widow.

Gabriel has always been a meticulous planner. It doesn't come as a surprise that he has his funeral organized to the last detail, leaving nothing for me to do but mourn. Dressed in black, with Kris by my side, I stand at the edge of a grave as an empty coffin is lowered into the ground. As long as Gabriel is not inside that coffin there's a chance he's alive. Until I see his body with my own eyes, I refuse to believe it. Dr. Engelbrecht says I'm in denial, but he doesn't feel the bond I feel with Gabriel. He says denial is the first step in the grieving process, and it's perfectly normal, but he doesn't know I've been grieving since I turned thirteen. If he knew my intentions, he'd say nothing about what I feel is normal and I should be locked up in an asylum. I intend to spend every cent at my disposal to find the man who stole me. In my heart, I'm certain he's alive, even as Rhett assures me every day that Gabriel entered that building. Rhett went as far as to get the tapes from the street security cameras that monitor the building, showing Gabriel's broad shoulders disappear through the door. My husband must be Houdini, then.

A touch on my arm pulls me back to the present. Diogo's face hovers over mine.

"I'm sorry for your loss, my dear. Now that you're alone, let me know if you need a shoulder to cry on."

Rhett, who's never far, steps forward, but I hold up a hand. "No, thanks. I tend to avoid rapists."

Kris jerks with a start. She looks like she wants to say something, but Diogo places his body between us, blocking her from my view.

He laughs, the sound soft and hollow. "Careful with the accusations. I may decide to sue you for name slandering."

"I'd never make an accusation without the evidence to prove it. As it happens, I have the footage from the security cameras showing you with your dick hanging out trying to *jump* me against the wall. Isn't that how you put it?"

He glances around and lowers his voice. "No need to get your claws out. I'm only offering my support."

"Your support is unwanted. If I find you and your support anywhere near me again, I'll splash that tape in all the places that matter and turn you into an overnight news celebrity. I'm sure one of the boys will enjoy *jumping* your ass against a prison wall."

He points a finger at me. "Watch it, little girl. I don't take to threats kindly."

"Oh, it's not a threat. It's your new reality. If anything happens to me or anyone related to me, those files go footloose. Call it my personal insurance against *jumpers* like you."

Rhett and Quincy are enjoying the show, but their smiles don't diminish the ferocity of the warning looks they fix on Diogo.

Fire shoots from his eyes. All that's missing is smoke billowing from his nostrils as he twirls around and stalks away.

Inside, I'm shaking. Of course, it's all bluff. I don't have the tape. I don't enjoy playing this game, but I expected it. When someone as powerful and wealthy as Gabriel goes down, the vultures move in.

Captain Barnard, who's standing nearby, walks up. "I'm sorry about your husband."

"Thank you."

"This isn't the time or place, but call me in a couple of weeks if you'd like to clean up the loan shark business. We'll strike a deal. I'll offer you immunity in exchange for information."

"I don't need immunity. I'm not guilty of anything."

"Of course not. I sense an honest, good woman in you, Mrs. Louw. I hope you'll do the right thing."

"So do I."

When he tips his hat and walks off, Michael and Elizabeth Roux step up to offer their condolences.

Elizabeth stares after Barnard. When he's out of earshot, she says, "What did Diogo want? I bet it wasn't to offer sympathy."

"Nothing," I say.

"If he as much as looks at you again..." Michael leaves the threat hanging.

"Don't worry." Quincy takes my arm and pulls me away from Michael. "We've got her back."

"Anything you need," Michael continues with an unfazed air, "you just have to say. Elizabeth and I are here for you."

"You're coming to our place for dinner on Friday night," Elizabeth says.

"That's very kind, but--"

"No buts. I'm cooking, so it won't be anything fancy. Just a dinner between friends where you can be yourself and let your guard down." She glances at Rhett and Quincy. "Since they don't seem to let you pee alone, bring your bodyguards, too."

"They're not bodyguards, not any longer."

"Whatever." She turns to the men. "You're more than welcome, guys. Take care of her." She kisses my cheek. "Call me anytime you need a friend."

"Any last words?" the minister asks as the crowd starts to thin around the grave.

I stare at the heap of freshly turned earth. "This isn't over, Gabriel Louw."

The minister gives me a piercing look, but he doesn't say anything. He's probably happy this is over so he can go home to his comfortable slippers and newspaper.

"Ready?" Rhett asks.

"Yes." I turn away from the open hole in the ground.

"Where to? Home?"

Gabriel stipulated in his funeral plan there was to be no reception after the ceremony. I'm thankful I don't have to put on a show for the vultures.

"I'm going past the clinic to see Connor."

"I'll drive."

"I have a car."

"I'm not letting you go alone." He says it like he means business.

Kris comes around and takes my hand. "He's right. We'll both come with you, and then I'm cooking you dinner at home."

I only nod gratefully. I can do with her support, even if she's already given me so much.

As we make our way to the cars, there's a part of me that stays behind in that graveyard. It hurts, but not the kind of hurt when you lose the love of your life. It hurts with loneliness, and at the same time it burns with hope. Tomorrow morning I'll take Gabriel's ring to a jeweler to have it fixed and polished.

THROWING my full weight into dealing with the aftermath of Gabriel's *disappearance* as I came to call it helps me cope. There's enough to keep me busy so my mind doesn't dwell on his absence. For starters, there's Connor. There's always Charlie. There's my work at Kris' practice, which I put on hold. We agreed to employ an assistant, and now that Kris is earning more she can afford to employ another vet. The most challenging tasks are taking care of Gabriel's estate and the business.

As it turns out, I inherited everything––the houses, the cars, the business, the assets ... and the debt. I don't think Gabriel realized the dire situation the business was in. The Louws lived well above their means, and bribe money made a big dent in their coffers. Magda did a good job of hiding it. Because of the ongoing investigation into the sabotage, Gabriel's assets and estate are frozen. My only income is the salary Kris pays me. Thank God for paid maternity leave.

The house will have to go. There's no way I can sustain it on my salary. The mortgage Magda took out on her house in Parktown to keep a drowning business afloat requires that the house be sold. One week later, both houses go on the market. I call Sylvia to ask if she wants anything––maybe there's something of sentimental value to her––but she slams the phone down in my ear.

The big, old place in Parktown has to be packed up. It takes Kris, Charlie, Quincy, Rhett, and me a full week of strenuous labor to wrap precious crockery and glassware in paper and ship sealed boxes to antique stores. I use the money I get for the furniture and houseware to pay off the most pressing debts. That same week, to my great joy, Connor comes home.

Our house is next. As soon as I secure a buyer, I rent a modest house in Northriding, a cheaper area, but still in the safer, northern suburbs. Then comes the hard part of paying off the staff. Marie left when Magda passed away, and Gabriel got rid of the guards who remained on Magda's property. I terminate the contracts with ours and pay them a bonus to soften the blow. When I propose the settlement to Rhett and Quincy, they stubbornly refuse.

"I can't pay you what Gabriel paid you," I say. "In fact, I can't pay you at all."

Quincy crosses his arms. "I'll settle for profit share."

"In what? The loan shark business is in so much trouble it'll take years to recover."

"Then I'll settle for years." He winks. "What can I say? I have faith in your business ability."

"I'm with him," Rhett says.

"It's a foolish decision, guys."

Rhett raises a brow. "This is what Gabriel would've wanted."

"What about what you want?"

"Profit sharing sounds good to me."

With that, our discussion is settled. Rhett and Quincy stay on to protect me and Connor, sharing one of the two bedrooms in my tiny, rented house, while Charlie, Connor, and I share the other. It isn't right, but no matter how much I argue and bargain, they won't change their minds.

With the move behind us, I dive headfirst into the business. Not knowing enough about finance, it soon becomes clear that I'm going to need a financial adviser to help me navigate through the minefield of contracts and debts. Michael and Elizabeth are a great help, going through the legal jargon and explaining things to me in simple terms. Gabriel was busy after Magda's death. He cleared the illegal portion of the business, cutting loose the government and police officials who received regular kickbacks from Magda. He settled territorial squabbles by putting contracts in place that operate on a commission basis. Conveniently, all evidence of corruption and crime was destroyed in the explosion that leveled the Brixton office, leaving me as safe as I can be in this city and business. If I had dirt on the big shot politicians and judges, I wouldn't have lived long. Disturbingly, Christopher, the hypnosis psychologist, disappeared after Magda's death. I can only hope he fled for his life and not that Gabriel revenged his underhanded dealings. In any event, all traces of Magda and her cronies are wiped out. What is left is the legal side, albeit a business I don't care to exploit. It still involves using crippling interest rates to rob already poor people.

Acting against Michael's advice, I lower the interest rates across the board and write off the debt of those debtors who already paid interest equal to their capital loans. There will be no more bone breaking and violence. I close all the offices except for the one in Auckland Park to save expenses and retrench the staff. Magda hired them, and I don't trust them. Rhett and Quincy help out with the bookkeeping, even if it isn't their forte. We can't carry on like this indefinitely, and I can't afford to simply shut everything down. I need money to pay Rhett and Quincy, and I need to survive. I need a future for my child and brother. I need *lots* of money if I'm to find Gabriel. What I need is a change of direction and a CFO. The problem is that I can't afford to employ a decent CFO. I need a different strategy. I run my idea past Michael when he pops in to see how I'm coping, which has more or less become his Monday ritual.

"I need a bright, young university graduate with ambition and nothing to lose."

Michael regards me from across the desk in my office with a doubtful gaze. "On a minimal wage?"

"Don't forget the profit sharing."

"Your business is unstable, and you're an unknown player with no connections. The country's economy and politics are in shambles. No local or foreign investor will give you the time of day. What you should do is collect the interest from your active lendings."

I glance at Charlie who's playing cards at a table in the corner and lower my voice. "I'm not going to put people out of their houses or slit their throats if they can't pay."

"What *are* you going to do? I assure you, the majority won't pay unless you put the fear of the devil in them."

"Write it off as bad debt."

He taps his fingers on the desk. "You're not running a charity, Val."

"I won't do to others what happened to me."

He sighs heavily, leans back, and straightens his tie. "Your intentions are noble, but you're heading for bankruptcy."

I rub my forehead, feeling a headache coming on. "I know." This is more frightening than I thought, but I won't sink to the level of crime or violence. Never.

"Why don't you just accept my offer?"

Connor starts fussing in his carrycot on the carpet next to me. I pick him up and throw a cotton blanket over my shoulder so I can feed him discreetly. I don't have an issue with public feeding, but if Gabriel didn't want Michael to kiss my hand, I think he would've been jealous of sharing the intimate image of Connor on my breast, and it's extremely important to me to protect Gabriel's feelings, even in his absence. Especially in his absence.

"Val?" Michael raises a brow, reminding me he's still expecting an answer.

"I can't take your money." Michael kindly offered to take care of me and Connor as a way of paying his last respects to Gabriel, but my pride will never allow me. I have to make it on my own. This is my mess to sort out.

He sighs again. "You're adamant about this, aren't you?"

"Absolutely."

He pinches the bridge of his nose. "I have a contact at the business school. I'll speak to him and see if he knows any suitable candidates."

My smile is all teeth. "Thank you."

"Don't get your hopes up." He gets to his feet. "If you pay peanuts..."

"Yes, yes, I know." I roll my eyes. "I don't want a monkey. I want a clever worker who'll help me grow the tree to harvest the bananas in good time."

He makes a face. "That's the worst analogy I've ever heard. Please don't mention that in your interview."

"You brought up the peanuts."

He laughs and shakes his head. "I have to go. Dinner, our place, Friday night?"

Like every other Friday night, I accept. Our dinner dates became a standing arrangement, just as Saturday nights at Kris' place turned into a weekly institution. Charlie, Rhett, and Quincy are always included. I can't go anywhere without them, anyway. It's my friends' way of taking care of me, and sometimes those nights are all that keep me sane. I miss Gabriel with brutal intensity. Every day without him is torture. Work keeps my mind off him during the day, but it's at night, alone in bed, that I break a little more with each passing hour.

Michael kisses me on the forehead. "Hang in there. It gets better."

I can only nod. If I speak, my voice may break. I wave goodbye as he blows me a kiss from the door and calls out a greeting to Charlie.

Quincy walks in as he leaves. "I brought lunch." He places a plastic container with a fork on my desk and another one on Charlie's. "Pasta and cheese salad."

The salads are his and Rhett's humble effort at cutting costs. I know they miss their double burger take-outs.

Blinking away the tears that always come when I think of Gabriel, I give him a grateful smile. "Whatever would I do without you?"

He winks. "You're welcome. When that little man has done eating I'll take him for a stroll so Rhett can do the vacuuming."

"I can do the vacuuming."

"No sweat. You're busy."

Connor has stopped suckling. He's about to fall asleep on my breast, so I remove him gently and adjust my clothes. "You don't need to coddle Connor. He'll probably sleep right through the vacuuming."

Quincy looks at me as if I'm mad. "With that noise? You can't expose his ears to that. Nah, give him here." He takes my little bundle, sniffs his butt, and declares solemnly, "He's clean," before buckling him into his stroller and tucking a blanket around his body. He adjusts the umbrella that attaches to the side of the stroller and pulls the protective plastic cover over the hood.

"For the pollution," he says, taping a disposable hospital mask over the holes of the breathing gap.

While I dig into my salad, he loads a baby bag with diapers, wet wipes, a bottle of expressed milk in an insulation tube, a rattle, and a burp cloth. Lastly, he adds a variety of pacifiers, probably all the models on the market. I don't know why he still bothers, because Connor always refuses them. By the time he's ready, Rhett walks in with the vacuum cleaner.

Rhett drops the vacuum and stalks to the stroller. "He's not covered enough." He takes his mobile phone from his pocket and checks the weather. "It's only twenty degrees with fifteen kilometers of wind." He starts unfastening the plastic cover. "Put another blanket and a beanie."

"He'll be too hot under the plastic," Quincy protests.

"Ho–hot," Charlie says.

"He'll get sick with the wind coming through the gaps. I told you we should've taken the Chicco model. The plastic fitted all the way to the footrest."

"But that one had four wheels, and my research stated clearly that three wheels are easier to manipulate. Don't forget that Maclaren is better on the baby's back."

"The frame can't fit a carrycot or car seat like the Chicco."

"Guys," I get up and round my desk, "Connor is happy. Look at him."

They both look down into the face of innocence. Connor is sleeping, his little chest moving with strong, steady breaths. With that angelic face you'd never think he could lift the roof with clenched fists and angry bawling when his food doesn't come fast enough.

You're so much like your daddy.

Rhett slams a hand on his forehead. "Dickhead, Quincy. You haven't changed him before he fell asleep, and now he'll get diaper rash."

"You think?" Quincy shoots me a worried look.

"He'll be fine." I push Quincy toward the door. "Bring him back if he starts crying, and be safe."

If it weren't Quincy, I would've objected to taking my baby for a walk to the park opposite the street. It's much too dangerous to walk outside, even in broad daylight, but Quincy is not the average man, plus he's armed with three guns, a couple of knives, and Bruno.

The minute they're gone, Rhett starts vacuuming with the speed of superman while I go back to the books, pouring over balance statements.

He nudges my feet with the vacuum pipe. "Lift."

I cross my ankles on the desk, waiting for him to finish. The gun he always carries in the back of his waistband shows as the hem of his sweater shifts up with his movements.

When he switches off the machine, I say, "I'd like to start training again." Even if Gabriel cleaned up the business, it still remains risky because of the old stigma. People may hold vendettas. Besides, the city will always be dangerous.

He props his hands on his hips. "I agree."

His easy agreement surprises me. I expected him to argue, but the fact that he doesn't, tells me how volatile and vulnerable my situation is.

"What does Dr. Engelbrecht say?" he asks. "Are you ready?"

"I'm ready."

"Tonight." He seals the deal with a nod. "I'm going to check on Quincy." He pulls the gun from his waistband and leaves it on my desk. "Lock the door behind me."

I haven't been to Berea since the day Jerry gave me a stolen car, but it doesn't mean Berea won't come to me.

I HAVE an hourly interview with the five candidates for the CFO position I got from Michael's contact at the business school. Rhett is rocking Connor, and Quincy is playing darts with Charlie in my office. Not the most professional image, but both men refused to budge for the interviews.

The first man is in his fifties. He lost his job when the company he worked for folded, and at his age, especially with the high unemployment rate and affirmative action law, it will be tough for him to find another job. As he has a family to feed, my terms don't work for him, so we move on to number two.

A young graduate, I take an immediate like to his enthusiasm. He's not overly keen on working for a minimal wage with the long-term, uncertain promise of risky profit shares, but before he can make up his mind, Rhett shakes his head.

"Uh-uh. He won't do."

I turn in my chair. "Excuse me?"

"He's a no go." Rhett takes a threatening stance, which has the guy opposite me cower.

"Can you please give us a second?" I direct the young man to the entrance and close the door. "What are you doing, Rhett?"

"He was checking out your boobs."

"What?"

"He looked at you in *that* way."

"I agree," Quincy chirps in. "He won't do."

"Jeez, guys, give me a break. I'm trying to employ someone for the lowest of salaries to help us make big money."

They both give me their obstinate stares.

"Can we just get through the interviews without any comments from you?"

Neither answers.

I sigh and stick my head around the doorframe. "You can come back in."

The young man gives me an apologetic smile. "I thought about it while I waited, and I'm sorry, but it's not for me."

He leaves without saying goodbye.

"Now look what you've done," I exclaim on a huff.

They look too damn pleased with themselves, as if they fought a wolf off a lamb.

FOR FAR TOO LONG, I avoided the Brixton site. I choose a Saturday when I can leave Charlie and Connor with Kris. I don't want either of them to witness this.

Quincy and Rhett flank me next to the second-hand Honda I took possession of this morning. I sold the Porsche to minimize expenses. The three of us stare at the destroyed building. Emotions float between us. Of all the people in the world, they're the only two who understand what I feel, because they must be feeling a part of it. Rhett takes a shaky breath. He was guarding the street when the blast hit. The roof and parts of the walls are missing. What used to be the windows and door are gaping holes, revealing an expanse of blackness inside.

When I take the first step, the guys follow. They let me go at my own tempo, staying a step behind. The power of the destruction is devastating. Going through the doorframe is like walking into a vortex of death. Everything is a shade of black––shiny onyx and matt charcoal with smears of greasy oil. Guilt suffocates me. I wanted a way out. At some point, especially during the early days, I would've wished for this. Not so, now. I only want Gabriel back. Broken filing cabinets lay on their sides, their drawers flung out. The cushionless frameworks of upside-down chairs surround us. It's like standing in the eye of a twister of pain. My heart rate spikes, and my breathing quickens.

"There's nothing for us here," I whisper.

"Let's get her the fuck out." Rhett turns me in the opposite direction and propels me through what used to be the door.

In the street, I gulp in air, fighting to contain the panic attack. Feeling sick, I rest my hands on my knees.

"It was a bad idea to come," Rhett says.

Quincy hands me a tissue. "She needed the closure."

This isn't my closure. This is only the beginning. If it's the last thing I do, I will find Gabriel. I just need to make some damn money.

A scruffy pair of heavy-duty, construction boots fall in my line of vision.

"Hey," Quincy draws his gun, "stop right there."

My gaze trails up over mustard-colored pants and a white shirt with oil stains to a round face supported on a double chin.

"Howzit, Val?"

I wipe my mouth and straighten. "Hello, Lambert."

"You know Roos?" Rhett asks with a hint of surprise.

It's Lambert who answers. "We're childhood friends. Grew up together in the hood."

I never expected to see him again. "What are you doing here?"

"Just wanted to say I'm sorry." He looks at his feet. "I heard you married big."

"Sorry for what?"

"For never saying something."

"Who told you?"

"Marvin. Said he'd kill me if I open my flytrap, and if he couldn't get to me, Mr. Louw's people would."

"It's history, now."

Quincy and Rhett's heads turn between us. I want to leave the past in the past, not flaunt it at their feet.

"Does that mean you forgive me?"

"You didn't have a choice, Lambert. There's nothing to forgive."

"You're not going to come with your goons," he looks at Rhett and Quincy, "and shoot me in the back while I'm sleeping?"

"No."

"Okay." He shoves his hands in his pockets and rolls on the balls of his feet, still not meeting my eyes.

"Goodbye, Lambert."

"Yeah. Cheers, I guess."

Rhett gives him a look that says, 'Don't fuck with me,' as we walk back to the car.

"Who's he?" Quincy asks.

"My almost-fiancé."

"Jesus. Good riddance," Rhett mumbles. "If he looks in your direction again, I'll put a bullet in his––"

"No more violence," I say.

"I was going to say a bullet in his big toe, out of self-defense, of course, if he attacks."

I can only smile as Rhett holds the door for me.

"I wonder where he could hide?" I muse to myself as I start the engine.

"Your almost-fiancé?" Quincy asks.

"Gabriel."

A thick silence descends on the vehicle. Neither of my companions says a word.

At home, I work out in the gym we set up in the garage, building my strength and endurance as I do every day now, and enjoy the luxury of a long, uninterrupted shower with no baby fussing or hungry hurls before we head out to Kris' place for dinner and to pick up Charlie and Connor. When I step into the kitchen, Quincy and Rhett are leaning on the counter, their arms crossed.

"I know this look." I prop my hands on my hips. "What have I done?"

"We think it's time you go on a date," Quincy says.

"Whoa. I thought men were strictly forbidden."

"Assholes are. The others who aren't assholes have to pass a test."

I huff. "Thanks for offering your assistance, but I don't need a date."

"We know a guy––" Rhett begins.

"What are you?" I tap my foot in annoyance. "A dating service?"

"It'll do you good," Quincy says.

"No, thanks. Can we go? Kris made chicken a la king, and I'm starving."

Rhett is nothing if not insistent when he wants to be. "Why not?"

I lift my left hand and splay my fingers to show my wedding ring. "Because I'm married."

"Val," there's a plea in Quincy's voice, "you're widowed."

"One date," Rhett says. "If you don't like the guy, we'll find someone else."

"Thanks for your concern, but if I need an escort service, I'll let you know."

I don't give them time to answer. I stride to the garage as if I don't have a care in the world when I'm tearing up inside. I can't stop hurting. I can't stop wanting Gabriel back. Three months have passed, and I haven't made any headway in tracing him. I did my own internet searches and asked around, but nobody has seen Gabriel since the morning of the explosion. I need a PI. For that, I need money, and for money I need the business to work. I refuse to give up on Gabriel.

"All in good time," I say to myself.

"Yes," Quincy agrees eagerly. "In good time."

He has no idea.

ANOTHER CHRISTMAS COMES AND GOES. Kris employs a new practice manager. We agreed it's better that I resign to focus on my inherited business. It takes me four months to understand the funds in which Gabriel invested the capital and return on investments, and another month to analyze them. A small, maverick type stockbroker company, McGregor and Harris, made the best return at a growth of twenty-five percent. The bank is paying a measly one percent on our tied capital, and our long-term investment policies are losing money at minus eight percent.

I call McGregor and Harris and set up a meeting with one of the two shareholders, Herman Harris. Their office is a humble room in a brand-new office block in Midrand. Harris gives my guys, as I came to call Quincy, Rhett, Charlie, and Connor, a curious look when we pile up in the narrow hallway in front of his door.

"Charlie and I'll take Bruno for a walk," Rhett offers, taking Connor from Quincy's arms.

Harris stares at my baby. "You call him Bruno?"

"That's the dog," I explain.

"Wow." He scratches his head. "You brought a dog, too?"

I shrug. "My entourage."

"Come in." He steps aside. "We only have two visitor's chairs."

"That'll be enough."

I study Harris as he directs us to two office chairs. He's a lot younger than I expected. Definitely still in his twenties.

When Quincy and I have taken our seats, I dive straight into business. "Mr. Harris, you've––"

"Herman, please." He runs a hand over his suit. "I'm a casual guy. I only dressed up for this meeting. Usually I'm in a T-shirt and jeans."

"Thank you, although, it wasn't necessary. I don't mind casual. As I was saying, you've been running one of my husband's investment funds for the past five years."

"My condolences. My partner and I were shocked when we heard the news."

"Yes. How do you make twenty-five percent when other companies make five?"

"Your late husband gave us a small amount of money to invest at high risk. The high risk paid off."

"You play the stock market exceptionally well."

"We study the trends and know how to predict them." His eyes sparkle. This is clearly his passion. "All our clients are low capital, high risk investors, which allows us to play around quite a bit. We invest the combined capital of our clients by buying up low-cost shares that show potential for big growth."

"How does your process work?"

"If I tell you, I have to kill you." He laughs at his own joke.

"What I mean to ask is how can you be sure of your predictions?"

He swivels a big computer flat screen toward me. "We wrote a software program that takes various internal and external socio-economic and political factors into consideration. It's better than any other software program out there. It maps trends we can analyze and feed back into the program, always bettering itself. Then there's this." He wiggles his fingers. "The magic touch. Intuition. I have a nose for these things."

"I have a proposition for you. I want you to scrap the trust fund management fee you charge us."

He scrunches up his nose. "You want us to manage your investment for free?"

"Not for free. I'm prepared to pay you ten percent of the profit you make on our invested capital."

He laughs and scratches his head. "That's a clever business proposition, but ten percent of what you earn in profit won't cover our fee."

"What would you say if I told you I want to move all of our investments to your company?" By law, I can't cash out the money before the investment term is up, but I can transfer it to a different investment fund.

He sits up straighter. "All of it?"

"Everything."

"How much are we talking about, exactly?"

I take out my phone and email him the document with our investment summary I prepared before the meeting. He opens the message when it pings on his computer screen, his eyes moving from left to right as he reads. When he gets to the bottom, his mouth hangs open.

He looks back at me. "All of this?"

"Herman, I'm going to be honest with you. I don't have the cash flow to pay your fee. In fact, I don't even have the money for the monthly investment debit order. If I don't take a risk, and I mean a huge risk, I'll lose everything. You may not lose much when one of your small investors goes under, but you can win so much more if you get this right. The way I look at it, it's a win-win for us both. Besides, I believe good, hard work should be rewarded, and I like what I've seen of your work so far."

Quincy speaks for the first time. "It's a young company, Val. You don't know if they're going to make it."

"I don't know if we're going to make it, either. Magda's company came from Gabriel's father's father, but it's not the same company, any longer. With all the changes I implemented, it's as rookie as it gets. At least this way Herman and I are both personally invested."

"I love your balls." Herman gives me a look of approval.

This could be the biggest business mistake of my life, but since we stopped killing and threatening, our debtors aren't paying, just like Michael predicted. It's either this risk or closing our doors.

"Is that a yes?" I ask.

"Deal."

He extends a hand, and we shake on it.

"I'll have the paperwork drawn up," he says.

Less than fifteen minutes after entering the office, we leave, adrenalin pumping through my veins.

"Damn, Val." Quincy shakes his head. "I hope you know what you're doing."

"So do I." Quincy's profit is on the line too. "By the way, I have something for you and Rhett." I take the contract from my laptop bag and hand it to him.

After reading, he looks at me much like Herman did, his mouth agape. "Twenty-five percent?"

"Yep. We're splitting it four ways––me, you, Rhett, and our future CFO, if we ever find someone willing to work for dubious profit shares."

He lowers the paper. "It's too much. The company is yours."

"We're equal partners, all of us."

"But you have Charlie and Connor to take care of."

"One day you'll have your own family to care for. Let's just hope the gamble works."

Rhett and Charlie, who spotted us waiting by the car, return with Connor and Bruno.

"Come on," I say. "We're going out."

"Out?" Rhett bends his knees to put us on eye level. "Out where?"

"Wherever you want to go. We have shit to celebrate."

"Val!" Rhett frowns at me. "Don't cuss in front of Connor. What celebration?"

"Your contract." I give him the piece of paper. "Sign on the dotted line so we can go."

He gapes at me as if I have alien antennas on my head.

I strap Connor into his car seat while Rhett and Quincy seem to search for words. When I'm done, I straighten, stretching my back. The week has been rough. I can do with downtime and greasy comfort food. "Whereto, guys? It's your call."

"Spur," they say in unison.

"The Spur?"

"Spu—Spur." Charlie bounces up and down. He loves the Spur.

"You want to go to the Spur?" I repeat.

"There's a baby playground," Quincy says, "with face painting and everything."

"Connor's too young for face painting," Rhett says, "and you don't know what toxins are in that paint."

"I bet he'll love the slide."

"He's not going on that microbe infested super tube."

I bundle them in the car while the arguing continues.

"Mil—milkshake."

"Fine. Forget about the damn slide. There are games."

"Dude, he's not playing computer games until he turns eighteen. It's bad for the brain."

"He can't be a social outcast. Guys play games. It's what *we* do."

Connor cooes as if he knows he's the center of the heated discussion.

I text Kris and invite her to join us. Then I put the car into gear and lose myself in the safe bubble of squabbling voices. My body warms with a pleasant feeling of friendship and acceptance. If Gabriel weren't gone, my happiness would've been complete.

THE MONEY from Gabriel's estate eventually comes through when the unresolved police investigation is closed and his assets are no longer frozen. It's barely enough to pay off the last of our debts, but it prevents me from having to declare the company bankrupt, which will leave me financially crippled for the next decade, as I wouldn't be able to get a loan or buy anything on credit.

Michael questions the wisdom of my moves, but he does send more candidates for the CFO position my way. After the twentieth interview, I finally meet an MBA graduate who's willing to take the plunge. Simon Villiers is clever, optimistic, and energetic––all the qualities I want in a man who is about to start his first job with barely enough money to make ends meet and twenty-five percent of––for the moment––worthless shares.

The spikes in the wheel are Rhett and Quincy, as usual. As shareholders, I need their agreement to employ Simon. I can almost see how Rhett's head is working as he studies the attractive blond man sitting at the opposite side of my desk.

Rhett gives Quincy a small shake of his head. "Too attractive. Did he look at her in *that* way?"

"I think he did," Quincy says.

Simon shoots them a puzzled look.

"You're in?" I ask Simon, eager to draw his attention away from the sideline comments.

"I'm in."

Rhett hooks his thumbs in his belt and takes a step forward. "Hold on a second. This interview isn't over. My turn."

I sigh inwardly.

"Do you have a girlfriend?" Rhett asks.

"What?" Simon's face scrunches up. "What does that have to do with my competency?"

"Just answer the question," Quincy says.

"It's discriminative," Simon retorts. "You're not allowed to ask me that."

"Well, guess what, cupcake?" Rhett advances more. "Whoever is going to fill that chair," he points at the desk next to mine, "is going to become part of the family, so excuse me for wanting to understand how *your* family is mapped out."

"All right." Simon gives Rhett a dashing smile. "Actually, I'm gay."

The looks on Rhett and Quincy's faces are priceless. All I can do is sit back and enjoy their reaction.

"Oh." Rhett glances at Quincy. "In that case, he'll do."

Quincy, who sits on the sofa in what we call our relaxing corner, pushes the stroller over the carpet with a gentle kick and reels it back in with a rope he tied to the handlebar, his invention of putting Connor to sleep. "Yeah, definitely."

"How about you, Rhett?" Simon asks in a seductive voice, getting his own back. "Are you single?"

"I'm ... uh ... yeah. I'm straight."

"Okay." Simon turns his attention back to me. "Where do I sign?"

I would've hired him from the way he handled Rhett alone. "Here." I push the paper over the desk to him. "Welcome to the company."

SLOWLY BUT SURELY, with Simon's help and the Harris investments, the money starts coming in. We're relying on legal loans with reasonable interest rates and make our profit through clever investments. It's exactly like running a bank. The business is not my passion, but it pays for what becomes my passion--finding Gabriel.

I don't tell my business partners or friends about my search. They don't believe Gabriel is alive, and I'd risk getting locked up in an asylum for insisting he is, so I keep my mouth shut. When there's enough money in the bank to pay for the roof over our heads and the food on our table without going into overdraft, I use what I can from my income to hire a private investigator. We start with checking passenger lists at the airports and finding a match for Gabriel's description. With his physique, it would be hard to go unnoticed. For months, nothing turns up. I go as far as endorsing Captain Barnard's efforts to clean up the areas of the city where we have branches so that he pulls all the street surveillance tapes of the day on which the explosion took place. I want to be sure I missed nothing. The tapes show Gabriel entering the building, the blast, and nothing else, but there's a blind spot at the back of the building where the cameras don't reach. With no exit at the back, he would have had to either go over the roof or underground. Barnard gets me the blueprints of the building from the municipality, but that only shows the structure. No secret passages. No sewerage or drain systems. No fire escapes from the roof.

I'm starting to lose the last thing I have left. My hope.

19

Gabriel

S taging my death was easy. After climbing through the trapdoor in the ceiling, all I had to do was move the roof tile above the hole I made beforehand and scurry over the roof and down the back of the building where the street cameras aren't angled before setting off the explosives via remote. The blast wiped away my tracks as well as all evidence that could have incriminated me or endangered Valentina's life. Rhett, who was keeping watch in the street, didn't know about the body I recovered in Hillbrow the previous night and stored in the bathroom at the back. I placed the corpse close to the explosives, knowing the explosion wouldn't leave fingerprints or dental records, and fit my wedding ring on the dead man's finger. The fire would wipe out any identifiable traces, but not the platinum band that betrothed me to Valentina for life.

For life.

Leaving Valentina and Connor is the hardest thing I've done after saying goodbye to Carly. It chops away at my insides, leaving me as broken as the people I'd tortured. Keeping Valentina forever was a dark, dubious, and beautiful dream, but that life is over. With the money from my will and the inherited business, she and Connor can live comfortably. I'm one hundred percent sure Rhett and Quincy will stay on in her employ. They love her enough to follow her to the end of the rainbow and beyond. The business is clean. I got rid of the bad elements, cut the ties, and blew the evidence to pieces. Valentina can run the loan office without being arrested or murdered by the Portuguese or Jewish mafias.

I wanted to confide in Michael, but it would've been too risky. No one can ever know. To the world, I'm dead. Valentina needs the money and a fresh start—without me.

Damn, the thought hurts. I press a hand on my chest, rubbing away the physical ache where I lie in a hospital bed in Switzerland with my body and face in bandages. New technology allowed for extensive corrective surgery to my face and hip. When I recover, I'll have new features and an almost-good body.

The self-sustained *injuries* are not as much a gift to myself as a way of bringing me back to life. I've already taken on a new identity. I'll go back to South Africa to keep an eye on Valentina and my child. This is my new life purpose, and the only motivation that keeps me going. There are too many dangers out there for a woman alone. Not that she'll be alone forever. Not a woman like her. She's much too appealing. Too beautiful. Too strong. Too loving. It will be tougher than burning in the flames of hell, but I'll endure seeing her in the arms of another man as long as she's happy. For the rest of my miserable life, I'll hide in corners and shadows, following the woman I love, ensuring she's safe on street and in her bed at night. I'll watch over her and Connor like a guard dog. I'll always love her, but this time only from afar.

Weekly updates about her welfare reach me via email. My informant is an ex-Recce. The guy is a nutcase, but he's one hundred percent reliable. Reading the latest report, I utter a loud curse. The nurse, who is changing my sheets, gives me a reprimanding look, but I don't give a fuck. I pay enough for the private room to swear as loudly and as much as I like. The pain from my surgery that's usually acute turns unbearable. It happens whenever I clench every muscle in my body.

The reason for my self-directed anger blurs on the screen in front of me. I blink and reread the last paragraph. My assets are frozen, an unfortunate result of the forensic investigation, which I didn't have the damn foresight to predict. Until the case is closed, Valentina is penniless.

I ache to be there. The need to take care of her is overwhelming, but I'm unable to come near her. All I can do is watch her struggle from a computer screen on a different continent, and it fucking destroys me.

IT TAKES another nine months of excruciating waiting, physiotherapy, and healing before I can close the distance between Valentina and I. Needing a new source of income, I launched an investment company while I waited to heal. It's awkward not to be able to buy what I want without reflecting on my balance statement, such as airfare to South Africa. By the time I leave the clinic, the small company I manage online starts showing a profit. Before my *death* I researched various offshore companies and came up with a list of promising startups. I anonymously invested money in a company manufacturing a relaxation drink, more or less the opposite of Red Bull, which proved to be an instant success. A little bird in Johannesburg told me that the gold resources are almost depleted, hence I bought up shares before the crisis hit, and the gold price skyrocketed. By fluke, I stumbled upon and acquired a small insurance firm on the brink of bankruptcy that specializes in diamonds and gemstones. I also went to considerable lengths to create a cyber history for my new identity.

When the bruises on my face are healed, I have enough money to buy a ticket to South Africa and lead a modest life. Standing in front of the mirror of my one-bedroom, rented apartment in Zurich, I study the man staring back at me. Instead of a full beard and moustache, he has a goatee. The skin on his cheeks is smooth. The scar that used to cut from his eyebrow to his jaw is gone, and the gap in the eyebrow once more covered with the same dark brown color as the hair on his head. His cheekbones are higher and his nose straighter. His eyes are green, thanks to contact lenses, and his features are set in symmetrical order. Where his left eye used to sag a fraction, both eyes are now aligned. The man is attractive, handsome even, and a complete stranger.

Perfect.

If I don't recognize myself, no one will.

The new suit is cheap, but it fits. Even in the clinic, I stayed in shape, working out every day as much as my wounds allowed. The strict exercise regime has nothing to do with vanity and everything with being able to protect my family. With a last look to ensure my tie is straight, I grab my fake South African passport and a single suitcase before closing the door on the Zurich flat forever.

⸻

MY FIRST PRIORITY when I arrive on South African soil is to secure a place to live. I rent a small house in a security complex in Midrand and buy a secondhand car with cash. Furnishing the two-bedroom house takes no more than a couple of hours at a big chain store. The next day, a fridge, recliner, and bed are delivered. Getting my hands on a firearm is a lot less complicated than what it should be. I know where to go, where no questions are asked. I don't care that the weapon isn't licensed or probably stolen. I only need it for extreme measures, in case Valentina or Connor's life is in danger, and I don't plan on getting caught. At least not alive.

On day two I'm like an animal in a cage, pacing from the kitchen to the bedroom and back long before the sun rises. I shouldn't go near her, not until I have my shit together, but I can't wait a second longer. Fuck that. I won't get too close. I'll only watch her from a distance, make sure she's all right. I shower and change into my only suit, brush my hair to perfection, and then mess it up again. I'm as nervous as a teenager going on his first date, and I'm not even going to speak to her.

My hands shake as I pull the car out of the garage and take off in the direction of Northriding. I park three houses from hers and wait. It's Saturday. There's no telling at what time she'll leave the house, if at all.

At seven-thirty, the front door opens. I move to the edge of the seat, clutching the steering wheel so hard my hands hurt. I hold my breath, counting in my head. Counting calms and helps me focus. It's a habit I perfected in the Zurich clinic.

One, two, three, four--

A man steps out.

My vision explodes in shards of black fury. I knew it was a probability. Every man will be on her like a bee on honey. I told myself I'd deal with it, but I didn't take into consideration how the reality of actually witnessing a man in her house will play havoc with my emotions. I battle to hold it in. I count to ten and back to one. I want to tell him to stay the fuck away from my wife. Only, she isn't my wife.

She's your widow. Get a grip, Gabriel.

She has every right to date, but fuck it. I can't face it. I'm about to put the car into gear and drive away when the man turns. Rhett. Relief bursts like a tide in me. A second later, Quincy exits, carrying a car seat with a baby strapped inside.

My heart stops beating. I strain forward for a better look. Connor. He looks just like the old me. He is so damn perfect, not because he resembles the face I was born with, but because he is part of me and *her.*

A dainty foot clad in a black boot steps over the threshold. A long, slim leg follows, and then a woman walks onto the porch. The pieces of my fallen-apart world snap back together. Nothing matters, not the old life I worked so hard to delete or the redefined one I so carefully constructed. As before, as every moment in her arms, there's only her. She's wearing a pair of tight jeans with a fitted red polo neck jersey and a black coat. Her body is toned, slimmer than I remember. Curls the color of ruby wine and dark chocolate tumble over her shoulders and frame her delicate face. I pivot to her like a planet in orbit. I want to jump out of the car and rush over the lawn, take her in my arms and kiss her dizzy, but the husband she had is nothing more than a bad memory. I slam my palm on the steering wheel, feeling the pain in my soul. This is the price I bargained for her life, and I'll be damned if I don't honor my vow.

The trio loads Connor and shitloads of baby stuff into a Honda. I don't know how they fit everything, but eventually they're all in. Valentina drives. Keeping a safe distance, I follow them south. It's when we near Bryanston that I understand their destination. Parking in the lot of a weekend bio market, they take their load from the car. I stop two rows away where I have a good view and roll down the window. First Rhett assembles the stroller and lifts my son inside. There's a great deal of bickering between him and Quincy about whether the cover should be up or down. Eventually, Valentina puts a diaper bag in Quincy's hands and a basket in Rhett's before taking the stroller from the disgruntled men and pushing it over the grass toward the stalls.

"He needs another blanket," Rhett calls after her. "It's only sixteen point seven degrees with a wind at five kilometers per hour."

She ignores him, swaying her hips as she maneuvers the off-road stroller over the polls of wild grass and dry heaps of upturned earth as if it's a breeze.

"Val!" Quincy runs to catch up. "Put up the umbrella. He'll burn."

I can't help the smile that creeps onto my face. It's the first time since *dying* that my mouth curves into anything that remotely resembles warmth or friendliness. The pussies. I never imagined they'd turn into two such fuss balls, but I'm right there with them, suddenly worried that Connor will burn in the autumn sun. This is South Africa, after all. There's a big hole in the ozone layer right above our heads.

A young guy in a beige trench coat stares at my woman as she strolls past.

That's my wife, you dickhead.

The vulgar ogre turns his head to look at her ass. I'm about to jump from the car and rub his face in the dirt when Rhett and Quincy give him a glare that makes him look away.

Good.

I breathe easier. I should stay in the car, but my desire to get a closer glimpse is too big. Connor is bundled up in blankets, so I couldn't get a good look to see if he's grown taller. And Valentina... She's changed. There's a new kind of self-assurance about her. If I didn't know her so well, I'd have missed the tight set of her shoulders, indicating that her life is far from easy or stress-free. She's a token of strength and resilience, of the love and loyalty that drew me to her in the first place.

I get out of the car, lock up, and trot toward the rows of stalls. Snaking my way through organic pumpkins, jams, honey, and home-baked breads, I follow the small group. They stop at a coffee corner to greet a couple who are having scones and what looks like Rooibos cappuccino. The woman has bleached blonde hair and the hulky man wears a washed-out Spiderman T-shirt over a sweater. Kris and Charlie. After exchanging a few words, Valentina and her entourage leave Kris and Charlie. Valentina stops at various stalls, conversing with the vendors while Rhett and Quincy keep an eye out and carry the produce. I'm relieved that my men are protecting her like blood-hounds. To the unknowing eye, they're just two guys trailing after a woman, but I know they're scouring the area and sniffing the air for danger. From the reports I received in Switzerland, I know Valentina can't afford to pay them, which means they must stay out of loyalty and love, the very characteristics I admire in my wife. It looks like she cultivates them in everyone who crosses her path. Look at me. Here I am, tailing her like a hungry wolf, desperate to protect and care for her.

Circling around the farm produce, I move one row up and walk down the other side so I can cross the object of my obsession for a closer look, but when I reach the spot where they were seconds ago, they're gone. Shit, where are they? I turn in a quick, frantic circle, and smack into someone with my back.

Twirling, I catch the woman I bumped into before she stumbles. The apology dries on my lips. Valentina stares up at my face. For a defining moment, the world falls away as we look at each other. My body goes as stiff as a stick. Will she recognize me? Her eyes search mine as if she's trying to make a connection, but then they go blank. My disguise works. She doesn't have a clue. Holding her so close, literally in my arms, makes me heady and drunk. Every follicle on my body pricks, coming alive with static electricity that crackles over my skin. A whiff of delicious raspberry reaches my nostrils. The silkiness of her hair brushes over my fingers where I still clutch her arms. Her lips part slightly, dragging my attention there. It takes every fiber of my being not to bend down and suck those lips into my mouth.

Valentina finds her tongue first. "I'm sorry." She steps back, breaking our awkward stance. Her eyes remain friendly, but caution slips into her expression.

Good girl. She's right to be wary of strangers, especially strangers who touch her and stare at her for a few seconds too long.

I drop my arms and force a smile onto my face. "The apology is mine. I didn't see you." God, I can't get enough of her. I don't want her to go yet. Just a bit longer to drink in her face and the warmth of her presence. Before she can turn away, I say, "I hope I didn't hurt you."

Her laugh is soft. Husky. "It'll take more than that."

Rhett and Quincy step up from behind, giving me the evil eye, but I ignore their thunderous faces, plunging on before she gets away.

"Is this your baby?"

Warmth floods her voice. "Yes. This is Connor."

I peer inside the stroller and almost choke on my emotion. My son gives me a full-blown smile. A smile. He smiled at me. I swallow down my pansy tears and jubilant laughter, keeping my voice even. "How old is he?"

"Ten months."

Connor grabs the finger I hold out greedily. I chuckle. "He's handsome."

"He is," she says with pride. "Looks just like his daddy."

Something pierces my heart. I straighten and look at her left hand.

She's still wearing her wedding ring. I grow warm and fuzzy inside like I have no right to. I have no right to be happy for her grief or loyalty, not that she'd give me either.

Not ready to let her go, I grope around for a subject in my head when my gaze falls on the overflowing basket in Rhett's hands.

"You don't joke around with the shopping."

She wipes a stray curl behind her ear. "It seems like a lot, doesn't it? But my guys," she winks in Quincy and Rhett's direction, "eat like horses. I prefer to support the local farmers, plus it's organic."

That sounds just like her.

"What about you?" She eyes my suit. "You're not dressed for market shopping."

"I'm meeting someone."

"Oh, I better let you go, then."

Don't.

Tilting her head, she regards me with a quizzical expression. "Have we met?"

The mask on my face stays in place as I hold out a hand. "Gregor Malan."

She accepts my proffered hand and gives a firm shake. "Valentina Louw."

More warmth spreads over me as she uses the surname that stamped my possession on her, like my lips, my cock, my belt, and my seed. Fuck, I need to get a grip.

"It was a pleasure bumping into you, Gregor Malan."

Her smile is so fucking sweet I want to lick it from her lips. "Like the apology, the pleasure is all mine."

Only pure willpower enables me to take the first step, and the second, and the third, each farther away. I shouldn't look back, but I'm only human and a lustful man at that. When I glance over my shoulder, Rhett and Quincy are on my ass. Good boys. They'll come second if they're stupid enough to take me on, but I sure as hell appreciate that they keep the wolves at bay.

Rhett blocks my way. "We'd like a word with you."

I glance at Valentina. She stopped at a fruit stall with her back turned to us. "You left your friend unprotected."

Quincy widens his stance. "It'll only take a minute."

"Are you interested in her?" Rhett cocks his head in Valentina's direction.

This is the part where he plants a fist on my jaw for saying yes. I look him straight in the eyes. "Yes."

"Why?" Quincy asks.

What the fuck is this? "What do you mean, *why*?"

"As in a nice piece of ass for tonight or as in an amazing woman for life?"

My anger surges at the mention of her ass. "If you ever speak about her like that again I'll break your arms and legs."

Rhett and Quincy look at each other with big grins.

"I think he'll do," Quincy says.

Rhett looks me up and down. "Worth the shot, maybe."

"What's your fucking problem?"

"Here's the deal." Rhett comes closer and lowers his voice. "Valentina's had a real tough time, lately. Her life's been pretty much shit. If you checked her out because you think she'll be a nice diversion, we're going to bust your balls and break your dick. If you're good husband material, we're prepared to set you up on a date."

I can't believe my ears. "Set me up on a date?"

"Consider it a preliminary testing," Quincy says. "We'll hang out with you, you know, check you out. If you meet our criteria, we'll let you see her."

Rhett pushes a finger in my face. "Only if your intentions are serious. You play with her, you play with me."

"She's a young mom, recently widowed," Quincy continues, "so show some respect."

"What are you guys? Her dating agency?"

"Friends," they say in unison.

"I see." I don't. I want to bash their heads in for setting Valentina up on a date with a man she doesn't know, even if that man is me.

"Aren't you supposed to keep men like me away?"

"She's a good woman," Rhett says. "She deserves to have someone."

As much as I'd like to jump at the opportunity, it will make me the man I used to be, the man who manipulated her into wanting and loving him. The whole idea of dying was to set her free.

"Some friends you are," I bit out. "Keep men like me the fuck away from her, do you understand?"

"You're not interested?" Rhett asks.

"Damn." Quincy wipes his brow. "That's a damn shame. I like him."

"Guys?" Valentina walks up to us. "What's going on?"

"Nothing," Rhett says. "We just talked men stuff."

"Shall we go find Kris and Charlie? Connor is hungry."

"Yeah." Quincy takes the bag of fruit from her. "Let's go."

As nonchalantly as I can, I walk away, focusing hard on not showing the slight limp that remained.

Don't look back. Keep going.

Shit, I can't do it. When I turn, Valentina stands quietly between the hand-dyed tablecloths, watching me.

20

Valentina

The breath is trapped between my ribs. I can't draw in enough air to make my lungs work. There's something about Gregor Malan. His face is not Gabriel's and his walk is different, but he has a limp, albeit slight, and his build is the same. Everything about him screams Gabriel. If Gabriel himself didn't tell me he couldn't risk more plastic surgery, I would've bet my life the man who bumped into me is my husband. Either that or the angels had pity on me and sent me a lookalike to relieve the burning pain always present in my chest. Only, no substitute will ever do. If I can't have Gabriel, I don't want anyone. My love for him is too complete. Too perfect. I guess he finally broke me. Ruined me. For everyone but him. Yes, I'm damaged beyond repair, the broken toy destined for the garbage dump, but I'm *his* toy, and broken or not, he *will* take me back. As soon as I can find him.

"Everything all right?" Kris asks when we get back to her and Charlie.

My smile is automatic. "Fine."

"We'll put the stuff in the car," Rhett says. "Come on, Charlie, give us a hand."

The men walk off with our shopping and Connor, considerately leaving Kris and I alone.

"Out with it," she says, pulling me down in the chair next to her. "I know that look."

"What look?"

"You're brooding."

I clutch my hands together. "I just saw someone who reminded me a lot of Gabriel."

Caution flickers in her gaze. "Val, don't go looking for him in another man, because you'll only end up disappointed. No two people are the same."

"Exactly. I can't be with anyone but him."

She cups my hand. "It's only been ten months. Give it time. Someone else will come along."

"My mind feels screwed up. The things Gabriel did to me, I hated him for them, and now I crave the pain that brought me pleasure. What other man in his right mind will understand what I need?" I rub a finger over my amputated thumb. "My body is mutilated and my stomach scarred with the stretch marks of his baby. Don't you see, Kris? I'm damaged in every possible way. No one else can ever want me. Gabriel was my monster, and he made me imperfect and broken in his image. We're perfect for each other."

"Don't talk like this." She pats my hand. "You fell in love with him. It's natural for you to feel this strongly about him, even if what he did was wrong."

"I didn't fall in love with him. I'm addicted to him, but if—*when*— I find him, I'm planning on falling head over heels for him like I couldn't the first time. This time, there'll be no holding back."

"Oh, Val." Her look is concerned. "You need to see a psychologist who can prescribe antidepressants to help you cope. There's no shame in relying on medication. You don't have to get through this on strength and willpower alone."

"I don't need a doctor." I push out my chin. "What I need is a date."

"I thought you said you didn't want anyone else."

"I don't."

Her eyebrows pinch together. "I don't understand."

"I need a date with the man I met here."

"No, no, no. You're not going on a witch-hunt for a Gabriel incarnation. That's just plain unhealthy."

"Told you I'm damaged. There's not a healthy thought left in my head."

"I don't know what you see when you look at yourself, but I see a beautiful, strong, generous, and loving woman, a woman who'll unselfishly do anything for her brother and child."

Quincy calls from across the field. "Val, let's go."

I give Kris a quick hug. "You're a good friend. Have I told you how much I appreciate you?"

"All the time."

Quincy comes jogging toward us. "I changed Connor's diaper and gave him his bottle, but he's starting to complain."

"It's his nap time. He must be tired." I get to my feet. "Thanks for meeting us, Kris."

"See you Saturday?"

"Sure. Come over for dinner and a board game in the week."

Walking back to the car, my step is lighter than what it has been in ten months as a plan takes shape in my head.

TRACKING MR. MALAN IS EASY. From what I can find on the internet, he runs a one-man, obscure insurance company specializing in high-valued gemstones. It's a risky business, but with only a handful of topnotch clients such as De Beers and Anglo American he must be making a good living. According to his social media profile, he grew up in central South Africa, near Kimberley, which, on paper, explains his connection to the diamond industry. I have my doubts about the bland and straight-lined history mapped out on my computer screen. Mr. Malan obtained a business degree from the

University of Bloemfontein, after which he ran a small jewelry manufacturing business that dissolved with the owner's death, hence his new project. There's only one way to find out if my suspicion is founded.

Closing the office door for privacy, I balance Connor on my lap and dial the number listed for Dimension Insurance.

He answers with a short-breathed, "Yes?"

Everything about that voice makes me go still inside. The way the deep baritone vibrates through my body sends sparks to my nerve endings. Every follicle contracts. Every hair stands erect.

"Hello?"

I jerk back to life. "It's Valentina Louw. Did I catch you at a bad time?"

The pause on the other end of the line lasts only a millisecond, but it's enough to notice. "No. I was just working out."

I can hear the uncertainty, the questions, and the hunger in his voice. We're too much in tune, the nuances too clear for me to imagine them all. "I can call back later."

"That won't be necessary. What can I do for you?"

"I looked you up on the internet."

He utters a dry chuckle. "I gathered." More caution. "Why?"

"You run an insurance company."

"That's right."

It sounds as if he's opening the fridge. A can pops. The sound is followed by soft swallowing. My imagination does wicked things to me, putting images in my mind of Gabriel leaning against the counter, drinking beer. His Adam's apple moves as he swallows. All the while he watches me with the sexual intent that tells me he's going to bend me over the counter and take what he wants, but not without giving me what I crave, first.

"Mrs. Louw?" I swear there's a cocky grin behind the carefulness in his tone.

I fan myself with a piece of paper from my desk. "I have business for you."

"What kind of business?"

"Diamonds. I prefer we meet to discuss this in person rather than over the phone."

"I..." His sigh is filled with regret. "I'm not the right man for the job."

His words can't be further from the truth. "I'll be the judge of that. Tomorrow, four o'clock?" I close my eyes and hold my breath.

"I work from home." He makes it sound like a protest.

"Not a problem. I have your address."

"Of course you do." This time, he sounds downright amused, but then his tone changes, again. "Mrs. Louw, I--"

"See you at four tomorrow, then."

I hang up before he has time to conjure a reason why I shouldn't knock on his door. If Gregor is Gabriel, I plan to expose him. He better be ready. I'll barge through his door like he once did through mine, swinging a weapon much more powerful than a gun.

ALL THROUGH THE NEXT DAY, I have a lump of concrete in my stomach. Since we're fumigating the office, we have to close early--the perfect excuse to go home and get ready. While Connor naps, I shower and change. My hands shake when I apply make-up and dry my hair. Even the weather plays along for ambience with a powerful thunderstorm, probably one of the last before the dry winter spell. The thunder wakes Connor. I feed and change him, and get in some quality cuddle time. At three-thirty, I button up my trench coat and grab an umbrella. Connor should be good for a couple of hours. Carrying him downstairs, I go in search of the guys and find them playing poker in the kitchen.

Rhett gives a wolf whistle when he sees me. "Wow. You cleaned up nicely."

"It's only make-up." I shift Connor to the other hip, suddenly feeling self-conscious. Have I gone overboard?

"Pre-pretty."

"Thanks, Charlie."

Quincy's gaze runs over me. "Stockings and heels? I didn't know we're going out."

"Ou–out." Charlie looks at the window where thunder lights up the sky. "It's rai–raining."

"We're not going out. I am."

"Uh-uh." Quincy pulls his mouth in an obstinate line. "You're not going anywhere without one of us." He pushes back his chair. "I'll come."

"You can't come."

He gives me a baffled look. "Why not?"

"I'm going *out*."

Rhett stops stuffing his mouth with potato chips to look at me. "Out as in on a date?"

"I guess you could call it that."

"Oh. Wow. Yes. Okay." Quincy and Rhett exchange a look. "Great."

"That's cool." Rhett says. "I'll drive you."

"Rhett." I lift my brow.

"What?"

"I'm not going to relax knowing you're sitting outside in the car."

He scrunches his forehead and rubs his lips together, as if he's thinking. "It's dangerous, out there."

"You taught me how to handle myself, didn't you?"

"Yes, but––"

"Don't you have confidence in my ability to defend myself?"

"You're mean with those tiny fists and a gun, but…" He rubs the back of his head. "I don't know."

"I appreciate how well you're looking after me, guys, really I do, but if you want me to go out and meet people, you've got to give me a bit of freedom."

"She's right," Quincy says on a sigh. "We can't chaperone her on a date."

"I'll be out a couple of hours, max."

"All right." Rhett seems simultaneously happy and uncomfortable with the words. "Call us if you're running late."

"Do you mind watching Connor? I would've asked Kris, but she's working."

"Of course not." Quincy holds out his hands. "Come here, big guy. Uncle Charlie is going to teach you how to play poker, and Uncle Quincy is going to teach you how to win."

"Be careful on the road with the rain," Rhett says, his expression worried.

"I'll be fine. Thanks for Connor."

"Don't mention it." Quincy winks. "Go on. Have fun."

"There's a bottle in the fridge if Connor gets hungry before I'm back. If he gets difficult, call me."

"We know how to handle a baby." Quincy balances Connor on his knee and shoos me away with one hand. "Off you go."

"You guys are the best. I don't know what I would've done without you."

"You're making me all emotional now," Rhett complains.

"Later, Charlie." I blow him a kiss and leave before my nerves fail me.

On the drive to Gregor's place, I contemplate the outcome. If he's not Gabriel, he may not appreciate my approach, but I'm certain it's him. I can't help but feel sure of myself.

Gregor's house is in a neat, raw-brick security complex. I have to sign in at the gate, and the guard has to call his unit for permission to let me through, which warns him of my arrival. Gregor may still refuse me, but after talking on the intercom system, the guard pushes a button that lifts the boom.

As I take the long driveway up to his house, the electronic gates open. I drive in and park in front of the garage. The front door opens before I'm out of the car. Gabriel—Gregor—stands in the frame, dressed in dark slacks and a fitted shirt. The sight of him takes my breath away. This new model of Gabriel has a shorter beard and hair, but the color is the same. His face is strikingly handsome, throwing me somewhat off kilter and adding the spark that fuels my doubt. Beneath the clothes, I can guess the lines that define his muscles.

His stance is casual, but his shoulders are tense. He watches my approach with a boredom that's feigned, because his eyes miss nothing. They look at me in the way Gabriel first looked at me in Napoli's and the way he did when he broke into my flat. Like that first time, he tears open my soul and looks right through me, but there is one difference. The roles are reversed. This time, I'm coming to him as the hunter, and he's the vulnerable prey.

He doesn't speak until I'm right in front of him. "Mrs. Louw."

"Mr. Malan."

His green eyes scrutinize me. The color is disconcerting, not the iced blue I'm looking for, but he's wearing contact lenses.

"I think this is a mistake. Whatever you think my company--"

I climb onto the step, putting my body flush against his. "I'll have a glass of water, please."

The sharp intake of his breath is all I get before he backs away, giving me clear entry into his house. Prowling around, I take in his domain. The lounge, dining room, and kitchen are open-plan. The space is furnished with nothing but a reclining leather chair and a fridge.

He regards me from hooded eyes as he walks to the fridge and retrieves a bottle of mineral water. Taking a glass from the cupboard, he pours the water and hands it to me.

"Thank you." I make sure our fingers brush when I take the glass.

His eyelashes flutter. "About your business--"

"So, you're from Bloemfontein."

His eyes narrow, and his lips twitch. He doesn't like it when I defy him by interrupting and controlling the conversation, but he lets it slide.

"What else did you read about me?"

I take a sip of the water. "Everything I could find."

For a second his gaze fixes on my lips as I drink, but then he drags it away.

"How about you, Mr. Malan? Did you read everything about me?"

"I didn't have to."

I take another sip. "How so?"

"You're a known figure in this town."

"I am?"

He walks around the island counter, stopping short of me. "You said you had business. I did my homework, too. Your specialty is high-risk investments. I didn't see diamonds in your portfolio."

I lift my left hand and show him my wedding ring. "I'd like to insure this. It's very valuable to me."

He stares at it. "I don't deal in personal insurance. For that, you'll have to call Auto and General."

Leaving the glass on the counter, I place my palm on his chest and slide it down his rock-hard stomach to his even harder erection. When I cup his length, he remains motionless, regarding me with expressionless eyes, but his cock twitches in my hand.

"And for this?" I whisper. "Do I have to call someone else for this, too?"

His green eyes darken at my words, but he doesn't take the bait.

Gently, he removes my hand and puts a step between us. "As there seems to be nothing I can help you with, I think it's better that you leave."

"Nothing?" I start to unbutton my coat. "It's been a long time. Ten months, to be exact."

A vein pulses in his throat as he follows my actions. "You don't want to do that, not with a man like me."

"You wanted to find me. Didn't you come looking for me at the market?"

His eyes snap back to mine. "What do you mean?"

"Divine intervention. It's as if we were destined to meet."

"You don't believe that, beautiful."

"My husband used to call me beautiful."

He blanches a little. "Look, I--"

When my coat falls open, so does his mouth. The words he was going to say drop off the tip of his tongue and dissolve in the thick air between us. Heat burns hot in his eyes as they settle on my attire-- sinful pink and black underwear with thigh high, lace-trimmed stockings and killer heels. The bra makes my breasts spill over the cups, and my nipples are visible through the sheer lace. His hands clench at his sides as he looks me up and down. His chest moves rapidly. His nostrils flare. If his cock could get any harder, it just did. The outline is clearly visible under the fabric of his trousers. He swallows and meets my eyes. His are smoldering with desire. He wants me. Crap, if I'm wrong, I'm going to have sex with a stranger in his kitchen.

Please, don't let me be wrong.

When his hands reach for me, I almost falter, but I have to know, and there's only one, sure way to discover the truth. One thing a man like Gabriel can't alter or fake is the way he fucks my body. Strengthening my resolve, I lift my chin and push out my breasts.

His expression twists with raw agony. Grabbing my arms, he turns me toward the door. "Leave. Now."

I lean back, cushioning his groin with my ass. He offers no resistance when I rub against him. The dip of his knees and the ragged groan that tears from his chest as I drag my ass over his hard-on tells me I won. His reaction makes me confident enough to walk to the island counter and hop onto it. I don't have to say a word. All I have to do is spread my legs.

He charges like a lion. There's a growl on his lips when he twists my hair around his fingers and pulls to the side, exposing my neck. Like a predator, he locks his teeth on the soft spot where my neck and shoulder meet. He doesn't bite down, just holds me in place as he sucks on my skin, marking me. When he lets go, I'm sporting a love bite. Satisfaction washes into his expression when he stares at the mark. Gently, he drags his tongue over it, moaning as he tastes my skin. He runs his nose up the length of my neck to my jaw, inhaling deeply.

Using my hair to keep me in place, he kisses and nips his way down from my ear to my shoulder. Each kiss turns more frantic than the next. He wedges between my legs and lets go of my hair to catch my face. Holding my cheeks between his palms, he plunders my mouth with the pent-up fever of a man who's been denied for too long. Our tongues tangle as he explores the depth of my mouth and the shape of my lips. He eats me as if I'm his last meal.

I can count the times Gabriel kissed me without total control on one hand. His seductions were well thought out and executed. This man is kissing me without an ounce of constraint, like Gabriel kissed me when I told him I didn't want Michael. He's kissing me like Gabriel did the day he married me against my will. I moan into his mouth, my body preparing itself for his possession by growing warm and slick.

He tears his mouth from mine and jerks his shirt from his pants. "Tell me how badly you want this."

My gaze drops to his pants. "I want to taste you."

His fingers reach for the buttons of his shirt. One by one, he pops them with shaky hands. "You can have my cock anywhere you want it."

When the edges of the shirt fall open, he pushes our upper bodies together, skin against skin. It feels familiar. It feels right. He flips down the cups of my bra, letting the curves spill over, and takes a nipple in his mouth. His tongue is heaven and hell. He sucks on the tip, sending a spasm straight to my clit, and then he follows it up with a white-hot arrow of pain when he bites down. A few repetitions and my core is a melted puddle of arousal. He doesn't let up until he's given the other breast the same treatment. I'm panting and boneless, unable to support my weight when he lifts his broad hand from the small of my back. With his fingers curled around my neck, he pushes me down on the counter. The touch is dominant and possessive, just like I remember.

I gasp when he pushes the elastic of my panties aside and draws a finger over my slit.

He bends over me and hums his approval against my lips. "So wet."

When he parts me with one digit, I cry out harder.

"Is this what you want?" He works his finger inside up to the second joint.

"Yes, oh, God."

"I'm going to give you what you came for."

The promise is more beautiful than erotic, because what I really came for is *him*. He doesn't give me more time to think, because he starts moving his finger at a maddening slow pace. I push up on my elbows to look down at the sight, and he eases the pressure of his palm on my throat to let me. I want to see him claim me. As if sensing my need, he rips off the panties and drops them on the floor, staring intently at the wicked work of his finger.

"God, you're beautiful."

My clit tingles when he presses the pad of his thumb on the bundle of nerves. Gathering my wetness, he starts a slow and gentle massage that has my toes curl.

"Stop." I grab his wrist. "I'm going to come."

His smile is calculated. "That's the idea, beautiful."

"I want you inside me when I come."

His eyes widen a fraction. His jaw flexes the way Gabriel's used to when he fought for control. "You will."

Using the V of his fingers of one hand to open me wider, he adds a second finger to the first. My muscles clench around him.

"Fuck, yes."

His thumb goes back to my clit while his fingers prepares my channel for his cock. Gabriel is long and thick. This is something he'd do. A few hard thrusts combined with the relentless, circular move-ments of his thumb and I come with a fierce orgasm, crying out my pleasure. I'm still riding the wave when his mouth is on my pussy, his tongue taking over from his fingers. He feels so good. He knows exactly how I like it. He alternates gentle licks and sucks with nips of his teeth. Like Gabriel trained me, I come again quickly, this time in his mouth. He sucks me through the shockwaves until my body is a quivering mess.

"Good girl," he praises, planting a kiss on my mound.

I turn even wetter when his hands go for his belt. At the same time my heart throbs in my throat. This is about more than lust. This is about a gamble. The belt falls away. The button of his slacks pops. Thank God for the hasty way he pulls down the zipper, because my nerves can't handle the suspense. Taking my hands, he pulls me into a sitting position before gripping my hips and lowering me to the ground. He doesn't have to ask. I go down on my knees, like I did countless times with Gabriel, bringing the elastic of his briefs with me. When his cock jumps free, I sit back on my heels. He's thick and long with manly veins, the head broad and smooth. I almost cry with relief and thankfulness. He's exactly like I remember.

He's Gabriel.

Whether he knows that I know isn't clear. The moment is too consumed with his need. His desire is the sole focus of his attention as he drags his fingers through my hair and waits. Knowing my history of abuse, Gabriel never pushed himself into my mouth. My soul soars as I cup his balls and pull him closer. When my lips fold around him, I get back the pieces of myself I left in the debris of the explosion. Flicking my tongue over the slit, I lap up the pre-cum he spilled for me, reveling in the taste that is uniquely Gabriel. My heart flutters with joy too powerful to contain as I take him deep. Sucking Gabriel off has always been one of my biggest turn-ons. I love the way he groans when my tongue swirls around his thickness and traces the vein on the underside to his balls. I revel in the way his knees buckle and his hips jerk, knowing I'm the cause of his pleasure. Having him in my mouth is like a homecoming. It's the truth, the only truth I know. He lets me take him how deep I want, and he doesn't hold back. He comes quickly and hard, spilling his seed down my throat. I savor every drop, feeling the same interconnectedness I felt during oral sex with Gabriel.

He's Gabriel.

I stare at him, my soul bursting in wonder, as he rides his pleasure to the end. When his body goes still, he pulls his cock from the suction of my mouth. Without breaking our frantic chase for each other's pleasure, he grips my arms and drags me to my feet, crushing our mouths together briefly before bending me over the counter.

He positions my arms so I'm stretched out with my fingers touching the edges. "Hold on, beautiful."

Grabbing the cold granite for leverage, I brace myself, knowing when Gabriel takes me from behind it will be hard. Exactly how I want. His fingers play over my folds, gathering moisture and lubricating me. The broad head of his cock nudges at my opening. He's already hard again. One hand is guiding his shaft, the other gripping my hip. Seeing that it's been a while, he enters me slowly, as considerately as only Gabriel can be. After every inch he stops, giving me time to adjust while playing with my clit. By the time he's fully lodged inside, we're both panting. I don't have to tell him I need more. He knows my body inside and out. He knows my needs better than I know them myself.

When he starts moving, it's with the grueling pace I need to push me toward another climax. He slams into me, pivoting our groins together, and shifting my body up and down over the smooth surface. My need climbs high and fierce. When my inner muscles clench around him, he rolls my clit between his deft fingers, taking me over the edge. Coming around his cock, I scream out my pleasure.

He covers my body with his, putting his chest against my back. "Fuck, yes. You're beautiful when you come."

My reprieve only lasts a few seconds. Aftershocks from the orgasm are still rippling through me when he pulls out and flips me over.

"I want to look into your face."

So do I. I want to see his eyes when he comes. There was a time he didn't look at me when we had sex. It was the time he only fucked me from behind, hiding his scarred face and his true person, but I never wanted a different face or another soul. Only him.

He spreads my legs and bends my knees. His expression is tender as he rubs his palms up my inner thighs to the center between my legs. Parting my labia with his thumbs, it's on my eyes he focuses when he pushes inside. I don't hesitate to bare my heart. My feelings are etched on my face for him to read. For his eyes only. I show him my ecstasy as he fills me in the only way that makes me complete-- with his body and soul. I show him my reverence as he starts pouring everything he has inside of me. Our desires, emotions, dreams, and essence intertwine as we move together. I take what he gives when his thrusts become more powerful, but I also give back in return. For every shove, I clench down on him, dragging him deeper and holding him tighter. My hands travel over his strong arms and his hard chest, tracing the familiar grooves. I adore every part of him, inside and out, and I'm falling harder than I imagined possible. The sensation is wild and vulnerable, beautiful and frightening in its intensity. I need his arms around me.

"Hold me," I whisper.

He doesn't hesitate. Without breaking his pace, he laces our fingers together and lifts my arms above my head. His chest presses against mine as he claims my lips in an incredibly soft and lingering kiss. I embrace my feelings, letting the love explode and grow inside of me until there's nothing but him. He fills my senses. His kiss tells me what I want to know. He cares. He still cares for me and not just as a possession. I'm pinned under his strong body, a damaged being, but I'm here out of my own free will, and that makes me more than a broken toy. I'm more than a vendetta or a debt, and he's more than The Breaker, because he kisses me like a husband. Right now, he's only a man who loves a woman, and I'm the woman who loves him back. Falling in love--the giddy kind--after deep and eternal loving may be doing things in reverse, but Gabriel and I have never been the norm. Perhaps we weren't meant to be the norm. We're us, and I love us.

"Valentina."

His whisper brings me back to him, to the sensation where our bodies are connected. It's too much and too little. I can't bear more, and I can't stop. My fingers clench around his as a strangled cry of pleasure leaves my mouth.

"I've got you, beautiful."

He does. He always has. He slows his pace a fraction and tilts his hips, changing the angle of his penetration. There. Oh, God. My lips part on a soundless gasp as he hits the right spot.

"Come with me."

It's a plea, not a command, and I obey it more eagerly than I obeyed any of his orders. My vision blurs as my body explodes. He's right there with me, giving me his all. His back arches, and his hips jerk as he holds my gaze. His eyes are open and his soul exposed as he shows me what I do to him. Our connection is perfect. There are no thoughts about the past or the future in my head. What I feel is too intense to leave space for worries and fear. There's only this moment. As his arms come around me to cushion my back and hold me close, I allow myself to fall apart, heal, and for the shattered pieces to come together. I weep in the crook of his neck, unabashedly, for the greatness of this gift, for having him again.

Lightning flashes outside, and the storm erupts in full force.

When he lifts on his arms to look at me, his cock slips free. I moan, not wanting to lose him, yet.

"Cold?" He rubs my arm.

"No."

He kicks his shoes free and removes his pants. I watch with mesmerized fascination as he undresses. There are still scars on his body, but they are different, now. Whatever he did, he underwent severe surgery. I don't care what he looks like, but I miss the marks I got to know, the ones that defined him. No matter. I'll get to know his new scars.

Catching my gaze on him, he says in a low voice, "What are you thinking?"

"That my husband had scars like that."

He doesn't offer an explanation, and I don't push. What I don't want is more lies between us.

"Take this." He helps me to pull on his shirt. I can't help but inhale deeply. The clean, spicy smell is from before Gabriel became Gregor.

Lifting me into his arms, he carries me to the reclining chair, settles down with me in his lap, and covers us with a throw from the chair back. Our cocoon is safe and warm. Together, we listen to the sound of the rain on the roof and watch the sky darken through the window.

He strokes my hip under the throw. "Where's your son?"

"With friends."

He tenses. "Reliable ones?"

"The guys you met at the market."

His tension doesn't ease. "Can they handle a baby?"

"As good as any mom I know."

"You sure?"

I can't resist teasing. "For a first date, you're very concerned about a single mom's baby."

He brushes a stray hair from my face. "He's cute." He says it like it explains his interest in Connor. "You said a *single* mom." He hesitates. "Are you?"

"Would I have been here if I wasn't?"

He doesn't answer.

A part of me wants to dive into this relationship and grab everything with a sweep of my arm, but I remind myself to be patient. I'm not doing this by force or manipulation. This time, it will be out of both our free wills.

I turn his wrist to the light to read the time on his watch. It's past five. "I have to go, soon."

His arm tightens around me. "Already?"

"I said I'd be back to feed Connor before bedtime. His bath is at six."

My heart contracts painfully for the longing that flashes in his eyes. He looks at me for a long time, and when he finally speaks, he pushes the words out, as if they are hard for him to say.

"Valentina, you're a very desirable woman."

"But?"

"But this wasn't a first date."

"What was it?"

His eyes search mine for something I can't name. He takes a breath and licks his lips. "A mistake."

Hurt twists my heart, but I brush it aside. I won't allow him to derail me. "This may not be a conventional date, but it wasn't a mistake."

"You don't know me, and when you do, you'll run. This is every kind of wrong."

"What we just did in your kitchen, did it feel wrong?"

"No. Every bit of it was right, but that's not what I meant, and you know it."

"Then we'll just focus on what feels right."

"No, Valentina." His voice is harsh. "It won't work."

I was so ready to tell him I know the truth, but he's not ready to hear it. I believe he's ready for us, or he wouldn't have come back and looked for me, but if I force things, I may screw this up.

I push on his chest to get up. "I have to go."

He locks me in a tight embrace. "Not while it's raining so hard. Too unsafe on the road."

"Connor--"

"Nothing will happen if you're thirty minutes late. Call your friends and tell them you're waiting out the storm."

Always protective. God knows, I need the extra time with him. "I'll get my phone."

"Stay put." He shifts out from under me and fetches my bag from the kitchen.

I use the opportunity to study him more. If he thought I wouldn't recognize the chiseled perfection of his ass, he really didn't know that each part of his body is forever imprinted in my mind. I don't care what face he wears, scared or handsome, I want the man underneath.

"Here you go." He hands me my bag and gives me space to make the call.

While I speak to Rhett, the smell of freshly brewed coffee fills the space. When I cut the call, he carries a steaming mug to me. Two sugars and milk, just the way I like.

"I would've offered you wine, but I don't want you to drink and drive."

"Thanks." I smile at his protectiveness. "That's very considerate."

"Would you like something to eat?"

"I'm good."

For the remainder of the time, we sip our coffee in comfortable silence while he plays with my hair, almost like in the days when I sat at his feet in his study at night. When only a light mist rain remains, he helps me gather my clothes, but shoves my ripped panties in his pocket. He buttons up my coat and walks me to my car, holding my umbrella for me.

His kiss is passionate and desperate, as if he's saying goodbye. "Be safe."

"You too."

He opens my door but grabs my wrist before I can get in. "Valentina."

I look back at him. "Yes?"

"Thank you for coming."

"I couldn't stay away."

His smile is both sad and tender.

Guilt attacks me on the way home. I feel bad for leaving Connor with the guys so I could have sex with my dead husband. What kind of a mother does that? What if Connor is hungry or feeling cranky? My worries are unfounded. When I get home, I find Connor playing happily in the playpen and Charlie folding the laundry. Rhett and Quincy give me curious looks.

"You look ... different," Rhett says. "It went well, then?"

"Yes." I smile, but offer nothing more. Things between Gabriel and I have always been complicated, and it's no less so now. I can't even define what we have, let alone explain it to my caring partners.

"Someone we know?"

"What he means is," Quincy says, "is it someone we'll approve of?"

"I think so."

"Wait a minute." Rhett scrutinizes me. "Is it the guy from the market?"

"Yes. Why? Do you approve?"

"I like him," Quincy says.

"Ditto."

"Good."

They're going to see a lot more of him in the future. I'm determined to make it happen. The question is will Gabriel admit the truth? Will he come back to me as my husband or as a stranger?

21

Gabriel

Damn me to hell and back. How could I give in so easily? Touching Valentina was every jaded shade of wrong. I should've kept my distance. Running into her screwed up everything. I'm not arrogant enough to believe she's attracted to me or my new face. She merely acted on the instinct I trained into her. Valentina needs pain with her pleasure. Dominance in bed. She's drawn to the sadist, the monster. Sensing what I am underneath the polished veneer of a man is what brought her to my door. This is who I am. I can't change it any more than a cat can turn itself into a dog.

After she'd left, I pace the floor. The faint smell of raspberry contracts my chest, reminding me of what I'm missing, and that I'll be utterly alone for the rest of my life. So be it. I don't want anyone else. My purpose is protecting her and my child. That's enough. I'll feel better when I can make up for the financial hardships she suffered after my *death*. Once enough profit from my company rolls in, I'll invest anonymously in her clever company. My heart swells with pride. I always knew she'd survive, and the fact that she's making such a good job of it without me fills me with a pang of sad jealousy. No man wants to be expendable, dispensible, replaceable. All I ever wanted was to take care of her, and look where that got us. It's better that I stay far away from her, even as every cell in my body pulls toward her with a force near impossible to resist. I exchanged her life for freedom. I have to hold onto that oath when I feel weak. Which is all the time.

Of course, I'm tempted to take the golden opportunity she presented me, to claim her as a different man, but that will be just another lie, another manipulation, and I'm not going down that road with her again. Ever. I repeat the mantra, hoping it will sink in and that my dick will eventually get the message. Just being near her makes me hard. Fuck, thinking about her does the job. I clench and unclench my fingers, fighting a sudden urge to go after her and throw the truth at her feet, kneel, and beg her to forgive me and take me back. God, I'm such a selfish bastard. No, I won't blow my cover and her new, hard-earned life to hell. There's only one cure for taming my uncontrollable desire. I pull on my sweatpants and a T-shirt and punish myself with a grueling workout in the gym. With every weight I lift, I try to expel the memory of her taste, her sounds, and how she felt under my hands, but it's futile. The more I push, the deeper she seeps under my skin.

After a shower, I set out to do what I've been putting off since getting back to Johannesburg. I buy a bunch of white roses and drive to the graveyard. Visiting Carly's grave rips me to pieces. I was afraid to come here, and now that the full force of the loss tears the patched-up grief wide open again, I sink down on my knees in the mud and weep over the stone of my beautiful girl I couldn't save. Raw cries tear from my chest. For the first time after her death, I let them out. The violent emotion is far from healing. I'm simply lifting the lid on the simmering pain I carry inside of me. This, too, will always be a part of me, like losing Valentina and Connor. I accept it. This is what I deserve, to be an unhappy man with a whole face and a broken soul. Drying my face on my sleeve, I kiss my fingers and press them on the cold stone.

"I love you, Carly."

I won't fail Connor if it's the last thing I do. He'll never know me, but he won't know need, either. No one will lay a finger on him as long as I live. Allowing the resolve to give me strength, I push to my feet and go back to my house, which feels emptier and colder than ever now that Valentina has marked it with her presence.

ONE WEEK GOES BY. I work myself to a standstill, if not with work, in the gym. I keep a tight watch on the woman and child who give meaning to my existence. I keep my distance, ensuring I don't make the same stupid mistake, so when I come home from the gym on Saturday morning to find Valentina's car parked in front my house, anticipation mixes with trepidation. I'm surprised, and I'm not. I made her physically and emotionally dependent on me when I first took her. It's only natural she'll look for someone to replace that dependency. A darkness rises inside of me when I think of another man fulfilling that role, but the turbulent feeling is quickly squashed when she gets out of the car with Connor on her hip. The sight of them stills me. A deep-sated pain tightens my chest. I press the remote to open the gate, pull into my driveway, and exit my car warily.

"How did you get in?" The words come out more harshly than I intended.

Valentina doesn't bat an eye at my angry voice. "I smooth-talked the guard."

"He's not supposed to let anyone in without permission." I'm pissed off that he disobeyed the rules. It's dangerous. I'll have to speak with him.

"Connor helped," she says with a smile.

I stare at him with barely disguised pride. Yeah, it will be hard to resist that drooling, two-toothed grin. I make a conscious effort to soften my tone. "Why are you here?" Shit, is something wrong? "Is everything all right?"

"I'm taking Connor for a picnic. I thought you might like to come."

"Valentina…" It comes out like the warning I intended, but God, it feels good to say her name. The problem is I want to scream it with her submissive body under me.

Not giving me time to elaborate, she pushes Connor into my arms. "Hold him for a second, will you?"

The lure is too strong to resist. When my arms go around my son, something inside of me snaps. The world tips, and all the wrongs fall into place as I hold his small body against my chest, inhaling his baby smell.

Valentina lifts a diaper bag from the backseat and gives me an apologetic look. "I just need to change him before we go. May I please use your house?"

I'll never deny my son anything. "Go ahead."

Balancing Connor in one arm, I unlock the door and let her in.

She walks over to the only piece of furniture in the lounge. "Do you mind?"

"No."

While she spreads a protective cover out on the reclining chair, I carry Connor to her. For a second I cling to him, reluctant to let go, but she's standing there with the diaper in her hands, so I lay him down. Warmth travels up and down my body as I watch her take care of our child. I devour the intimate moment like a starving man. When he's clean and dry, she turns to me with a smile that holds both friendly warmth and passionate heat, neither of which I deserve.

Her tone is sure. "Ready?"

Despite how I sent her off after our lustful encounter, she doesn't doubt that I'll agree, and she's right. How can I now that I've had a taste of Connor? I desperately want more. I want more of the self-assured woman standing in front of me, too.

My smile is tight. My weakness burns in me. "Give me a minute to shower and change?"

"Of course."

I rush through a shower and pull on a fitted white shirt and slacks. By the time I return to the lounge, she's sitting on the chair, breast-feeding Connor. I stop in my tracks. Looking down, her expression is nothing but loving. There's no resentment in her features for the child she didn't ask for or planned. My eyes slip to my son. His suckling is surprisingly strong for such a tiny creature.

"Ouch," Valentina says, flinching as he hollows his cheeks.

He fists his little fingers in Valentina's jersey, holding onto his source of food for life. Little sighs, groans, and hums of approval infuse the swallowing noises he makes. He has a cluster of dark hair, not curly like mine, but silky like his mother's. Even at ten months, he looks impossibly tiny. Fragile.

Before I can stop myself, I'm standing in front of them, caressing Connor's hair. Why this particular scene moves me so much I don't understand. Maybe it's because my own mother never took care of me. There were nannies for that.

Valentina stares up at me. "He's almost done."

"Take your time." I mean it. I can stand here and look at them all day. "Isn't he on solids, already?"

"Oh, yes. I still breastfeed because he needs all the natural immunity he can get. He's really only eight months old, if you consider that he was born two months prematurely."

She hands him back to me and adjusts her clothes.

"We'll take my car," she says, "because I have the car seat."

The minx successfully bullied me into an outing without even putting up a fight.

"Do we need to stop for supplies?" I ask.

"I've already packed a basket. It's in my trunk."

I offer a hand to help her to her feet.

She drives us to the zoo, a place I used to visit often when I was little. Not much has changed in thirty-eight years. Connor is too young to appreciate the animals, but we follow the path past the monkeys and birds, walking side by side in a comfortable silence. Under the shade of a willow, she spreads out a blanket and puts Connor on his tummy, leaving plastic toy blocks within his reach.

"He's almost sitting by himself," she says proudly. "He's a little behind on this milestone, but the doctor says its normal with preemies."

She's good with him. She makes a great mom. I shouldn't touch her, but I can't help brushing a strand of hair behind her ear. "How is it?"

"How's what?"

"Motherhood."

"It's tough, sometimes, but I'd never want it any other way."

"I'm sorry it's been hard for you." I mean it with all of my soul.

She shrugs. "It's a matter of finding a routine that works for everyone."

"I'm sure it's not that simple."

"It's not so bad. I have flexibility in my work, and I can take Connor to the office."

"Do you enjoy your job?"

"I appreciate it. It puts a roof over our heads and food on our table. Talking about food…" She reaches for the basket. "Are you hungry?"

"Starving." But not for food. Like a fool I stare into her eyes, getting lost in their murky darkness.

Don't touch her.

Ah, fuck.

I cup her face and push her down on the blanket. It feels natural that my body should cover hers. I ache to taste her, to feel her soft lips, and smell the intoxicating perfume of her skin. Holding her eyes, I bring our mouths closer together. If she wants to back out, I'll give her the opportunity. She closes the last hairbreadth of distance by lifting her head. When our lips touch, the same deep ache as always takes root in my chest. Instead of getting her out of my system, I'm getting more entangled in her than ever. It's all the sweeter when this time she chose me. I didn't kick down her door and drag her here against her will. I'm not seducing her with pleasure to look past my scars. She came to me. I kiss her like a drowning man, so thankful for her free will I can hardly breathe. All the emotions I felt when I was nothing but a cold and empty shell are because of this woman. She taught me the meaning of gratitude. I feel it now, for giving me this moment with her and Connor. There's so much pleasure in having her consent. Not some fucked-up, manipulated version, but the real deal.

I pour my heart into the kiss, and my body responds, going hard and hot everywhere. We're in public, but I don't give a damn. I'm getting deliriously drunk on her and the addictive feeling of happiness.

A gurgle from Connor pulls me back to earth. Reluctantly, I break the kiss. Her face is prettily flushed.

I chuckle. "I think he approves."

She gives me a radiant smile. "Oh, he definitely does."

"Thank you."

"For what?"

"For today." *For allowing me time I don't deserve.*

"You're welcome."

Connor starts to fuss. In less than a second, he goes from happy to crying. My protective instinct goes into overdrive. Perplexed, helpless, I fall over myself to reach him. "What's wrong? What happened? Is he hurt? Is he ill?"

As calm as ever, Valentina takes a bottle from the diaper bag and hands it to me. "Want to feed him?"

Connor wails with a voice that would've lifted the roof had there been one. Pride swells my chest to the point of exploding. When I put the nipple in his mouth, he starts sucking with greedy gulps.

"Again?" I ask. "He just ate."

She smiles at me. "He gets hungry every two hours, more or less."

It's like floating on a cloud. The moment feels surreal. A feeling that matches my joy at just having kissed Valentina surges through me when my son nestles deeper into my arms. He weighs nothing. His body is so small his head fits into the palm of my hand. His mouth latches firmly around the nipple, and his cheeks hollow as he makes hungry little sucking sounds. I swear there's a groan somewhere in the mix and something keen to a growl when I lose my grip on the bottle and break the suction. A deep laugh rumbles in my chest. I cuddle him closer, holding him to my heart.

"You're the man," I say on a chuckle, planting a kiss on his forehead.

As he drains every drop in the bottle, I'm fully in the moment, devouring each second of the precious gift.

"First time giving a baby a bottle?" Valentina asks with a twinkle in her eyes.

"Hell, yeah."

"Not too bad." She winks and plants a kiss on my cheek.

Just like that, my resistance crumbles. All of my supposedly steadfast intentions fall like battle-beaten soldiers. One more kiss, a fleeting moment of weakness, a never-ending memory, and I'm dating Valentina Louw, the woman who knocked my feet from under me, the mother of my child.

IN THE WEEKS THAT FOLLOW, our *dating* becomes official. Regular. We're an item. With the start of winter, we go to indoor playgrounds with Connor. When Kris or Rhett and Quincy can watch Connor, we stay in and make love. I touch Valentina every second I can. Every moment is like borrowed time. Treasured. Whatever we do, I always let her take the lead. She introduces me to her friends as Gregor Malan, and they accept me without question or resistance. Everyone is eager for her to find the happiness she deserves, and I'm flattered that they think I'm the guy for the job. The only issue that spoils this new development is the lie that stands big and ugly between us.

The closer I grow to Valentina in this new relationship, the more torn-up I become. My deceit punishes me in every waking hour and pierces my heart at night. Guilt finds me even in my dreams. She deserves better. She deserves the truth. As my love keeps on overtaking every other emotion and purpose in my life, I know what I have to do.

I have to come clean.

I have to lose her.

Again.

The evening I make the decision, I spend the night on my knees. I kneel on the tiles with my forehead on my fisted hands, wishing for forgiveness and knowing I won't get it. When I face her tomorrow, she'll hate me.

Waiting until a decent hour, I call and ask her to come over after work. Alone. I don't want to do this in front of Connor or my ex-bodyguards. What I have to say is meant for her ears alone. For the rest of the day, I pace around the house, reciting my speech in my head, but no words sound right. Finally, I settle for the simple truth.

"I died to give you freedom. I died because I love you. I'm still dying, a little every day, and I'll keep on doing so if it'll give you the happiness I stole from you."

Too damn dramatic.

I face myself in the bathroom mirror, trying again. "I'm not the man you think I am. I'm…"

Fuck.

I drag a hand through my hair. Who am I? "I'm a ghost of the man who kidnapped and impregnated you." Scrap that. "I'm the man who loves you."

She'll hate me more than before, but it's the right thing to do. Maybe the most honorable thing I've ever done in my life. I give the strange face in the mirror a glance before I head for the shower to get ready. If this is the last time I face Valentina, the least I can do is pay her the courtesy of looking presentable.

Valentina

UNTIL TODAY, things moved slowly between me and Gabriel, or Gregor, as I got used to calling him. We date like two normal people. There have been plenty of opportunities to tell him I know the truth, but I want him to tell me when he's ready. I can't tell him how I feel until he confesses. If he's not ready to listen to me as Gabriel, he's not ready to listen to me as Gregor.

Then came his phone call today. There was something in his tone, a faint tremble in the deep timber of his voice. My hands shake as I fit the new red dress and twist my hair into a bun. What if he doesn't want to see us any longer? No, I have to be positive. Gabriel may not love me like I love him, but he needs me. He wanted me alive, enough to make me pregnant. That counts for something, doesn't it?

Connor coos on the play carpet. I pick him up, burying my nose in his hair. "I love you, baby. So much."

A pang of sadness invades my heart as it always does when I have to leave him, even for a few hours.

"He'll be fine," a voice says from the door.

I turn to take in Kris' soft, compassionate smile. Wonderful Kris who always understands.

She holds out her hands. "Give him here and go have yourself some fun."

I kiss my baby's head before handing him over.

Kris looks me up and down. "You look beautiful."

Absentmindedly, I rub a finger over the stub of my thumb. "You think so?"

"Perfect." She gives me an encouraging nod. "You're running late."

She knows I'm stalling. I'm stalling because I'm nervous. How will this night turn out for us? For me, Gabriel, and Connor? When she leaves with Connor, I slip the gift I kept for Gabriel in my bag. Depending on what he says, I'll offer it to him or bring it home. A part of me wants to put tonight off, but we can't carry on living in our make-believe world.

I say a quick goodbye to the guys. It's pizza and movie night, so Charlie is sorted. Then I drive to Gabriel's house.

He waits outside, dressed in dark slacks and a white shirt. As always, my mouth goes a little dry. He's perfect in every physical sense, but to me he's still the scarred man I fell in love with. On the inside, he's as torn up as I am, and that pain is a bond we share.

Instead of getting the door for me like he usually does, he remains standing on the lawn, drinking me in with a hungry expression as I walk up the path. We don't need words. I know what he's thinking just as he knows what I am, because his eyes drop to the hard points of my nipples under my dress. I stop short of him. My emotions are raw, but so are his. A war rages in his green eyes, the color so wrong and so right. His hands flex as if he's trying not to touch me, but then the fragile cord of his restrain snaps.

Grabbing a fistful of my hair, he jerks me closer. The action makes me stumble into the hard barrier of his chest. He catches me with one arm around my waist, trapping his erection between us.

"Fuck." He buries his nose against my neck and runs it along my jaw. "Just one touch."

That hurts. He says it like a farewell greeting.

"I need you inside the house. Now," he whispers in my ear.

Taking my hand, he leads me to the door. When it's locked behind us, he turns on me, one hundred percent Gabriel. "That's a very pretty dress." For all of one second, he looks indecisive, as if he's fighting an internal battle, but then he takes my face between his hands and kisses me hard.

"Aren't you going to tell me to take it off?" I ask when he sets me free.

"There are things I need to say."

I want to hear, and I don't. I'm afraid of losing him, forever, this time, but I'm not afraid to fight for what I want. I'm not giving up, yet. I push the straps from my shoulders and let the dress fall to the ground. Not wearing underwear, I stand naked in front of him, except for my shoes.

His gaze caresses me with approval, but the battle continues to rage in his eyes. "You came here like this?" He closes the distance, staring down at my mouth. "Why?"

We both know why, but he wants me to say it. "I want you to fuck me."

The taut skin of his cheekbones darkens. "How?"

"Hard. Rough." I deal my trump card. "While you spank me."

The lines of his face turn rigid, and the green of his eyes becomes smoky. "Why?"

"Because it makes me come harder."

His chest deflates with a breath of defeat. "I can't deny you."

"Then don't."

He cups my breast, flicking a thumb over my nipple. "Lie down on your back and spread your legs."

I shake my head. "If you want it, you're going to have to take it."

His body tenses. "I don't want to hurt you, not any––" He bites back the rest of his words, giving me a pained and needy look.

"It's what I need."

His resolve crumbles like a dry piece of bread. His carefully guarded lust unravels, giving me a part of the true man as he folds his fingers around my neck and pushes me to my knees. Holding me in place with one hand, he unzips his slacks with the other, leaving the waist buttoned but freeing his long, heavy cock.

He lets go of my neck to grip my hair. "Touch it."

Our position turns me on beyond anything I've ever experienced with me naked on my knees and him towering over me, fully clothed. Gathering the drop that spills from the slit, I rub the wetness around the crest before dragging my nails along the underside. His skin is hot velvet, his flesh hard granite. I catch his eyes as he stares down at me, reading me like the open book I am, knowing exactly what I need.

"Lick it."

At the permission, I drag my tongue over the head, all the way down and back up. I don't want to play nice, today. With a look of defiance, I suck him deep into my mouth.

His expression is approving even as he gives a small shake of his head. "Naughty, greedy girl. Did I tell you to suck my cock?"

Instead of replying, I gently rake my teeth over him.

He shivers. "We'll take care of your punishment later. If you're going to suck, do it like you mean it."

I do. I curl my tongue around him and touch his length where my mouth doesn't reach. Taking him as deep as I can, I urge him wordlessly to remove the last barrier between us, the point to where he hasn't pushed me, yet. I need this. I want everything from him. I want him to understand he healed me, and that I'm willing to go anywhere for him. He pulls out and shoves back faster. I let him fuck my mouth like I've never done with any man, savoring every stroke he pushes into my mouth. I want to swallow for him. I want to choke and have my eyes water. I want him to take me all the way. Changing the angle of my head, I make him pierce my throat instead of my cheek. My reward is magnificent. His eyes grow large with a heated light, and his erection twitches in my mouth. He pushes harder and deeper, stretching my jaw to the limits.

"Breathe through your nose, baby."

This is all the warning I get before he snips the final cord of self-control he's always maintained while fucking my mouth. Gripping my head between his large hands, he holds me still and starts fucking my lips in all earnest. When I gag he pulls back, giving me only a brief reprieve before continuing his grueling pace. The way he uses me is so hot. I'm salivating around him, making disgusting noises in the back of my throat, and he loves it. Blinking away the moisture in my eyes, I focus on taking deep breaths through my nose.

"Look at me," he grits out.

I lift my eyes to his, letting him see my smeared mascara and lipstick, laying my vulnerability at his feet.

"You love this, don't you?"

I can only moan around him, feeling him tighten in the way he does before he comes. Instead of giving me his seed, he pulls out. I want his taste in my mouth, but he keeps his cock inches away from my face, taunting me.

Gently, he massages the joints of my jaw until the ache subsides, and then he folds his strong fingers around my throat and pushes my back to the floor, my legs bent under me. Resting his weight on one arm, he stretches out over my body and takes my lips in such a delicious and languorous kiss that my toes curl. While his tongue soothes my brutalized mouth, his hand explores my breast. He kneads the soft flesh between needy fingers, a bit too rough to be comfortable, until moisture coats my folds. Soft kisses land on my cheek, jaw, neck, and collarbone while he grips my nipple and pulls. The sting is delicious. His fingers trail over my stomach to my mound, lightly grazing my clit. We moan into each other's mouths when the pad of his thumb slips through the wetness gathered there for him.

A soft nip on my bottom lip announces the end of the kiss. He pulls away a fraction to look at me. "I'm going to take everything you've got."

I can barely manage a hoarse, "Yes."

He lifts my arms above my head and arranges my hands with my palms showing up. "Keep them there."

He moves down my body, kissing every inch of my skin until I writhe in need. When he finally reaches my pubic bone, he doesn't press his lips on my clit like I crave, but straightens my legs, relieving the pull of my muscles. Taking his time, he massages my thighs and calves. Just when my muscles start to relax, he pushes my legs open, exposing my pussy. He pulls my folds apart with his thumbs and sits back on his heels to study me.

"So pretty," he muses. "So perfect." He thrusts his middle finger inside, burying it up to the knuckle. "So tight." A few hard pumps make my hips lift off the floor. "So wet."

I whimper, needing more of that friction, but he removes his finger. A smile tugs at his lips at my protesting moan. His head lowers slowly until his tongue teases my clit, mercilessly gentle. I lift my hips, trying to make him take more, but am rewarded with a bite that sends a shard of pain through my clit. My cry bounces off the walls, a plea to stop and give more. Then he starts eating me in all earnest. His tongue, teeth, lips, and fingers are everywhere, until I can't tell the nips of pain from the carnal pleasure. A finger eases into my ass, not carefully, but urgently, without holding back. I strain down to claim that feeling, making it mine as he fills me with everything but his cock. A few pumps and my release starts coiling, pulling my lower body tight. He growls with satisfaction as I come in his mouth, my pleasure exploding around his tongue and finger. My arousal coats his lips as he pulls away, giving me a possessive and victorious grin. I'm his, not only in this moment, but always. I want him to drive into me and fill me with the physical knowledge.

"Take me," I manage on a croak.

"I'm the one giving the orders."

To emphasize the statement he flips me on my stomach and lifts my hips. My ass is high in the air, an offering to him, and I already know what's coming before he gathers my moisture and massages it into my asshole. An involuntary moan escapes as he stretches me impatiently with two fingers. I breathe in and out as two becomes three. One hand caresses the globe of my ass cheek as the other punishes me inside.

Bending over me, he kisses my shoulder. "You've been a bad girl, coming here naked under your clothes. The wind could've blown up your dress, and someone could've caught a glimpse." Possession is thick in his tone as his fingers trail over my exposed folds. "And this is mine. All mine."

I revel at the declaration, knowing he'll claim me regardless of what his guarded expression meant when I arrived. No, I don't want to think about that, now. All I want to focus on is him inside of me, around me, fucking me.

The slap that falls on my naked butt comes unexpectedly. My ass clenches, trapping his fingers inside. The heat scorching my skin sets every inch of my body from my waist down on fire. I push up, offering him more, and he takes it, spanking and pumping. My cries are fierce and desperate. I already need to come again.

"My greedy, beautiful girl," he groans. "You want my cock in this tight asshole, don't you?"

The last time he took me like this was on our wedding day. I know it's going to hurt and that I'll love it, but right now I'm craving the sting of his palm too much to focus on anything else. My breasts are heavy, swaying with each slap he delivers to my bottom. The pattern moves from right to left and back again, firing up the skin on my backside and turning my pussy plump and wet. My folds swell and throb. My clit feels overheated. The spanking stops, but not the fingers pumping in and out of my dark entrance.

"You won't walk around without underwear again unless I tell you to."

"No," I whimper. My thighs quiver.

"Good girl. I'm going to take this beautiful, spanked ass." The fullness of his fingers disappears, leaving a burn behind. "Keep still."

Leaning my forehead on my intertwined fingers, I try to oblige, knowing it will be impossible. The broad head of his cock teases the tight ring of muscle.

"I'm going to take you like you asked me," he says in a voice thick with lust. "Fight me."

I know what he means. He doesn't want me to give anything. He wants to take my ass, showing me his true nature without holding back, and he wants me to do the same. Carefully, he stretches me, driving the broad head of his cock past the first barrier of muscle. God, it burns. Perspiration beads on my forehead as he prepares me with shallow strokes, giving me just a taste, and then he spears into me, making my back arch and forcing a choked cry from my throat. He gave me permission to fight, so I try to make my body flat, escaping the harsh pace by lowering my pelvis to the ground, but his arm wraps around my waist, holding me in place. Fueled by my resistance, he slams harder, jamming his cock into my forbidden entrance until my eyes water and my backside burns like the fires of hell. I try to crawl away, but his grip tightens, and his fucking intensifies. His balls are slapping my pussy, and his cock hammers inside of me, driving my need higher with an animalistic mixture of pain and pleasure. The farther I try to move, the harder he fucks me.

"You'll take my cock," he hisses before kissing my shoulder.

I can say stop, and he will, but instead I clench my asshole, pushing him out. The act of defiance triggers the response I want. His hand curls around my throat, cutting my airflow. Oh God, I missed this. I don't care that it's deprived or strange or fucked-up. I want to give him my air, pleasure, pain, and ecstasy. I allow him to half-strangle me while he slides in and out of my ass, feeling nothing but trust and a deep sense of peace, knowing he'll take care of me. As I start seeing white spots, he eases his hold marginally, allowing me to breathe, and then his fingers are on my clit, pinching, rubbing, spanking. A twisted sound escapes my dry throat as I explode in shards of painful pleasure, my pussy contracting around empty air. I reach behind me, trying to find his cock. I need him where I'm empty.

He grabs my wrist and lifts my arm above my head. "Not until I tell you."

He runs a finger around my asshole, making the muscle contract, and then he pulls my globes apart, his fingertips digging into my ass cheeks. Glancing over my shoulder, I see him standing on his knees, his cock rigid and thick. He points it at my pussy and spears my folds. My inner muscles shudder as he drives home, giving me all he's got. Over and over, he takes me, all the while rubbing circles with his palm over my clit. He changes his angle and finds the sweet spot that sends me over the edge every time. It doesn't take long for another orgasm to build. When it breaks, I clench down on his cock, squeezing him until he curses and jerks, but he doesn't come. He thrusts into me, hard and unapologetic, taking because I asked him to. He fucks me bone and senseless, until I lose track of time and place. I'm hardly conscious of my body being used, because I'm drifting in a space of belonging and pure Gabriel. Pure, warped us. I only realize I collapsed flat on my stomach when the force of his fucking shifts me over the tiles. He carries on, pounding into my pussy and palming my breasts until his cock swells and twitches, and warm jets spurt into my channel.

"Fuck." He falls over me, holding his weight on his arms. "Sweet Jesus." Desperately, he pumps twice more, deeper, hitting the barrier of my cervix. "Valentina." He kisses my neck and rests his forehead on my shoulder. "Fuck, Valentina."

My body feels bruised and thoroughly loved in the most delicious way. A lethargic relaxation claims me, turning my muscles to jelly. My lover pulls out of me, causing warm semen to run down my thighs. If I had the strength, I would've pushed up on my arms to look at how he marked me, but I know he's watching.

"Beautiful," he mutters, running his hands through the stickiness gathered on my inner thighs.

Incapable of doing anything but lying on the cool floor, I focus on his hands as they rub over my ass, back, and shoulders. He covers me in gentle kisses and whispers words of praise for how good I've been. Then he gathers me in his arms and shifts me onto his lap, rocking me gently while he strokes my hair and keeps on showering me with compliments. We come down from our high in each other's arms. The aftercare is as much part of Gabriel as the fucking, and I love him for showing me how much he cares. His approval seeps into my skin and past my defenses, making me feel safe and cherished in my own warped way.

When I'm sated on his lingering kisses and soft caresses, he carries me to the shower and washes my body and hair. Afterward, we lie naked on the recliner in the dark, listening to the sounds of our breathing and the crickets outside. The earlier peace is starting to slip, because I have to get back to Connor, soon.

When I stir in his arms, his hold tightens.

"I promised Kris I'd be home before midnight," I say reluctantly, simultaneously eager to see my baby and wishing I could stay the night.

"Valentina…"

The way he says my name is a warning, and somewhere in that tone lies damnation. This is the moment where he either tells me the truth or chooses omission. If he sends me away with a goodbye instead of the truth, my battle of wooing my husband is lost. I shiver, feeling the weight of our future settle on my heart. It makes me feel cold. I turn to face him. I want to look into his eyes, his unreal green eyes, in our moment of truth.

His finger traces my jaw. "Valentina, I have something to tell you."

Despite the gentleness of his touch, his body is tense, his muscles hard and stiff.

I wait silently for him to continue.

He hangs his head for a moment before meeting my eyes again. "I lied to you." When I don't reply, he says, "I deceived you in the most unforgivable way, and I don't want to be that man any longer."

I splay my hands over his hard chest. "Tell me."

He winces, as if in pain. "Just know I acted in your best interest, even if it caused you pain." He takes a deep breath and catches my

286

fingers as if he's afraid I'll pull away. "There's no easy way to say this, and I don't want to hurt you more than you've already suffered."

"Tell me," I repeat.

His brow twists. "Promise me you'll hear me out. Please."

"I promise."

He gives a tight nod. "Valentina, I..." He swallows, his eyes measuring my reaction. "I'm the man who robbed you of your life. I'm Gabriel."

Gabriel

THE NAKED WOMAN in my arms isn't an open book to read. I just told her I'm her dead husband, but her body language tells me nothing. I can deal with a slap, an insult, blame, and anger, but not the level, sober look she gives me. It leaves me defenseless, because I don't know what words she needs next. Do I soothe her? Apologize? Beg? Explain?

My gut knots when she doesn't reply for several long seconds. She can't forgive me. The deceit runs too deep. Her emotionless state can only mean she's finally weaned off from Gabriel. He doesn't matter. Maybe he never did. Only an arrogant asshole would hope differently. I still owe her the truth, so this is what I give her, starting from the day I discovered the evidence of her rape and ending with my plastic surgery.

Not once does she interrupt. She listens quietly as I confess, her attention acute and focused. When I come to the end of my guilty monologue, she finally stirs. My nerves raw and my heart bleeding, I watch her get to her feet and walk to where her bag lies on the floor. She'll gather her clothes, get dressed, and leave. I'll never see her and Connor again, and I can't blame her. I did worse to her than the enemies whose bones I've broken. All I can do is drink in the soft lines of her perfect body. A painful flashback of her hanging from a rope with her underwear around her ankles pierces my mind. She still has those same, gorgeous S-lines, like the ethereal subject in a painter's portrait.

Taking something from her bag, she turns and watches me in the way she listened––with silent concentration. As she walks to me, the strength that makes her the most remarkable women I know shows. Every step is laced with confidence. Does she hold judgment? Will she condemn me? I will take whatever I get, whether it be hate or acceptance, but I don't expect forgiveness. My only hope is that we won't part on ugliness. Nothing to soil this perfect, last moment. A part of me wishes for her to walk away like this, saying nothing, while another part of me screams to know what she feels, what she thinks.

She stops close to me, way too close. "I've been waiting for a long time for you to tell me this, Gabriel."

She says my name softly, purposefully.

My heart starts beating furiously, blood gushing through my veins, burning my skin. "You knew?"

"From the first moment."

If she knew, why did she allow things to go this far? Why didn't she kill me, hurt me, or got one of my ex-bodyguards to take care of me? Where is her revenge? My eyes drop to the object she clutches in her fist. Whatever it is, she waited for my confession before handing it to me. It could be damnation or absolution, but I suspect the first.

I shouldn't touch her, not after what I admitted, but I can't help myself. My hands are drawn to the curve of her hips. I cup them and pull her between my legs, staring up at her huge, brown eyes, afraid of what I'll find there, but there's no anger, blame, or hurt. Only something beautiful I don't deserve. I should plead, beg, explain more, try to put the shambles of feelings twisting and tumbling in my heart into sentences, but the only word I can force from the hollowness in my chest is, "How?"

"I don't need a face to know you."

Hope blooms inside me, but I squash it. "Why didn't you say something?"

"There's only one thing I want to say, and I couldn't do it until you were honest with me."

What can she possibly say after everything I told her, after everything my family did to her? Her gaze is soft and filled with something that makes my heart jerk. I never want to forget how she looks, right now, because for the first time in my life someone stares at me with love and loyalty. She will fight for me like no one ever has.

Her lips part with a featherlike breath. "I love you, Gabriel."

My world and pitiful existence collapse, every defense I cemented into the wall of my life crumbling around me. Regret, joy, hope, disbelief at my incredible, miraculous luck that this amazing feminine creature can love me pour out of me, condensing in big, shameless tears that run over my face.

She leans against me, pressing our skins together. "I tried to tell you, a long time before you left, but you didn't want to listen. Now, with only the truth between us, you have to believe me."

I press my face into her stomach, holding onto her like she's my salvation. "I love you, Valentina. With everything I am. God knows, I tried to stop, to set you free, but I can't."

Where do we go from here? How do we pick up the pieces and build a new life as a family?

She answers the question when she opens her hand and holds her palm out to me. "Gregor Malan, will you marry me?"

The platinum of my wedding band makes a perfect shining circle on her skin. I stare at it in disbelief, battling to digest her words.

"Where...?" I look from the ring to her face.

"The police found it in the debris."

She hung onto it. She never stopped fighting for me. Overwhelming, bigger-than-life love crashes over me. "You suspected?"

"I knew you weren't dead. I never stopped looking."

I fold my arms around her. I'm a drowning man, and she's my sea. "Don't let me go. I promise I'll never leave you, again."

Her lips tilt into a faint smile. "Is that a yes?"

The burdens of my past lift from my shoulders. For the first time in my life, I feel truly happy. Light. I set my kitten free, and she came back to me.

"Yes." I smother her stomach in kisses. "Yes, fucking yes."

"Give me your hand," she orders.

When I hold out my left hand, she pushes the band that symbolizes our lifelong union over my ring finger, where it belongs. The fit is perfect. We're perfect, like I always knew we'd be. She's my life, my love, my redemption. Not my property, but my wife. Not for nine years, but forever.

EPILOGUE

Gabriel

The day is one of those cooler summer ones with a hint of a brewing thunderstorm on the horizon. The Johannesburg skyline with the Brixton, Ponte, and Auckland Park tower landmarks is visible from the Emmarentia hill, but it's not the view I'm focused on. It's the woman standing in front of the stately old building, her ruby brown hair blowing in the breeze. She's wearing a yellow dress that accentuates the glow of her golden skin. For a moment, her eyes find mine, connecting with me and me alone, and then she's scooped up by the mob of journalists and politicians who all want a piece of her.

I tighten my hand around Connor's, making sure I don't lose him in the crowd, and balance Sophia on my hip. Sophia will be nineteen months tomorrow, and we have a third on the way, although it doesn't yet show in the gentle swell of Valentina's belly. We decided to announce it to the world after today. Today, Valentina didn't want anything to compete with the opening of the center for the disabled.

As much as our children, this is her baby, something she worked hard on during the past year, and even though many families and mentally challenged individuals will profit from her project, she did it for Charlie. The old hospital was turned into a nurse hostel years ago, and when government funds to maintain it ran out, the beautiful three-story building stood empty for almost two decades, the structure dilapidated and its once manicured garden overgrown with weeds. As the city's new mayor, this was one of Valentina's first initiatives. Yup, she came a long way.

The work she did with her company is commendable. After growing it into one of the country's most successful businesses, she started plowing money back into the community to help people who suffer like she used to, people who come from where she does. It came as no surprise that those people came to love and revere her, selecting her onto the local municipal council and now as the Johannesburg mayor. Her connections to Barnard and other clean state officials helped, as did the anti-criminal operation she undertook in Berea. My little pet is a strong, fair, and compassionate leader. It doesn't take a scientist to see she was born for this.

I shift the weight of the diaper bag on my shoulder, staying on the outskirts to give Valentina room to speak to the press as well as to admire her from a distance. Watching her operate, I can never get enough. I'm not the only one. She's a people magnet. Quincy and Rhett, now married with their own families, are crowding close. They're no longer her self-appointed bodyguards, but we remain friends, honoring our standing Saturday poker nights at Kris' place. These days Rhett runs a successful security business while Quincy provides protection for the touring stars of rock concerts. They know me as Gregor. Nobody except for Valentina knows my secret. Kris is here, too, always supporting Valentina in her official and non-official ventures. Her practice in Orange Grove became a benchmark in the industry with such a phenomenal growth that she opened five franchises throughout the city, as well as the biggest animal rescue center in the country. She's also the sponsor of a full bursary for underprivileged veterinary students.

A series of flashes go off as my wife poses for the cameras with the newly appointed president of the Association for the Mentally

Disabled. Charlie beams at his sister's side. He comes to the center every day to work as a mail sorting clerk, and the work does him good. He loves dividing the letters into neat destination bundles. The center provides employment opportunities, ranging from filling envelopes to preparing promotional flyers, as well as support and guidance for the members and their families. People like Charlie can find a sense of belonging and purpose here, as well as government sponsored treatment.

Charlie lives with us in the new house we built on an acre of property on the border of Kyalami. It's a family house with toys scattered over the floors, a swing in the garden, and a bicycle on the lawn. We have five dogs, all strays, and an array of cats that come and go, some staying longer than others. Oscar is still with us, but Bruno sadly died of old age last year.

All of our lives revolve around the small woman in the center of the spectators. Another flash goes off as the Minister of Home Affairs shakes her hand. Last month Valentina was on the cover of every magazine and newspaper, and this week she's been invited to a congregation of leaders who hope to vote her into government on a national level, but she already decided to decline. Like any couple with their own business, two young kids, and another on the way, we lead a hectic life, but one I wouldn't exchange for anything. I wish Carly could have known her half-brother and sister and share this incredible moment, but I believe she's here with us.

Since Valentina became busy with city council business, I run her company. My main focus is still protecting her and our children, but I'm happy to have something in which I find purpose, something I enjoy. Something clean. No more breaking. No more violence.

Sophia starts to fuss. I know this particular cry. Soon, she'll be bawling. I lie her down in the stroller to check her diaper and drop the bag to the ground.

"Be a big man and get me your sister's bottle, please," I tell Connor.

He unzips the bag, locates the item, and holds it out proudly. "Here, Daddy."

I ruffle his hair before taking the bottle from the insulation holder and testing a drop of milk on my wrist to ensure it's not too hot.

My little girl takes a greedy gulp when I put the nipple in her mouth, first swallowing air. A soft hand falls on my shoulder, and Valentina's voice washes over me.

"Are you managing?"

I grin at her. "Always."

"You're a good daddy."

I steal a chaste kiss, careful not to tip the bottle and break Sophia's suction. "You're a better mommy."

"Thank you." Her words are soft-spoken.

My gaze rakes over her body. "For what?"

"For doing this," she motions at our baby girl, "so I can do that." She flips a hand at the people enjoying the cocktails and finger food set out on the lawn.

"You're welcome." Truth is, I love daddying my kids, and there's nothing I won't do for my clever, industrious, pretty wife.

"Just a few more minutes and then we can escape."

Connor runs off to Charlie. I keep one eye on him and the other on my daughter. "Go mingle and do whatever mayors are supposed to do. Sophia doesn't need to nap for another hour. I can go home with her and Connor if you'd like to stay longer."

"I was thinking we could put the kids down for their nap and catch up."

My body is immediately interested. "Catch up, huh?" I shift behind the stroller to hide the untimely hardening in my pants.

A pretty flush heats her cheeks. "Um, yeah."

I know exactly how I'm going to catch up with her, and from the way she lowers her lashes and works her lip between her teeth, she knows, too.

"You better get your sexy butt in the car. Now."

I use enough of the assertive tone she loves in the bedroom to make her eyes snap back to mine. Her pupils dilate a fraction, and her nipples turn into two hard points under the soft fabric of her dress.

She clears her throat. "Give me a minute to say my goodbyes and to get Charlie."

"I said now. You disobey me, wife." I lower my lips to hers, not kissing her, but breathing the words over the plump curve of her bottom lip, loud enough for only her to hear. "There will be consequences."

"Promise?" she asks in a breathy whisper.

"You can count on it."

She stares at me with the heated, adoring look that tells me she loves me for who I am, and that no matter what, she'll always be there for me.

"I love you, too," I say as she makes to turn.

"I didn't say I love you," she says with a mischievous smile.

"Yes, you did."

In a few minutes she'll be screaming it, too, in the only language that matters.

A language that surpasses words and time.

A language of love and forever.

Our unique language.

~ THE END ~

ALSO BY CHARMAINE PAULS

Standalone Novels

(Enemies-to-Lovers Dark Romance)

Darker Than Love

(Second Chance Romance)

Catch Me Twice

Diamond Magnate Novels

(Dark Romance)

Standalone Novel

(Dark Forced Marriage Romance)

Beauty in the Broken

Diamonds are Forever Trilogy

(Dark Mafia Romance)

Diamonds in the Dust

Diamonds in the Rough

Diamonds are Forever

Box Set

The Loan Shark Duet

(Dark Mafia Romance)

Dubious

Consent

Box Set

The Age Between Us Duet

(Older Woman Younger Man Romance)

Old Enough

Young Enough

Box Set

Krinar World Novels

(Futuristic Romance)

The Krinar Experiment

The Krinar's Informant

Seven Forbidden Arts Series

(Dark Paranormal Romance)

Pyromancist (Fire)

Aeromancist, The Beginning (Prequel)

Aeromancist (Air)

Audiobooks

Standalone Novels

(Enemies-to-Lovers Dark Romance)

Darker Than Love

Diamond Magnate Novels

Standalone Novel

(Dark Forced Marriage Romance)

Beauty in the Broken

Diamonds are Forever Trilogy

(Dark Mafia Romance)

Diamonds in the Dust

Diamonds in the Rough

Diamonds are Forever

Box Set

The Loan Shark Duet

(Dark Mafia Romance)

Dubious

Consent

Krinar World Novels

(Futuristic Romance)

The Krinar's Informant

———————

ABOUT THE AUTHOR

Charmaine Pauls was born in Bloemfontein, South Africa. She obtained a degree in Communication at the University of Potchefstroom and followed a diverse career path in journalism, public relations, advertising, communication, and brand marketing. Her writing has always been an integral part of her professions.

When she moved to Chile with her French husband, she started writing full-time. She has been publishing novels and short stories since 2011. Charmaine currently lives in Montpellier, France with her family. Their household is a lively mix of Afrikaans, English, French, and Spanish.

Join Charmaine's mailing list
https://charmainepauls.com/subscribe/

Join Charmaine's readers' group on Facebook
http://bit.ly/CPaulsFBGroup

Read more about Charmaine's novels and short stories on
https://charmainepauls.com

Connect with Charmaine

Facebook
http://bit.ly/Charmaine-Pauls-Facebook

Amazon

http://bit.ly/Charmaine-Pauls-Amazon

Goodreads

http://bit.ly/Charmaine-Pauls-Goodreads

Twitter

https://twitter.com/CharmainePauls

Instagram

https://instagram.com/charmainepaulsbooks

BookBub

http://bit.ly/CPaulsBB

Printed in Poland
by Amazon Fulfillment
Poland Sp. z o.o., Wrocław

80088156R00172